HARMON GENERAL

A NOVEL BY KIMBERLY FISH

Enjoy!

Kimberly Fish

Harmon General
Book Two in the WWII Historical Fiction Series: Misfits and Millionaires

Published by Fish Tales
303 West Loop 281 STE 110
PMB 216
Longview, Texas 75605

Cover design: Holly Forbes
Cover photo credit: Longview News Journal,
Gregg County Historical Museum
Back cover photo credit: Bryan Boyd
Formatted by Enterprise Book Services, LLC
ISBN-13 9781719234962

Other Books by Kimberly Fish

Misfits and Millionaires Series:
The Big Inch

Comfort Plans

Snippets from *The Big Inch* Reviews:

"The Big Inch" is my kind of brain candy and Kimberly Fish delivered. I loved it and can't wait for the next one in the series." --Sydney Young, blogger, Lone Star Literary

"With an eye for detail, Kimberly Fish weaves a compelling story of a war widow who finds herself in Longview, Texas, in 1942. Reading Kimberly's novel was a bit like going back to a cloak and dagger time, and I enjoyed the local references. Longview was an amazing place to be during WWII." --Van Craddock, *Longview News Journal*, Columnist

The Big Inch has plenty of excitement, action, and intrigue that will keep readers engaged -- I read it in one sitting. I am extremely impressed with the writing. Texans must read this book, but it has wide appeal to anyone who loves a great story. Highly recommend." -- Kristine Hall, blogger, Lone Star Literary

"Kimberly Fish's unique writing style snatched me out of my easy chair and plunked me down into the middle of her character's life where I was loathe to leave when my real life called me back. Her descriptive visual writing drew me in on the first page. Can't wait to read more stories by Mrs. Fish." --Vickie Phelps Author of *Moved, Left No Address*

"If you live in Texas you will definitely want to check this one out! Also, anyone interested in World War II. I give The Big Inch by Kimberly Fish 5 stars!" --Kara Lauren, blogger, Lone Star Literary

"Kimberly Fish has a gift for combining conflict, emotion, and characterization to create a compelling story. Readers will enjoy her books from start to finish." --Louise M. Gouge, author of *Love Inspired Historical Four Stones Ranch* series

"If you enjoy suspenseful stories infused with historical facts and intrigue, then this is one novel you won't want to miss." --Susan Sewell, Reader's Favorite book reviews

Snippets from reviews for *Comfort Plans* winner of a 2018 Best Historical Romance award from Texas Authors:

"Author Kimberly Fish has a writing style that feels fast and fresh. There is nothing unpolished or simple about this story, but she makes you feel like her words flowed effortlessly from her keyboard to your eyes. Collette feels dimensional, and as a reader, sympathizing with her struggles seems as natural as offering your best friend a reassuring hug and a glass of Merlot after a rough day." –Melissa Bartell

"The hidden German letters in the fireplace firebox add the finest part to this story, after Cornbread of course. Comfort Plans is a good weekend read that will draw readers into Collette's winding life of work, finding love, Cornbread, and discovering if the letters lead to hidden treasure." — Christena Stephens

"Kimberly Fish is back with the same rich writing and flair that I fell in love with in her novel, *The Big Inch*. *Comfort Plans* offers something to which every woman can relate, and riding along on Colette's journey feels familiar and comfortable – and is worth every minute spent doing it."— Kristine Hall

"Kimberly Fish serves up a unique novel with a Texas gal and guy, a Texas setting, and a Texas mystery. But the icing on the cake is that the author takes her talents and keeps them in familiar, and not so familiar, territory. Texas is a big place. San Antonio and the Texas hill country are as romantic and idyllic as they come."– Sydney Young

"The author knows how to weave a tale and this book is a wonderful mix of romance, history, and a splash of mystery.
We give it 5 paws up!" –StoreyBook Reviews

To my parents, Betty and Powell Johnson,
who inspire me in countless different ways.

ACKNOWLEDGMENTS

Thank you to the readers of <u>The Big Inch</u> whose kind remarks gave me the courage to take another too good story to forget and refit it for a contemporary audience. This novel is about the second amazing World War II project in Longview, Texas—an Army hospital to treat war wounded that not only flipped the town with five-thousand new residents, but made major contributions to modern medicine. For those who read The Big Inch, I hope you enjoy reacquainting yourself with familiar characters and "the rest of the story" regarding the Big Inch Pipeline. For those new to the series, please visit my website, **www.kimberlyfish.com** to tour the pages and read about the back story and nostalgia related to the WWII era in East Texas. Please subscribe to my newsletter and let's keep in touch about upcoming book news and events.

I owe a huge debt to the folks who let me interview them about their family members who worked at Harmon General; the patient staff at various libraries, including LeTourneau University, LSU-Shreveport Library, Longview Public Library; and the archivists at the Army Medical Museum on Ft. Sam Houston, Texas, and the Gregg County Historical Museum. There's almost no better resource than old newspapers and I'm thankful to be able to read through dated Longview News Journal editions at the Longview Public Library.

Mel, Mike, and Laura Fish are my forever muses, they are the gifts that make my life real and true. I'm grateful for the people who've stood beside me through difficulties and celebrations—and, especially, for a Grand Cru who are willing to travel to far-off places and be adventurous too. Big hugs to my first friend in Longview—Lisa Ross, who rang my doorbell with a chocolate cream pie in her hand (how do you not instantly love someone like that?) Many friends have poured something of themselves into my life and I cherish them for their kindness. But when it comes to the craft of storytelling, I need people who aren't afraid to wield a red pen. I'm indebted to Kristine Hall, Jody Morse, Vickie Phelps, Jill Phipps, and Jeni Chappelle for keeping this novel focused, and out of ditches. If this book has any redeeming value, it's because I write, ever in hope, of pointing to God.

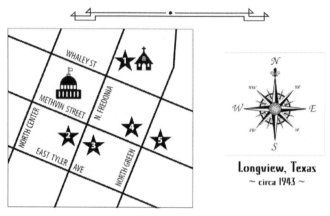

Longview, Texas
~ circa 1943 ~

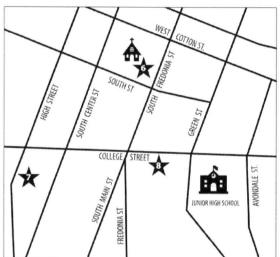

1. First United Methodist Church
2. Lassiter's Menswear
3. Between the Lines Bookstore
4. Gregg Hotel
5. Bramford Building
6. First Baptist Church
7. Kennedy's Boarding House
8. Campbell's Boarding House

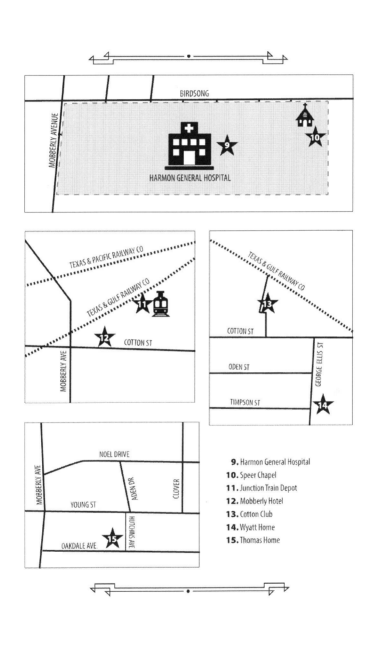

BIRDSONG

MOBBERLY AVENUE

9

HARMON GENERAL HOSPITAL

10

TEXAS & PACIFIC RAILWAY CO

TEXAS & GULF RAILWAY CO

11

12 COTTON ST

MOBBERLY AVE

TEXAS & GULF RAILWAY CO

13

COTTON ST

ODEN ST

GEORGE ELLIS ST

TIMPSON ST

14

NOEL DRIVE

MOBBERLY AVE

ADEN DR

CLOVER

YOUNG ST

HITCHINS AVE

15

OAKDALE AVE.

9. Harmon General Hospital
10. Speer Chapel
11. Junction Train Depot
12. Mobberly Hotel
13. Cotton Club
14. Wyatt Home
15. Thomas Home

The Parrish Family of Valdosta, Georgia:
Lane Mercer (Louisa Jane Parrish Mercer): Delia's daughter, Roy Mercer's widow, and agent with the Office of Strategic Services
Delia Parrish: daughter of Little Momma and Big Daddy
Edith Thomas: Delia Parrish's youngest sister, Lane's aunt
Victor Thomas: Edith's husband
Abigail, Beatrice, Chloe Parrish: Delia's older sisters
Big Daddy and Little Momma Parrish: Delia's parents,

Residents of Longview, Texas:
Ezekiel Hayes (Zeke): attorney, and scratch golfer
Molly Kennedy: owns the boarding house where Lane and Emmie once lived
J Lassiter: owns a menswear shop on Fredonia Street
Judge Israel Wyatt: club owner, self-appointed community leader
Mrs. Wyatt: married to Judge Wyatt, (her mother lives with them)
Patrick LeBleu: associate of Judge Wyatt's
Arnold Smith: associate of Judge Wyatt's
Jewel Carter: jazz singer staying with the Wyatts
Velma Weeds: secretary for an oilman, worked in the Bramford Building
Lola Jones: Miss Kennedy's maid and head cook
Marco Abastini: reported mafia leader

Office of Strategic Services
Colonel Theo Marks: senior officer in charge of European operatives, Office of Strategic Services
Mary Magdalene Tesco (Emmie): a senior OSS agent assigned to Harmon General Hospital
Roy Mercer: former OSS agent, Army Captain, deceased
Dr. Brown: OSS's chief psychiatrist

Washington, D.C.
Major J.R. Parson: coordinator of PAWS federal project, The Big Inch Pipeline
Slim Elliott: welder hired by J. R. Parson

Harmon General Hospital
Dr. Stuart Lemming: pathologist, Colonel in the US Army, and friend of the Mercers
Roland Peale: medical technician in laboratory, Sergeant US Army

Prologue

Mary Magdalene Tesco—Emmie to her friends, Sergeant Tesco to those who met her after she assumed an under-cover role at the new military hospital—tilted her nurse's cap as much to catch the eye of the soldier on the front row of attendees as to block the sun from searing her corneas. She needed that soldier to wink.

With a dozen or more soldiers wearing eye patches, the flirtation would defy the wound he hid under black silk. As it was, with the sun reflecting off the clapboard siding of headquarters, it would make it impossible to tell if his twitch was a wink or just a reaction to unrepentant sunlight.

Perspiration dripped between her shoulders, soaking her blouse.

She hated Texas.

The light was altogether too bright, the weather too unpredictable, and the people too friendly for her taste. Give her London fog any day of the week.

"Today we honor the bravery and courage of Colonel Daniel W. Harmon, a distinguished medical officer of the Regular Army and commander of the Army and Navy general hospital thirty years ago, by naming this massive military hospital to Harmon General Hospital, and officially activated today by the United States Army."

The two-star general droned on about the speed with which the 156 acres south of Longview was transformed from farmland into a service hospital specializing in psychiatry, surgery, pathology, and care in hand therapy, eye reconstruction, and malaria-related conditions affecting soldiers wounded in combat.

"And in conclusion—"

That soldier didn't wink.

Emmie stepped behind the row of nurses, whose job the last few months had been setting up the equipment needed to treat the thousands of wounded who'd arrive by special rail. She'd been one of those servants, working in overheated, pre-fabricated barracks labeled as everything from psychiatric wards to dental clinics. Despite the nurse's uniform, her primary job had been to blend in and glean information from conversations. Clues to the name of the man who was bent on destroying this hospital.

Colonel Theo Marks, her boss in the espionage agency—Office of Strategic Services—had said the man who escaped capture at Walter Reed Army Hospital was a grade A priority and his only defining attribute was his yardstick build. Because of his brutality with injured soldiers, experimental tests that altered treatment outcomes, and an affinity for the Nazis, Theo had code named the devil Doctor Death.

Apparently, Doctor Death was on his way to Longview—if he wasn't here already.

Intelligence reports indicated he intended to dismantle the 8th Service Command's commitment to discovering cures for communicable diseases. Word from Walter Reed was that the former field soldier, who could impersonate a lab technician or a surgeon general, thought Hitler could succeed if the Axis crippled the Allies with airborne or otherwise communicable diseases. She shuddered, imagining the devastation if bombs came loaded with biological hazards.

As Theo liked to say, the sooner they eliminated that particular soldier, the sooner they could cripple the Nazis. Finding this target had been her obsession since she'd arrived in Longview in June.

At first, she'd questioned Theo about why this seemingly insignificant hospital would be a hotbed for intrigue, but he'd reminded her, with not a little bit of patronization, that the best research facilities were in remote locations. Bletchley Park, in the English countryside, was a prime example.

She hated that tone. And that he was mostly always right.

Since being given the assignment, Emmie had thrown herself into an Army nurse's role, a skill that she truly loved and happened to be quite good at, due to her training and a nursing certification. After stepping off the train at the Longview Junction, she'd befriended every department head, doctor, nurse, and janitor assigned to the medical campus, searching for her mark.

Once she identified Doctor Death, she'd need time to stage an accident. Nothing obvious. She couldn't afford the newspapers to headline a tragedy. Something simple, effective, and preemptive.

Sweat pooled under the collar of her uniform. Ignoring that inconvenience was one of the many skills she'd acquired over the last few years, but it didn't make the stickiness less of a nuisance.

Scanning the crowd of politicians, assorted guests, and curiosity-seekers gathered in front of the flagpole, she looked for the newcomer, an impossibly thin man. The nurses' gossip said an odd Captain processed in through headquarters this week. One built like Ichabod Crane. Apparently, that Captain wore an eye patch, too. A clue making her think the new man was her mark and he aimed to blend in with about a fourth of the wounded soldiers at Harmon.

She'd not be fooled by a disguise. Seeing beyond the obvious was her special skill set, one that she was commissioned to teach other female recruits at the OSS's field school. Theo had said she was a natural-born leader—but the part no one talked about was how, with those second-nature skills, she'd committed so many atrocities in the name of war that her conscience had grown numb to the consequences.

Mostly numb, she corrected. Watching one of her girls get dragged through French streets by Gestapo agents had ripped the scabs off any semblance of indifference…to the point she'd fled Marseilles and tried to disguise herself as an opera singer travelling to Portsmouth, offering to work for passage on a British cruiser bound for the States.

But Theo was rather good at seeing through disguises, too. He should write those bloody recruiting posters, she'd suggested as she'd surrendered to his cuffs.

Failure. The stench of it lingered in her memory.

Here she was, six months later, working with a hospital staff who had a pitifully slim knowledge of what their patients had lived through on the front lines.

Emmie released the button under her tie, allowing a bit more air to move against her throat. Her steps retreated behind the row of nurses enduring the speech, and she let her thoughts pound with each heel against the sidewalk.

Failure—was that going to be the epitaph on her headstone?

It was what her father decreed all those years ago. She was nothing but a big, fat disappointment—an embarrassment to her parents, the ridicule of her brothers, and an insult to the family name.

Ironic, but she'd not allowed herself to think of that last conversation in a long time, years even. But here, surrounded by happy families, many with money to ride out the rationing, she was taunted by snippets of what she'd walked away from when she exited Mrs. Goddard's Home for Unwed Mothers and walked across the street to the nursing school for women, needing a second chance.

She drew in a gulp of autumn air and nearly choked.

Enduring memories was not her style. Certainly not ones that made her remember taunts when she turned her back on becoming the society girl whom she'd been groomed to aspire to.

Blinking away sweat that dripped from her hatband, she focused ahead on the familiar gait of Dr. Stuart Lemming, Harmon General's senior pathologist. Always hurrying from one place to the other, the nurses were sure he was inventing lab tests with each new case. Apparently, he was bored by the speeches and ready to get back to the cooler climes of his laboratory.

The brass band played The Yellow Rose of Texas in what she'd have to assume signaled the end of the formal dedication. Security would be nominal, as no one really thought a military hospital treating syphilis and malaria, amputees, and psych patients would be a security risk. What she'd learned about Longview in these last few months would not leave her so naïve. She'd seen that the cover of rural Texas provided rich soil for those dealing against the law. If it was fertile for gambling and booze running, it would be ideal for a Nazi sympathizer with medical expertise.

Ahead, just at the corner of the headquarters barracks, a dreadfully thin man leaned against the downspout. His arms were folded across his chest as he studied the crowd gathered for the ribbon cutting ceremony.

Her breath caught in her throat.

Could that really be her target, Ichabod Crane aka Doctor Death, waiting, without any cover?

Emmie glanced at the cloudless sky, almost as if asking God to validate that she was going to get a break after all these years of chasing men into dark corners, illicit bedrooms, and woods where bodies could be hidden.

There weren't enough rosaries for her to get heaven's attention these days so she'd have to trust her gut. Her instincts were usually spot on and, unfortunately, not something she could teach. One of her OSS trainees had bragged that she'd get a leg up just by imitating Emmie Tesco. As the sweat on her throat cooled, Emmie regretted that the girl had been so wrong. Imitation had led to capture.

Emmie turned her ring, the one she'd especially designed in Rome two years ago, upside down releasing the secret hinge. She felt a whizz of air against the inside of her finger as a poisoned needle descended from the bejeweled box.

Somehow, she'd have to pierce her enemy near his jugular, as his uniform was too thick for her weapon.

Her heart rate kicked up, but her limbs became as steady as a lion's as she stalked her prey. One quick glance into his eyes would reveal if he was a murderer or just a man who'd missed too many meals during this god-awful war.

If that man was her mark, Doctor Death would never see the equipment being installed for biological testing or the dark rooms where molds were growing for penicillin strains. He'd not see the wards prepared for soldiers damaged with disease, infectious wounds, or amputated body parts. He'd never discover the technology being developed to recreate a human eyeball for those who'd lost eyes to injury.

She straightened her shoulders and stilled her breathing.

Timing was essential.

The man leaning against the wall shook like a willow branch. She could see the black band of an eye patch under his military-issued hat. Rarely had a mark just stood in one place while she approached. They were usually trying to kill her first.

Honeybees had been swarming the rose bushes a few minutes ago. That meant the natural enemy of the bee would be in the area too. She would put it into the gossip pool that she'd swiped at a wasp but she'd been too late and the man had been fatally stung. Yes, that just might work. Simple and un-messy.

As she approached a few more feet, he didn't move from his perch, even though her heels whispered against the concrete. Lifting her right hand, she aimed for her quarry, her fingers splayed to swat at his neck.

He turned toward her.

Surprise bloomed in his good eye—one that was glassy and bloodshot. Twig-thin shoulders poked up through his uniform, revealing the barrenness of his bones, as if he might crumble in a breeze. His hair, what little she could see, was the same odd shade of maple as her brother's, and his one apparent iris was a bottomless brown. A color she'd not seen since holding an infant swaddled in a blue cotton blanket.

This man was no murderer. He was some mother's child.

She dropped her hand in the nick of time and missed scraping her needle against his exposed skin.

"Sorry," she gasped. Her thoughts ricocheted between shock and destruction, causing her arm to fling around in the air. "Shooing away a wasp."

The soldier, with an awful orange-yellow cast to his whiskerless chin, offered what might pass for a smile. "Thank you, nurse. You saved my life."

He spoke with the inflection of a well-educated New Yorker. A college man, most likely derailed from a degree by a war blazing on multiple continents.

Emmie's gaze darted to another nurse rushing over.

"I swiped away a wasp," she said, defending her stance, as she folded the needle back into its tomb.

The soldier collapsed against the side of the barracks, the exertion making him cave to his knees. "I swell when I get stung."

The other nurse tucked her hand under his elbow to shore him up and glanced at Emmie. "This one just arrived. Got some horrid version of malaria in the Pacific, and the docs are going to try to cure it, once they figure out which strain it is."

Guilt clogged Emmie's throat. She covered her mouth to prevent spewing apologies on a young man who had no idea what fate she'd imagined for him.

Darker thoughts followed the breach caused by impetuousness—ideas that the child she'd never wanted might be leaning against some barracks on some far-off battleground, praying for someone to save him too.

An ache rose from a box of memories Emmie never revisited.

She swallowed the trembling in her throat and tried to sound nurturing as she focused on recovering her misstep. "Good luck with the treatments."

The other nurse felt the soldier's forehead for temperature. "He wanted to see the festivities. Said it had been a long time since he's been around town folks who knew how to roll out a welcome to strangers."

"Folks here are known for their generosity." Emmie brushed a crease from her skirt, disguising the pummeling of what remained of her control. "I'll put in a good word for you with the Gray Ladies."

"Gray Ladies?" he asked.

She regretted that, even without her assault, he might not live long enough to meet them. "They're local housewives who want to make soldiers feel at home in Longview. You'll see them wearing gray uniforms and carrying home-baked pies."

Hurrying, she looked back once to watch the nurse helping the soldier limp away. Once was too much. It unleashed bitter tears, threats from her parents, and her vows of revenge. Memories from a childhood splattered by the stains of rebellion. The tapestry of Hudson Valley legacy finally torn in two by the dishonor she'd caused her family.

Tripping, Emmie reached for the wall of the Bachelor Officer's Quarters. Air choked in her lungs, but she only paused for a moment. She had to keep moving or risk exposing her steps to the scrutiny of others. Theo was counting on her to finish the job, and that still meant something to the woman who had scorched all remnants of her soul.

She swatted at a mosquito that buzzed her ear, annoying her already over-stimulated nerves.

She really hated this state.

Chapter One

April 12, 1943 10:00 a.m.

Lane Mercer moved deeper into the corner of the lobby of the Gregg Hotel. Seeking somewhere away from the humid breeze blowing in every time the doors opened, and hiding behind the potted palm provided a cover she enjoyed. Running her fingers through the soil stirring dirt molecules into an already fetid atmosphere—and sneezed.

"God bless you," the doorman offered.

She smiled to acknowledge his kindness, and then scanned the hall one more time. Had this been one of her OSS assignments, she'd have already botched the job.

A handful of weeks off active duty with the espionage agency, the Office of Strategic Services, and she'd grown careless. But that was the least of her problems this morning.

The breakfast crowd milling from the hotel's restaurant had thinned, and anyone walking across the marbled floor would think that she was meeting someone. Despite her efforts at being unmemorable, she knew that almost everyone stopped to admire the fabrics and draperies in this corner—it was designed by Conrad Hilton to be a conversation spot.

The musician playing a version of I'll Be Seeing You on the grand piano winked at Lane, acknowledging that he remembered she'd been involved in infamous events in this same hotel lobby just a few months ago.

Yep, she thought, her former cover was toast.

Racket near the doors caused Lane to flinch. She spun her attention toward a family piling their luggage in teetering stacks. A little girl fell to her knees, jerking the arm of a doll trapped between two heavy trunks.

Lane bit her lip, and looked away.

Another obstacle to dodge, should she decide to flee before her appointment.

Tourists arriving for the city's crush of springtime garden tours, parties, and reunions—the annual Friendly Trek Homecoming—were filing into this hotel, and she'd assume others all over the area.

She glanced toward the coffee table with the brochures advertising the schedule for garden tours and the parade that boasted floats, marching bands, and speakers giving tribute to the founders of Longview. Her aunt and uncle were part of the brigade hosting rounds of parties for all those Longview ex-residents who'd come home for the tradition and spectacle. Lane's gaze darted to the windows overlooking the busy sidewalk, noticing the shrubs blooming in pinks, whites, and reds, offering a show-stopping welcome to those meandering on a warm spring morning.

Her gaze shot to the filigreed pediments decorating the ceiling, and she squeezed her tense fingers together. If she went to that homecoming parade, she was doing it as a spectator, not an operative.

Lane's newly-acquired bookshop was intended to operate as a safe house for moving agents across the Texas transportation grid, and her government-issued knife—her dependable stiletto—and multiple fake passports were hidden under a floorboard, never to be needed again.

She'd been told to blend in to the community, enjoy a reprieve from duty. Theo had told her to relax.

She picked at the torn cuticle on her thumbnail.

Despite Colonel Theo Marks predicting she could breathe easier with OSS operations being little more than a bed and breakfast offering, she didn't entirely believe him. He'd left Emmie Tesco in Longview. That meant something wasn't resolved.

The pianist's gentle playing soothed her anxiety. Maybe her appointment this morning wasn't going to be the nightmare she'd envisioned when she and her Aunt Edith had gotten into a row this morning.

She glanced to her right, noting the concierge trying to explain the hotel's floorplan to the parents who ignored their offspring climbing like monkeys along the staircase.

The glass door of the Longview Flower Shoppe opened from the other end of the hotel lobby, and a woman she assumed to be the owner, Mrs. Francis, stepped out wearing a fitted blue suit, navy glasses, and a small silvery cap set among her curls.

"Mrs. Mercer?" The heels of the lady's pumps echoed off the marble as she approached. "I was wondering if you were coming today."

Despite thinking thoughts meant to distract her from the task at hand, Lane still wanted to duck behind the palm. She stole one final glance around the faces of those sorting luggage, wishing one of them would pull a fire alarm.

"Mrs. Mercer?"

The pianist merged into a version of I'm in the Mood for Love. She was in the mood for a one-way ticket to California.

"Mrs. Mercer?"

Lane's gaze shot to the woman standing on the other side of a console that boasted maps and travel guides.

"Sorry," Lane stammered, feeling ridiculous. She'd stared down Gestapo agents. She should be able to handle a florist. "I hope I haven't kept you from something?"

The lady smiled as if her day was Lane's to manage. "Of course not, dear, but your aunt was quite anxious."

Lane gasped. "Aunt Edith is already here?"

"Mrs. Thomas arrived fifteen minutes early for the appointment, said she wanted time to explore my new, walk-in refrigerator and see what the spring inventory offered. She has a discriminating eye for color, you know."

Lane's panic had nothing to do with flowers. It was, in fact, generated by a sapphire-and-diamond ring squeezing the third finger of her left hand.

She conjured a picture of Zeke Hayes's face and tried to remember if his eyes were more slate than bluebonnet? It had been six weeks since he left for the East Coast, continuing the work of the Big Inch Pipeline project with Major Parson. She remembered the feelings he generated even if she couldn't quite pinpoint the shade of his eyes.

But her dread this morning was born from the ashes of her first marriage, not Zeke's twinkling gaze.

Her short stint as wife of Roy Mercer had scribbled over any remnants of the fairy tale that there was such a thing as true love. Even after all she knew, she still wondered if she'd just been born unworthy. That a bastard child should never reach above her station. And reach she had—twice actually. Her thumb skirted the diamond.

Zeke was a savvy attorney, and one knock out of a golfer, but he'd never been married before. He had no idea that taking her on included a boatload of ugly history, secrets she'd never be able to speak of, serious trust issues, and more hang-ups than even the Office of Strategic Service's staff psychiatrist was willing to touch. If she were him, she'd run.

Eight months ago, Lane had never thought she'd last a week in this town; much less become engaged, live with her Parrish family relatives, and take on the remodel of a bookshop. Some days she looked in the mirror and didn't recognize herself.

After six weeks, she wondered if Zeke would either.

To speed along the moment, Lane ignored the ring, the fiancé, and her crazed thoughts as she gripped the leather handle of her purse like it was a lifeline. "My aunt does have a high estimation of her decorating abilities. It's a constant theme as she plans these home parties."

"You are the daughter she never had, and she's excited to spoil you," Mrs. Francis said as she wrapped her hand around Lane's elbow to steer her away from the seating area. "Mrs. Thomas is in her element planning this event. She's told me she sees you wearing an organza dress, maybe in a pale blue, to bring out your eyes."

The need to flee was so tangible it tasted metallic—like a train engine running off the rails.

"I'm afraid I don't have as much time this afternoon as we'd originally discussed," Lane said, making a decision to avoid a repeat of the breakfast argument with her aunt. "I was going to stop by and tell you we'd need to reschedule. You see, I have an author who is passing through Texas soon, and she has agreed to do a reading and book signing at my shop. I'm consumed with details."

Mrs. Francis winked. "I understand, dear. Not every bride enjoys the pre-planning process."

"No, it's not that at all." Lane was pushed through a doorway into a room scented with roses and tapered candles. "I'm just busy, and we—my fiancé and I—haven't settled on a date."

"But Mrs. Thomas has already reserved the church. She told me, not ten minutes ago, that she stopped by the church and signed the papers."

Lane's feet skidded to a stop inside the shop. "That can't be."

Her gaze zeroed in on the feather on the top of Edith Thomas's hat as she struggled to remember their last conversation about potential wedding dates.

"We were meeting with you today to find out what the next few seasons looked like on Longview's city calendar," Lane said feeling the walls close in around her. "To determine if an autumn or winter wedding made more sense."

"It appears June twelfth suddenly became available at Trinity Episcopal. Your aunt snatched it this morning." Mrs. Francis's face bloomed. "Congratulations, dear. You're going to be a June bride."

Lane mentally assessed the construction schedule for the bookshop, including the renovations to the upstairs apartment, and saw her calendar go up in flames. "But that's two months away."

"With the war, weddings come together much faster than they used to. Most couples are so grateful if they can snatch a few days for a honeymoon that they don't even care where they get married. You'll have the benefit of one of the most beautiful sanctuaries in Longview. It's quite a coup."

Lane clenched her fingers wondering how she'd been trumped.

Mrs. Francis patted Lane's shoulder. "Don't worry. It will all come together in the end." She leaned closer and whispered, "And if it hasn't worked out, it's not the end."

Lane didn't have time for homilies. She needed breathing room. "I can't stay. I have a pressing engagement."

"But what will I tell your aunt?"

"Tell her whatever you want." Lane shoved her shoulder against the shop's door. "It doesn't appear my words will make much difference anyway."

The bell's tinny ring was an unfortunate epilogue.

Lane's steps couldn't keep up with the fury inside her head. How had she lost control of what she'd told Edith would be a quaint ceremony in autumn? Her friend from the Big Inch Pipeline project, Slim Elliott—welder extraordinaire and self-taught preacher—was supposed to officiate, and he'd said all he needed was the bride and groom and a mostly coherent witness. Flowers were a nod to Edith's dictate for tradition. Somewhere between that loose conversation about potential plans and today, a June date had taken on epic significance.

Why was she petrified by fifteen-minutes and a minister?

The marriage was going to happen eventually…right? So, was June any worse than November? Lane couldn't explain away her panic, but she knew, like she knew the detailed cleaning procedure with a revolver, that there was some detail she'd missed. Some grain of dirt that would cause a misfire if she loaded this bullet.

Pushing through the hotel's twin doors, blinded by the light in a break of clouds, she stepped on the boots of a man in a khaki uniform.

"Excuse me," he offered as he braced his hands around her shoulders.

Mortified that she'd plowed into a soldier, Lane hurried to apologize and recognized a man she'd not seen in over two years. Maybe a lifetime ago.

"Stuart?" She blinked three times to make sure he wasn't a mirage.

"Lane?" Stuart Lemming squeezed her upper arms, as if making sure she was flesh. "I can't believe it's you. How long has it been?"

Since her husband's funeral, but no need going back to that day when all that was left of Roy Mercer's life had been reduced to a wooden box of Army medals, letters of condolence, and a flag that had flown over the American Embassy that fateful day of the bombing. "Ages."

Stuart stepped backward on the portico to get perspective. "You look wonderful. Seriously, I'm not sure I'd have recognized you if you hadn't mowed me down."

Her qualms about weddings were captured and stuffed under her armor, as her brain spun through all manner of responses to the friend she'd gained when she started to date Roy back in D.C., and then promptly expunged the moment she joined the OSS.

"Ungallant still." Insulting him wasn't kind, but it would prove that she'd not lost all her wit in the seasons since they'd last commiserated about gas rationing and Post Exchange privileges.

"You'd be disappointed if I'd changed." He removed his hat embellished with a brass eagle. "How is it that you're in Texas when I last left you in D.C.?"

Lane patted her throat, feeling sudden perspiration. An encyclopedia of memories fanned open, and dust from all those pages tickled her senses. She didn't cough. Instead, she tried to slam the book shut before the weight of it brought her to her knees. "I could ask the same of you."

"Good ol' Uncle Sam, I guess." He shrugged. "I riled too many established procedures at Walter Reed Army Hospital. They promoted me to Colonel and shipped me into the field so I could learn the errors of my ways."

The twinkle in his eye told a different story. The son of a World War I officer, he was well-versed in the bureaucracy of a federal machine—it was one of his and Roy's favorite complaints when orders were issued and new procedures invented to muddle what should have been a straightforward assignment.

"And how is that going for you?" she asked.

"With the exception that we're at war and soldiers are sick and dying, I'd say good. I'm stationed here at Harmon General, and have full control over a brand-new laboratory." He leaned closer to her ear. "And I'm too far from Washington to be a bother to the old guard."

She knew the hospital, having tagged along with Edith and some of her friends as they were recruited to become Gray Ladies. "It's an impressive facility—barracks trucked in by rail nearly overnight, right?"

"It was a little more complicated than that to build an Army hospital out of a sweet potato field, but as I showed up at the end to lay claim to the lab, I can't take credit for any of the work." He stuffed his hands in his pockets and rocked back on his heels. "I say, this is a wonderful surprise. Seeing you after so much time. We have to catch up. Are you free for dinner this week?"

Lane stepped aside to let a couple pass into the hotel. The seconds bought her a moment to consider the risks of visiting with someone who remembered her from the days before she was drafted into Theo's agency.

She twisted her engagement ring under her finger and stuffed down the misgivings that her aunt would grill her for having dinner with someone other than her fiancé. But Zeke wasn't in Longview, and she was stunned by how much seeing Stuart took her back to a time when she felt less jaded.

"Of course," she said, before she could overthink her response. "For an old friend, I'd drop just about anything. Where are you staying these days?"

He stepped out of the way of two more guests entering the hotel. "I've rented rooms in the Campbell's boarding house on South Center Street. An easy bicycle ride after working all day at the hospital."

"And I'm living with my aunt and uncle." A figure that just might bully through the doors any second, demanding that Lane return for the appointment with the florist. Feeling itchy to leave, she said, "Let's meet here at the hotel for dinner. I'll call the hospital this week to get in touch and make arrangements."

"A take-charge girl." Stuart's gaze roamed her face, her prim brown suit, and green hat tilted to disguise her profile. "I never knew you had it in you."

He was remembering those crushing days as they'd waited for the report that would explain Captain Mercer's fate in the bombing that destroyed a city block in London. Lane had been crippled by grief, barely able to leave her bathrobe. Then she'd met Colonel Theo Marks.

"War makes us do things we never knew we could."

Stuart's eyes clouded. "I still miss Roy so much."

Lane found it odd that of the two of them, she was the one who'd moved on. She almost never thought of her husband. Certainly, not intentionally. When a pregnant barmaid claimed that he'd fathered her child, her memories had been stifled. Thankfully, after a few discreet interviews, she found there was no British child carrying her husband's legacy into the future. That didn't erase the scars, or the unease that she'd somehow missed sensing his instinct to be unfaithful.

"You were as close as brothers." If she focused on Stuart's earnest face, she could almost revisit the days the three of them would meet at the park for picnics, bouncing around ideas for how the war in Europe could end so much earlier if only the generals would follow their advice. "Every one of Roy's best stories involved you."

"I was always the straight man, trying to talk him out of mischief."

"And failing miserably, as I recall."

Stuart smiled.

Lane could see that he would love nothing more than to rehash those days when they were idealistic. She would rather have her tooth drilled. Memories of Roy were tied too much to her reasons for agreeing to Theo's outrageous offer to join the agency. "I hate to run off so soon after seeing you but—"

"And I'm late for a meeting with a medical journal publisher, someone interested in the documentation I'm doing with laboratory tests, but let's get together soon," he said, looking at her like he was cataloguing her changes. "I don't work late on Fridays, if I can avoid it."

"Friday it is, then. I'll call you and confirm the details."

As Lane watched Stuart disappear through the doors of the hotel, she wondered what would come of reconnecting with Roy's college roommate. Outside of her aunt, she'd not encountered any other people she knew before the days she'd enlisted in the Office of

Strategic Services. Living in view of a man who employed microscopes might be the biggest test of all regarding her new identity as a former agent of the OSS.

Lane hurried down the steps and stopped at the curb. A Ford breezed past, leaving a trail of oil-burnt fumes. Gripping the light post, she'd guess she had a fifty-fifty chance of maintaining her cover of a widowed secretary who now owned a bookshop.

Seventy, if she never saw Stuart again.

But first, she had to dodge her aunt and somehow keep Zeke from penciling in the twelfth of June.

Chapter Two

April 14, 1943 10:30 a.m.

"Can you connect me to Sergeant Tesco, please?" Lane propped the phone's receiver under her chin. The orderly's voice cracked as he yelled, asking if any of the nurses on duty knew how to find Tesco.

While she waited, she glanced at the scribbles on her desk blotter, moving aside the letter she'd received from the celebrity romance novelist's publisher. The letter had been filled with items she needed to address in order to accommodate Mrs. Roberta Harwood on this new stop during the promotional tour.

Lane didn't want to review that list, so she reached instead for the last letter she'd received from Zeke. It was postmarked Indiana. He was travelling on tasks related to negotiating contract disputes between the railroads and oil companies. Lifting the pages to her nose, she breathed in a hint of sweet tobacco. He'd been smoking a cigar while writing, and the fragrance made him feel close. She couldn't wait for Sunday afternoon when they'd scheduled their next, ever-so-expensive, phone call.

It was ironic that she was still fascinated by the details of the federal pipeline project she'd helped Major Parson begin, and even though she was no longer his secretary—or running interference between him and Harold Ickes, Secretary for the Department of the Interior—she relished all the scoop, particularly as documented by Zeke's acerbic perspective.

Her ear was still tuned to the phone's receiver, hoping to hear someone pick up on the other end. Until then, she sorted her mail; stacking bills from the light company and the telephone service in contrast to sales fliers from various publishing companies.

No one had warned her that managing a bookshop would have so many details, but that lack of knowledge was precisely what her across the street neighbor—Mr. J Lassiter, the letter J, he explained, given him by a mother

15

who couldn't be bothered to spell—was going to save her from. Or so he promised during their second introduction. Lane glanced through the shop's bay window, overlooking Fredonia Street, and saw her mentor, Mr. Lassiter, tidying the window box that drew attention to his expensive menswear establishment.

He was the only man she knew who could look impeccable while dead-heading petunias. As her gaze drifted back to the blotter calendar, she saw a red circle around this week's Wednesday date with an arrow pointing toward the words: "Mahjongg at M. Kennedy's."

Lane squeezed her eyes shut, fending off the guilt. She'd promised that she wouldn't forget this time.

The slick news release list from Pocket Books was handy, and she tapped it against the sales cabinet, running through a list of plausible excuses for an invitation that Molly had insisted Lane accept.

She leaned forward, paying attention to the noise in the phone's background: the rolling gurneys, shouts of instructions, heavy footsteps, and clatter of metal pans. She wouldn't be at all surprised if someone walked by and hung up the telephone, since it seemed the orderly had walked away after leaving the receiver on the counter of the nurses' station.

Reading through the titles of westerns and mysteries being offered by the Pocket Books editors, Lane regretted the missed opportunity to spend time with Molly and her friends from the Women's Federation—a group that had feted her as a celebrity, calling her one of the most interesting ladies of 1942 for having upended a local assailant in an office building.

Louisa Jane Parrish Mercer knew otherwise. She was a simple girl who happened to have quick observation skills and a fascination for solving problems with the least amount of bloodshed—not that anyone ever asked about the notches on her lipstick tube.

She switched the phone, propping it under her other ear as she glanced again at the circular. Maybe she needed to order more paperback westerns and fewer hardbacks. Maybe she needed to call Molly and apologize. Maybe she needed to send Zeke a letter begging they put off their wedding until . . .Was 1944 too soon?

"Sergeant Tesco speaking."

Lane snapped the phone to her mouth. "Emmie, it's Lane. How are you today?"

There was a significant pause. "To what do I owe the occasion of a phone call?"

Lane recognized the prick of curiosity in the agent's voice. No doubt, Tesco was anticipating some coded message or instruction from Theo's office, but those days of secret communications were over. At least on Lane's end. She picked up a cloth and dusted the edge of her counter.

"Nothing special; I just needed your help tracking down Dr. Stuart Lemming, a pathologist there at Harmon."

The background noises of orderlies shouting instructions carried across the line.

"Dr. Lemming, is the pathologist here, Lane. Kind of a big deal, if you ask the nurses."

"Because he's so handsome and polite?"

"Because he's demanding as the devil and absolutely always right. Surgeons don't operate without his diagnosis." Tesco sounded pleased.

Lane knew Emmie delighted in pointing out mistakes, but she ignored the dig and stuck the pencil behind her ear. For reasons she didn't want to explore, she was curious about the direction Stuart's life had taken after the funeral. Lane nibbled on her thumbnail. Just professional curiosity, nothing else.

"I'm not surprised," Lane said. "He was always the guy everyone wanted on their team for charades. He could guess an answer before most people had finished acting it out."

"Well, isn't that a fact I wouldn't have expected you to know about our Dr. Lemming." Emmie's censure was final.

Lane could imagine Emmie's brow furrowing, marring a perfect complexion. "He's an old friend from Washington, and I was trying to reach him to arrange dinner for tonight. When I called the lab, they said he was too busy to come to the phone for a nonemergency."

"So you called a busy nurse on the prosthetics ward that just received an influx of soldiers transferred from Atlanta?"

"You do tend to make things happen when no one else can."

Emmie's sigh echoed along the line. "Your praise is a little flat. I have saved your rear end. Twice."

"Will an apology get me a message to Dr. Lemming? He already knows about the plans. I just needed to let him know what time for the reservation, and I didn't want to call his boarding house on account of the matron might know Molly Kennedy."

Emmie lowered her voice. "Is your fiancé still out of town?"

The nervy bubble that had been chasing through Lane's bloodstream popped. She didn't question Zeke about who he dined with while away on business, and she doubted he'd question her. They weren't jealous teenagers.

"I'm sure this military line isn't supposed to be tied up with trivial conversation," Lane said, picking up a musty edition of The Making of Modern Britain from the edge of her desk and fixating on the mildewed binding. She squeezed its soft middle to diffuse the tension in her hands. *"Would you help a friend and pass along the message? Eight at the Gregg Hotel, dinner is Dutch treat."*

"You'll owe me."

"Don't I always?" Lane replied.

"I'll be around soon to start collecting on your debts."

"Well, bring a paintbrush. The painters left half a job upstairs, and I'll put you to work." She knew she'd not see Emmie if it meant being part of her grand reopening scheme. The nurse had made it clear she thought bringing in a celebrity author was a ridiculous suggestion for a shop that was supposed to be a safe house. "You do remember how to paint, don't you?"

"Goodbye, Mrs. Mercer. I'll pass along your message." Emmie added, "Most likely."

Lane set the phone back into the cradle and flexed her taut fingers. She lifted her engagement ring toward the desk lamp. The glint of light from the diamonds encircling the sapphire reminded her she'd sold Roy's wedding band and sent the money to Georgia to help with her grandmother's hospital bills. Good from bad.

The bell over her storefront door jingled and the venetian blinds rattled as two women walked in, questioning each other as to whether they could spare the time since school was due to let out any minute.

Lane regretted that dust motes danced in the sunlight. It would take a miracle to clean this store to a shine, but at least these women had actually entered during construction. Maybe teased by the pot of red geraniums she'd positioned on the sidewalk.

"Hello, is there anything I can help you find? I have some new books that I'm still inventorying." Lane slowed down her words because J Lassiter taught her it's better to *welcome a customer as if into her home. "I've just unpacked A Tree Grows in Brooklyn. It's featured on bestseller lists."*

The two ladies gazed around the narrow walls lined with a remnant of books, their eyes seeming to tally the warped shelves, the rusty library ladder, and the worn rugs at their feet. With a work scarf tied around her hair, Lane was sure she'd come up short in their estimation too.

"We're here to meet Mrs. Mercer."

"Oh, that's me." Lane folded her hands over the book catalog.

They clutched their handbags, eyeing each other uneasily.

"Is that sign in the window true?" the one wearing white gloves asked. "Are you really having Roberta Harwood here for a book signing?"

Lane weighed her options. A long-ago echo from the previous book clerk reminded her that many in Longview viewed Mrs. Harwood as something akin to contraband: bootleggers, gun runners, and romance novelists.

"Yes, she's a part of my grand reopening celebration." Lane grabbed a book of sermons to foil the impression she was a seller of corruption. "Mrs. Harwood is taking a train trip across the southern United States in doing research for her new western series, and she's stopping along the way to visit with fans."

"That's unfortunate," the white-gloved one said. "We don't approve of her books. She's led many women into thinking that being a wife and mother is not a satisfying honor."

Lane had read three Harwood novels and hadn't seen any of those messages. There were oodles of unrealistic expectations about men, their proclivities toward moonlight and women who wore skimpy gowns, and more candlelight than was prudent for houses built of wood. But most of the heroines were, in fact, subject to the whims of fathers and guardians.

"Her characters always end up in a marriage," Lane offered.

"I wouldn't know. I don't read that kind of trash, but that's not why we're here to visit with you."

She'd not been in the book business long, but even she knew that to walk into a shop and declare that there were other matters to attend to, other than buying a book, usually resulted in something unpleasant.

The resident cat, Stevenson, wove his body between her legs. She hoped he wouldn't hurl a fur ball at their feet. Many of the neighbors on Fredonia Street scolded her for keeping a pet in a business, predicting she'd disgust customers. Based on the revulsion of these ladies, they might have been right.

"How can I help?" Lane said, toeing Stevenson toward a skirted table.

The one wearing white gloves brushed something from her skirt. "We're from Longview Junior Service League, and we've brought you an application to join."

Lane was sure some sort of ripple in time had just warped. She sniffed the air: book mustiness, floor wax, and mildew. She was standing in her little store.

"I don't understand." Lane questioned how she could be offered something considered valuable to most society women in Longview. "I haven't lived here long, and I don't think I've been to any of your teas."

"Your aunt told us that you were getting married in June, settling down after having helped with the pipeline project. She thinks you're a veritable war hero and worthy of membership in our organization. We, at the Junior Service League, are fond of helping with the war effort."

Remembering their argument in Riff's Department Store about wedding trousseaus, June twelfth, and the role of a modern wife, she doubted her aunt was as apt to make such an endorsement now.

The lady wearing a brown dress said, "You should have heard her carrying on. She's quite proud of what you've accomplished."

Lane was familiar with how her aunt could carry on. They'd lived under the same roof for the last several months. Setting the book on a table, she turned toward the shelves behind her sales cabinet where she'd propped a sun-faded globe next to a stack of dictionaries to remind her that there was a big world out there. Spinning Antarctica helped her focus on the circumstances Edith had set in motion.

A wedding date and now membership in an exclusive club—neither of which she had asked for. This was a change for a girl who just last year was mucking through the fields around Beaune, France, trying to get messages from the frontlines to her counterparts feeding information to British troops.

"There's an interview process," the lady continued. "But of course, with a recommendation from your aunt, you'd get in fine."

Lane spun the globe, reminding herself that she'd willingly sought out civilized town life after being in the trenches with the OSS. The idea of being tidy, ordinary, and connected to a community was something that would stabilize a girl who hadn't a permanent address until she moved in with her grandparents at age thirteen.

The white-gloved one gestured to the warped shelves. "And she said you'd be selling this shop after you got married. You were just helping out the family that lost their father to the war. So after the wedding, you'll be looking for volunteer opportunities, and we have plenty. We're just fascinated with how we can all be Gray Ladies. What a worthy cause— spreading friendliness and a bit of home cheer with those poor, wounded boys."

Stung, Lane wasn't sure what hurt worse—being told that Edith thought the bookshop was a short-term convenience or that the life goal for her new normality should be baking pies and knitting lap rugs for soldiers.

"You were generous to help that family," the lady in brown said. "This was the only bookshop in the area."

Lane stuffed down the argument that boiled under her skin. The conversations she'd eavesdropped on lately hinted that everyone thought women would return to their places in the kitchens, nurseries, and laundries once the war was over and a magic wand was waved over America. If President Roosevelt knew what was good for him, he'd wrap up this war business and put families back in their natural order—or so Victor and Edith opined over the dinner table.

She wasn't an expert in social science, but she didn't think anything would be like it had been before. The war rearranged normal.

Lane saw both ladies in a dimmer light, filtered by a passing cloud. "There's an application?"

"We're a professional organization." The lady with white gloves set the papers on the counter. "Very select."

The other lady nodded. "We have socials. Why, your new husband would meet many important people, valuable connections and all."

Lane put her hand on top of the papers, her ink stains contrasting the white gloves. These ladies had probably never gone any farther afield than

Dallas. She'd heard from Molly that there were a few local girls who'd volunteered for women's auxiliaries aiding the branches of the military but not enough women to have changed the culture in a town as Southern as any she'd known on the other side of the Mississippi River.

"Thank you for stopping by." Lane slid the application under the desk blotter, telling herself she'd think about this invitation when she wasn't riddled with questions about what she was doing with the bookshop and what Zeke expected her to be, as his wife.

"But don't you want to ask us questions, find out how best to navigate the interview process?"

"Shh—" the gloved one whispered. Resting hip against the cabinet. "Now, tell us about your fiancé. I'm afraid I don't know Mr. Hayes at all. Is he in Rotary?"

Was Zeke in the Rotary Service Club? Lane had no idea. She knew few business details about the man she'd pledged to marry. That was among the many questions that niggled her brain in the middle of the night. Had she taken his ring because it represented security or because she really felt like he was the most wonderful man in the world—Edith's standard for all romances? There'd be no answers right now. That was the only thing she knew for sure.

Lane glanced at her watch. "Oh my, look at the time. I have to go. Terribly important appointment. Please stop again when you have more time to shop."

"But we're not—"

Lane moved around the sales cabinet, steering them toward the door. As she pulled the crystal knob, a glass edge bit into her finger. "It's been lovely chatting with you. I'm sure we'll have to visit again."

As she shepherded them to the sidewalk, she could see the expression on J Lassiter's face from across the street. Straightening the sandwich board outside his menswear shop, he took one look at her sales fiasco and shook his head in disapproval. He'd be over later to offer another course in customer service.

See flipped the sign to closed and pulled the shade. Leaning into the shelves, she sighed. She wasn't even sure where to begin to set things right with the turmoil in her heart.

The obvious choice was her aunt, but thus far, telling Edith that June wasn't a good wedding date hadn't worked. Trinity Episcopal was too valuable a location to lose just because Lane wasn't ready to get married, her aunt had lectured yesterday. There was plenty of time to "get ready" after the marriage, Edith had said. Apparently, Uncle Victor didn't even know half of what it meant to be a husband until at least a year after their first anniversary. Lane had stopped her aunt from going into specifics.

Zeke hadn't weighed in on the option of wedding dates or setting up a household, as he was still negotiating details for the Petroleum War Administration contracts in New Jersey. Major Parson was threatening to send him to Washington to deal with the Department of the Interior too. Lane knew that would be a coup for his resume, but a misery for his chronic back pain. She'd not wanted to burden him by telling him of Edith's insistence.

Lane glanced around the bookshop, filled with another man's treasures and his moody cat. This purchase hadn't been a financial salve for the former owners. It was her exit strategy from being a field operative. A grace she'd given herself.

Glancing around the shadows, she heard the last strains of an album of Mozart concertos echo from the gramophone in the back of the shop, a space that functioned as office, storeroom and access to the upstairs apartment. She pledged she wasn't letting this shop go just because it was socially inappropriate for women to own retail.

Besides, Theo had invested in renovating the apartment into a safe house for his agents and guests, she—contractually—couldn't let it go. He was paying for the improved plumbing and reflective window coatings upstairs for covert assignments, and she was paying a little extra to carpenters to improve function in the bookshop.

There was a laundry list of tasks to be done before she was fully prepared to welcome prospective shoppers—those who loved books, maps, and scratchy records.

Lane walked back to the office and lifted the stylus off the disc before the crystal needle cut a trench into the label. She stared at the delicate arm, dangling the needle. The incongruity of such a tool bringing concertos to a room was a mystery she identified with on a personal level. If she was serious about fashioning a life she wanted to own, one that was played out on her terms, that would mean pushing against grooves others had drawn for her.

Lane chuckled. For the first time in weeks, she felt a little bit more like the old girl who'd signed up for the OSS. The one she recognized from underground missions, and covert maneuvers. A girl she'd long since lost touch with.

Walking over to the roll top desk, Lane picked the phone from its cradle. There was one other woman she'd met in this town—besides Emmie Tesco—who understood the thrill of pushing against preconceived expectations, and Lane hoped she'd take the call. Dialing the three-digit number to connect her to the boarding house on College Street, Lane knew she'd have to grovel first, but Molly Kennedy was more than a society matron—underneath that strand of pearls beat the heart of a silver-plated rebel.

Despite their loner reputation, rebels stuck together.

Chapter Three

April 16, 1943 1:10 p.m.

"I don't usually try new restaurants before they've had a good run, but since you stood me up for Mahjong, I was willing to indulge you—if only to find out what could possibly be better than spending time with me." Molly Kennedy pulled lightweight gloves over her arthritic fingers. "And, by the way, you were right about the cook, Eloise. A reliable chicken salad is the staple of southern cuisine."

Lane dropped her wallet back into her purse and nodded goodbye to Linda at the counter. The restaurant was a short walk from the Hurst Clinic, and as it had turned out, Molly had a doctor's appointment earlier. The timing for today's meeting couldn't have been more perfect.

"I buy some of their cookies every few days and keep them under a cake platter in the shop," Lane said. "Trying to lure in customers one treat at a time."

Molly's glance took in Lane's beige skirt and white blouse. "I'm not sure putting sugary fingers in proximity to your books is a good idea, but what do I know? Maybe adding sweets to your inventory will help with sales."

"Mr. Lassiter says I have to give customers three reasons to come to my shop, so I'm thinking through what else someone might need when they're on the hunt for a good book. In these days of rations, I think cookies would be a plus."

Molly narrowed her papery lids. "Do you spend a lot of time with Mr. Lassiter? I've always thought he was a confirmed bachelor."

Lane didn't know enough about J's backstory, but she'd bet Molly had a dossier worthy of Theo's files. Once she was past the machinations of her aunt, and the Junior Service League, she'd tackle getting Molly's information.

"At the moment, he's my business professor," Lane said. "But if there's something you feel I need to know, don't hold back."

"Nonsense, dear." Molly clutched her belt. Her mouth pinched as if lunch was coming back to repeat. "I'm sure he's a lovely man. He's just not from around here, now is he?"

The more Lane lived in Longview, the more she understood the caste system. Outsiders were a commodity best endured with distance.

"Are you okay?" Lane gestured to the sidewalk. "You look pale."

"I'm always pale. That's the signature of a lady." Molly's smile returned to its normal suspicious pose. "Now, what was all that hubbub about wanting my help to get out of the invitation to the Junior Service League?"

"Those weren't my words, exactly." Lane had been digging for more details about how it might go for her as a shopkeeper and new bride, wondering if she could do both with equal success. "I merely asked if you thought I'd have the time to do volunteer work and attend meetings."

"You seem to have always found time to do the things you want, like that nonsense with Major Parson and following him all over Texas and Arkansas last year."

Lane waited while a line of cars eased through the intersection at Whaley and Center streets. Though Molly might deny it, she looked winded from the brief walk out of the diner. The park benches at the courthouse lawn might be the ideal place to continue this conversation.

"That was part of my job," Lane said in defense of travel.

"Oh," Molly snarled. "Like it's part of Emmie Tesco's job to sneak out of the house at all hours of dawn and dusk?"

Lane had kept up with Emmie's surveillance work, surprised she'd yet to catch her quarry. How Lane had finished her Parson mission successfully, while Emmie had not, was a recurring theme of Theo Marks' conversations about the elusive nature of espionage. But it was not one repeated. Emmie didn't indulge questions. Or anything else that was viewed as a peek into her private life.

Thankfully, Major J.R. Parson was safe, the pipeline project was almost completed, and soon the Department of the Interior would be escorting tankers of Texas crude oil to the troops in Europe.

Emmie's task was trickier.

"She's a busy nurse, with a hospital that seems to have a revolving door of emergent needs," Lane said, shading her eyes to find an available bench on the courthouse lawn. "You can't be surprised by the hours she keeps after all the months she's been living in your boarding house."

"I'm used to the phone ringing at odd hours, but now she's got a male friend knocking on my door; I'm certainly not in favor of that. Why, he's so gruff, he scares my cook, Lola."

Emmie had male friends stretched from here to Hong Kong, if the stories were to be believed. "So, you think Emmie is sneaking around with a man?"

"She's inviting him into my parlor, then leaving him there for me to entertain while she drags out her wardrobe changes. Honestly, if I wanted to talk to a Bible thumper, I'd have gone to the street corner and stopped those boys who are always yelling out about brimstone and fire."

Lane could just imagine what Molly might have to say to someone who questioned her right to go to Heaven. "So, she's seeing a preacher? That doesn't seem like a good fit."

"It's worse." Molly looked around at the faces dropping donations to the collections box for aluminum recycling, then leaned closer to Lane. "He's a welder. Worked on your pipeline project. That's how they met. Through you, of all things."

Lane ran through her list of known associates who met the description of welder and preacher. There was only one man who worked the Gospel as easily as he shaped hot metal. "Are you telling me she's seeing Slim Elliott?"

"Apparently, you introduced them at the East Texas Chamber banquet. I, for one, think he's being incredibly forward." Molly turned up her nose. "Let me just say, he's not that attractive. With a face like those Rocky Mountains in the LIFE magazine photos, I do not see why Emmie even gives him a minute of her time. She could have a nice man if she'd stop skulking around."

Lane's memory blurred as she tried to think through those days when the pipeline team had been awarded Business Partner of the Year. Longview had been filled to the rafters with oil executives, pipeline workers, and a few politicians cashing in on the support for a federal project. But that was not the part of the banquet to which Molly was referring. She must have heard the story of Emmie walking in on Major Parson's arm as if they were more than friends.

"Slim and Emmie argued in the same conversation where they said 'how do,'" Lane said, remembering the sparks firing off their stares.

Molly's brow lifted. "I wouldn't know, as I wasn't invited."

They'd mingled in the Pinecrest Country Club lobby, sipping cocktails, and Slim had said something insulting about the cut of Emmie's dress not being fit for a business dinner. She'd replied that someone so grizzled by welding flames had no business passing judgment on fashion. Major Parson had to negotiate a peaceful exit. Lane hadn't imagined they'd ever speak to each other again.

She rubbed a new worry from her forehead. Slim was fragile and vulnerable beneath his crusty exterior. If Lane was any friend to him at all, she needed to warn Emmie away from flirting with a man too sensitive to deal with a spy.

"Shocking though that is . . ." Lane guided Molly off the sidewalk and into the grass growing thick. "Emmie's shenanigans are not why I invited you to lunch."

"She needs both of us to be more involved. We may be the only family she has," Molly said, as if she'd suddenly become quite fond of her unconventional boarder. "I've heard it firsthand that she's estranged from her mother and hasn't seen her brothers in years. A tragedy, but that's what happens when women start working outside their homes. It's the downfall of our American way of life."

Lane pointed out an available bench. "Emmie could no more be a housewife than you could be a fireman."

Molly stopped and propped her hands on her hips. "I'll have you know, missy, that I once put out a grass fire using nothing more than a water hose and my grandmother's quilt."

"So maybe you could be a firefighter." Lane steered Molly to the seat. "But we do not need to be a net for Emmie Tesco. She can take care of herself. I'm sure of it."

Molly looked at her with skepticism then settled on the bench, arranging her skirt to cover her knees. "That's crazy talk," Molly huffed. "Thinking you don't need anyone, that you're the new American miss and can do it all."

"I'm not that foolish. I know I can't do a lot of things." Lane glanced over the crowd milling on the courthouse steps, taking one last study for suspicious characters before she sat next to Molly. "But I've learned I can do some things, just like Emmie has. We had to learn to depend on ourselves. I mean—"

"The sooner you admit you need someone, the sooner you remember that underneath all that linen armor, you're a human being just like the rest of us."

Lane glanced down at her beige skirt, buttoned so tightly that there wasn't even room for her stiletto, but that was due more to her aunt's cooking than a matter of self-sufficiency. "I know my faults."

"Do you?" Molly's brow quirked. "Your shell is getting flinty, Lane. Something about this business has turned you."

Her mind spun with images from Washington to France that might justify Molly's position.

"Granted, I didn't know you before you moved here last summer," Molly added. "But nicely raised young girls from the South come with a less jaded disposition. It takes years to grow steel in our stems."

Lane wouldn't confess a single detail of her not-nice childhood. If growing up under her mother's influences had made her flinty, so be it. Longview was about making her life softer, sweeter, not adding iron ore.

"So, you wanted to know how to dodge the Junior League-ers?" Molly let her gaze wander among the tourists admiring the courthouse lawn. "I was in the Junior League, and you should be too. It'll be good for you. Get you to meeting some of the fine young wives in our city, bring you out in the open, make you direct all that energy you seem to have toward civic projects, and it'd be good for Zeke too. Lord knows he needs a bit of polish."

Lane liked Zeke as he was.

"And," Molly continued, "it would keep you from becoming hardened like Emmie."

Ah, the crux of the issue.

"Emmie and I couldn't be more opposite." Lane didn't know much about the nurse's life before the OSS had changed her destiny, but she'd bet a new shipment of books that Emmie had made the choice with her eyes wide open. "We didn't even agree on radio stations when we both lived at your house. I doubt there's much cause to worry that we're going to become lifelong buddies."

"Or do you tell yourself that because you happened to snatch an attorney and get a ring for your finger?" Molly rearranged herself on the bench, seeming to need a more comfortable perch. "You marry that boy sooner rather than later, you hear. Let all this business about the bookshop and the Junior League fall into its own natural pattern."

Lane loosened the button closing the blouse against her throat. "I never said I wasn't going to marry Zeke."

Molly made a humming noise behind her teeth, much like her cook, Lola, did when stirring the roux thickening in the big soup pot.

"I'm going to marry him," Lane insisted, sounding a little unconvinced, even to her own ears. "He's a gem."

"And he's a thousand miles away working on that pipeline project." Molly took note of the faces she recognized by offering a cool smile. "Don't you fall into the trap of thinking some Yankee girl is going to leave him alone because he's promised in Texas."

"What?" Lane turned to face Molly. "Have you heard something?"

Molly patted Lane's knee. "I didn't get to the point where there are an obscene number of candles on my cake and not learn a thing or two about men. You marry Zeke and get about the business of having babies. That's what is important—not whether or not you have cookies in a bookshop."

Frozen by candor, Lane turned around to face the people scurrying along the sidewalk running parallel to the courthouse.

"Yoo-hoo! Aunt Molly, I've been looking for you."

Lane turned toward the teenager approaching from the sidewalk. The girl's polka-dotted dress, bright blue belt and matching shoes made a fetching picture of spring against the backdrop of city commerce.

"Darling girl," Molly said to Lane, as she waved the brunette over. "My sister's baby girl," she added as an explanation. "Laura is a Baylor University student, bright thing. Takes after my side of the family. Here's hoping she doesn't chuck it all to go sign up with the military auxiliary recruiter who was in town yesterday."

The girl, Laura, reached down to Molly. "I've looked all over for you. Momma told me to meet you at Hurst Clinic and bring you back to the house, but I guess I was late because, well, here you are."

"You're an hour late." Molly kissed Laura's cheek. "But all's well that ends well because I was chatting with my friend, Mrs. Mercer."

Lane and Laura exchanged greetings.

"I could tell a Longview hush-hush was going on." Laura winked as she settled next to her aunt on the bench. "What is it this time? Are you still talking about that secretary that poisoned her boss? What was her name, Velma?"

How did news of Velma Weeds' treachery make it to a university in Waco, Texas?

"The hush-hush?" Lane couldn't resist asking.

Laura nodded. "The mothers in Longview don't spread nasty news that might be bad for morale. They keep their gossip on the quiet. All their little hushed conversations are usually where the juicy stuff is told."

"Molly," Lane chided. "You were holding out on me. Is this what goes on at mahjong?"

"I have no idea what the girl is talking about." Molly fanned her face. "This new generation is much too forward and disrespectful."

Laura laughed. "I learned my best moves from my aunt."

Lane had no doubts. It was the information network that kept both women from the OSS fascinated by the older lady who seemed to a have spoon in every local pot.

Molly planted her hands into the bench in an effort to rise gracefully. "Laura is in town for the Friendly Trek event, I obviously need to put her to work in my garden so she'll forget this foolishness."

Laura helped Molly find footing on the lawn. "Nice to meet you, Mrs. Mercer."

"You too, Laura." Lane stood. "I'll catch up with you later, Molly."

Molly waved but held on to her niece's arm with more weight than Lane expected. What was the illness that seemed to be diminishing her friend?

Lane watched the crowds move across the sidewalks, some headed for the courthouse, others to the offices and shops. Cars honked as they jockeyed for parking spaces, and a line formed outside the bank. She checked her watch. Two o'clock. Time for business deposits.

The Chamber's postcards advertised tall trees, cool lakes, and rolling hills, but she knew that a number of out-of-towners stopped along Highway

80 for more nefarious reasons. Things the "hush-hush" didn't want their daughters to know about. Things she was trying to forget.

Out of habit, she reached for her beltline, but her fingers found nothing more steely than a button that had come loose. This skirt didn't leave room for compartments. By her own choice, she was exposed, vulnerable, and for the foreseeable future, alone. Until Zeke's work was done.

Missing him more now than ever, she realized as she watched Molly and her niece amble away, that she wanted friends. People she could laugh with and share a little hush-hush.

Edith might fall into that category one day but they were at such odds over the wedding tug-of-war that she didn't feel as inclined to inviting more Parrish scrutiny into her business. Lord knows, she'd been running from the family nosiness most of her adult life.

Despite her training that the only one she could depend on was herself, Lane felt it was time to ease that rule. She was a civilian now, with a thin connection to the agency. It was time for a new normal.

Glancing around, she promised herself she'd do better about inviting people in, and making acquaintances. She had to.

Chapter Four

April 16, 1943 8:15 p.m.

Stuart held open the Gregg Hotel's door for Lane. "I'm so glad you called. I was afraid you'd forgotten our dinner, and I had no way of knowing how to get in touch with you."

Lane held Edith's black netted hat against her hair as wind gusted along Methvin Street. She covertly glanced over her shoulder to see who might witness them entering the hotel together. Although she'd written a letter to Zeke yesterday telling him she was having dinner with a friend, she was concerned that an eyewitness account could set the wrong impression in motion.

As one who had created those sorts of false reports, as an agent, it was tempting to assign motives to the people scurrying through the doors of the car dealership and dress shops across the curb. Was that a new policeman leaning against the corner of the Bramford Building smoking a cigarette?

Maybe she was overthinking Zeke's network of legal associates who would be lingering around Green Street tonight. Still, when she smiled at the doorman, she made sure she stood far enough away from Stuart that it didn't look as if they were on a date.

"A cocktail first?" Stuart nodded toward leather-covered doors of the hotel's lounge.

Lane listened to the muted sounds of men's laughter. "That's not the place a lady should be seen, so how about we go on to dinner?"

"Sorry, didn't know." Stuart guided her toward the maître d. "I'm still getting the hang of this town. The guys I work with tend to drive to Kilgore as often as they do into Longview, so I'm out of touch with the locals."

It was ironic that in short order she'd become something of an expert. In the months since she'd stepped off the train at the Junction Depot, she'd come to know the nooks and crannies and more than a few places that would make her relatives blush. Obviously, she felt safe too, but with her training and skills, few places would have unnerved her.

"You're not dating anyone?" she asked as they passed the pianist playing his own version of Night and Day.

Stuart touched the back of her waist and winked. "Not yet."

Lane read the warmth in his brown eyes. She'd have to tell him about Zeke at dinner and hope that didn't kill off the years of memories they'd collected in Washington.

They were seated next to a large window that overlooked the sidewalk, leaded glass panes reflecting the table's candlelight. The fragrance from the roses in the budvase made her think of the blooms in Victor's garden. Her aunt and uncle had given her a room in their house, and she wasn't going to begrudge their hospitality by getting in the center of another rumor mill. She fingered her engagement ring so it faced upright.

Ice clinked as the waiter filled their water goblets.

Stuart leaned into the table. "Where do we start? All I know is that I came back from a training exercise in Baltimore and found you'd moved out of your apartment. Your landlady said you'd paid rent through the end of the month, but one day you were just gone. Not even a forwarding address left for mail."

Lane was thrust back to that address on 19th street, a one-bedroom walkup. A love nest, Roy had called it. More of a bird's nest. An actual tree branch grew into the eaves, and the bathroom ceiling leaked when it rained. They'd moved there after their wedding, but barely had time to make it a home before he was shipped to London.

The three tiny rooms had always smelled of blight. It was easier than she'd have imagined to leave that address when Theo gave her orders to travel to Virginia for new recruit training.

"Who was going to write to me? You and Roy were the ones with all the friends." Lane added wistfulness to her shrug. Taking a sip of water helped swallow the memories she'd worked hard to never remember.

"I'm embarrassed to admit I didn't even know your family name," Stuart said. "Much less where you were from, or where you worked inside the Library of Congress." He held the stem of the water glass, as his eyes lingered on her. "Some friend I was."

Rearranging the silver fork with the engraved H for Hilton, Lane sighed. "Don't be too hard on yourself. There was a lot going on in those days. Remember how you were trying to get a fellowship with that doctor at Johns Hopkins?"

"I wouldn't be where I am today if that had worked out."

She rearranged the butter dish. "Disasters have a way of plucking us off one dead-end road and putting us on a new path."

"The voice of experience?"

"The story of my life." Lane picked up her knife and tapped it against the butter plate, thinking of a story that sounded plausible to a man who could determine a diagnosis on a cellular level. "That's how I got to be an executive secretary with the Petroleum War Administration."

"How does a war office have anything to do with Longview, Texas?"

Drawing in a breath tainted by patron's cigarettes, meatloaf, and sizzling potatoes, she looked at Stuart and channeled a bit of that secretary, Claire St. John, who'd inspired Lane's performance in Major Parson's office. A bookshop owner wasn't nearly as sexy as an executive secretary, but—if she played the part right—it would be efficient in stifling more questions about her background.

"The better question is, how quickly is East Texas oil going to help the troops shut down the war in Europe?" Lane cocked one shoulder like Claire would do when pretending she didn't know as much as did. "You know about the pipeline project, right?"

He revealed that he didn't. During the dinner entrée, Lane retold an edited version of the story related to the birth of an above-ground pipeline destined to move uncountable gallons of crude oil to New Jersey and the Allies beyond. It still boggled her mind that the chessboard of logistics had actually worked.

Swallowing an oddly nervous titter, Lane ended her dialogue by saying, "That's how I met Ezekiel Hayes."

Stuart laid his fork and knife across his empty plate. "Who's this mysterious Hayes?"

The moment felt so unpracticed. She'd never had to explain Zeke Hayes to another person. Even Victor and Edith had known of his legal exploits long before she mentioned his name in conversation with the pipeline project. The people she knew in Longview were well aware of Zeke because either they admired him for his golf handicap, or they'd read the newspaper headlines about the unconventional capture of Velma Weeds inside the Bramford Building. Stuff of the hush-hush.

Lane moved her left hand toward the center of the table. "He's my fiancé."

Stuart's face blanched. "You're getting married?"

He took her hand and turned the ring toward the flickering candlelight.

"I believe that's the normal procedure," she said, with a lightness that might be more mimicking of Claire than a true read on her emotions. "He's still in New Jersey working out the last of the contracts and construction details, but when he returns to Longview, we'll get serious about making plans."

Stuart released her hand and leaned back in his chair. "But Roy—"

Lane wasn't prepared to talk about the man who'd destroyed her notions of what happily ever after was supposed to look like. "Roy died in a bomb explosion two and a half years ago. Though I thought I would die without him, somehow, I found the strength to go on. Zeke is part of that going on."

He studied her with the same intensity he might show a slide of cancerous tissue.

Unnerved, she glanced at her half-eaten dinner roll. Picking up the bread knife, she slipped it into the butter and sliced paper-thin slivers. She wondered how convincing she sounded, since this was the first time those words had been given a public airing. The sentiment was true, though. A romance with Zeke had brought spontaneity and laughter into a void that had long since forgotten that there was more to living each day than avoiding death.

"I'm sorry, Lane." Stuart reached for her hand again. "I wish I'd been there for you. This war has ruined more friendships than I can count. It's to my shame that I wasn't in Washington to wrap you up and make all the awfulness of those months go away."

Those fingers gripping her hand were warm and secure. They were an appendage of a man who'd known his whole childhood that he was destined for medical school. Had he ever questioned his sanity? Or felt like the universe hated him? Probably not. Stuart, like Roy, had been born under a lucky planet.

"There were times I loathed Roy." Stuart's voice reverberated with iron. "He never appreciated the gift he'd been given when he met you. Roy was still a playboy even after you were married, and I could never understand how he could look at you across the table night after night and not give up his reckless ways. I'd never have treated you so cruel."

Lane gazed beyond the candlelight to sketch the reminiscences of the three of them in D.C.; wandering museums, laughing in movies, impromptu picnics, and last-minute seats at baseball games. But in sorting the pictures for a new study, she remembered how Stuart was always the one explaining Roy's absences and picking up the tab when Roy's work got in the way of their plans.

Now, with what she knew of her husband's proclivities toward women, she doubted there was a mystery at all. For reasons she might never know, Roy had married her and promptly accepted an assignment shipping him off to England. What this said about her charm as a wife was quite appalling—Zeke should be warned she was a dud.

"Roy was too charming for his own good." Stuart threaded his fingers between Lane's, holding her hand in a way that defied Zeke's ring. "And I was too dumb to know he'd never outgrow his need for the thrill."

Blinking, she processed his explanation, and let the plea fall over scars surprisingly still tender. She had to stop Stuart from saying anything else that might cause her to reexamine the man who'd severed the last cords on her ability to trust. Delia had taught her that desertion was the preferred strategy for dealing with messy people. Roy had left such a quake after his funeral that she'd closed the door on the rubble of their short life together, and locked it with a key she no longer recognized.

"Then you'd like Zeke." Lane pulled her hand from his and returned her sensibilities to something more relevant. "His thrills are limited to winning golf games. He's called a scratch golfer, but as I don't really know what that means, I can't brag too much. Word on the street is that he's quite good."

"Don't do this. Don't rush into a marriage because our country is at war. Wait for the right man." Stuart's gaze bored into her face. His brown eyes beamed with concern—and something else.

"What makes you think I rushed?"

He leaned closer, his voice barely above a whisper. "Because you haven't said you're in love."

Songs and poems put so much emphasis on "falling in love," notions that Lane was sure were created by a huckster, that she almost wondered if she and Zeke were the odd ones for insisting they were ready for commitment simply because they found peace in each other's company.

She often thought of his intelligence and determination as a safe haven from the things she wanted to ignore—but there was no denying their chemistry either. If passion could equate to love, they had plenty to spare.

Before she could defend her engagement, Lane grew aware of a shadow blocking the light from the chandelier.

"Well, well, well. Isn't this cozy?"

Lane saw Emmie Tesco clothed in a cocktail dress, her hair rolled to mimic Ava Gardner. All hopes that this dinner would remain private vanished.

The only redemption from a moment that had to have been calculated in Hades was that there was a tall, skinny man with long silver hair standing just behind Emmie. He had a face weathered by flame and wind and eyes that could see through stone. She fully expected him to drive a chariot.

"Tea Cup?" Slim Elliott stepped around Emmie to pat Lane's shoulders. "Didn't know I'd lay eyes on you tonight."

Lane tried to stand, but the weight of Slim's palm pressed her back into the velvet chair. Her eyes darted around the dining room, tallying those who might gossip about four strangers invading the clubhouse for the East Texas oil families.

Emmie held her hand toward Stuart. "Dr. Lemming, what a pleasant surprise."

"Nurse Tesco?" Stuart stood, shaking her hand with enthusiasm. "I almost didn't recognize you outside the hospital. I forget sometimes that people have a whole life that has nothing to do with charts, patients, or bloodwork."

Slim offered his hand to the doctor also. "I'm one of Lane's nearest and dearest, and I know you're not her fiancé."

Stuart had the grace to dip his head and dim his smile. "An old friend from our days in the nation's capital."

Slim's eyes narrowed on the doctor before he peered back at Lane. "Tea Cup?"

"It's not what you're thinking, Slim."

"I'm not one to judge. You know that."

She was sure Slim would give her the benefit of the doubt. Emmie made no promises.

Lane rushed a question before Emmie could fire a barb. "What brings the two of you out together on a Friday night?"

"He's trying to convert me, and I'm immune to his ways." Emmie took a step away from Slim. "But since it was a free dinner, I wasn't going to pass up the opportunity to eat out. Harmon General's cafeteria is hardly gourmet."

Emmie's eyes were overly bright, and Slim's were cautious. Lane had seen Slim evangelize roughnecks and pipefitters along the Big Inch Belt, but this was the first time she'd seen him on a date. He didn't wear the suit and tie well. Slim was meant for denim, straw hats, and wide-open spaces.

Women who traded in secrets should go nowhere near his goodness.

"I recommend the meatloaf." Lane motioned to her empty plate. "It's even better than what's served at Molly Kennedy's house, and that's saying something."

Slim eyed a waiter's tray as it passed by. "I'll be so glad when this dang war is over and we go back to eating real meat."

Emmie kicked Lane's toe under the table, saying, "Could I visit with you for a minute, maybe in the lobby?"

Lane wondered what saying yes might cost her.

Stuart waved his arm toward the door. "Go freshen up. Isn't that what you girls do when you want to talk about the men?"

Slim sighed. "I'll get our table, Miss Tesco. Looks like we'll be eating meatloaf."

Lane pushed her chair out. "I'll be just a minute."

Stuart nodded as he stood, waiting for her to exit.

Slim grabbed Lane's elbow before she followed Emmie. "Don't let that filly run for higher ground, okay? I'm lucky she finally agreed to dinner."

Lane didn't understand the attraction, but she knew this wasn't the time, or place, to question anyone's motives. "I'll tie her to the coffee urn if it means that much to you."

Slim didn't chuckle. "I'm serious as a grand jury. I don't want to ruin this."

Lane knew too much about Emmie to imagine the two of them would ever have a second date. Slim lived by the Good Book. Emmie stepped all over its pages with high heels. If she was having dinner with Slim, it suited her purposes to do so.

"Anything for you," Lane said.

"You're a blue chip, Tea Cup."

She had her doubts about that endorsement, but the ropes of the OSS were being pulled by one of its best operatives. If Emmie needed to talk privately, it meant that there was more going on in Longview than tourists coming for the Friendly Trek to see the azaleas and catch up with classmates. There would have been a new development at Harmon General Hospital, and the only official OSS agent on duty needed a backup.

Lane's blood sizzled with new energy. Hate it though she did, agency work was a narcotic that was hard to wean off.

Maybe normal was overrated.

Chapter Five

April 17, 1943 4:32 p.m.

Lane picked at her fingernail, thinking she was the stupidest woman in Texas. After her heartfelt conversation with Molly about how she wasn't going to end up like Emmie Tesco, here she was standing outside the Service Man's Center on South Green Street, wearing the uniform of a military nurse. She rested against Emmie's Chevrolet, searching the faces of the soldiers and hoping one of them was the man Emmie wanted Lane to photograph this afternoon. She brushed pollen from her backside and bet that this wasn't actually Emmie's vehicle. Knowing the agent, it was hotwired from some parking lot, stolen for this mission.

But that wasn't why Lane was questioning her sanity.

No, the fact that she'd fallen for Emmie's trap was where she'd gone off the rails. She should never have indulged the dolled-up nurse in a private conversation, because Emmie turned easy into a nasty four-letter word. Worse yet, she'd fallen for the threat that Emmie would track Zeke to the ground and report a dinner date far more salacious than the meatloaf special.

Idiot, she muttered to herself.

The whole reason she was on this "easy assignment," standing in the sweltering sun, fanning away mosquitoes and flirtatious come-ons, had more to do with her inability to wean off the danger inherent in the OSS and less to do with Emmie's extortion.

And the situation wasn't helped by Edith rolling out more wedding details with each sunrise.

Victor Thomas actually encouraged the madness, winking that his wife was like a kid in a candy shop with plans for the ceremony. Had anyone bothered to ask Lane if she wanted her aunt planning her wedding? Of course not. Parrish women did not ask permission.

She stared into the Green Street azaleas, imagining how she'd stand up to her aunt and demand a stop in the rush toward June twelfth—much like she'd persuade Emmie to call Theo and asking for actual agency support at Harmon.

Lane would have laughed at the image, but she slapped her arm and annihilated another blood-sucking insect.

She supposed the bigger question was why she hadn't planned a wedding herself. If she had to guess, Lane would say that she'd grown too accustomed to independence to hold another bouquet of hydrangeas and submit her will to a man who then had the power to wound her heart. Again.

No doubt those nagging worries were why she'd agreed to Emmie's scheme last night. Like an addict, she needed one last attempt to be an agent before she settled down for good. Before she tried to find ordinary.

Theo would call her all sorts of names for interfering in the protocols for the Harmon General mission, but she couldn't help herself. A year ago, she'd been nearly crushed by the failure to see that her clandestine removal of four key French Resistance officers had been sabotaged. The black hole that had formed in her confidence was at the root of why she'd been assigned to Longview in the first place. Now, she wanted one more stab at doing something good for the greater good before she wore another wedding band.

A swarm of nasty bugs buzzed her throat and she couldn't swipe the skeeters fast enough.

A bloodletting was her payback.

Lane picked at the uniform bunching at her waist. The skin on her legs begged for fresh air as they choked in thick, white hosiery. How nurses wore this getup every day was a mystery she didn't want to solve. Somehow Emmie did it, and since she'd been rumored to have been the paramour of a French couture designer, it must have been the ultimate patriotic sacrifice to wear such ill-fitting clothing.

She checked her watch. If her mark didn't arrive in the next ten minutes, she was leaving.

Lane's nose followed the scent of sizzling hamburgers as the aroma drifted over a nearby fence. The soldiers assembled at Service Man's Club were anticipating a barbecue. Those arriving by city bus or cabs were already making catcalls, hoping that Lane and any other available women would be part of the evening's social agenda.

But women were not allowed at the house on Green Street.

The ladies of Longview did not fraternize with soldiers, outside of organized dances at the USO. Edith had made that lesson part of the bigger one where she'd explained which parts of town to avoid for the bootleggers, prostitutes, and Negros. And in case Lane wasn't terrified enough, Edith had listed the streets where hobos and vagrants tended to gather after riding the trains into East Texas.

Lane was familiar with them all.

Standing here now, dressed in one of Emmie's uniforms and holding an OSS-issued purse that disguised a camera, was taunting the fates. One of the residents living on Green Street was destined to recognize her profile and report the sighting to Edith.

Clutching the purse against her waist, Lane snapped the button sewed into the embroidered pattern, taking photos of two men arriving by car. She hoped one of them was tall enough and skinny enough to be the one Emmie said she was hunting—someone code-named Doctor Death.

Lane checked her watch again, noting scant movement of the minute hand. The men chain-smoking cigarettes on the front porch acted curious about the nurse lingering at the curb—but none matched the description Emmie had suggested. She'd stay a few more minutes, hoping the nemesis had a hunger for hamburgers and root beer.

In a moment where she wasn't thinking of her own problems, she'd felt a tide of sympathy for soldiers gathered on the porch who were most likely not going back to the frontlines. If they even recovered from their injuries. Those who did improve enough to be useful would be reassigned stateside to some support role, and it might be years before they made it back to their homes.

Another cab pulled close to the curb, and she turned and studied the man whose long legs reached for the sidewalk. As he emerged, she leaned her hip into the door and applied lipstick, all the while photographing his arrival.

He spoke to no one, save tipping the cabbie. Staring at the fraternity of men under the porch, he then opted to walk around the shrubbery to enter the yard's side gate. Lane snapped a few more photos, wishing he'd turn toward her. She dropped her keys, leaning down for a better camera angle.

As the gate closed behind him, a man in a striped shirt and dress slacks exited the front door and announced to the soldiers that dinner was ready. Lane took that as her cue to leave and walked around to climb into the driver's seat.

A hand banged against the passenger's window. "Give me a ride, sister?"

She glanced over to see an earnest expression on a green-eyed man with a bandage across his nose and a half-smoked cigarette dangling from his lips. Maybe he wasn't a fan of free root beer.

"Where to, soldier?"

"Train depot at the Junction. I'm catching a ride to Dallas tonight."

The April temperatures were climbing to the nineties, so she didn't blame him for wanting a ride instead of melting during the two-mile walk.

"I can take you as far as Mobberly, you okay with that?"

He opened the door and slid into the front seat. "Suits me. I got to get out of this town, too many people poking their noses in my business. You know what I mean?"

Lane did indeed.

Picking up the bottle of warm soda she'd left tucked between the seats, he asked, "You gonna finish this Coca-Cola?"

She watched him drink the beverage before she could answer. Good thing he didn't know about the case she had stashed in the back, the box she was going to be delivered to Molly Kennedy later. Edith was sure that this would be good medicine for her friend.

As she pulled away from the curb, and turned left on College, she felt something sharp dig into her waist.

"Don't flinch and I won't hurt you."

Who was it that said no good deed goes unpunished? Like second nature, her mind went into personal security mode, although she made her expression appear helpless. Her eyes narrowed on the stop sign ahead. "What do you want?"

His laugh reeked of darkness. "I'd say a romp in the hay, but this town is short on barns. Drive out, away from the town, and we'll make it up as we go."

Emmie would owe her big time for this favor. Even if Slim Elliott had bought two non-refundable tickets to a Shakespeare production in Kilgore, there was no call for throwing a fellow agent to the wolves. Lane formulated a plan and ran through the operation needed to recover from this soldier's plot.

Yes, Emmie would hear about this situation for sure.

The private dug the knife deeper into her uniform to punctuate his words.

"Momma told me never to pick up strangers," Lane whimpered. "I guess this was the reason why."

"We don't have to remain strangers. I intend to get to know you quite well."

She rounded her eyes and turned her head quickly to let him see her fear. "Please don't hurt me. I'm too scared to be any trouble to you."

He leaned close as if wanted to sniff her neck, but his cigarette's smoke filled her nose and she started coughing as a way to dodge his attempt.

Timing, as she well knew, made the maneuver. "Please." Her voice wavered. "You're frightening me."

"Do as I say, and maybe you won't get hurt too badly." His smirk belied his words.

She'd delight in using his cockiness against him. Not all men who wore uniforms were heroes, and this one was about to discover that not all women were victims either. She hoped it was a lesson he'd remember forever.

Lane saw a break between a tow truck and the curb at the parking lot for First Baptist. There was a pile of directional signs left over from the morning's parade, and the stack was tall enough to cause damage to a car's front end. Remembering a similar maneuver with a tractor and a German soldier harassing a winemaker, Lane jerked the steering wheel to the left. The sudden shift to the axle caused the passenger's side tires to pop up on the curb and whack into the pile of sandwich boards.

Fragmenting wood ricocheted through the car's interior.

As the soldier rocked back and forth in the front seat, Lane grabbed his wrist, bent it backward and at an angle, hearing small bones splinter into shards no surgeon would want to repair. Her foot slammed the brakes, as his scream pierced the chaos. His sobs were echoed by a hiss from the tire that had punctured in the pile of wood and nails.

The car settled into the debris, and Lane leapt from the driver's seat and ran toward the church. With the purse clutched under her arm, she turned back to see the car sliding from the heap. Folks hurried out of a nearby restaurant, wiping their fingers with napkins as they surveyed the commotion.

With speed she hadn't used in months, Lane skirted a decorated automobile dragging aluminum cans, announcing "Just Married." Blending in with the crowd filing out of the sanctuary, she slowed down and tried to catch her breath.

People emerging from the church were jolted by the commotion at the intersection. Lane glanced that way too and saw a cook helping the soldier from the car.

Hoisting Emmie's purse strap high on her shoulder, Lane snapped a photo of the creep. She'd want to warn Emmie that though this private was no Doctor Death, he was worth turning over to the MPs.

Once the wedding guests remembered their duty to toss rice at the bride and groom, Lane scooted toward the alley running beside the church and hugged the shadows cast by the businesses along the east side of Cotton Street.

Hiding among those waiting for the matinee at the Rembert Theatre bought her a few moments to figure out what had happened and how she would explain the car's demise to Emmie. Parched, and irritated by hosiery, she let her mind traverse a mental map of downtown, searching for the quickest route to relief. This late in the afternoon, the Rita and the Arlyne movie houses would be great places to hide inside their air-conditioned theatres, but the bookshop was just a fifteen-minute walk away.

It boasted a secure phone line to Theo—a card she could play though Emmie would hate her for it—and a stash of bourbon hidden behind a first edition C.S. Lewis.

If she took a path over Cotton and hurried north on Fredonia, maybe she could dodge anyone who would remember her from the Green Street house. It was a better plan than trying to return to her room at Oakdale Avenue and explain this costume to Edith.

Pacing her steps, Lane lowered her head, hoping to avoid eye contact. Young women in Longview had volunteered for the Red Cross and the Gray Ladies, proudly wearing their uniforms, so maybe no one would take notice of her.

As her feet led her along Fredonia Street, her brain unraveled why Theo would leave Emmie without a backup at a hospital with a would-be murderer, German POWs working as orderlies, and soldiers who seemed to transfer in and out of Harmon with the speed of a revolving door. Lane would enjoy asking Theo to explain this, but in her assignment as a safe house hostess, she wasn't authorized to know about holes in a mission across town.

Tempted by the aromas from a street vendor's push cart advertising icy Coca-Colas and steaming hot Jiffy dogs, she set aside Emmie's problems for the call of her stomach.

As if led by memory she didn't own, she reached into the purse and found several coins and a gum wrapper. Stepping closer to the vendor, her nose filled with the scent of salty hotdogs. Her stomach growled. She'd been starving since smelling those hamburgers on Green Street.

"I'd like to buy a soda," she said, her accent catching on a dry vocal cord.

The vendor chuckled as he lifted the lid of his cart. "Ma'am, we don't carry soda, around here. I got Coke, IBC root beer, a few 7UPs, some TruAde Grape, and of course, Dr Pepper. Stocked up for the Friendly Trek trade."

Major Parson had kept a stash of Dr Pepper in his credenza behind his desk, and she often looked at them, wondering about the appeal.

"I'll take a Dr Pepper," she said, hoping no one would report her to Uncle Victor, the manager of the local Coca-Cola plant. "And a dog with the works."

The man whistled while he prepared her order. Lane glanced to her left at a family holding hands with their boys as they walked toward a food market's double doors. The mother handed her basket to one of the children and told him he could be her special helper.

With those words, a memory of canning tomatoes rose from the summer she'd moved in with her grandparents. She'd been Little Momma's helper so many times the special had calloused over her fingertips. A reward for those chores had occasionally been a ride into town and a cream soda from the counter at the local drugstore, a sweet she'd craved while famishing in France.

Adding a nickel to the man's total, she held the warm paper wrapper in one hand and swallowed her first swig of Dr Pepper. The carbonated bubbles tickled her throat with sugar and some distinctive fruity undertone.

"Thanks for taking care of our boys," the vendor called out as he picked up the arms of his cart and moved farther down Fredonia Street.

It wasn't the first time she'd been credited with something she didn't earn, but his praise reinforced her fraudulence. Because she couldn't afford for J Lassiter, or any other shopkeeper, to see her in this getup, she hurried toward a break between the buildings and slipped down the dark shadows of Bank Alley.

Turning behind the bank, the lettering on the back entrance to Between The Lines bookshop glowed like a homing beacon.

Completing the series of locks and pushing her shoe against the kick plate, she entered the stockroom, instinctively checking the newspaper left scattered on the floor and angle of the bathroom door—prompts she'd positioned to clue her in if an intruder had wandered through the shop since she left at half-past three. Satisfied, she reset the knobs back into their locks. Lane leaned against the wall and breathed in the familiar scent of book bindings and floor wax, at peace for the first time since a messenger delivered the paper-wrapped package from Harmon General.

As soon as she was out of Emmie's disguise, she could sort through the memories of the last two hours to categorize what was significant and what didn't need to be included in the follow-up report regarding the stakeout on Green Street.

Lane set the hotdog and soda on the desk then reached under the skirt to unpin the miserable hose from her garter, rolling them down to her ankles. She tossed them in the trash bin without any of the usual qualms regarding wastefulness. Those things were a torture device. Treating herself to another swig of the soft drink, she flipped the switch for the overhead light and saw the space illuminated for the rat's nest it was: book boxes were stacked in teetering piles, the desktop swayed with the weight of business, and ugly wallpaper was concealed by book reviews, articles featuring authors, and a collection of cartoons from bygone issues of the The New Yorker.

It was the safe haven she would have dreamed of had anyone told her that she could reach for whims too fantastic for a child formed of Georgia's red dirt.

Even the scent of new pine boards filled her head with notions of a better life. The narrow twisting stairs that curled up to the apartment above were littered with construction materials and acted as a chute for the two-by-fours that were part of the remodel.

No one ever commented—at least not in a kind way—about this catchall for the bookshop, but it centered her thoughts to sit in the squeaky swivel chair and stare into the ledger books that would map her future. She loved the ink and coffee grounds that seemed embedded in the walls. This was the address for the world she wanted to inhabit, one where she could dream and no one would mock her for it. She was both manager and janitor, and the roles fit her like second skin.

Stevenson wound around her ankles, reminding her that he shared the space too, and had staked a longer claim.

Pulling another sip of Dr Pepper over her tongue, Lane savored the stack of new inventory to be shelved, and the pile of stickers which she would use to handwrite the prices of books. A little white-hot sizzle of excitement replaced weariness as she found the correspondence that had been in Saturday's mail. She picked up Zeke's stationery and smelled the edges again.

Essence of cigar, no doubt a medicinal whiskey was splashed on the envelope too. He wrote to her late at night when his thoughts were unwinding from the stress of brokering other people's arguments, and she'd always pictured him writing in his pajamas and his hair mussed.

Setting the letter on top of the blotter, Lane sighed, knowing she had work to do before she could indulge in a second read of his words. Biting into the bread, an explosion of mustardy flavors flared in her mouth as she chewed through the pickles, onions and cheese melted over the sausage. She moaned in delight.

As each bite restored the balance of craving and adrenaline, Lane could better make sense of things that had eluded this afternoon—like why she still felt torn about her junkie's need for danger when she should be thinking about bridal attire.

Swigging the drink, she decided that she didn't have to have all the answers today. Coming out of the OSS was a process, and she wouldn't fight it, any more than she was going to fight her reservations about a wedding.

She'd been through a dark valley last year and, maybe—at the ripe old age of twenty-nine—she didn't need to have every question answered. People like Zeke and Stuart, who adored having details figured out and in a labeled place, would laugh at her ambiguity. But the space felt right.

Nodding like she agreed with herself, Lane glanced around the chaos of her shop remodel, and guessed she was undergoing a renovation too. Whether Zeke or Edith were the contractor, she wouldn't say, but someone was overseeing this project and the sooner she surrendered to it, the better.

Wiping her fingers, Lane decided that the best news of all, after that fiasco with the soldier in the Chevrolet, was that she wasn't quite as broken as she'd previously thought. Somewhere the seams of healing had held, and maybe she was ready to move forward.

Chapter Six

April 18, 1943 9:12 a.m.

Emmie shook out the wrinkled uniform and craned her neck to look at Lane. "I didn't expect this back so soon."

Lane leaned into the desk behind the Harmon General nurse's station positioned with views of both halls on the busy psychiatric ward. An unfamiliar energy bounced off these walls, offset by the smells of urine and burnt hair.

Arranging her thoughts, Lane said, "I brought it back today because I'm never wearing it again."

"We're not peers anymore. You quit. Remember?" Emmie folded the uniform into a parcel. "You don't get to call the shots."

Lane resisted the urge to say something biting in response, and slid the camera purse off her arm, placing it beside the desk. "I used all the film. I hope I snapped a photo of the man you were looking to find." She glanced down to watch Emmie's white shoe scoot the purse under the desk's kneehole. "And in case it comes up later, the Chevrolet has been impounded at the police car lot."

Emmie clutched the clipboard to her chest. "You'd better have a good explanation."

"I do, but for the moment, I'll call it a simple matter of self-preservation." Lane watched an orderly push a soldier in a wheelchair. They both looked as if they were shell-shocked by the ward they'd just exited. "Don't bother calling me again. I won't get the apartment ready in time if you distract me with your errands."

Emmie came around the desk to stand close enough to Lane that she could pinch her silk blouse and the skin underneath without anybody noticing. "You'll do what I need you to do because you don't want to risk lover boy finding out that you're carrying on with Dr. Lemming."

46

Lane closed her eyes and imagined the outcomes of Emmie's threat. The pain at the back of her arm stung less. "I'm sorry this assignment is too much for you, nurse, but you'd better call the Colonel if you want backup. I'm no longer available. I've got a grand opening to plan, a remodeling to oversee, and an aunt to distract."

Emmie skimmed a pencil over her clipboard as if she were writing notes. "You're going to die of boredom as a civilian."

Lane chuckled. "I welcome boredom with open arms."

"As I recall, you didn't adjust well to it after Roy's death. Wasn't that how Theo worked his magic?"

Roy? That slap across the face woke Lane from thinking she could outwit a chess master. "Your memory serves you well."

"To be fair, your husband's legacy in the agency is not one many will forget." Emmie searched the hall for potential eavesdroppers. "It was unfortunate that you unraveled from the Beaune Incident in front of so many spectators at the Gregg Hotel last autumn. You and Roy both tested our agency more than most."

The Mercer legacy had not been a one-act play. Roy had bowed out with his death in London, and her exit finally came at the hands of an unhinged woman with Fascist sympathies and plans to avenge her father's death. Neither went unseen by witnesses.

"No need to bring up my husband's name now." Lane watched soldiers sleeping in their wheelchairs. "That's just mean."

Emmie dipped her head to the side to get a better look at Lane. "I use whatever tools are handiest to get me where I want to go."

"And what is it you want from me?"

"Cooperation." Emmie scanned Lane's pale pink suit. "And I wouldn't be averse to some information."

"I'm sure I don't know anything that would help you," Lane said, fingering away the sudden bursts of perspiration from her brow. "I have limited resources between Oakdale Avenue and Fredonia Street."

Emmie smiled slowly. "Ah, but you have an old friendship with a certain doctor I'm interested in."

Lane gasped.

"Not interested in that way, although I'm never opposed to a flirtation," Emmie said *with even more slyness. "But in this case, I think he might lead me to my quarry. His last duty station was Walter Reed, and that detail fascinates me."*

Lane wasn't sure she could trust herself to be around Stuart again. Just hearing him laugh was enough to take her back to a time when she had no idea how to hotwire an automobile, much less send a veiled message via Morse Code. No. She'd not court Stuart's friendship to make efforts easier for the nurse.

"You're on your own with that one." Lane felt around for the clasp of a pearl earring clipped to her lobe, making sure she was still intact for her appearance at First Methodist in half an hour. "I have no doubt you can do just fine without me."

Emmie stepped aside to let an approaching nurse have access to the chart rack then nodded to Lane to follow her toward the doors that led outside. As their heels left imprints on the recently mopped floor, Lane wondered—and not for the first time—if they could have ever become friends, or if the tangled competition of men and missions would have always stood between them.

Roy's face flitted behind her eyelids, reminding her that, despite her efforts to leave him in a graveyard, he was still tripping up her struggles to move forward. Even here, so far away from where he'd delighted her and Stuart both.

"Do you ever imagine your life after all this?" Lane motioned toward the swing doors at the end of the lobby, the ones with black lettering indicating only the authorized personnel were admitted beyond. "What you might do if you could walk away from all that's happened in the last few years?"

Emmie sighed with the weight of a thousand memories. "Why would I waste my time with such drivel?"

"Because it's a healthy distraction, or so the agency psychiatrist told me when I came back from France."

"Oh, please. The psychiatrists don't know as much as you'd think. They make up a lot as they go along." Emmie waved her clipboard to the rows of bath robed soldiers slumped in wheelchairs, staring at a wall lined with movie-star pinup posters. "Like this is a brilliant stroke of therapy."

Lane had kept her eyes singularly focused on finding Nurse Tesco fifteen minutes ago when she'd picked out the psychiatric ward from the lineup of barracks. She'd not allowed herself the liberty of looking around, fearful that she might see men as twisted as their minds. There was no avoiding the confrontation now, and what she saw wilted something in her spirit.

Men, many of them barely voting age, vacant from the shells of their bodies. Some bent in unlikely positions, gnawing on fingers, or picking at their hair. Embarrassed by their bald agony, Lane tried to ignore the images mirrored here, those of her mother at the mental hospital in Milledgeville, Georgia.

Delia's shell of spine and clavicle had housed what was left of a beautiful woman who'd long since surrendered to the belittlement of drugs, drink, and abuse. Blinking fast, Lane whipped those memories away.

"I have to go," she croaked.

Emmie reached for her arm. "I need you to get me closer to your friend. At least you have to give me the details of where he travels and who he meets with."

"I'm not planning to see Dr. Lemming again." Lane denied the note that was stuffed into her evening purse. The one where Stuart had scribbled the telephone number for the Campbell's boarding house and the hours easiest to reach him. "I'm too busy with the shop."

Emmie winked. "Theo would tell you this is important."

Theo hadn't checked on her in weeks. His main concern was that she completed the apartment improvements before his next guest arrived and to not go over his budget.

"Then you tell Theo you need help," Lane said with a quieter voice. "Admit to him that you've worked for months with little to show for it."

Emmie's face blanched. "I am not a failure. I've cut off two rogue outfits selling prescriptions to the black market and stopped a thief from embezzling medical supplies. The MPs think I'm the Sherlock Holmes of Harmon."

Lane adjusted her straw hat to keep her hands busy. "Then fine, you track Stuart. I'm a respectable member of society now. Even the Junior Service League wants me to join."

"Well, la-di-da." Emmie took two steps away from their conversation. "Give my love to the Gray Ladies."

Before Emmie resumed her rounds, Lane followed her for a beat. "Hey, something is wrong with Molly Kennedy. Pay her attention the next time you do more than run through the boarding house. She belches like a sewer." Checking her watch, she knew there were seconds to chat if she were to catch the next bus running the route to downtown. "Please."

Emmie fingers wrapped around the clipboard. "I'm not blind. I've noticed she's not well."

"Well, after all she's done to hide our odd comings and goings, don't you think we owe her a little something in return?"

"I suppose you're not talking about that nonsense about the two of us marketing silk hose to her network of friends?"

"I think the Women's Federation is satisfied now with the nylons coming out of Dallas." Lane could tell Emmie wanted to say more, so much more, but they were in a public space so words were trim. "Keep an eye out for her. Molly looks weak, and she's our best resource for knowing the gossip about who's moving around Longview. If her network of friends doesn't know the scoop, it's not there."

"Is that all?" Emmie's brow quirked. "I've got to get back to work." She reached into her pocket, pulled out a vial of pills, and rearranged her chart before she turned toward the men without saying goodbye.

The reminder that this was not Lane's first go-round with the broken was almost tangible. After years of being shuttled around Delia's world, she could have diagnosed her mother, if only she'd known the medical vocabulary.

Lane's fingers fisted against the door.

Looking toward the soldiers one last time, she wondered if her mother's care in Milledgeville was much different from this factory-style approach to comforting the forever lost. Delia had never recovered her mind, even after she'd sobered. That's how her Aunt Abigail, the oldest of the Parrish sisters, had explained it to Lane when she met her at the bus all those years ago. Delia, though breathing, was sleeping like she was gone.

Backward in so many ways yet wise beyond her years, all Lane knew was that she'd been turned over to a foster mother after Delia started waving a shotgun at the school principle who'd come to check on a sixth grader's unexplained absences. Delia's violent outbursts subsided after she went to the hospital in handcuffs, but by then, it was too late.

Lane had been told that her mother would never return. And she never did. On any level.

It wasn't until the foster mother told the sheriff that she couldn't keep the girl anymore that Lane was shepherded onto a Valdosta-bound bus by a deputy, given a hand-me-down coat, and told to not ask too many questions of her relatives. She'd accepted her Aunt Abigail's explanation that day and only remembered the words once she started researching diseases of the mind during her lunch hours at the Library of Congress.

Lane let her gaze stray to Emmie, who was helping a soldier sit upright in the wheelchair, manhandling him to settle him in the middle of the seat as opposed to falling over the arm rest.

"Nurse Tesco?" Lane couldn't stop the impulse any more than she could stop breathing. "They're going to forget what they've seen in the war, aren't they?"

Emmie's cap bobbed as she fought off the advances of another soldier in a nearby wheelchair. "It's why we do what we do, Mrs. Mercer."

Lane closed her eyes and hoped that if there was a God listening to garbled prayers, maybe He'd do something good for these men who couldn't help themselves. Something better than Delia's fate.

Chapter Seven

Lane walked outside the nave of First Methodist and lingered on the wide steps, waiting for her aunt and uncle to follow the crowd dispersing like sheep released from their pen. Conversations were hushed, occasionally punctuated by high-pitched laughter from the teenagers who'd been unmoved by the sermon.

She would be hard-pressed to give a good accounting of the preacher's message either. Slipping into the church after the choir's anthem, she'd found an open seat in the balcony and let her mind bounce over the colorful hats below instead of following the Scripture passages. The rituals were a comfort, and she'd found that being next to people who believed helped lift the weight of her thoughts that were still mired in what she'd seen in the psychiatric ward.

Services in Longview were more formal than any others she'd witnessed. The church she'd attended with her grandparents was made up of cotton farmers and a circuit-riding preacher who'd take a singular verse and turn it into a three-hour lesson. Back then, the reward for that endurance was a potluck lunch and cousins who'd turn the clapboard church into a reunion of mischief makers. As a girl who had scant knowledge of how to make friends, she had valued the acceptance that came courtesy of Little Momma's wing.

Much like what Aunt Edith had offered here.

Nodding hello to some of the ladies in Edith's supper club, Lane stepped closer to the carved door, knowing her relatives would be some of the last to leave the sanctuary. Victor usually had to have a special word with the preacher, and Edith always pinched the drooping blooms from the altar arrangement.

"Mrs. Mercer," Molly Kennedy announced. "Come meet my guest."

Lane's gaze hurried to find Molly leaning heavily on the arm of a stout woman in a black suit. "Morning, Miss Kennedy."

"This is Mrs. Robertson," Molly said nodding to the woman beside her. "She's arrived not two hours ago from Lufkin, said her son was injured in an accident last night and she hurried here to check on him. She's going to stay with me for a few days since the hotels are filled with the tourists in town."

Lane smiled at the mother. "I'm so sorry for your son, will he recover soon?"

"I hope so," Mrs. Robertson said. "He'd been injured in North Africa, and I was so grateful the Army assigned him to recover at Harmon General, but he was in a car accident yesterday and shattered his wrist."

This couldn't be the same soldier. Surely not. Lane kept her tone level, asking anyway, "Was it a bad car accident?"

"Rather freakish, if you ask me," Mrs. Robertson said, glancing at Molly as if they'd already discussed the oddity. "He somehow ended up in a crash among parade signs. I brought him some home baked bread and jam to soothe him."

Molly patted Mrs. Robertson's arm as they eased down the church steps

Lane knew that the solider needed a whipping behind the woodshed, not jam.

"Darling girl," Edith called from a few paces back in the line of those ambling from the sanctuary. "I'm so relieved you made it to services. I had no way to let you know we were going to the club for lunch afterwards."

A gentleman who'd overheard Edith's remark leaned closer to Lane as he passed and smirked, "Aren't you the lucky one?"

She might have disagreed. Going to the club with her aunt was tantamount to being put under a spotlight where it was rude to contradict opinions, suggestions, and anything else that might be construed as ungrateful. At least there'd be pecan pie.

Edith approached and wrapped Lane in a hug. "I wasn't sure how you were going to make it from that hospital to here in time, but I should have known if anyone can do the impossible, it's you."

Lane was glad for the hug. That meant the argument about wedding dresses had been forgiven. "Thank God for a reliable bus timetable, right?"

"Oh, honey, we thank God for everything," Edith said, weaving her arm with Lane's and leading her down the steps toward the sidewalk. "Even this war, I guess. But I'm having a hard time with that one. My sister, Beatrice, just sent a letter saying her grandson is missing in action, and he's only twenty. I just can't imagine how God is going to make sense of all of this madness."

Lane tried to avoid theological discussions with her aunt on the premise of her lack of knowledge. She looked over her shoulder to the few people lingering at the doors. "Is Uncle Victor going with us to Pinecrest?"

"He's gone to get the car." Edith pulled a handkerchief from her purse and dabbed the moisture at her temple. "With all the new people in town, church is so crowded he had to park a block away. I can't tell you how unhappy he is about that."

"I can almost see the fumes coming from his ears." Victor didn't do well with change, and Longview seemed to be evolving every week. "But it must be good for the congregation to have new folks."

Edith scrunched the embroidered cloth into her palm. "Got a lot of Yankees coming to this town to work at Harmon General. Not sure how we're going to find common ground, if you know what I mean."

"I wonder if Yankees like to buy books."

Edith swiped at Lane's arm with her handkerchief. "Listen to you, only thinking about the almighty dollar when your head should be full of wedding plans."

Any bliss she'd felt for being in a church vanished. "About that, Zeke and I haven't even talked—"

"Don't start now. I have the worst headache and can't stand to hear you go on about why you don't want a dress and flowers." Edith offered a tight smile to the teen pushing an invitation to the Friendly Trek All Church Singalong in the evening. "Although, maybe not the organza anymore. I think, given the slim fabric options these days, tailoring a beautiful suit might be our best option. Why, I even called your little friend from Riff's, Minerva, to see if she could find us a reputable seamstress. If we find a pretty suit on our trip Wednesday to Dallas, she could have it altered."

Lane folded the flier into her purse, next to the letter she wrote to Zeke last night, the one she was going to drop into the post box on the corner. "We're not spending money on a fancy suit for one day of my life."

"It's going to be my gift to you, so I don't want to hear another word."

Cars passed in an orderly fashion, and at the next break, they crossed the street to wait at the corner where Victor usually picked them up after services. Lane reached for the drawer pull on the post box, and deposited Zeke's mail.

"It's not that I don't appreciate your generosity," Lane said, feeling perspiration that had nothing to do with temperatures. "But Zeke and I haven't discussed what we want to do about a ceremony, much less set a date."

"The date is set." As were Edith's lips. "You just tell him to get himself back to Longview by June twelfth, and I'll take care of the rest. He won't even have to buy a suit. Victor and I'll make that our gift too."

"No, absolutely not." Lane imagined how J Lassiter might enjoy outfitting Zeke like Gary Cooper, his idol for all things rugged. "You can't pay for our wedding clothes."

"Why not?" Edith propped a hand over her brow as if searching for Victor's car in the line that had stalled at the intersection of Fredonia and Whaley. "We have plenty of money thanks to the military shipping our Coca-Cola every which way. Plus, we have no children, so you're my one shot at having a society wedding."

Society wedding? Lane's mind filled with photographs from the magazines she'd seen, featuring the offspring of oilmen and politicians. She was the illegitimate daughter of a woman who'd died alone in a mental hospital. Girls like Lane didn't have society weddings.

"We've asked Slim to do our service, and if he can't, we'll go to the courthouse." Despite being someone who'd stood up to Gestapo agents and recalcitrant Frenchmen, her knees quaked. "That's what we want."

"Pshaw." Edith waved her handkerchief at the traffic, seemingly signaling Victor. "You're not getting married at the courthouse. Why, I know that fancy Major Parson and some of his oil friends would want to come to your wedding. It's going to be beautiful at Trinity Episcopal. I even talked to some of the violinists who were here for a party at the Bramfords' this week. They're willing to play at the wedding too."

Lane's stomach flipped. She was sweating. If her worries were only for uncomfortable shoes and a veil then she'd probably be able to get over the reservation. But her jitters seemed to be shake deep roots. She couldn't ignore the feelings anymore. She had to figure out why she didn't want to get married. To Zeke.

After Roy's death, she'd buried her heart deep enough that no one could injure her anymore—a move perfected for the OSS missions that led her to the underworld of human behaviors. She'd vowed to never fall again for mothers with a crooked kind of love, charmers with promises of instant happiness, or those who bartered futures painted with impossible dreams. And she hadn't.

Zeke was solid gold, not plated brass, and when she said yes to him it was with as pure a heart as she'd ever had. She wanted what he had. Or at least, she did then. Now she wasn't sure she was the type to last until a twentieth wedding anniversary.

A ghost, with Delia's bourbon-syrup accent—no doubt brought out of internment from the memories opened at Harmon—reminded her how men were all users and that a golfer who had fought for everything he'd earned wouldn't think kindly of a wife who kept part of herself reserved. He'd want all or nothing. Delia would have lit a cigarette and blown out one of her famous smoke rings before reminding Lane of all the evidence she'd gained to prove that men didn't like independent women. The clingier, the better was her business model.

Lane reached out to open the chrome handle of Victor's Hudson when someone called her name.

She let go and turned to see Stuart hurrying along the sidewalk, dodging church families, his uniform in pristine order and the Colonel's eagle shining brightly on his hat.

"Oh, my," Edith whispered. "Who's that?"

Too late to run, Lane said, "That's just an old—very old—friend, Aunt Edith."

"How can you have an old friend in Longview? You haven't been here a year yet."

"The same way as anyone these days," Lane said, running through plausible excuses for explaining Stuart Lemming to her aunt. "The war."

Stuart stopped at the corner where Victor's car idled. Out of breath, he reached to the stop sign to steady himself. "I couldn't believe my good luck in finding you here. I've been wanting to see you again since Friday."

"Friday?" Edith clutched the open door and gave Lane one of those glances, offset by a raised brow, that demanded answers to questions yet to be voiced.

"Stuart, this is my aunt, Mrs. Edith Thomas." Cars were beginning to back up behind Victor, honking overriding the after-church glow of equanimity. "And Edith, this is Dr. Stuart Lemming, one of those Yankees who've descended on Longview with the hospital."

A horn blared from behind the Hudson.

"Hurry and get in," Victor yelled from the driver's seat. "We're holding up traffic."

"Do you mind if I ride along with you for a while?" Stuart ushered Lane into the back seat and crawled in behind her. "I'm trying to dodge one of the Gray Ladies who wants to take me home to meet her daughter."

"Who in the world are you?" Startled, Victor whipped his head around.

"Just drive, Uncle. I'll explain." Lane rolled the passenger window down, turning her face to the wind.

Stuart settled onto the seat and removed his hat, balancing it on his knee. "Thanks for the lift, sir. I'm trying to get back to the Campbell house for Sunday lunch, but a matron with a daughter got ahold of me after services and wouldn't hear of letting me go. I thought my goose was cooked until I saw Lane standing there. Thank God for being saved by familiar faces. Am I right?"

Lane grimaced. "Yay for me."

Stuart leaned into her shoulder and winked. "Yay for you."

Edith, turned fully around from the front seat, demanded, "Now, explain to me how you know my niece."

It took three blocks and a long wait at a stoplight before Edith understood Roy and Stuart's college friendship that turned into a threesome when Lane married the tennis champ from Asheville, North Carolina. Oddly enough, until Stuart said it, she'd forgotten that Roy's childhood involved tennis trophies. But then, there were a lot of things she'd forgotten regarding the man she'd lived with for a quick six weeks.

Edith whacked Victor when his lead foot caused the car to lurch over the railroad tracks. "And how did the two of you reconnect here in Longview?"

Stuart grinned. "Lane ran into me. Literally. As usual, her mind was a million miles elsewhere, and she wasn't paying a lick of attention to where she was going."

So that was how Stuart remembered her.

She'd always thought she'd just been shy, but now she guessed Stuart and Roy had thought her absent-minded too. He'd have been stunned to discover that the psychologist's test she'd taken as part of her entrance to the OSS indicated she had above-average intelligence and observation skills that trumped most men.

"She is juggling a lot these days," Edith said and pursed her lips. "Her bookshop's reopening is a few weeks away. Then, of course, there's her wedding in June."

Stuart turned to face Lane. "You didn't mention that the nuptials were that soon."

"It's not confirmed."

"It's confirmed," Edith huffed. "I've paid the deposit."

"Paid what deposit?" Victor asked, his hands clenching the steering wheel. "I'm not made of money, you know."

Edith pinched the bridge of her nose. "As I was saying, her wedding is in June. Should I add you to the guest list?"

"I'd be honored." Stuart held his hat more securely in his lap. "And as one of her oldest friends, I'm happy to walk her down the aisle, if her father isn't available."

A stiff hush reverberated in the cab.

"Oh, look." Lane pointed to the sign for Center Street. "Turn here, Uncle Victor. This is where Stuart is staying."

"I'm flattered you know the way," Stuart said, patting Lane's knee.

"My old boarding house is close by. I used to walk this way on my way over to the shops on High Street."

Edith's gaze rested on Stuart's hand as it hovered over Lane's skirt. "Tell me more about the time with you and Lane and Captain Mercer. She's close-lipped."

"I'm the one who talked Roy into marrying this little sweetheart." Stuart winked at Lane. "I told him he wasn't going to find a better girl if he searched all of Maryland and Virginia."

Lane leaned into the seat cushion. Roy had to be coerced into marriage? This shouldn't have surprised her. The girls at the Library of Congress reference room were sure there was an illogical reason that handsome Roy Mercer even looked twice at the girl with mousy brown hair and unfashionable shoes. Delia always told her that eyes were unforgettable, but Roy almost never complimented her eyes. Now that she thought about it, he'd not complimented her much at all—save to say she was a great listener.

"We never actually met Captain Mercer, you understand," Edith said as she grabbed the seat, holding on as Victor took the turn too quickly. "We haven't even seen a photograph."

Lane turned her head toward Stuart when he gasped.

"Lane? How could you not have those pictures we took after the Army-Navy football game?" Stuart pointed out Judge Campbell's house to Victor. "I'll have to dig through my rucksack to see if I have a copy. They made a fine pair, Mrs. Thomas. I can prove it."

Edith turned around to situate herself better in the front seat, staring through the windshield. "Well, I'd like that, Colonel Lemming. It'd be nice to see if he holds a candle to Mr. Hayes—a fine-looking man, in his own way."

Stuart pushed the passenger door. "Thank you for the ride, Mr. Thomas. A pleasure to meet you, Mrs. Thomas." Then he rose from the seat. Before he stepped away, he leaned back in through the car door and smiled to Lane. "I hope to see you again soon, Mrs. Mercer."

Lane hoped to fall into the next available pit.

"She's busy, Colonel." Edith folded her arms across her spring suit. "But maybe we could have you over for dinner one evening. The preacher said it behooves us to show kindness to strangers."

Stuart winked goodbye. "I hope not to be a stranger for much longer."

Lane watched him walk the grass-worn path to the wide porch bracketed by white columns, grateful that neither Stuart nor her relatives knew about her work with the OSS. Those secrets were easier sealed for the fewer folks who knew that she was more than just a girl who once worked at the Library of Congress.

Victor put the car in gear, asking, "We're still on for lunch at the club, right? I'm starving. And I have to get a good meal in me before I take off for my trip."

Lane felt around in her pocket for a handkerchief. Not only was her throat dewy, her forehead seemed to have burst from the weight of all the heavy thoughts this morning. Patting at her skin, she watched Victor in the reflection of the rearview mirror. "How long will you be out of town, Uncle?"

"Who knows? Could be a while."

Edith harrumphed. "Says it's a company meeting, but I always go with him for those."

"You've got to stay home and take care of Lane and all those fandangle wedding ideas you got floating around in that head of yours."

"They're not fandangle, Victor Thomas. They're the wedding you and I should have had in Georgia, were it not for my sister's funeral."

Lane closed her eyes against the breeze blowing through the open window. So Delia's death all those years ago forced her youngest sister to forego a lavish reception. One more crime to lay at the headstone of a woman who'd never mastered the art of living well.

Edith turned to stare out the window at the passing houses. "You'd better not get into trouble without me," she warned her husband. "That's all I'm saying."

Her uncle's smile stretched even wider across his cheeks. The rearview mirror didn't show his eyes, but she'd seen enough in those seconds to know that Victor was quite content to travel without his wife, with no promises made about his behavior.

She could almost hear Delia cackle and say, "See? I told you. Users, every last one of 'em."

Chapter Eight

April 20, 1943 7:26 a.m.

"You should consider stacking the books by genres and then go alphabetically." J Lassiter propped his hands at his waist, his thick, black glasses nearly halfway down his nose as he stared at her bookshelves. "Put fiction at the front of the store. With public libraries popping up in most towns, I don't imagine you have a lot of customers coming in for reference materials anyway."

Lane studied the sketch she'd laid on her sales counter and scratched through the model she'd drawn. Once again, J's ideas were superior to anything she'd created. "Should I put all the fiction on the wall under the sliding ladder, if that's the most popular section?"

He nodded. "Who doesn't love a little ride on a ladder as they read the titles? But before you do anything significant, this shop has to be taken apart and scrubbed to the baseboards. And if I haven't said it before, the cat has to go."

Stevenson leapt up on the sales counter and settled on a newspaper. The feline seemed to be daring the menswear merchant to reissue the threat to his whiskered face.

"The cat stays." Lane scratched Stevenson behind the ear. "For now."

"It's a ridiculous affectation." J turned back to face the stacks. "But it's not the biggest of your problems."

Lane sighed, fearing she'd never get a good grade on the weekly business lesson. "And my biggest problem is?"

J pointed his index finger toward the tin-paneled ceiling. "Those workmen upstairs are adding dust to your shelves with every dropped wrench. When are the carpenters going to finish that apartment?"

"Soon, they tell me." Lane had thought it would only take a month to get the bathroom brought up to 1940s' standards. Then a bit of cosmetic work on the paint and windows. "Mr. Crocker grumbles that he keeps losing workers to the Navy recruiters. He's hired some older men who don't mind the carpentry and plumbing, but the downside is that they're slow workers. They tend to break for fishing expeditions whenever the weather is nice."

J removed his glasses and wiped the lenses with a handkerchief. "You're too nice to tell them they won't get paid if they go fishing?"

A box dropped on the stairs, followed by a muffled curse.

"I tried that, but Mr. Kyle laughed and said he doesn't need the income." She picked Stevenson up off the headlines and set him on the rug. "Seems a lot of folks who used to have to work to make ends meet have oil leases that came in strong a few years ago. Now, they're mailbox millionaires."

Her uncle regularly complained that he wished he was one of the lucky ones who'd turned farmland over to an oil company for drilling. Edith reminded him that he'd chosen to invest in government bonds, and that was the safer commodity. The oil was going to run out any day now.

J folded his linen square and returned it to his pocket. "I had a similar problem when I leased the dry good store and had to convert it into my version of a British club." He put the glasses back on his face. "But patience isn't a virtue when your livelihood depends on bringing customers back to your shop. You'll have to stand up for yourself."

She'd told J that she was having the apartment done over for a renter with health problems, that was why she needed specialized details installed—like a reflective film on the windows and soundproofing insulation to keep heavy footsteps from disturbing shoppers below.

"The wallpaper should be in from Dallas later this week." She poured Darjeeling tea into a china cup and handed it to J. "Once the workers are through upstairs, I can finish getting the downstairs organized."

"I recommend burning most of these out-of-date books, but I guess you could donate them to the soldiers recovering at Harmon. Lord knows they can't all hobble over to the Post library." He flicked dust from his suit sleeve. "Certainly, not the Negroes. I'm not even sure they are allowed in the library, much less the Post Exchange."

Lane had wondered about the Negro soldiers too. She'd seen a lot of white men in the psych ward but not a black or brown face among them. In France, there'd been scant room for segregation, but in the States, certain conventions were still observed, even, it seemed, in the military.

"I have a friend who's a nurse at Harmon. I'll ask her if I can bring some of these to the men—any man, who wants to read."

J sipped from the china cup. "You grew up in the South, didn't you?"

She nodded, tempting the hot tea with her tongue.

"I did too," he said. "But I thought Texas was going to be different."

"How so?"

He set his cup down so gently it didn't even wobble the saucer. "When it was time to leave South Carolina, I chose Longview from the stops listed on the T and P rail line, in large part because of the oil boom and the customers who would have cash in their pocket and a desire for my fine haberdashery services. But also because I'd believed all the stories I'd heard of larger-than-life people who made big things happen in Texas. I wanted to meet interesting folks."

Lane would put Major Parson on that list, followed by Slim, and of course, Molly Kennedy.

"But at the end of the day," he said, "it's every bit as Southern here as it was in Greenville."

She watched him reach for the teacup and stall, like he was lost in his memories. Not for the first time, she wondered why he had to leave South Carolina. Most of their conversations revolved around running a small business and marketing a luxury item to a customer base that couldn't trust that they'd still have money tomorrow. But one evening, he'd told her about his father's general store and how he'd seen the potential to do business differently. In the end, he was punished for his spirit.

"Doesn't that play to your strengths?"

He looked up from the tea. "What's that, dear?"

"This being a Southern town." She noticed that he had the kind of skin that made it hard to guess his age. Based on the silver threads at his temples, she guessed he was at least Theo's age, maybe older. "You understand what the customers will want to buy."

"For today." He sipped another drink. "But tomorrow, who knows? These soldiers are travelling to places and seeing products that they've never even dreamed existed. Those young women volunteering for the women's auxiliaries and whatever other organizations are sending our girls to far off places are going to come home wanting the silks, the perfumes, the beverages they sampled overseas. The only way Southern towns, or any town, will survive is to anticipate how this war will change their tastes and interests and accommodate for it."

Her tongue craved the bitter coffee she'd grown accostomed to in France—maybe he was right.

J Lassiter was the most brilliant business man Lane knew. Sad and lonely, but a visionary. She'd try not to begrudge his pop-in evaluations and lectures. He might help her become a financial success.

The phone bleated a ring and she paused, listening to see if the tones had the interrupted pattern that would indicate Theo calling from a secured location. It did not. She hurried toward the desk at the back of the store and reached for the receiver.

"Between The Lines Bookshop." She tried to remember the rest of the catchy phrase J had taught her. "Here to solve all your book buying needs."

"Hello, beautiful."

Lane wilted into the desk chair. Two days of wild thoughts and midnight wonderings crashed between her eardrums, much like the tower of lacy oatmeal cookies she'd baked yesterday for Edith's tea party—the pile that tipped from the crystal cake plate, too fragile to recover.

Lord, this man's voice always trailed sugar and spice in its wake.

"Zeke, what a surprise! It's not even Sunday." Lane had the giddiest sensation of being found after losing her way. "To what do I owe an expensive, long-distance phone call?"

"It's not enough to say I miss the sound of your voice?"

"It is." The strange dust of the last few days settled in her mind. "I sure have missed the sound of yours."

Crackling pops littered the connection and reminded her of the days she knew the Germans and the British were tapped into every phone line.

She wrapped the phone's heavy cord around her finger, twisting a tourniquet on the rush of second-guessing. There'd be time to analyze his words and her reactions later, when she had the shop to herself. For now, she'd soak in the sound of her fiancé's voice and forget she'd ever imagined giving his ring back. "Where are you this week?"

"At the moment, I'm in Oklahoma City. But after I finish a briefing with some of the major oil company executives this morning, I'm scooting over to the train station and starting the long ride home."

She sat up straighter. Her elbow knocked over a pile of book catalogs. "Home—as in Longview?"

"Where else would home be? Parson says I've worked like a steam engine this month and I need a break before I start going off the rails. He gave me the rest of the week for a vacation. You and I are going to make up for lost time."

Joy and dread bloomed in her heart with equal color. She glanced to the ceiling as if she expected the carpenter to drop a bag of nails and she could use the distraction to buy moments of planning.

"Lane, honey? I was expecting a shout of hallelujah, not silence."

"Oh, I'm happy, happier than I can say." She squeezed her eyes shut to think through how she was going to keep workers on the job and Emmie's blabbing tongue away from Zeke's ear for a whole week. "When do you plan on getting here?"

"I don't know for sure if I'll make all the connections, but if I do, I could be in Longview by five. With an hour to get to Melton Street and changed then gas up the pleasure mobile, I can be at your aunt's house by seven."

Lane checked her wristwatch to judge how many hours she had and if she could intercept Zeke in Dallas so they could jump a train to San Antonio instead. Tempted, it would only delay the inevitable. She'd learned to deal with problems head-on at the agency, and that would be a good lesson to dust off for today.

"Should I dress for a dinner date?" Fingers crossed that he wouldn't want to go to Pinecrest.

"I'll make the dinner plans, but you won't need a pretty dress." His voice became huskier. "I'm going to take you somewhere the crowds won't follow."

A sizzle started in her toes and worked its way up to her heart. "Do I need a suitcase instead?"

His chuckle carried warmth, even with all those miles separating. "Now, I can't go getting blamed for starting the honeymoon before the wedding day. But while I'm home, let's get those plans nailed down. You know, I'm a big fan of sooner rather than later."

Lane chewed her bottom lip. "June is too soon, don't you think?"

"I don't have a problem with June, but I'll need to check my calendar. That's prime golf tournament season."

She bit back a curse. "Well. . ." She paused, thinking through a new strategy. "We don't need to decide anything right now. This call is costing you precious dimes." She could kick herself for even bringing the wedding up. "So, we'll table all that until later."

"All that matters to me is you."

With no effort whatsoever, Zeke's face materialized in her memory with its slightly crooked nose, usual faint sunburn across his cheeks, and a day-old growth of whiskers to keep him from being too pretty. But it wasn't his looks that gave her a charge. He'd found her at her absolute worst and gave her the space to unpack the baggage she'd brought back from France. A man who could let a woman unravel and then fall in love with her while she rewound the threads was unforgettable.

"I can't wait to see you, Zeke. I mean it. I've gotten a little self-consumed here with the bookshop business. Hearing your old twang makes me remember that there are better days coming."

He laughed, and then they hung up before the phone bill ate into his travel fund. Lane set the phone back onto the cradle while her hand lingered on the receiver—as if his voice still hummed through the line and could keep the tingle going a few moments longer.

Stevenson wound his lumpy body around her legs, breaking the spell with an unfortunate odor of soured milk.

"There's a man at your door who says he has a special delivery for you," J said, leaning into the stockroom from the shop. "Insists you sign for the box."

Filing her anticipation into a folder that would be closed until closer to five, she stood and shooed Stevenson from her footsteps. "Thanks. I can't imagine what I've ordered that would require a signature."

"New inventory?" He scanned her stockroom's stack of cardboard boxes imprinted with the brands of popular book publishers. "I see that you took my suggestions for improving the offerings of paperback westerns."

She regretted that the shelves weren't ready for the display of new books, but there was a checklist of cleaning tasks to accomplish before she brought out shiny covers and crisp bindings.

Stepping around J, her focus went to the front door and the man wearing a government-issued trench coat, and woolen fedora—dipped low over his brow. His pursed expression would give away no secrets.

"Mrs. Mercer?"

"Yes." She didn't recognize his face and wasn't sure which agency sent him. "What can I do for you?"

He held a clipboard forward. "Just need your John Hancock for receipt. Special delivery."

She ran through a mental list of procedures Theo had briefed her would be the protocol for running a safe house. Part of that included deliveries from other agencies.

Lane read the man's face for information but found him to be as blank as any chalkboard in the summer. She took the forms, lifted the metal clasp holding them against the board, and read the attached paper for indicators of what, or who, she'd been assigned. A Maryland address was listed as the sender, but the quasi-government logo met the profile for an FBI cover operation.

"As long as it's not a COD," she said, taking the pen he offered and scanning the inventory sheet.

"No, ma'am. I'm not trusted to carry cash anyway," he said, bending down and pushing a wide box across the floor, closer to Lane's shoes.

She tried to pick it up, but it weighed more than she expected and clinking clatter indicated the shifting of bottles inside. He reached down for it and set it on her sales counter.

"No returns," he said sternly. "Company policy."

Nodding, as if she knew the policy well, she ushered him to the door and held it open for him. "I'm sure the bill is enclosed."

"You've already paid in advance," he said, stepping through the door onto the sidewalk and pulling his hat lower on his forehead.

J followed the man across the threshold, holding the door opened as he watched him disappear into the crowd. "I didn't like that one bit," J said, shutting the door so firmly it made the blinds rattle. "That man looked like he dealt in monkey business."

Only if zoos were filled with government agents.

Lane glanced at the box, taped shut, and stamped porcelain. "I'm pretty sure this is a birthday gift my uncle ordered as a surprise for my aunt. He'd said something about having it delivered here so she wouldn't get suspicious." Lane hated to lie, but she couldn't tell J that she was receiving supplies for a transition house. Not only was that forbidden information, but J would read her the riot act for bringing single men into an establishment run by an unmarried woman. "You know how some folks can't resist peeking."

J pushed his sleeve up his wrist and checked his watch. "I'll keep an eye on your door today. What with the construction workers coming and going, you never know who might wander through."

That was part of Theo's master plan. He was going to dress overnight guests in some sort of repairmen attire so a passerby wouldn't be alerted to an unusual pattern. She'd have to warn Theo about J's protective streak.

"I'm sure it's time to be at your business. Don't let me keep you," she said, looking out her window to see if anyone was peeking at her poster advertising the author event.

He smoothed his shirt and righted the cufflink. "A gentleman from Henderson said he'd be here by eight a.m., so I'd better get the coffee brewing." He shuddered. "Coffee. What a pedestrian beverage."

"And yet so popular."

J smiled benevolently. "It's up to you and me to keep the refined arts alive. Thanks for the cuppa."

"Always a pleasure."

As she closed the door behind him, she turned the lock. She couldn't afford a stray customer seeing whatever was so important to have a personal delivery.

Stevenson meowed his disdain for such early morning activity, as she carried the box to the back office. Cutting into the paper wrapping, she opened the seal to find three bottles of vodka, labels written with Cyrillic letters. Below that were cans of what appeared to be Russian caviar and some obnoxious-looking vegetables pickled inside a jar.

Smelling the jar's lid, Lane would bet her next client for the safe house spoke Russian. Lumbering with the package, she opened the door of the closet, pushed aside boxes of accounting records, and made room for her stash of imported goods.

Theo would, no doubt, be in touch soon. And so would Zeke.

Chapter Nine

April 20, 1943 7:06 p.m.

Late afternoon light painted Oakdale Avenue with burnt orange, as Lane pushed back the gold-striped drapes her aunt insisted were the latest rage in décor. Her aunt did have marvelous taste. Her tea party guests had told her so earlier. Lane's focus narrowed beyond the fabric to the tufts of grass at the curb and Zeke sitting in the driver's seat of his Jeep, his hand hovering over the radio dial. She guessed he was probably catching the last bars of some Bob Wills tune.

With mild temperatures and sunshine, it wasn't hard to imagine him letting go of every strain that had been digging into his shoulders these last weeks. Contracts, contentious construction vendors, government officials, and the broadcasting hounds—to name a few. His letters home had been filled with the detritus of a man shaking off his work. Her correspondence in return had glossed over the wedding conversations with her aunt, describing instead her crash course in sales and marketing and various bits of glamour related to the guests returning to Longview for the Friendly Trek. To her surprise, an array of famous people called Longview home.

She smoothed the pockets of her denim dungarees and rolled her toes inside the sneakers he'd suggested she wear tonight. He'd dictated her wardrobe so she'd not overdress for their date. Zeke did have an affinity for the dirt roads of Gregg County. After months of riding shotgun with her uncle, flagging a cab, or catching a crowded bus, she could easily anticipate the delight of a Jeep with no roof and a dodgy transmission that conveniently choked for moonlight and shooting stars.

She'd ride in a wheelbarrow if it meant laughing with Zeke.

And that was what she had to keep telling herself.

It was a weird blip in her mind that was giving her what Victor and Edith had labeled cold feet.

She loved Zeke. She did.

This emotion wasn't the insanity of Roy's first kiss or the faith of what she'd witnessed among friends in France who had married with bombs showering rubble over bell towers. But it was something solid. And solid was good. It meant security and friendship. Forever.

Lane squeezed her lashes together. So why was a red light flashing behind her eyes?

Edith bumped into the table still set with remnants from the garden club tea. She pulled the curtain farther aside and looked at the World War I military-issue Jeep parked at her curb.

"You're lucky to be young and in love." Edith picked lint from the drape.

Lane shifted her gaze from the golden-haired man climbing from the driver's seat to the woman with steel curls pinned behind her ears. Her aunt's expression had been set in stone this afternoon, and nothing Lane could say seemed to budge the tension holding her eyes in a vice.

"We're not that young," she said, taking a step away from the overpowering scent of lemon oil that was embedded in the fibers of Edith's apron.

"You have your whole lives ahead of you. That's more than the rest of us can say." Edith folded her arms across her apron.

Lane suspected the V between Edith's brows had nothing to do with nearsightedness. "Any word from Uncle Victor today?"

"Not a thing." Edith dropped the curtain and stepped around the chair she'd recently bought, making her way toward the door. "You'd think that a man I've known for this long couldn't surprise me, but he goes off on a trip and wouldn't even let me pack his suitcase." She pulled at her earring. "Like I don't see right through that story about sugar rationing and the Coca-Cola people looking at sweetening substitutes. That would take half-an-hour's conversation on the phone, not an open-ended trip to somewhere he wouldn't even say."

Victor had mentioned Atlanta at lunch, but when his wife had pressed him for more details, he'd waved her off and said a man was entitled to privacy every now and again. Based on Edith's slow simmer, she'd never gotten him to confess his plans.

Lane had seen a letter in Victor's car, fallen between the seats, from a woman in Macon, Georgia, suggesting she knew something he'd want to hear about. So perhaps her uncle was travelling beyond the capital city to lanes farther south. It was his prerogative to tell Edith, not hers. In light of Delia's history, Lane decided that maybe wives didn't want to know about mysteries that could only be solved by confrontation and pain.

One last glimpse through the window revealed Zeke's stride eating up the sidewalk. Would they ever get to the point that they'd been together so long they were desperate for time apart?

She tried to imagine Zeke gray-headed, maybe with a gin-drinker's nose or a belly. Would they snarl at each other about bills? Argue over the living room color? Would there come a time when he wasn't faithful?

Edith pulled the door wide open and leaned over the threshold.

"Hurry in before the skeeters follow you through the door," she said, waving to soften the demand.

Zeke brought brightness into the house. He wrapped an arm around Edith and drew her close. "Do I have to dodge Mr. Thomas this evening? Last time, he said if I showed up again, he'd have a shotgun pointed at my gut."

"Lucky for you." Edith's smile hardened. "He's not here."

Lane nearly tripped on a footstool hurrying to Zeke's side. Wrapping an arm around his waist, she leaned her cheek against his denim shirt and said, "I, on the other hand, am incredibly thrilled you're here and that no one is bearing firearms."

He draped his arm around her ribs and kissed the top of her head. "Now that's the kind of welcome a man wants."

With her ear against his heartbeat, she could blink and almost imagine them on a deep front porch, rocking in chairs, fried chicken and sweet tea on the table nearby.

She didn't know why she was prone to forget the comfort he communicated, but it was worth reminding herself that the man who'd been the bane to her soul last year was now the only person who occupied her imagination. That was why she'd said yes to him in February, and it was why she was going to say, "I do." One day.

Her heart fluttered with his nearness, and she vowed she'd not bother Zeke with her troubles. He only had five or six days in Longview, and he needed those days to be fun—filled with golf and home-cooked meals. Telling him her woes would only weigh him down.

There'd be plenty of time for confessions after the pipeline project had been signed and delivered.

Edith stepped backwards and surveyed their denim with scorn. "How come the two of you aren't dressed for a night at Curly's? Surely when a fiancé comes home from working on a war project, a night of dinner and dancing at the hottest club in town is in order."

Zeke fitted his arm around Lane. "We're going to eat. And go dancing," he said, pulling Lane closer.

Edith made a point of looking at Lane's sneakers.

"I told her what to wear on account of how we're taking a slightly unconventional route to the whole dinner experience." Zeke's smile turned just a tad bit wicked.

Lane assumed a run through Top Burger in Greggton was on tap, but the rest of it was up to Zeke's fancy. Maybe they were going to go look at those forty acres he had his eye on in Gladewater.

She didn't care. She needed more of him before she'd be able to determine what to do about Emmie, Doctor Death, the bookshop, and a wedding that had been booked for June twelfth.

Lane kissed her aunt goodbye and hurried over the threshold, Zeke in tow.

As soon as the door closed, he spun Lane in his arms and kissed her with a passion pent up by distance, complicated negotiations with the railroads, fickle deals with oilmen, and threats from international enemies.

"Don't ever stay away from me so long," he said against her lips.

She wrapped her arms around his neck. "I'm not the one who left Longview."

"You could have come with me."

"Only if we'd stopped by the Justice of the Peace first."

"An oversight we can rectify tomorrow morning."

She dropped her arms, stepping back. Distance was critical.

His eyes twinkled. It wasn't his usual playful expression hovering in anticipation of a zinger—he was serious. She'd seen that expression when he talked of PGA sudden-death playoffs and the prospects for University of Texas football.

"Let's not bother your first night home with talk of a wedding," she said, leading the way off the stoop. He'd never understand her reservations. She doubted anyone would. She grabbed his hand again and tugged him across Victor's prized lawn. "Let's go have some fun."

"Okay, but I'm saying we will settle on a date before I go back east, if we haven't done the deed by then."

June was two months away. Surely, she could think of some creative redirect before Trinity's minister looked for her to walk the aisle.

"I hear Top Burger has a limited number of chocolate milkshakes again." She gave him a coquettish smile. "First one to the Jeep claims the biggest cup."

He chased her across the grass, catching her at the curb, lifting her up, and swinging her around in the air. As he dropped her into the Jeep's passenger seat, his hand lingered around her ribs, moving quickly to reacquaint himself with her shape.

"Aunt Edith is watching from the window," she hissed.

He kissed her, nipping again at her bottom lip. "Let her watch."

Lane put a hand over his racing heart. "Let's not give the neighbors one more thing to talk about. They're still miffed about the horse manure I brought in for Uncle Victor's garden."

Zeke crossed the front of the Jeep, pointing back to her through the windshield. "When we're married, you can mulch our garden with whatever crap you want."

He hopped over the driver's door and winked at her while turning the key in the ignition. The idea of them living together had been on his mind. He'd mentioned marriage twice in the last five minutes.

Why did Lane feel like a bag of coal had settled on her gut?

Squeezing her eyes shut for the briefest second, she wished she could enjoy this preview of their life together and stop analyzing every wrinkle. Her aunt spent most mornings sitting on her porch, surrounded by wet laundry pinned to a line, rocking in a chair with the Good Book open on her lap.

Surely, Edith's secret for getting through could become her habit too— even though she hadn't lifted a Bible since the day she'd placed Delia's well-worn version in a South Georgia casket.

Lane tried for glib banter—something that wouldn't clue Zeke in to the misgivings that draped her like Little Momma's hand-me-down shawl. "Why does this sound like I'd be the only one doing yardwork in this hitherto unseen garden?"

Zeke's chuckle carried over the pop-pop-pop of the engine firing to life. "Because these hands," he held his right hand out for her inspection, "hit hundred-dollar golf balls. They don't cart around dung for a Victory garden."

"Said every amateur golfer ever." She reached up and wove her fingers around his outstretched hand. "Don't think you can use that excuse to get out of washing dishes either. I'm on to you now."

He kissed her knuckles before letting go of her hand to shift gears, as they prepared to turn right onto Mobberly Avenue. He waved to the firemen washing their hook-and-ladder truck at the station then reached for her hand again.

The affection was short-lived as the start-and-go traffic creeping along Mobberly Avenue kept him shoving the temperamental stick between second and third gear.

Zeke stomped the gas pedal as they approached the traffic light on the corner of Cotton Street and through the intersection as the light turned red. The policeman's strident whistle followed the Jeep's tail as they approached the busy train station known far and wide as the Junction. As they followed the dip in the asphalt, under the bridge holding up railroad lines, Zeke yelled out, "Go Horns Go!"

His requisite shout of affection for the University of Texas echoed until they came to idle at the intersection with Methvin.

"Don't look, baby. Don't want you seeing the ladies of the night who are already hustling for business."

Like she'd be scarred by seeing women in skimpy attire standing around a bus stop. As the Knight of her Sensitivities, Zeke should never hear her confession of the things she'd seen and done in the name of war.

They hurried forward through Fifth and on to Fourth Street, and made the turn by the cemetery, approaching Gregg Memorial Hospital. The airflow off the windshield whipped his denim shirt against his chest and she could see that the pipeline project had exacted a toll. His shoulders were thinner, and his skin was the color of day-old grits.

As they turned onto Marshall Avenue, she tightened the knot on the scarf she'd brought along to keep her hair contained and tried not to stare too much at her fiancé. Despite his hours working indoors at a desk in New Jersey, Zeke was still her eye candy.

The only photo she had of him was one that was framed on her nightstand—a fuzzy snapshot, courtesy of the East Texas Chamber photographer who had taken pictures of them the night of the Big Inch Pipeline appreciation dinner. That evening, his hair had been slicked back, his chin clean-shaven, and his dinner jacket molded to his body. Movie stars had less sex appeal.

This version, with wind thrashing his hair and a day's stubble softening his jaw, was more the man she'd worked alongside on the pipeline project last year. Lane wished she had a camera so she could always remember that it had been a night much like this one when she realized Zeke might be the antidote to her blues.

"Do I have a growth coming out of my ear?"

She wasn't embarrassed that she'd been caught studying him. "Yes, and I've been trying to find a nice way to tell you that it's time you gave it a name."

He patted her knee. "You name this one, and I'll claim the right to choose a name for our firstborn."

Lane shivered, but she made it look like she'd caught a cold air current. Children were a topic she'd never contemplate. With her background, she didn't want to consider that she'd ever be a fit mother.

"It's bad luck to talk about babies. Don't you know anything, Hayes?"

"I know I love you."

Lane leaned over the gearshift and kissed his cheek. "You're a gem."

"Diamond in the rough is more like it." He cupped his hand over her kiss, acting as if her imprint were priceless. "What have you been doing while I've been held hostage by Major Parson?"

She folded her hands in her lap. The list was long, but she'd not bother him with drudgery—he'd never been briefed about her real role with the OSS, and she wasn't about to inform him now.

"Oh, you know a bit of this and that. Mostly waiting out the construction workers until I can thoroughly clean for the grand reopening, learning the business trade from J Lassiter, and getting ready for Roberta Harwood to descend on us lowly Longview-ites. And let me just say, ordering book inventory from New York publishers is not for the faint of heart."

"I'm sorry I won't be here for the book signing," he said over the roar of the Jeep's engine. "We'll be finishing details for the ribbon cutting on the last stretch of the Big Inch."

"Not to worry. I'm sure it will be a paltry attendance. Apparently, Mrs. Harwood's fame precedes her and not in a good way. I've been warned I'm courting evil incarnate."

"Well, that's got to be good for publicity."

"It might be." She'd been surprised when J Lassiter told it was a brilliant stroke of marketing to bring in an author with a scandalous reputation. He'd assured her the fascination with infamy was almost as tantalizing as a tent revival meeting. "The newspapers say they'll send reporters. But I don't hold out much hope. I'm sure there will be a robbery, fire, or war report that's far more important than my event."

Zeke shifted into fourth gear as he outran the slower traffic, seemingly thinking about her predicament while they left behind the motels, gas stations, and drill supply shops of Longview. Passing the inky trees that came right to the edge of the highway, she let her gaze drift to the woods bordering Highway 80, wondering what they'd find to talk about when the war wasn't central to every sentence.

After nearly hitting an oil tank truck turning blindly onto the road, they drove Highway 80, a stretch of road some in the East Texas Chamber of Commerce were nicknaming the miles of smiles. The pine trees became farms, and traffic thickened as they came to a town famous for its Presbyterian church and a Negro man's BBQ stand. The congestion through Greggton was backlogged with Longview shift-workers heading home and a bus painted to advertise a five-piece band that must have been playing at one of the honky-tonks.

Zeke started snapping his fingers to the song on the radio. She marveled that he was in such good spirits, having been on trains all day, but she shaded her eyes against the western sun and accepted that Zeke's happiness could be hers, too, if she'd embrace impulsiveness: things like spontaneous dinner dates, five days with no worries other than keeping up with her fiancé, and a future that could actually be free of major dramas.

She released a breath that rattled through her ribs. Yes, maybe she could be happy too.

Zeke guided the Jeep toward the parking lot of the Top Burger restaurant. He ground the gears down and bumped over a pothole.

"You want to come in with me?" he asked whipping into a narrow opening between a farm truck and a spiffed-up Model T. "I'm going to get our hamburgers for take away, but you might want to walk on the hallowed grounds while they get everything wrapped for the road."

"Tempting though that is—" She motioned to the oil-topped lot filling with teenagers and big, throaty-sounding cars. "I'll grab a few minutes of people watching. Don't forget that I was the one who won the bet for the chocolate shake."

Zeke pumped his foot against the brake, hiccupping the gears forward and backward before the Jeep finally settled. He smoothed his hair into some sort of order. "It's early yet, but later on, there will be drag races between here and the Golden Point burger joint in Longview. Those Lobo fans have to avenge the loss of bragging rights after the Pirates spanked them during basketball season."

Lane watched Zeke chat up some kids as he ambled into the restaurant. She pushed a stray hair back under her scarf, guessing that in time she'd know the names of the local high school teams and which rivalries were blood and which were just for mild entertainment.

Through the plate-glass windows, she could see teenagers stuffed into booths inside the Top Burger. They were skinny as rails, with big, trusting eyes and more hair than could be controlled by slick products and headbands.

Had she ever looked that innocent? Been so naive that her complexion didn't speak of anything more strenuous than yearbook photos and math tests? She thought back to Valdosta High School and remembered the bony girl who'd been bullied for her awkward social skills. What the jocks and glee club girls couldn't see was that Lane had been seasoned by a life of pretending and what she lacked in formal education she more than made up for in wits.

Not knowing where the next meal would come from had a way of teaching proficiencies that no high school class was authorized to grade. She'd mastered imitating accents for her mother's laughter, reading body language, and dodging a backhand—all before she'd learned long division. It was almost as if the patterns of romances, mean girls, and youth group chessboards was a third act to the violence she'd witnessed in the back rooms where she'd crouched, waiting out Delia Parrish's visits to her sugar daddies.

After Lane had moved in with her grandparents, Big Daddy wouldn't let anyone utter Delia's name in their home. Few asked about the things she'd endured. Lane's aunts would wrap her in a hug and a mess of collard greens, as if Sunday dinner could erase the haunt of men who'd come through her mother's door—the snake-eyed charmers with pills in one hand and belts in the other.

"A chocolate milkshake for the Queen of the Sabine."

Startled, Lane locked down memories she'd worked hard to forget. There'd be no indulgence for Delia tonight.

Zeke leaned over the driver's door with a box filled with drinks and sacks of greasy burgers. He handed her one of the cups.

She licked the whipped cream dripping onto her fingers as she caught up with his thought processes. "That nickname is only good if you buy the property along the river in Gladewater."

"In my mind, it's a done deal."

Lane watched him stash their dinner behind the seat braced by a cracked leather bag of golf clubs. "Does that mean you have the farm under contract?"

He jumped into the driver's seat and surveyed the parking lot before he jockeyed the gearshift, searching for reverse. "Now, I can't tell you my strategy without some preamble." Once out of the space, and digging the gearshift into first, he added. "That's how us attorneys like to do things. We need a panting audience and a stage with plenty of room to command."

The Jeep lurched into a pothole.

Lane grabbed for the door handle. "Forget the BS, are we heading out to see the property now?"

Zeke laughed. "I can see you're not going to flatter me." He shifted into second gear, yelling over the grinding noise, "I've got someplace special to take you tonight. A place unlike anything you've ever seen." He grandly gestured to the woods along the highway. "You might even say it's a sparkler in the necklace of magical places in East Texas."

As the pavement settled into tar-topped smoothness, she licked more cream off the top of her milkshake, feeling a moustache form above her lip. "That's what you said about the lake outside Longview—Lake Lomond."

He winked. "Stick with me, kid. I'll take you to the top of the world."

She'd seen enough of the world to satisfy her for a lifetime, but she'd not been this far west in Gregg County. Once they passed the Premiera Refinery, she'd be in new territory. She knew Simon Deason's house was close by, as she'd sent messengers with documents for Major Parson there often enough. But the rows of shopping centers and gas stations stringing Greggton together ran out of ribbon around the massive refinery.

Without Major Parson to point out what was what, she didn't recognize the family names on rig repair businesses or pawn shops that fanned out from the airplane runway at the edge of Primiera's property. Zeke didn't seem to be in an explaining mood either as he had to manhandle a Jeep that wasn't aligning with its lane. Lane leaned her head back against the seat, letting the wind whip away a week's worth of worries as she counted the pump jacks, speakeasies, and dives stacked between the trees. Good markers if she had to find a way back to civilization.

Chapter Ten

April 20, 1943 8:04 p.m.

Hearing the Jeep gear down, Lane sat upright in the seat. When she looked through the bug-slapped windshield, she could tell the sun's glare had lost some its starch. They must have been driving longer than she realized. A stench of burnt-off oil fumes circled the Jeep, a calling card from some nearby refinery. Zeke turned off the highway onto a slower paced farm-to-market road. She curved around to see what the sign marker posted for road identification and watched sunburnt kids gleefully riding horses along a fence line. Pump jacks and work sheds interrupted the fields of sweet potatoes.

"Is this Shangri-La?" she asked, settling back into the seat.

Zeke patted her knee before he had to grab the gearshift again to slow for a turn. "We're so close, I can smell it."

Lane still sniffed an odor of eau de oil production.

The Jeep bumped along a driveway as he pointed out a sign identifying the property as the Liberty Country Club.

"This is your idea of a date night?"

"Baby, golf is always the right choice."

Lane would have disagreed, but contained her comments out of indulgence for his obsession. This was Zeke's week off from work, and apparently, he needed to reconnect with his holy temple.

She peered through the gaps among thin pine trees, and thought the place looked as if a goat patch had been groomed to become a nine-hole course. Lanes of spotty grass were fitted around nodding pump jacks and oak trees that bore the scars from previous ice storms. The club seemed aimed at roughnecks rather than the elites who preferred the long, cushioned course of Pinecrest Country Club.

Zeke pumped the brakes to keep from hitting a truck backing out from under a shade tree. After a curse to the clueless driver, he waved his hand with the same aplomb J Lassiter used when showcasing new bolts of fabrics recently arrived from England. "I give you. . ." He paused for effect. "Nirvana."

Lane set the milkshake on the floorboard and untied the scarf knotted under her chin.

"Or, the backside of the moon," she murmured, looking to large patches of sand connecting gaps in the grass on a putting green.

"Not a believer?" He hopped over the door, landing with no indication the last ten miles ate into his backside. "I'll change your mind."

He handed her the greasy burger bags then pulled golf clubs from behind the passenger seat.

A shack with a wind-whipped green awning and a gaping window was steps away from where they had parked. Behind the shack, men lined up like toy soldiers on the driving range—some hunched over their tees, some whacking at balls, and the rest staring into the horizon like they were waiting on a divine hand to move their target a little closer to the right or left, as the case may be.

"We're going to have to redefine magical." Lane sighed. "The lake had more to offer and that was with the charm of potential snakebites."

"Don't judge." He hiked his worn golf bag higher on his shoulder. "Not all diamonds are obvious at first sight."

She could see two men leaning against the plywood counter that advertised baskets of golf balls for the driving range. Around their chewed cigars, they wore expressions that bordered on insulted as they watched Lane approach.

"If you'd told me I was coming to watch you play golf I'd have dressed more appropriately."

Zeke pinched her bottom. "You look perfect to me."

Lane followed him toward a pair of picnic tables positioned near the driving range. The brick clubhouse in the distance was nice enough, but it wasn't going to host wedding receptions or Chamber banquets. She set the Top Burger bags on the table. Zeke added the drinks.

He propped his clubs against the bench. "We'll dine first, and then I've got something to teach you."

She groaned. "I don't want you to teach me how to play golf."

He opened the bag and pulled out a bag of fries. Offering her the wrapper, he chided. "Eat first, then we'll talk. I know how unreasonable you are before you've had food."

Lane stuck her tongue out at him.

He snitched a fry from her bag and popped it in his mouth. "That one was for a taste test. Can't serve you sub-standard fries."

It was dangerous being engaged to a man who knew her weakness for hot, greasy food. What else had he observed? She tugged down the bell sleeves on her shirt in case scars from the frontlines were more visible than she realized.

A soft air swirled around her shoulders, making her appreciate the benefits of getting out of town, even if a rural golf course wasn't terribly romantic. But since Zeke was so happy she wasn't going to begrudge him the evening. He'd carried a heavy load for the US government these past few months between bickering companies, attorneys, and the pressures applied by the president to get that pipeline finished. If a few golf swings helped him unwind, so be it. She'd save their heavy conversations, and the confession she knew she needed to make, for another night. Lifting a leg over the bench, she settled next to him and helped arrange the food.

Zeke bit into his burger, and she followed suit—enjoying the explosion of flavor from beefy patties and the ooze created when ketchup, mayonnaise, and mustard melded into an odd dressing flavored with dill pickle. All that goodness was almost enough for her to block out the thwack of golf clubs, the curse of missed shots, and the fragrance of cigar smoke drifting on the breeze from the driving range in front of them.

Wiping a paper napkin across her mouth, she watched the dimming light shadow Zeke's face. His slightly crooked nose, the tiny scar, his eyes shaded by life, and creases that spoke of countless hours of laughter, all punctuated by a half-tipped smile that, at times, had made her feel like she was the most fascinating woman in the world.

He was a handsome man. And he was hers.

"Are you going to eat that whole thing in four bites?" she asked, examining the remains of his burger.

"Maybe," he said around a mouthful of beef. "And I can finish yours too."

She hugged her wax-paper wrapper. "Not on your life. I haven't had one of these since the last time you were home. Edith doesn't approve of hot food stands. She says insects fall into the cooking oil and you might eat a grasshopper when you think you're getting an onion ring."

He shook his head. "Your aunt has some strange ideas."

"None stranger than us pulling together a wedding by June twelfth, am I right?" She was impressed that she didn't even stutter saying the date out loud.

"Seven weeks to order up a preacher and a new suit?" He glanced toward the pink-streaked clouds hosting the last threads of sunlight. "Not impossible, but I'd need to check the tournament schedule."

She pinched a fry into two parts. "June doesn't seem absurdly fast to you?"

"It sounds like my prize for getting this pipeline wrapped in record time. Word is Roosevelt is going to float all our names for government jobs because the pipeline team did what everyone said couldn't be accomplished."

Lane needed a new strategy if she was going to delay a walk down the aisle. Would he believe her if she said her reservations were more about her inadequacies to be a wife than his to be a husband? Honesty was foundational in a marriage, and there was a whole lot he didn't know about the woman who shared his taste in hamburgers. When would she tell him?

With cars parked under trees and scattered over a gravel lot, she reminded herself a public golf course was not the place to roll out the junk in one's heart.

She pushed back the ghosts that wanted a voice, and smiled instead— imagining Zeke going toe-to-toe with the bureaucrats who had bedeviled Parson last year. "I'm sure the last thing those oilmen want to do is work for the government. Parson probably wants to get back to his empire."

"Those oilmen do grumble and grouse about jumping through hoops, mostly because they miss their Mrs. Mercer, the wunderkind secretary who kept them off the Department of the Interior's dartboard." He winked. "And I'm the lucky bastard who stole their secretary from under their noses."

"Sweetheart—" She placed her hand on his forearm. "I wasn't stolen. I quit."

"As I recall it, you quit reporting back to the spooks in Washington about Parson. I didn't think you were going to quit being a secretary altogether."

She chewed slowly, thinking through the conversation in the lobby of the Bramford Building last winter when she'd blurted out to Theo that she was choosing to stay in Longview. Zeke had witnessed the whole episode, but he'd never asked for specifics about what exactly she was retiring from.

"Lane?" He crumpled the greasy paper that had wrapped his burger. "Has Theo Marks been sneaking around again? Has he lured you into another of his operations?"

How easily she'd forgotten that Zeke's razor-sharp mind could figure outcomes before most people had even finished speaking the next sentence.

She dipped a fry into a puddle of ketchup and mustard. "Like I could tell you if he had."

Zeke's eyes glared. "You said you were done with that life. That you weren't going to do his dirty work anymore."

Though the opportunity was right to speak truth, she glanced around at the people teeing up at the driving range and knew the location was all wrong for disclosures that might compromise national security.

"I haven't seen Theo in, oh, at least five weeks. Right about the time you left for New Jersey."

Zeke's gaze didn't look mollified, but he went back to finishing the fries, regardless.

Though the fog of depression had lifted when she shifted roles within the OSS, she was disgusted to remember how quickly she'd broken that soldier's wrist the other day—and walked away remarkably guilt free.

No, this was most definitely not the place to explain her past.

Her focus shifted to four men slinking from the screened kitchen door at the back of the clubhouse. Their long-sleeved shirts and ties, and expensive slacks looked at odds with the casual golf attire Zeke wore. Some men were backslapping the others, but all looked as if their pockets had either lightened or gained based on the outcome of some wager.

"Hayes?"

Zeke's gaze shot toward the men skirting the practice putting green. Lane thought she heard him groan even as his posture bolstered with bravado.

"There's the chump that lost me a pocketful of Andrew Jacksons."

Zeke wiped his fingers against his thighs and stood, extending a hand toward the foursome approaching their table. "They'll let anyone in this place."

The men gathered around Zeke, firing questions at him about his next tournament game, where'd he'd played golf last, who he beat at that club in Tyler last fall, and what were his prospects for a Calcutta bet at a tournament in Henderson.

Lane's head was circling, chasing the words that swirled around him. She listened to the mixed bag of admiration and risk they assessed as a result of his handicap.

One of the men set a foamy mug of beer on the table, the froth spilling from the combined pressure of gravity and force. She wiped the spill with a napkin before it slid toward her lap.

"Well, who is this little honey, Hayes?"

She knew, without looking up, that she was suddenly the speculation of five sets of eyes.

"This is my fiancée, boys." Zeke's voice radiated pride. "How lucky am I?"

The group speculation felt darker, no doubt a by-product of the idea of a honeymoon, and she folded inward, a maneuver designed to disguise her femininity.

"You bring her out here to show off your putt, Hayes?"

"Yeah, probably teach her a few moves that have scared off the pros running through East Texas?"

"She know what you can do with a driver, boy?"

"Of course, she knows. He's a G-D celebrity on the circuit. Has women fawning over him at every chicken dinner."

Lane didn't know about the chicken dinners, but she could guess that as a single man, with his natural charm, Zeke was the center of most parties. She watched him with theses cronies and wondered if she'd need to go with him to the tournaments to protect his virtue.

"Getting married is sure enough going to throw off your concentration. Better not let it affect your putting game."

Lane could imagine Zeke hearing various versions of this monologue at every course between here and Center. She doubted anyone gave him this much feedback in the courtroom.

"Now, boys," Zeke said, bringing down the volume. "We're having ourselves a special dinner date. I don't have time to bring Lane up to the finer points of golf when the sun's going to set in about thirty minutes."

One man backslapped Zeke with a hit that caused him to sway forward. "You want to put some money on that, Hayes?"

Zeke reached for balance on the table, and shot Lane a gaze that begged her forgiveness for the intrusion. "Excuse me?"

"Let's make it interesting."

The man's voice had signaled an alarm, and tension shimmied along Lane's spine. She watched one of the other men dig his hands deep into his pockets. This didn't look like a group that would easily back off, as a matter of fact, she rather thought they intended to stay.

"Yeah, I'd like to win back the five hundred I just lost."

Zeke stalled for a moment before saying, "Lane's never held a golf club. This wouldn't even be a contest."

Lane searched the faces of those at the ball shack. They were moving toward the picnic table as if drawn by the thin, smoky vapor of a wager, noses sniffing the air for fresh money.

"I say," one of the men said, "put her on that driving range and if she can even hit the ball, I'll give you a hundred bucks."

"I'll give you five hundred if she can get a ball ten yards." Another added. "Easy money."

Zeke held his hands up in surrender. "Fellas, Lane's not for sale. She's a lady and soon to be my wife. We don't bet on women around here."

"I say we do," a fourth man stepped forward. "I haven't seen you since that tourney in Nacogdoches, but you owe me for cheating me out of a cup."

"No one cheated you, Alfred. The officials proved it."

The golfer jutted his finger into Zeke's chest. "If you don't want me telling everyone on the circuit that you've gone soft, you'll take this bet."

Zeke growled some four-letter words before he shifted his focus to Lane, wearing an expression that pleaded for cooperation. "Honey, ignore these fools, will you? Let's pack up and go back to town."

Lane thought through her options. As his wife, she'd have to hear this sort of boorish talk for years to come. Should she end it here? Or, let Zeke leave with his dignity intact?

"I told you when we drove in tonight that this wasn't a night for a golf lesson," Lane said, packing up the trash from their dinner. "I'm here to spend time with you. Not hit golf balls."

Alfred laughed. "So, Hayes has already got a chain around his ankle and he hasn't even said 'I do.'"

Three others chuckled.

"Figures," a newcomer added. "He's too pretty for a real sport."

Lane watched a whole book of pain, anger, and hard-won lessons fan across Zeke's face. She might be the only person who knew he burned demons from his childhood on the greens of the golf courses he played. His happy-go-lucky demeanor had been won in the school of hardship and humiliation. She couldn't remember what mantra had helped him overcome all those boulders, but those shared experiences were the tie that bound them together.

She'd never met another human being who could relate to her childhood better than Zeke Hayes. Maybe that's why she entertained a thought that would help him save face.

One of the men said, "Let's up the bet to a thousand, just to make it interesting."

Zeke whipped around to stare at the man. "I'm not giving you a dime of my hard-earned money."

"Pansy," the man hissed into Zeke's face.

Zeke closed his eyes the same moment he folded his fingers into a fist. Opening them, he said, "I don't have two thousand to give you, Emerson. Unlike you, I don't have oil wells flowing into my bank account."

Emerson shrugged. "I know where to find you to collect. Humor us. Put your missus on the driving range and give her your three wood. Let's see what she can do."

"My three wood is the oldest stick in my bag." Zeke's face blanched. "You know I don't even play it anymore."

Emerson winked. "Why, now that you say that, I do remember you saying it was warped from that flood down in Beaumont."

Lane knew Zeke was cornered and a part of her wanted to leave before the drunk men turned uglier, but a part of her couldn't resist the challenge either. It was one of the few thing she liked about herself. Most people wrote her off as quiet and boring never knowing that a childhood hewn from couch hopping and cotton fields had been fertile soil for growing a surprising arsenal of skills.

The fourth man clutched Lane's elbow before she could step away. "Come on, honey," he said dragging her toward the mounded grass ridge pocked by divots and broken tees. "Give us old men something to enjoy. We don't often get to be on the front side of Zeke Hayes."

Lane tripped on the grade of the rise. She looked back to see Zeke's tortured expression.

"Lane, don't go along with this madness." Zeke stepped around the picnic bench, catching his shoe on the edge. "I'll take you home right now."

One of the men picked up Zeke's golf bag and found the wooden club. He brandished it back and forth as he walked the small distance to the open slot on the driving range.

"Stop." Zeke swung his arm out trying to catch the club from the fool. "I'll pay you each fifty bucks to go back into the hole you just climbed out of."

"No can do, buckaroo," Emerson yelled. "We're all in for two thousand each. Right, boys?"

The chorus of amens circled Lane.

Emerson passed the club on her. "You know what to do with this, honey? You hold it by the shaft, you give it a good squeeze, and then you pull it back for all your worth and hit the ball."

Lane hoped she'd remember this man's mottled face if she ran into him in Longview. He deserved to have his tires slit. "That sounds too simple."

Emerson wrapped his arms around her body as if he was going to teach her how to swing. His breath overheated the skin of her ear as he growled, "I bet you can manage. Just follow my lead."

Repulsed more by the way he leaned against her, than the beer and sweat that clung to him, she dug her heel into his toe.

"Lane, stop this minute." Zeke lurched toward the range. "I mean it, don't do this—"

One of the men grabbed him by the arms and held him back. "Get used to a woman taking all your money, Hayes. They're born with the talent."

Putting all her weight into her ankle, she heard the man groan. "Don't ever touch me again," she hissed to him, stepping away and prepared to do a knee block if he didn't understand her tone.

His eyes narrowed. "You'll pay, hussy."

As Emerson ambled back to his buddies, laughing like he'd done the best he could to set up the shot, Lane knew there was one way to end this. The cracked leather handle of the club dug into her palm and the skin of her fingers. "I'm only going to take one swing," she called out, knowing her voice sounded about thirteen and nervous. Little did they know she felt about a hundred. "Then I'm going home. Will that satisfy everyone?"

The men agreed, save one who grumbled about women not knowing their place.

Zeke sagged as if anticipating torture. "I will hurt the next man who touches my fiancé. I mean it."

Lane stepped up to the nearest tee box and reached for a busted wooden pick of wood. "Is this thing important?"

Zeke stood on his toes. "Lane, we can leave right this moment."

A golfer from another place at the driving green found a fresh tee and a ball and set the shot for her. "Those men are just having a little fun, sweetheart. They don't mean anything by it. Swing the club and give them a story to tell tomorrow around the water cooler."

Lane pitched the club between both her palms, feeling the weight of the wood. "This thing is heavy."

A swell of laughter washed over her as she addressed the tee. She flexed her knees and swung her hips to get a posture similar to those she'd watched earlier on the driving range.

She stood upright again. "Just one shot," she called back to the crowd. "Okay?"

Zeke rushed for her, but was held back by a golfer in a striped shirt.

"These are the most idiotic men I've ever met," she muttered as she gauged the distance of the driving range. "Okay, here I go," she yelled for the crowd that had formed around Zeke.

A memory from South Georgia brushed through her body. She pictured a prim man, more into fashion than she'd have thought for an associate of her grandfather's, but golf was a fascination that seemed to have drifted up from Florida, and those in Valdosta had not been immune to its fancies. Sometimes, when she carted for Big Daddy, she'd been more interested in the honeysuckle growing wild along the course than in how many yards it was to the green. But numbers and patterns eventually entertained her more than scents, and she learned strategy as much on the back nine as she did in any classroom.

Lane loosened her shoulders, flexed her knees, focused on the ball, and tucked her right elbow close to her ribs, getting the best angle to push her swing back towards the right, and on the follow-through, she hit the sweet spot of the ball, hearing the thwack crack the tension in the air.

Peeking over her shoulder, she watched the ball climb higher, follow an unseen arc, and land softly beyond the farthest distance marker on the range.

She'd never understood the fun of this game, thinking that the Scottish man who invented it must have had a lot of aggression and liked to hit things to make up for the inadequacies in his life. Even after all those summers playing golf with her grandfather, she still didn't understand the thrill.

Lane brought her arms down and turned to face Zeke. The collective awe was not something she was likely to forget, but this wasn't a moment of glory she'd savor. She'd pulled another con. Another agency sin she couldn't seem to shake.

"I'm going home now," she said, picking up the broken tee and tucking it into her pants pocket as a keepsake to mark that she knew she needed to stop lying.

Zeke's face broke into a hundred rainbows, his eyes as bright as any star glowing over Texas.

Cursing words barraged her like grenades as she stepped off the driving range, but she could let the insults roll off her back. Delia's men had said worse after discovering they'd been outwitted by her slip of a daughter.

As she passed Zeke, she leaned close and whispered, "I never said I didn't know how to play. Just that I didn't want a lesson."

Chapter Eleven

April 21, 1943 9:24 a.m.

Lane stood outside the blue door of the bookshop, wondering if she'd made a mistake in listening to her business mentor. J had suggested she consider moving the bookshop to the street to attract customers, and she'd taken him at his word. She'd rolled in Victor's wheelbarrow this morning, the rusted one with the sagging center—hoping he'd have given permission had he been around—and filled it with crumpled newsprint and children's Easter basket grass she bought on sale at Thompson's Department Store. She staggered not quite mildewed books like vegetables sprouting in a garden.

It had seemed like a good idea when it'd come to her in the middle of the night. Now, she tried different arrangements, none of which had any oomph.

If she shifted the pot of geraniums, it would camouflage the flattened tire and maybe also act as a prop if she wanted to open the door, inviting a breeze to sweep away the glue and dust particles that still lingered in the shop.

An old familiar sizzle in her gut caused her to pause. Like muscle memory, her intuition warned her that she was being watched. Leaning against the building, she pretended to study the wheelbarrow, but in fact she was surveying the windows that would have a view of this door. A black farmer carried a crate of vegetables into the alley, but he was the only unexpected person among the shopkeepers opening their businesses for the day.

Shrugging off the feeling, Lane reached into her tote bag and pulled out a sign—These Books Free to a Good Home—and propped it between a slightly warped medical reference and collected poems of Thoreau. Picking up a red leather book whose gold-leaf title had long since worn away, she leafed through the pages and saw in scroll art framing a quotation by St. Augustine, "The Christian should be an Alleluia from head to foot!"

Lane slammed the cover shut.

Instead of jamming the volume beside Thoreau, she folded it into the pocket of her apron. It wasn't that she wanted it, but Slim would like the gift. He'd probably relish knowing he was an Alleluia from head to foot. It was far better than how Molly labeled him.

She heard a heavy tread of footsteps, like someone was accommodating a bum knee.

"Folks don't trust free."

The resonant voice confirmed her intuition warning.

Rotating on her heel, she saw Israel Wyatt wearing a buttoned-at-the-throat starched shirt, vested suit, and fedora, even though the temperatures were already climbing to eighty. The beads of perspiration dripping along the thick folds of his ear were the only clue that the black man was overheated.

It had been a month since she'd last seen him, maybe more. Keeping up with the benevolent dictator of East Longview was not her primary focus now that he was not on hers—or the OSS—radar for information related to those with a grudge against the Big Inch Pipeline Project. Not that he'd ever welcomed her into his inner circle.

As a white woman with connections, she'd opened doors that would have been closed to him otherwise. Lane had helped a few of his young friends find means of travel between Longview and a welder's teaching facility for new pipefitters in Humble, Texas. They'd sent three waves of men to brighter horizons as oilfield gypsies or ditching laborers, depending on their aptitudes. War work was turning out to be great for Texas economics but lousy for those projects in remote places that still needed skilled labor. This human pipeline felt as critical as the one shipping oil to the troops in Europe. Plus, helping black men find jobs eased her conscience for the lives she'd not been able to save in France.

"You're an expert on sales strategies too?" she asked, wondering if Wyatt's complex portfolio of influence and business would ever be fully exposed.

He lifted his shoulders in what some might think was a shrug but what she thought actually bought him a more comfortable position for the sidearm tucked under his arm. "If it doesn't cost 'em something, they're not going to think there's any value."

Who knew? He might have been right.

In Beaune, she'd had to practically beg the farmers and wives to accept the military-issued coffee and chocolate bars she'd bartered in hopes that the trade would gain her access to the Resistance's secret meetings. The

French didn't trust her at first, so why would Longview shoppers be any different?

"Thanks for the tip." Lane folded a dust cloth into her palm. "I have to remove the warped bookshelves, and that means this old inventory goes too because Mr. Lassiter says cheaper paperbacks will bring more customers in."

Wyatt nodded like he understood J Lassiter's thinking. The self-ascribed judge, who'd never been elected to any post, had lived here long enough to remember days when customers bargained with credit and IOUs before cash flowed along with black gold. Based on what she'd learned about Wyatt's network of butchers, markets, and speakeasies, he still might operate on that model.

"Patrick is in trouble."

And with those quiet words, the Judge got down to business.

Lane leaned forward and moved Thoreau over to a section with other poets. Patrick Le Bleu worked for the Wyatts in a variety of roles, usually dependent on them to cover for whatever scheme he'd set in motion. She'd met Patrick when he was working Mrs. Wyatt's ambulance service, then later as a waiter for a private party at the Bramford estate. He'd been in and out of Lane's peripheral vision for months, always at the Judge's beck and call, but never on the list to move out of Longview for a skilled labor job.

In the months since Lane met Patrick, he'd proven to be reliable, even if he was usually steeped in anger. She wondered what he was today.

"Is he ill or in trouble with the law?" Lane pulled at the plastic grass. Sometimes, she'd learned, people shuttered their eyes thinking they wouldn't betray a move that way, but they'd forget that their voices give away a lot of information by tone.

Wyatt stepped closer to the shop's door, a move guaranteeing shade and privacy. "He's healthy as a horse."

Lane flipped through the pages of a mildewed dictionary. "Zeke is in town if he needs representation."

"This isn't a matter for Hayes." Judge Wyatt lifted the edge of his fedora, as if allowing a current of air to cool his brow. "I need you to help me find him a different line of work."

She wasn't sure how many employers were interested in a man with thug-like qualities, a patch over his blinded eye, and a perpetual bad attitude, but she'd guess there weren't many. "Has he tried the Marines?"

"You know he's not military material."

Lane replaced the book. Even if he had use of both eyes, Patrick wouldn't enjoy any line of military service. "He'd hate the uniform. Someone always telling him to spit-shine his shoes, and all that being-on-time business would probably drive him to use his fists."

A moment lapsed, and the breeze carried the scents of bread baking from the not-too-distant kitchen of the Brass Rail.

"I want you to connect him with the people you work for." Wyatt's voice was a whisper. "He'd be good doing secret stuff."

Recovering her shock, Lane pulled at the fake grass and shifted more of it around the dictionary. Wyatt knew, or thought he had guessed, many things about her activities and endless supply of contacts, but she'd never implied it was more than mere coincidence—an opportunity born out of being at the right place, at the right time. She'd been particularly careful to keep the OSS out of East Longview because what she knew of their culture from her days in Georgia implied few former sharecroppers and grandchildren of slaves trusted the government. "I have no idea what you're talking about."

"We don't have time to do that dance, Red Bird."

She glanced at him, seeing his eyes narrow as he took a step closer. When he used that ridiculous nickname, she knew he wanted her full attention.

"There's been a man at Flanagan's poker games asking about you." Judge Wyatt's whisper never faltered, but he might as well have been thumping a pulpit for his seriousness. "He's been to the Cotton Club, and my boys at the Junction say he's talking to the drunks and pimps about whether or not they've seen you around. Seems to think you work for a secret organization that spies on people and sells information."

A slew of blue words sailed through her mind, but she capped them for the bigger thought—who had outed her?

"Look at me." She waved her hand around her white eyelet blouse and navy skirt. "I'm about as ordinary as biscuits."

"You," his gaze scanned her body, "are no biscuit."

Lane reached into her tote bag and pulled out a marker. She drew a line through the word "free" on her sign and wrote "five cents" over it. She hoped he'd not see how her fingers shook. "Who in the world would be interested in me? I have few friends in this town."

Wyatt shook his head. "No information until you promise you'll get Patrick in with your people. He could be useful in that line of work."

Patrick was as subtle as a freight train on fire.

Though the OSS had recruited former convicts to its arsenal of employees, she didn't see how Patrick could master the art of mindfulness needed to carry out missions along dangerous military fronts. Theo wanted more soldierly types, but with those men being sent to the front lines he often had to take what he could get. Which was most likely how the organization ended up with so many women in the ranks.

What would the OSS think of Patrick? Could the grandson of a slave be called on to give his all for the flag? Could he be counted on to drag a fellow agent out of a hellhole, possibly at his own expense?

Even more frightening was the question, who had access to the agency roster? And why were they destroying her cover?

There were too many questions firing in her brain to come up with a pithy comment to put off Judge Wyatt. She'd have to think faster than the lawyer if she was going to retain any hand in future negotiations.

"Well, then, I guess we're at an impasse." She lifted a copy of *The Emerald City of Oz* which had an unfortunate water stain over the cover and offered it the Judge. *"Unless you want to buy a book?"*

"I don't read fiction."

"Don't or can't?"

His gaze hardened, as if he'd had to justify himself for far too long. "I have a law degree."

"Just checking. Not everyone who calls himself a judge really is one." This self-appointed leader had won the title for his ability to solve difficult problems for people with few advocates.

Wyatt was apparently bored with her because he started to move away. That was okay. She was totally mortified by his words and needed some breathing room too.

"I'll be back," he promised as he readjusted his fedora.

She watched him step toward the curb. "Just plan on buying books the next time you come. I'm going to have a famous author here next week. Tell all your friends."

He disappeared into the traffic filling the sidewalks.

Lane wiped her brow again, sure that the strain of disguising her stress was evident even to a child.

The shop door jerked open, and Edith peeked around the jamb. "Is that man gone?"

"Yes," Lane said, stepping through the door. "He was asking around to see if I knew anyone hiring."

"Like you would ever have a Negro working in here."

Lane reached back to get her tote bag and pulled it over the threshold. "He's not contagious. He just has a different skin color."

Edith tilted her head to the side. "I do not know where you get your mindsets. Always bucking traditions."

"Retail is not a tradition. Lots of people of all sorts of colors work in it."

"Not in the city limits they don't."

Lane dropped her bag on the table tucked under the shop's window, currently devoid of inventory. "You're probably right about that."

Edith moved her bucket of soapy water from Lane's path. "I washed down all the shelves, just like you asked. The next thing on your list was the window ledge."

Lane looked up to empty oak planks, glistening with shine and the room freshened by the scent of soap. While she'd been outside arranging her book display, her aunt had cleaned three cases that had been filled with the previous owner's dubious choices for reading material.

"I'm impressed."

"It's the Murphy's Oil Soap. It works magic."

Actually, Lane would give credit to Victor's continued absence. Since his departure, Edith had emptied two closets, donated clothes to the Red Cross, and reorganized the front break in the dining room. At this rate, they'd be lucky to have a doily that hadn't been starched decorating a chair.

Edith held a folded paper in her hand. "Why haven't you filled in this form? I told those girls to come see you. You'd be perfect in Junior League."

Lane filched the application. "I wondered where this had gotten to," she said, folding it into the apron pocket already stuffed with a book.

"It was sitting right under your calendar."

"Was it, now?"

She was reluctant to tell her aunt how the idea of joining a group of mission-minded women bent on making Longview a better place absolutely terrified her. She couldn't even explain it to herself. Except that it was too normal. Too Southern. And too much like what her mother should have done, had her mother not taken a leap off the cliff of Parrish family expectation.

"It would help you to make friends." Edith wiped the rag along the window ledge. "And be good for Zeke too. He needs to make business contacts. That way, when he's done with this pipeline project, he can come back to Longview and go back to being a real lawyer. Not that man who is always fishing clients out of jail. He needs to put that messiness behind him."

Lane wasn't sure what her aunt thought constituted an attorney's job description, but Zeke seemed happy enough doing what he was doing this year. She had her doubts that he'd be as content as an everyday attorney after the adrenaline of Washington, but they hadn't talked much about their job prospects last night. They'd been too busy containing the fire that scorched every time they got within kissing distance.

That was, when he wasn't furious with her for duping him about her golf skills. But she didn't want to talk to him about that eight-thousand-dollar swing or how many Saturdays she'd spent caddying for her grandfather. Georgia was not something she talked about. Ever.

90

The clatter of metal locks stunned her away from the red dirt of her past. She turned toward the stockroom and waited to see who knew how to bypass her security.

"Is that your back door?" Edith twisted water from the rag into the bucket. "You said you weren't expecting any more workers and that's why we could get the shop cleaned out. That's what you said, and doggone it, if this place hasn't been like a fire sale."

"I planned us a work day." Lane hid her exasperation by lifting the bucket and moving it closer to the giant cabinet that served as her sales desk. "But sometimes surprises happen."

"I thought we could iron out wedding details." Edith followed Lane, wiping water drips from the floor. "But it's so busy, I can't seem to get one flat minute of your time."

Lane squeezed her eyes shut. "Can't we spend time together without having to talk about the wedding?"

"Of course, but—"

"No, buts. I really need to see about this. . .delivery." Lane brushed her hands on her apron. "If you could work the dust out of these carved flowers, maybe get the pencil shavings off the paint, I'd be grateful."

As Lane hurried toward the stockroom, her aunt called out, "Grateful enough to go dress shopping this afternoon?"

Lane sighed as she steadied her balance by reaching for the archway and providing cover for the person slinking into the stockroom. "I have a million things to do before we can start that madness," she yelled to disguise the sound of footsteps.

Picking up the stylus on the gramophone, she added, "I'm going to set a record playing for you. It's something pretty to listen to while you're cleaning." And it would disguise the sounds of secret conversations.

After turning the volume dial to nine out of ten for the familiar Mozart concerto, she looked around the boxes of new inventory and the stack of books she'd planned to donate to the soldiers at Harmon General. Despite the rising crescendo of violins, there she was, alone in the space. Only one person knew how to circumvent her security system, and he was nowhere to be seen.

Theo Marks leaned around the corner of the stairwell wall and placed a finger against his lips. His suit was pressed, his hat tilted to an angle, and his eyes didn't bear any of the bags associated with one who kept the hours of an owl. Lane could assume he'd been in town a while. He nodded toward the upstairs apartment, his expression insisting she join him.

Lane glanced toward the shop, seeing Edith on her knees, wiping the front panel of the cabinet. Morning sunshine, diffused through the curtain at the bay window, painted Edith's concentration with a soft brush. Despite the dustups over the Junior League application and the ongoing battle about wedding plans, Lane was grateful for a relative who'd opened her absurdly neat house and allowed a messy girl to find refuge.

It was her childhood all over again.

Turning the volume up on the speaker, she scooted toward the stairs, knowing she wouldn't have much time until Edith started to investigate. Her aunt had barely accepted the explanation for Stuart Lemming's friendship; there was no way Theo Marks would get away without a full interrogation. Whereas Stuart sort of engendered trust and boy-next-door confidence, Theo's enigmatic eyes and half-lifted smile evoked every warning mothers gave their daughters about charmers and the destruction they left in their wake.

She could almost see Edith throw up her hands and demand an accounting for how many men Lane was dangling on a string. With Zeke right there, needing a wedding band too. She didn't have a proper explanation, for all these interesting men finding something of value in her, so she fell back on the most reasonable explanation and that was that she was doing work not expected of a girl, and for some reason, such doings engendered attention—sometimes, protectiveness.

Tiptoeing to the left, because that was the less squeaky side of the stairwell, she saw Theo's wingtips before she saw her boss. With a penchant for fashion, it was noteworthy that his shoes were marred with mud and that only added to the unease she felt about him "surprising" her.

His hand reached down to help her up the last stair. "Hello, love."

She smiled, putting her hand in his. "Long time, no see, Kemosabe."

"It's this brutal war." He stepped back to give her space on the landing that served as the foyer for an apartment never intended to charge rent. "I've been running from coast to coast with pit stops in New Mexico to check on top-secret test sites. You might be happy to know that your physicist, who stayed in this matchbox last winter is hard at work on something that we pray is never unleashed on the world."

"I don't know how you sleep at night." Lane never aspired to his level of responsibility. She doubted few would. "But on behalf of the known universe, I'll say thank you."

Glancing around at the dust-covered floor that was a puzzle of shoeprints, she flipped the light switch, illuminating the long room built into the eaves of the shop.

"What do you think?" Lane waved her hand toward the space that boasted a kitchen unit attached to a wall and a pony wall that gave some privacy between what she'd mapped out to be the living room and the sleeping area tucked under the half-moon window. "Can you see the potential?"

Theo took off his fedora and ran his finger around the rim. "As long as we have deadbolts on the doors, privacy film on that window, and some sort of fan to move the air around up here, I couldn't care less."

She frowned. "And here I was trying out homemaker skills by making it functional and pretty."

He laughed and patted her shoulder. "My budget for this place has been tapped. If you can do pretty and functional without costing me another penny, then knock yourself out."

Lane dragged her finger through the dust on the counter. "When you put it like that, I guess I can get the place mopped and a sleeping bag brought up."

Theo stepped back and opened the door to the remodeled bathroom, complete with a walk-in shower and a cabinet around the sink. He turned on the taps to watch clear water run from the faucet.

"I think your homemaking skills are going to get a good grade." He turned off the light and opened the closet, a makeshift space built between the stair wall and the eaves sloping toward the alley. "What's your groom think about all this? Is Hayes game to let you redecorate his bachelor digs?"

The ring on her left hand weighed heavy, and she hid her hands in the pockets of her apron. "He rents a room from a family, and I live with my relatives. Neither of us has a home to be redecorated."

Theo's gaze narrowed. "I guess that means you've not bought a place anticipating imminent vows."

Lane avoided his eyes. "You've guessed correctly."

"Surprising."

"What is?" She turned back to see his expression had gone from taskmaster to friend. His most dangerous look. The one she'd learned to avoid if she wanted to keep distance between them.

"If I were your fiancé, I'd not have let so much time get away."

She'd once felt that way about Theo too, but that was a long time ago, and life in between had changed the way she felt about men who chased thrills and intrigue. Another chalk mark in Zeke's favor.

"Well, as it turns out," she said, looking back toward the room that needed a sofa, a table and her fiancé, "my Mr. Hayes is quite the man around Washington and is doing his part for the war effort by negotiating contracts for the pipeline project. They're just days away from opening up all 1,400 miles of that monstrosity, and maybe then he can come back to Longview. To stay."

Theo stood shoulder to shoulder with her, folding his arm over his chest and gazing into the same void that she did. "He sounds like a paragon of legal expertise. But how smart can he be when he leaves a delectable young widow unchaperoned in a city teeming with soldiers and oilmen?"

"I'm not that delectable."

"Haven't you heard? Beauty is in the eye of the beholder."

Delia had been beautiful, but the rouge and costume jewelry couldn't cover the bruises. In the end, the ceramic pots of makeup were as empty as her mother's eyes.

Ignoring Theo's jibe, Lane sighed for effect. "I'm too busy with all this construction and keeping our friend Emmie out of the trenches to plan a wedding."

The half-truth sounded plausible. Edith wasn't able to complain otherwise either.

Theo was quiet, as if considering the burden of her life. "Were you happy with your first husband?"

Stunned, she blinked. Looking for something less volatile to consider, she walked over to the pile of trash and kicked insulation tags and bits of drywall towards the corner. "Who can say? We didn't actually live together for very long."

"Probably long enough. I knew Roy quite well. I can't imagine he'd have been an easy man to keep tied to an apron string."

Bristling from the insult—whether from yet another suggestion she wasn't enough of a woman to keep her husband satisfied or the one where Roy was painted as an ogre—her thoughts swirled for a defense. Theo had never previously shown much interest in her marriage once Roy's death certificate had been signed. She'd always assumed it was because he'd worked with Roy in the OSS and, out of compassion for her ingénue status with the agency, didn't want to poke a wound. That consideration, if it had been real, was officially over.

Now, Zeke was under scrutiny for letting her dictate the swiftness of their romance. She didn't see an answer that was sufficient to satisfy a man who knew almost every detail of her life and one who was remarkably cagey about his own. All she could own was that she was tired of being seen as a naïve girl who'd fallen for a handsome man during a time of national crisis. The echoing taunt that Roy would never have chosen her under normal circumstances was never far from her memories of him.

"I haven't thought of Roy in quite some time." She denied the specter that had dogged her since Stuart first spoke it into existence on the steps of the Gregg Hotel. "But when he was around, he was a lot of fun. I knew, even then, that it was odd he'd have chosen someone like me to marry when he could have had a show girl, but I guess I hoped he'd have decided that a long life together with someone who didn't demand much would be better than marrying someone who stared into the mirror all day."

Theo set his hat on the carved ball at the top of the stair's railing. "I've touched a nerve. I didn't mean to cause offense, but I was wondering if you had lingering feelings for your first husband—if that's why you weren't already at the altar with Hayes."

Lane closed her eyes to hide the flash of anger. "I wish people would stop rushing me to get married. There's no law that says one must walk the aisle three months after an engagement."

He turned the light switch off, casting the room in shadows. "I'd trust your gut over conventions." He loosened the tie at his throat. "But just so you don't waste any time wondering, Mercer wouldn't have stayed faithful to you. He was not a good chap."

A good chap.

That was Theo's moniker for the men he'd trust with his life—and there were precious few of those.

As one of the Army Rangers drafted toward the end of the First World War, Theo lived by a code that few Americans understood. He might appear cultured, but underneath that bespoke suit beat the heart of a man who could run black operations along enemy lines. If she'd not seen the duality, she'd probably not believe it either. So, if Roy, also an Army man, didn't make Theo's cut, she'd be thankful that widowhood kept her from a life of misery.

Her reservations for marrying again really weren't about whether or not she could trust Zeke—he was the opposite of Roy in so many ways—but it was as if some unseen hand was warning her to wait. She'd have thought her conscience scarred beyond recognition, unable to send intuitive signals after her mistakes that had cost the lives of four French Resistance fighters. But there was a ping, and it sounded every time matrimony came into a conversation.

Lane checked her wristwatch. She couldn't afford too many more minutes upstairs without Edith getting suspicious.

"There's probably something I should tell you about Roy," Theo said, with unusual reserve. "Something important, but I've never quite known how to bring it up."

She held her hand forward to stop another lock opening and releasing memories she'd stuffed under a headstone. The days with Stuart battered against her conscience, insisting she do something with the grief she'd long ago denied. Grief wasn't done with her, and she wasn't prepared to give it any advantages. "Don't bother. The less I know about Roy's past, the better. Maybe it's my pride, but I'd rather not hear that he was already more unfaithful than the woman in the London pub. And, I'd really rather not hear it confirmed that I was a mistake he couldn't wait to rectify."

Theo rubbed his thumb over his bottom lip. "Another time then."

"Yes, another time." Or not. Roy had been her fantasy come to life, and he'd been a solid body that she imagined going through life with—and for a girl who'd lived on the run—that meant the world to her. "Now, why are you here?"

"I need you to put on your hostess hat because I have a guest coming to stay in this birdcage, and I'm here today to check on the security measures needed to keep the man locked-in."

A million unfinished details took flight like origami on fire. Lane saw the hammer still on the counter. "I thought our issues were usually about keeping other people out?"

Theo cocked his head to one side as if relieving a crick in his neck. "This one. . .is special." His voice was anything but pleased. "We don't know a hundred percent, but there's suspicion that he's a double agent. The British would have killed him in Calais if our government didn't suggest that he could be useful to us in the end game."

Lane pictured the box of imported goods hidden in her storage closet. "You did manage to break through the locking mechanisms on the alley door just now; could he do that also?"

"I'm thinking your back door is the least of our concerns." Theo checked his watch. "What we really need is a bodyguard."

No one would ever ask her if she wanted to host a particular agency guest, the protocol was to do the job with the minimum of mistakes. Even if that meant harboring someone who'd let her countrymen die.

Lane breathed deeply, the paint fumes lingering in the space. The oily air might ease her reservations past the resentment she'd feel if she had to protect someone who would never be a friend to the United States.

The only other agent who'd stayed in this apartment had shown up in the winter and had been content to work out mathematical puzzles. This new one was creating havoc, and he hadn't even arrived yet.

A mallet started pounding behind her eye. Zeke would not be pleased to find out she was hosting a spy. He'd especially not be thrilled to find out she was still tied by financial strings to Theo Marks, either. The debacle last winter was supposed to have been the end of her work with Washington organizations.

Lane wondered if Theo could see the sudden twitch of her lid. "You're saying that there needs to be someone, other than me, who can babysit this guest?" She waved a hand toward the floor. "I still have a few workers getting the shop ready to open."

"I have seen your skill with a knife, but in this case, we'll need a man who can hogtie Boris if necessary." Theo slipped his hands into his pockets and rocked back on his heels. "Your shop renovation isn't a priority. Shut down whatever you've planned until after he leaves. Which, with good behavior, might be three days. Depends on when the Feds have a new spot for him."

"You do know there's a psych ward at Harmon General? It seems to be escape proof."

Theo picked up his fedora, passing it between his hands like he was deciding which was heavier; the hatband or his thoughts. "I've got enough problems with Emmie chasing her Dr. Death and trying to get extra staff out there to help her process the list of suspects, so I'll not add a malcontent Russian into the mix. Let's take a look at this apartment door and see how it might be bolted from the outside."

It was a hand-me-down door from the surplus store, one the carpenter had told her was too big for most new houses. "Where will this Boris go after Longview?"

Theo paused on the stair, his voice dropping to a whisper. "He's hoping his handlers will settle him in Reno, but Roosevelt wants him where we can use him for leverage. I imagine we'll keep him as bait, should the Germans follow through on invading Mexico."

She hung onto the handrail while Theo studied the apartment door's proximity to the support wall. "You think the Nazis will come up through the south?" she asked, picturing a worst-case scenario for Texas's unprotected border.

"At this point, I wouldn't put anything past them." Theo looked at her like he was communicating his deepest fears. "That's why we've got to do everything we can to stop them. And that's why this Russian is valuable. He's credited with knowing the strategy for those submarines hovering along the Gulf Coast."

Lane ran one hand through her hair, wondering how her life had gotten so complicated. "I think I can solve the bodyguard issue, but I'm going to need you to take a huge leap of faith on a guy that might not be your first choice. On a positive note, I'm pretty sure he's available immediately."

"I'm not hiring your fiancé." Theo straightened his tie and lowered his voice another notch. "I need someone who will knock a man down first, ask questions later. Your Mr. Hayes would cross examine Boris before he'd ever lift a finger."

Lane could hear that the concerto was almost to the end, so she stepped softly to the top of the stairs and listened for her aunt's footsteps, not putting it past her to eavesdrop if she'd heard their voices. There weren't any other noises other than the string section winding down.

Whispering, she tilted her head downstairs. "It's time for me to go. Lock up when you leave. I'm sure you know how."

She searched Theo's face, looking at each laugh line carved around his brown eyes for some clue as to how to navigate forward, but he wasn't as easy to read as he'd been in Europe. Time, distance, and her choosing Zeke over active duty status had put footers to a wall that was coming between them.

Lane put a soft step on the stair and looked at him again as she found her balance. Yes, Theo wasn't the same man she'd known from the front lines, any more than she was the same woman. He'd always be her friend, but he might not always be her ally. Hurrying downstairs, she rushed to the gramophone, lifting the stylus before the needle grooved into the center board.

"Tea Cup, I've been having the most delightful conversation with your aunt."

Lane froze, the stylus nearly dropping from her fingers. The sound of that deep voice resonating from the bookshop was terrifying. Leaning back on her heels, she glanced into the store to see Slim and Edith reading something opened on the cabinet.

"We've found a copy of Chesterton's sermons and are having the best time talking about favorite scriptures." Slim held his reading glasses in the air. "I'd do anything to be able to write like this."

"Slim, I didn't realize you were still in town!" Lane pushed hair behind her ear. "I thought your work with the Big Inch was keeping you in New Jersey, with Parson and Zeke."

Slim Elliott's wink was loaded with importance that had nothing to do with steel, welding bits, and over-worked men. "I had a better reason to slip back into Longview. Got a woman on my mind."

Lane hoped that woman was not a nurse-cum-spy with a bad attitude. Slim would be snapped in two by the bite of a woman with as much history as Emmie carried around. Maybe, he'd met someone else.

Too surprised to do much else, Lane waved. "Be there in a minute. Can't wait to see what book you found."

The whisper of Theo's footfall caused her to swing around toward the door.

"Bye, love." Theo nodded goodbye as he cracked the door wide enough to pass through. "Don't do anything I wouldn't do."

Lane hurried to lock the door behind him and leaned against the wood, breathing as if she'd run miles. Thoughts collided in her mind, and her biggest worry was not that she'd be incapable of keeping this twirling circus of situations from imploding—that was a given. Worse, what would happen if she did manage it well? And she still liked the thrill of espionage?

Lane heard Slim and Edith's laughter from the front of the shop. She let her eyes drift shut, imagining a future where she lived two lives at once through all the seasons of life.

Serving one's country had to have an expiration date, didn't it?

Chapter Twelve

April 22, 1943 1:55 p.m.

Lane parked her uncle's Hudson in the visitor's lot of Harmon General. She clicked off the radio, shutting down the war updates broadcast from KFRO. Her finger tapped the knob like she could somehow improve outcomes if she never had to deal with the realities.

Edith had recently stated that she'd refused to listen to any more news reports on the premise the announcers were sending her into despair. She'd started pressing flowers between the pages of Victor's books and remembered the new hobby every time her favorite radio broadcast was interrupted by the news service.

Lane's therapy of choice involved scraping rust off the library ladder and taking apart the warped shelves in the bookshop. Though she didn't enjoy hearing the bulletins, she knew that somewhere in the spin of words were the nuggets that would reveal the truth of what the generals had planned. It was in the sub-text where she'd better understand the threat facing Americans at home.

A gentle breeze whistled through the open windows, cooling her heavy thoughts.

"I'm going to look up one of my law school buddies in the commander's office," Zeke said, crawling out of the passenger seat and stretching his back as he stood on the tar-topped pavement.

Lane pushed open her door. "It won't take me long to touch base with this friend who called in tears because her boyfriend broke up with her."

That wasn't anywhere near the truth of why Emmie Tesco had called Lane half-an-hour ago, but it was the best explanation she could offer to Zeke. She hadn't expected him to insist on tagging along, but he'd said he wanted see the complex everyone was buzzing about, and how could she refuse, after he'd spent the morning helping her dismantle the bookshop?

"Do you want to meet at the PX? We can grab a cup of coffee," she offered.

"I'm not sure I can stay that long. I have a golf game this afternoon." He stared across a countless array of white clapboard barracks landmarked by a church steeple, a water tower, and a flagpole proudly waving Old Glory. "Maybe my friend won't be too hard to find in this box of dominoes."

Lane propped her hand at her back, still sore from the bookshelves they'd moved this morning. Checking her watch, she thought she could meet Emmie and be back to the parking lot within thirty minutes. Plenty of time for Zeke to wander around, if he didn't get lost.

"I've been to this hospital a few times before," she pointed toward a center building boasting a shingled roof, a postage stamp porch, and a modicum of native shrubbery. "That's Headquarters barracks. They should be able to help you find your friend."

Zeke ambled around the front end of the car, stopping just short of the large side mirror that blocked his access to Lane. He leaned over the chrome arm and kissed her.

"Don't you go letting some guy in a uniform sweep you off your feet, you hear?" He winked before setting foot on the grass. "I've got too much hope that we'll be living the American dream when this war is over."

Her lips tingled from his touch. "The American dream?"

LIFE magazine says we're the only country in the world where citizens aspire to make their lives better than their parents, own a house, tend a yard, and drive a car—not necessarily in that order.

She'd not have thought he spent much time reading magazines after all the legal documents he had to digest, but she appreciated the sentiment. She'd long ago vowed that she would never, ever live like her mother. "Who knew this was such a widely-held concept?"

"The folks at LIFE, that's who." He rapped the hood of her uncle's car. *"The upside is I'm marrying a girl who can drive. Which puts me square in the middle of needing to replace the pleasure-mobile with a sedan."*

"Or we could live in the guest house my aunt and uncle have started to build." Lane patted the car's roof. "And they don't seem to mind sharing their vehicle, and you could keep the Jeep."

"Your aunt is only having you drive Mr. Thomas's car because she's afraid the battery will die before he returns." He kicked the tires. "But I don't think we can count on your uncle wanting to share this baby after that. Or anything else, based on his patent dislike for me."

"I think you'll grow on him." Lane kissed him quickly, embarrassed that she couldn't resist his grin. "You sure have for me."

Zeke reached into his shirt's front pocket and pulled out a pair of aviator-styled sunglasses. When he slipped them over his eyes, he looked like an adventurer, a renegade, or someone she'd want to spend the rest of her life with—someone, she'd been reminded this week, who made her happy.

"What are you smiling about, Mrs. Mercer?" He pointed to her as he walked backward, somehow finding sure steps on unfamiliar ground. "I'm serious when I say no fraternizing with the officers. I hear they're famously charming."

"No one can be more charming than you, Hayes." She rose on her toes to wave him off. "I have it on the best authority."

"Who?"

"You!"

He chuckled, turned around, and set off for the Headquarters barracks. Lane drew in a steadying breath as her heels settled firmly on earth. She hoped he'd never find out about her meetings with Stuart. Zeke didn't seem to mind her conversations with Slim and he'd made peace with Theo, but he'd have a hard time understanding why a doctor from Washington felt a proprietary claim on her time.

She reached into the pocket of her skirt and pulled out the note where she'd scratched directions to meet Emmie. The nurse had sounded frazzled.

After walking past the Bachelor Officers' Quarters, someone's radio underscoring the racket from a nearby mess hall, she found the stacked, directional signs pointing this way and that way toward various buildings, specifically the ones she wanted—the laboratory and urology departments. The white arrows were much more professional looking than the ones cobbled out of armory boxes in military camps around France, usually marking the mileage back to New York and Philadelphia.

Beyond the sidewalk leading to the lab were a stash of three wooden picnic tables scattered under a shady tree and, just as promised, a nurse was smoking a cigarette and reading a novel. A breeze blew a scent of overcooked peas from the mess hall.

Lane climbed up the bench to sit on the wooden tabletop. "Whatcha reading?"

"Miss Holloway and The Sultan of Dubai." Emmie didn't look up. Her fingers, clutching a cigarette, turned the page as if Lane were little more than an ordinary nuisance. "I swear, I've never seen such a feeble excuse for a female, and yet she manages to outwit marauders, stop a cholera outbreak, and win the eye of the sheik all before chapter three." Emmie closed the book with a thud. "My life is so boring in comparison."

"A Roberta Harwood novel?"

"Gad, no. I wouldn't read that drivel." Emmie glanced to the spine, squinting to read the faded lettering. "This was in your free box that you sent here for the patients. I heard one of the guys laughing hysterically, and I just had to know what he was reading."

Lane took the book and read the opening lines. "Maybe I should have kept this one."

Emmie crushed her cigarette against the bench and stood. "I saw your lover boy rode shotgun with you today. Does he know what we're up to?"

"He thinks I'm checking on a friend who's so lonely and distraught that she needs a shoulder to cry on."

Emmie's smile revealed slightly crooked eye teeth. "I hate to disappoint him when he expects you to return with a mascara-stained hanky, but I think we have a real shot at narrowing down the list of suspects today, so I'm glad you're here to run interference in the laboratory."

Lane never figured out why the OSS didn't send backup to help with this investigation, as clearly, the resident agent was overtaxed, trying to determine which of the five thousand men on this campus might be the one with deadly intent. With 220 barracks, it was a logistical nightmare just to find a ranked officer, much less an enemy.

She glanced across a row of crepe myrtles, a softening embellishment to the countless identical buildings—and according to the lettered sign—the allee was a gift donated by local citizens in support of the hospital effort. Beyond the marker, she saw two buses idling at the curb of the main entrance, depositing visiting family members and shift workers. Disguising oneself for a covert mission at Harmon General was as easy as disappearing in a city center.

"As a nurse, don't you think you'd have more carte blanche poking around the laboratory?" Lane stood so she could be on a level-playing field with someone who liked to make plans on the fly. "I'm a civilian with zero medical background. They're not going to let me into the lab in the first place, much less nose around their staff."

"They will when you're on the arm of everyone's favorite, Dr. Lemming."

Lane waved her hand over her blouse, pleated skirt, and open-toed sandals. "I'm not dressed for a surprise tour of the lab."

"You'll have them so bamboozled with your Southern charm they won't notice."

Lane was exasperated that this was the extent of Emmie's plan. "You want me to interrupt a busy lab and drag the head pathologist around for a tour—so you can do what? Ransack their files? Look for the one lab tech with an eye patch?"

"Shhh—" Emmie jerked Lane's arm and pulled her toward the barracks and away from the soldiers strolling from the mess hall. "You're getting sloppy in your new role with the agency."

Lane pulled her arm free. "You're getting sloppy. You're so fixated on catching Dr. Death that you can't even see how ridiculous this has become."

Emmie's white shoes skittered on the gravel around the benches. "I'm doing my job."

"Are you?" Lane stared hard into the eyes of a woman who'd successfully maintained many cover identities in her career, but the one with a Texas address was slipping. "Then why do you want to kill this man so badly that you practically seethe with pent-up rage?"

Emmie's eyes flashed bursts of firecrackers as she scanned those within hearing distance. "I don't enjoy the kill. I just want to stop him before he sets biological warfare in motion and hurts innocent people."

Lane knew, like she knew that most criminals had crickets for brains that Emmie was pursuing this mission with more on the line than saving the world—she was out to save herself. Maybe, she was even hiding at Harmon to keep off the radar of someone who was chasing her.

"Besides, there's no place for seething feelings in the business," the nurse said as she scanned the yard for suspects. "We do our job. The American public doesn't need to know what evil lurks about while they live out their lives. That's what we do. Get rid of the evil." Emmie wiped a finger under her damp eyelash. "We're protecting them."

Lane wanted to reassure Emmie, but knowing the woman as well as she did, she kept her compassion to herself. "You're too smart to let this man get to you. You've analyzed patterns before. Ask for the reports from Stuart and find your connective thread."

"You're wrong." Emmie turned away, gesturing with a cigarette she no longer held. "This enemy is smarter than all the rest because he knows how we operate and he doesn't have a soul. He's just consumed by revenge."

"How do you know so much about the guy but can't seem to catch him?" Seconds before she could respond to the footsteps she heard hurrying across the concrete, a voice called out and shook her mind like a puzzle box that had tipped to the floor.

"Lane!"

Lane closed her eyes against the male voice, needing a moment to rearrange her features and buy some distance from the first authentic conversation the two women had shared in months.

"Colonel Lemming," Emmie purred as she turned to face the doctor who was wearing a blood-splattered white coat over his uniform.

Lane stared at the giant red splotches cascading from the shoulder of Stuart's doctor coat to his khaki pants hem. She'd never realized that pathologists encountered occupational hazards.

Stuart held his coat wide, letting a breeze weave around his body and absorb the moisture. "My lab tech and I got drenched by a botched blood transfusion. We're going to get fresh uniforms from the post cleaners."

That was when Lane noticed the man hovering behind Stuart, his head ducked so low his chin scuffed the linen facemask crowding his tie. His eyes were so fixated on the dirt that she wondered he didn't crash directly into Stuart's back.

Emmie nodded like blood bank disasters were routine, and maybe to a nurse, wearing someone else's tissue was part of a normal day. Lane was so disgusted by the notion of encountering bodily fluids that she shuddered even from ten feet away. Maybe that was why the tech couldn't raise his face—he didn't know how he was going to explain the mass outbreak of some hideous organism to the base commander.

She clutched her stomach. There was a reason she hadn't joined the Red Cross, and this was it.

Stuart's eyes warmed as if reading Lane's mind. "I'm guessing you didn't know that not everything stays contained in vials and bottles inside the lab?"

Lane shook her head.

"Accidents are not an everyday occurrence, but the quality of materials these days can be unreliable. We're just one of many Army hospitals needing supplies, and getting them here when they're desperate for them in Europe, and the Pacific, too, is getting trickier." He looked back at his tech. "That's why we're on the hunt for some local suppliers. Right, Peale?"

Lane had no idea what sort of supplies were needed in a laboratory. Emmie asked a few questions about sterilization techniques post blood spills, and Lane watched the medical tech. He listened intently to the conversation but never looked into their faces.

Lane thought that Emmie could get the information she wanted with much more success if she'd engage in a flirtation with Stuart, but the idea also rankled. She liked Stuart. He was her friend, and maybe her link to a past that she could barely remember. Emmie, with her gritty experiences, would dirty Stuart and alter his view of the world. He was one of the good guys. A hero. He didn't deserve to be a pawn in the OSS's game of chess.

No, Emmie would do better to employ her talents on someone a bit more corruptible, with less to lose from the encounter—maybe even the hunched-over, middle-aged technician. Peale, was that his name? Lane studied his long, narrow nose and short chin. The tech would probably cave to Emmie's manipulations within seconds. The novelty might be good for him—give him a spine.

Stuart reached into his coat and withdrew a packet of cigarettes and a matchbook emblazoned with the Harmon General Hospital logo, and a pencil. He opened the matchbook and scribbled a phone number on the flap. Handing the matches to Lane, he leaned closer. "This is my office number. Call me. We need to talk. Soon."

She folded the matchbook into her pocket, noting how the tech cut his gaze toward her. His eyes were an unsettling green shade, much like a shallow pool she'd seen in the gardens at Versailles.

"Of course," she chimed, ignoring the memory from her early weeks in France. "My fiancé, Zeke, wanted to meet you. Maybe we could get everyone together."

Emmie waved like she wanted to be included. "I'm free Friday night."

Stuart chuckled. "I'm sorry to say, I'm not. Taking the train to Dallas to hear a symposium on the latest in malaria interventions. Research isn't my specialty, but with this war, it's quickly becoming one."

Emmie winked and explained for Lane's benefit. "Dr. Lemming is working with the infectious disease specialists to explore ways to treat the troops before they go to the Pacific, so they don't contract mosquito-borne diseases. He's becoming quite the expert."

"I wouldn't say that, Nurse—?"

"Tesco."

"Nurse Tesco, that's right." Stuart's eyes warmed. "We've met somewhere recently, haven't we?"

"At the Gregg Hotel. You were dining with Lane."

"I knew you looked familiar." Stuart nodded, his head swiveling between the two women. "You were with some older man, and we were all part of the Lane Mercer fan club."

"Mr. Elliott used to work with Lane on another project." Emmie's eyes dimmed. "He's the fan. I'm just a former cellmate in a local boardinghouse."

Lane didn't like the turn of this conversation. The less Stuart knew about her life here, the less inclined he'd be to ask questions she couldn't answer truthfully.

"We'll try for dinner again another time," she said hurrying to close the conversation.

"Okay, but call me at your earliest convenience. I really need to talk to you."

Lane's mind whipped through scenarios that might involve Stuart wanting to have a conversation, and she almost forgot why she was on the military campus in the first place.

"Stuart—" Her mind flew faster than her mouth. "You must know that Nurse Tesco is regarded as one of the sharpest girls at Harmon. If you ever need a nurse to assist you in your lab, she'd be the one to ask for. She could be a real asset."

Everyone stilled. Even the breeze hushed.

Lane didn't have to be told she'd overstepped. Their collective silence reinforced the notion that she'd ruined the effort at getting Emmie closer to laboratory papers.

"I'm sure the head nurse will appreciate that endorsement," Stuart said, distracted by the orderlies hurrying toward the mess hall. "But we don't actually use a lot of nurses in my department. Field soldiers who can't return to their units get drafted to become lab techs, and eventually they get the hang of blood smears, don't they, Peale?"

Peale stared at the grass.

Emmie blew out her breath. "Well, you busy men need to get to the laundry. We've kept you way too long."

Stuart saluted in a gentlemen's bid to say goodbye and hurried across the yard. Peale followed, a good ten steps off Stuart's boot heel.

Emmie's face maintained the equanimity of friends chatting, but her whisper bit colder than a winter's frost. "You compromised my moves."

Lane reached into her skirt pocket and pulled out a car key, looking at the chain as if it were a talisman for the way out of this mess. "Your moves are as thick as gravy. I jumpstarted you."

"This is a delicate mission."

Maybe it was the heat. Maybe it was the hour she'd lost that she'd never get back, but Lane's patience was no longer on loan to Emmie Tesco. "We're in a war. Delicate went out the door a year ago. Are you losing it, or what?"

Emmie hissed, "How dare you?"

"I dare because whatever is at stake has you and Theo both in knots." Lane leaned closer. "And someone is asking about me down in the colored streets. Someone who knows I worked for the agency. So, if you don't find and deal with this character you've been chasing I may be in real danger."

Emmie's shoulders went stiff as a wooden hanger, but her eyes darted across the yard filled with wounded soldiers, family members carrying baskets, and nurses pushing wheel-chaired patients. A radio, propped on the eaves of an opened window, offered a tinny version of ragtime music.

"I'm not losing it."

Lane dragged in a breath. "You keep telling yourself that if it makes you feel better."

The fact that Emmie wouldn't look her in the eyes told Lane everything her silence couldn't. "Theo's moving a potential double-agent into my safe house this week." She blew out a breath, hoping the change of topic might ease the tension. "The mark will need a bodyguard. Do you remember Patrick Le Bleu from that incident at the Bramford Building last winter? He works for Judge Wyatt and can be terribly menacing. I think he'd make a great candidate. Do you think he can be cultivated for the agency with a day's notice?"

Emmie's rosebud lips formed into a smoke ring that was missing a cigarette. After a minute where she seemed to rein in her thoughts, she rolled her neck side to side and then stepped away from Lane, her sensible shoes leading toward the parking lot where Victor's Hudson glowed in the spring light.

Lane wasn't as deferential as Peale. She pulled alongside Emmie, scanning the yard for her fiancé as they walked around a bus, parked with its door open at the curb.

"Patrick has potential," Emmie finally replied. "But I don't think there's time to train him, and I have no idea how you're going to guarantee his trust."

Lane thought that was the sticking point. Theo always had some great secret to hold over a person's head that motivated them to buy into his espionage methods. She couldn't imagine what tool could be useful in securing Patrick's faithfulness. And there couldn't possibly be enough time to find out.

"Ladies!"

Like a dog trained to a whistle, Emmie spun on her heel and offered a generous smile to the male who had called out from behind them.

Lane turned toward the row of crepe myrtles too, but at least she had the advantage of knowing that voice well and wasn't just offering a smile to a generic baritone. Zeke strolled across the grass with a stride that had carried him across Washington, Austin, and the back nine of every golf course in East Texas. His confidence couldn't be contained behind those aviator glasses. It radiated off him like magnetic waves.

Other nurses, those gathered in front of Harmon General headquarters' building, seemed lured in by his charisma too, and they stared at the man in civilian clothes. As he approached, his arm reached for Lane's waist and corralled her against his side. He kissed the top of her head.

Emmie's smile faded.

"Glad I caught you." Zeke plucked the key from Lane's hand. "I had no idea how I was going to find you on this campus. It's like a maze of white barracks and brown dirt."

"Welcome home, Mr. Hayes." Emmie folded her arms across her uniform. "A lot has happened since you were last here."

"Really?" Zeke looked between Lane's expression and Emmie's narrowed eyes. "Nothing interesting ever happens in Longview."

"Oh, yes." Emmie's lips curled like a cat who found the bowl of cream. "For instance, Lane's dear, old friend, Dr. Lemming was just asking her—I mean several of us—out to dinner. I'm sure he'd include you too."

Zeke's jaw hardened as he looked at Lane. "I thought that guy was just passing through town a week ago."

Lane swallowed something she was sure was going to come back to haunt. "I told you Stuart worked at Harmon, didn't I? Old friend. Ran into him at the Gregg Hotel. He's terribly busy though. I won't see him often."

"Famous doctor, solves everyone's diagnosis." Emmie announced proudly. "And," she pointed down the yard to the laboratory. "He's close enough to drop in on, well, any old time."

Zeke's gaze skipped between Emmie's directions and Lane's silence before his expression hardened into the poker face he'd perfected for sudden death playoffs. He gripped her elbow and pulled Lane toward the automobile. "I hate to run, ladies, but I promised some guys I'd meet them at the tee box in twenty minutes."

Emmie waved her fingers. "Bye, now."

Lane jerked her arm free of Zeke and turned, rushing back to where Emmie stood. Inches separated them when she asked, "Why is it that every time I start to think we might be friends, you do something stupid to ruin every last ounce of sympathy I have for you?"

Emmie's eyes became blank slates. "You're just livin' lucky, I guess."

"Am I?" Lane took two steps away from the woman who, for reasons she couldn't fathom, seemed to hate her then turned back. "Or are you trying to sabotage me for some purpose that suits your evil ways?"

"Maybe I'm saving you from a disaster you don't see coming?"

Lane's gaze tapered on Emmie's mouth, which bore none of the tremors frequently associated with people who were lying. "What do you know?"

Emmie drew an imaginary key across her lips.

Lane groaned. Turning, she let her gaze find the Hudson in the parking lot and Zeke sitting behind the steering wheel, tapping his finger against the dashboard.

As she walked back to the car, she tasted salt and realized somewhere in the last few minutes she'd bitten her lip. A rookie mistake for dealing with tension. She wasn't sure whose American dream she was twisting in, but it sure felt like hers.

Lane opened the passenger door, and slid onto the hot seat.

Zeke speared her with his gaze. "I sure am glad I took a week off to come home. It seems there's a whole lot of interesting things going on while I'm off working the pipeline project."

Lane stared through the windshield, biting back what she wanted to say for what was expedient. "Emmie's shooting the breeze. She doesn't know what she's talking about."

"That woman doesn't waste time on breezes." Zeke turned the key in the ignition and stared hard at the Harmon General banner over the driveway. "Is there more to this business about putting off the wedding, other than it feels too soon? 'Cause I'm thinking that an 'old friend' might be at the root of your cold feet."

Lane reached across the seat and patted his thigh. "Stuart is part of my past. You're part of my future. My feet are not cold, it's just that we're both busy now, and maybe we should wait on setting a date. How do you feel about a Christmas wedding?"

He gunned the gas pedal and the car lugged backwards from the parking space. "Honey, we're not waiting that long. You'd better figure out something else, or call it off. But don't leave me hanging."

Chapter Thirteen

April 22, 1943 2:45 p.m.

Lane teetered back and forth in a rocking chair, staring across a yard bathed in afternoon light. This ode to Saturday relaxation—dappled sunshine lit the leaves stretching from the sweet gum trees on Timpson Street and even the hens pecking at the yard seemed happy—did very little to calm the tempest in her mind.

Emmie's intimidation had been hard to shake off.

A gap-toothed, barefooted child crawled over the neighbor's picket fence, carrying a slingshot in his back pocket. Though the twig of a woman sitting on the stool next to her shelling peas into a bowl didn't seem to look up, she did hum a warning refrain. As if the tuneless um-hmm meant someone was about to earn a whipping.

Lane wasn't sure if the caution was meant for her or the boy.

There couldn't have been many white women who found their way to the Wyatts' front porch, even fewer who hadn't been scared away by the maid who'd answered the door with a growl. The only house with any substance to it, and she'd not been allowed to wait inside. Merely told that the Judge would see her when he finished his dinner. In the meantime, someone assigned the woman wearing a bandana turbaned around her knobby head as neighborhood guard duty.

Lane glanced around at the small, clapboard houses nearby that were piled on stacked stones, or leaned against barns. No one would really call this a neighborhood, not this far out of town. More like a collective of cracker boxes.

The tempo of shelling peas took her back to a time when she'd sit next to Little Momma snapping beans or pulling silk off corn. That was a more positive spin on the moment than imagining Wyatt's crew spying on her from a guard shack.

"May I?" Lane held her palm out. Maybe busy work would take her mind off the distrustful expression on Zeke's face when they'd separated at her aunt's house. He'd taken the car to the golf course, and as she'd waved him with a smile, she'd been secretly plotting how to hire Patrick as a body guard for the Russian. Zeke must have sensed she wasn't going to be hanging laundry on the line. He'd cautioned her to be careful. "I can take some of those."

Eyes no bigger than raisins stared back at her from a face as riddled with wrinkles as a book with wet pages, questioning her generosity.

Lane usurped the natural order and reached into the paper sack anyway, pulling out a handful of pods. Thinking about Zeke right now would throw off her mettle, so she ran her thumbnail up the seam of the first pod, peeling back a watery shell that contained three pale peas. She popped the first one in her mouth and as she chewed, made a bowl with her skirt dipped between her thighs. Minutes later, she reached into the bag for more, careful not to tip her lapful. There was mud under her nail, and her nose was filled with mustiness, but her brain had steadied with the motions. No conversation had occured, but a rhythm of grace existed, knitting what society could not seam together.

No one had come to ask her any questions either. Wasn't that odd for a household unaccustomed to women on bicycles riding up in the middle of the afternoon?

Her fingers stilled. Her gaze shot back to the yard, scanning the perimeter for activity.

Yet, no one had acted all that surprised to see her at the screen door.

Had the Judge anticipated her running over in order to acknowledge the rumors he'd said were circulating? Had he placed bets on how fast she'd give up her cover?

If so, he'd underestimated his prey.

It was too soon to show her curiosity about who'd been asking questions in the speakeasies. She'd have to set that worry in a box far enough away to not reach into it and focus instead on what she did know. A Russian, with duplicitous skills, needed a bodyguard with equal knowledge of how a criminal mind might work. She couldn't guarantee Patrick's loyalty, but she could pay him a hefty fee, which would at least keep him tethered for the next three days.

Biting her bottom lip and feeling the tender wound she'd already created, she ran the traps on what might go wrong with hiring Patrick to protect a double agent. Tornados roared in with less danger. But she didn't have the benefit of time or a large inventory of available hog-tying types, so she'd have to hope Patrick was in an inventive state of mind—or desperate.

Lane flipped her wrist, the ticking hands showing that Judge Wyatt's lunch hour was going on three o'clock. At this rate, her whole day would be wasted. Zeke had said he'd want to see her tonight after the golf game. She hoped he'd be in a better mood. Juggling two lives was fast proving too complex to maintain.

Lane knew, like she knew that these peas would soak with a hambone and peppercorns, that Zeke wouldn't indulge her dragging out any sort of agency role. What was it he had thought she done during the time she worked for Major Parson—report to the spooks in Washington? Informants and agents were two different animals, and she doubted he'd have as much affection for the second one. Most men she'd met in Europe couldn't respect her as an equal in the field, even less if she knew more than they did about maneuvers. Zeke wouldn't be much different.

The falling out with Emmie had left her feeling dismal. The tension coiled in the other agent's shoulders was not something Lane could ignore either. It meant something was brewing at Harmon that was top secret, something possibly bigger than even Dr. Death.

Lane glanced at her bicycle propped against the fence. A long ride would help her sort through the questions in her mind and maybe work up a plan for how she was going to navigate the not knowing of agency business with the very real issue of how to tell Zeke the truth about the safe house. An old ulcer burst in her stomach.

She tossed the pod shells into the scrap bucket, tired of waiting on the Judge when she had bigger problems rolling her way. Besides, J had a butler who worked the haberdashery who was quite large. Paulo was from Argentina, so maybe the language barrier could work to an advantage when manhandling a difficult Russian.

Standing from the chair, her ear caught the sound of a transmission hiccupping through its gears as a mud-stained Chevrolet pulled into the driveway. The old woman never seemed to look up from the bowl of peas but issued another warning murmur all the same.

The car's radio cut off, and crickets' song was returned.

As the door pushed open, a woman with long legs and spiky heels rose from the driver's seat. As she stood, her full range of voluptuousness made the cotton dress she wore look like a showgirl's outfit. The woman stared at the porch then took in the rest of the yard, including the storage sheds and the makeshift ball field next door.

"Auntie," the stranger called out in a voice that carried rich melodies. "Is Mrs. Wyatt home?"

The woman shelling peas remained fixated on her task.

"Auntie?"

Lane watched the stranger climb the shallow steps and study the odd pair of women, as the two were unmatched bookends.

The stranger's brow arched a few more notches over skin that had the sheen of damp silk. "Wouldn't have thought there were too many white girls sitting on Mrs. Wyatt's front porch, but maybe there's more to Longview than I'd heard." She propped a heavy purse on the railing of the porch, as if its weight was too much for her arm. "This is the Wyatts' place, ain't it?"

Lane nodded but was reluctant to duel with the driver—she looked edgy after negotiating the roads. "This is the right address, but they're not in a hurry to entertain."

The woman adjusted her bra strap. "I swear it's hot as Hades in Texas. How do you people stand it?"

Another outsider. Someone who wouldn't go around town spreading rumors that she was waiting on the Wyatts' porch.

Lane offered a hostess-worthy smile. "I have it on good authority, we don't. Which could explain the irrational amounts of sweet tea consumed."

The woman smiled in response, showing large white teeth, which contrasted mightily with her walnut-hued skin. "Of course, tea would be the answer. This place is every bit as much the South as Alabama."

Lane detected a plummy accent underscoring the complaint, as if she'd been educated in an area known for lobsters and cold winters. Judging from the lack of response from the old woman, they were not, after all, related.

The visitor propped one hand high on the wood rail for balance and fanned her face with a handkerchief. "I don't really need this job. I could find a club in Dallas that would at least have better accommodations for the talent."

Lane reached down for her purse, guessing this was another jazz singer passing through the Cotton Club. "You were planning on staying here?"

"If this is Mrs. Wyatt's house, then yes. I'm booked for the next month, and she promised to put me up so I wouldn't have to stay out in a cabin in some god-forsaken woods." With a flourish, she allowed the handkerchief to drift toward her hips. "I don't do the great outdoors."

Lane guessed her social call on the judge had been ignored. "I'm about to leave, so you can have my seat."

"I'd prefer to stand."

"How long have you been on the road?"

"I drove in from Monroe, Louisiana, today, but prior to that, I was doing a gig in Vicksburg. Miserable place. Let's just say the Chamber of Commerce didn't roll out no welcome mat."

Lane's memories of Valdosta weren't so old that she couldn't imagine what it would be like for a colored woman traveling by herself through Mississippi. It was a wonder she escaped state lines.

"But if Patrick is still here, then it will all be worth it. That man owes me a second chance."

Lane stilled her exit. How many Patricks could there be who were connected to Judge Wyatt? This woman was the kind a man could forget, so why was she chasing him and not the other way around?

The screen screeched in protest as Judge Wyatt moved through the front door, rolling down the sleeves to his cuff as he accessed the three women on his porch.

The old woman stood, gripping the edge of the window sill for leverage. She clutched the bowl of peas and shuffled through the open door without any comment to the people occupying the space.

"Is she really your aunt?" Lane asked the tall woman.

The woman shrugged. "Never seen her in my life."

"Ladies," Judge Wyatt intoned as if he were standing at a pulpit. "To what do I owe the honor?"

The other woman didn't look him in the eye. She stared at his wingtips and with a much more conciliatory tone than the one with which she arrived, said, "Jewel Carter. A singer. I'm looking for Mrs. Wyatt. She offered me a few weeks of work at her club and said I was to be here by three o'clock sharp if I wanted the job."

The Judge pulled his pocket watch from his vest, opened the gold cover, and checked the time.

"Congratulations, Miss Carter. You're the first one here, so you can have the job. It's evening work only, but Mrs. Wyatt will find something to occupy your time during the day. I manage the club. She manages more respectable endeavors."

"Yes, sir." Jewel demurred. "Mighty kind of you, sir."

If Lane hadn't witnessed the transformation, she'd not have believed it, but Wyatt's influence must have its own long arm if it got this girl from the Northeast to bow the knee.

"Red Bird, what about you?" He turned those dark eyes on her and seemed to radiate right through the script she'd penned in her head. "You come about that project we discussed?"

Her first reaction was to answer, "Yes, sir," but she needed leverage if she was going to keep Judge Wyatt—and Patrick—on her playbook. If only he wouldn't call her that nickname harkening back to that gauntlet in the speakeasy last fall. That red dress had made her feel pretty, and it had been forever ruined by his barmaid. He owed her an outfit.

"I've given some thought to your suggestion that Patrick would be better off in my employ for a few days. I couldn't agree more." She rolled her shoulders back and clutched her purse so it hid the pea shell stains dirtying her skirt. "If you'll have him stop by the bookshop tonight, I can give him some instructions. Mind you, this is a temporary arrangement at best."

Judge Wyatt folded his arms across his belly. "We were looking for something more permanent."

Her knees were knocking, but as she'd learned in France, it was all about the attitude, even if the details were flimsy. "Be that as it may, the circumstance that has arisen is short term. If it goes well, who knows? But for now, I'll need about three days of his time."

"How far will he need to travel outside Texas?"

Jewel gasped. "Patrick is leaving town? I came all this way to apologize for breaking our engagement."

Wyatt joined Lane in staring at the woman with new scrutiny. Lane was shocked to find out Patrick had romantic inclinations. She'd rather thought him a coiled machine fueled by rage, but like with most people, there were deeper angles. Her fault for underestimating that fact.

"Patrick is needed at my bookshop on Fredonia Street." Lane measured the reaction of both and wondered what was going on that Judge Wyatt wanted Patrick out of town. She turned toward the singer and added, "I sure hope he's not planning on leaving town, either."

"Bah," Wyatt scorned. "That's not at all what we discussed, and you know it."

Lane turned back and regarded him with as much seriousness as she could muster. "It's the best I can offer at the moment."

Wyatt stuffed his hands in his pockets.

Jewel was remarkably silent, as if waiting for a pinball to land in a slot.

Lane knew she'd have to juggle a few lies to keep the Judge off Theo's radar, but if it salvaged the guest house operation, then it would be justified. At least she hoped this was a case where the end justified the means—those lines blurred in the espionage business.

"I know you folks don't know me from Eve," Jewel spoke, but her eyes were on the floorboards. "But I'd like to see Patrick Le Bleu, if this is the man everyone seems to be talking about."

With her part played as well as could be expected, Lane made a move to leave, but a large hand on her arm stopped her movements.

"Not so fast, Mrs. Mercer." Wyatt released her and said, "You've moved a lot of young men to places where they've found good-paying jobs. Why can't you do a better job by my friend?"

She was under a spotlight powered by two pairs of eyes, both questioning her intentions for the same man. "I don't have a magic wand, Judge. I just pass along information as it comes to me, and this is what is available. Seems like it could be in everyone's best interests at the moment." She offered a smile to soften the edge. "If Patrick wants to talk, you tell him where to find me."

Lane stepped off the porch with as much grace as she could muster, seeing as how she'd issued an ultimatum to a man who had underground connections across the three state lines. Her gut told her Wyatt was more friend than enemy, but that confidence would only hold for as long as she did things that benefitted his constituents.

Shaking off the stares of those who watched from inside the house, Lane walked over to her bicycle and started to push it toward the dirt road. Jumping on to the pedals once she'd passed the culvert, she blew tight air through her lips.

Once she was sure she'd passed the houses where the men who protected the Wyatts lived, she bent over the handlebar and pedaled as fast as she could. As the wind whipped through her hair, she breathed hard and kept her eyes on the paved side of the road. Edith's voice riddled through her memory, chastising her for the suggestion that she was taking the bike to check on the welfare of a wife of one of the carpenters working at the bookshop. Her aunt would faint if she knew the house in question was on the far east end of a street the Thomases did not visit.

Lane had not told Zeke where she was going either, and she regretted that she was so used to being on her own that she still hadn't learned the finesse of trusting a man who loved her. That would have to change after their marriage. No, she corrected, it needed to change before she walked the aisle. It was unfair to keep pretending that she was a solo artist in this circus. She had a partner for the tightrope, and she needed to start acting like it.

Pushing the pedals over rough road, she wondered if that wasn't at the root of her wedding day worries. Zeke would expect to hold power over her decisions and her choices, and he could demand things of her because she carried his name. She'd craved that dependence when she married Roy, but now, after two years of self-reliance, she wasn't sure she could change the shape of her will again.

When she crested Finch's Hill, where a family farm rolled out beside Cotton Street, she knew it was time to stop looking at what she would lose with Zeke and instead think of what she'd gain after a wedding. Lane coasted a bit, stretching out her legs to relieve the strain.

If Zeke were here, he'd be quick to remind her what she'd enjoy as his wife, and she smiled, imagining that there'd be perks to sharing life with a man who knew how to have fun.

A car approached from behind, the driver honking in warning. She looked over her shoulder and steered toward the grass, suspicious that this might be one of Wyatt's men come to change her mind about Patrick. The car passed with a family in the sedan, a young girl's face plastered to the window as they drove past.

She waved, remembering what it was like that first time she'd ridden in an automobile with her grandparents. Big Daddy drove as if he was half afraid the heavy Packard had a mind of its own, but Little Momma had told her to roll down the window and stick her nose out, smelling the honeysuckle threaded through every breeze in that South Georgia air.

She'd always been kept on a tight leash whenever that Packard stopped, as Big Daddy had always expected Delia's runaway nature to show true in her daughter.

And it did, just not quite like Big Daddy or Little Momma had feared. Running away from shame was so much easier than staying to sort things back to right. Though her grandparents never lived to see the type of disgrace she'd left in her trail, it was safe to say it was ten times worse than anything her momma had invented.

Lane assumed she got the itch to see the world from Delia, an expert in fleeing Valdosta. Except Lane had been smart enough to avoid the trap of beauty pageants and modeling; instead buying a one-way bus ticket going north—if one believed in patterns repeating themselves, one might say she'd not cancelled that ticket. The urge to run from conflict was ever-present.

Dodging a stray dog, Lane reeled in her thoughts. Zeke would be calling for her after his golf game, and he'd already hinted that they were going to drive north of Highway 80 in search of the most bodacious BBQ he'd ever tasted. He'd vowed his trip to Longview wasn't complete without brisket, and she wasn't one to doubt him. Although she wasn't sure how they were going to find a BBQ pit when he couldn't quite remember the name of the road to take.

Somewhere in all this she had to make arrangements to meet Patrick and persuade him to guard a Russian, as well as keep him from knowing the full extent of her role within the U.S. spy network. Patrick was strong, fearless, and had a chip on his shoulder, but that didn't mean he wouldn't run wild with the gossip that the shopkeeper was, in fact, a former secret agent.

She slowed her pedaling as cars thickened the intersection of Cotton and Tenth Street, her route for returning to Oakdale Avenue. Signaling that she was turning left, Lane eased across the road and onto the familiar streets that linked Edith to her supper club friends. She passed houses familiar to her from Sunday afternoon visits and climbed the hill that allowed her opportunity to exercise her legs in a way they hadn't been stretched since she rode a bike across the French countryside.

Lane approached Melton Street, where Zeke rented a carriage house apartment from a family with space to spare for single men, or soldiers. His Jeep wasn't parked along the curb, so he must still have been at the golf course.

Pedaling on, she had to figure out a way to keep Zeke, Judge Wyatt, Patrick, and even J Lassiter from finding out the real reason she was going to so much trouble to protect Theo's interests. She'd only just accepted that she was addicted to the danger the OSS provided, but beneath the adrenaline rush was the very real debt she owed Theo.

After the shock of Roy's death, he'd saved her with an offer of escape that gave feet to her need to run away—again. She'd learned to run away before she'd ever started school, and that kind of panic was hard to overcome. Especially since her romance with Roy Mercer had finally given her the hope that maybe, just maybe, she'd found someone who'd be a stable partner in the roller coaster of life.

Theo had been all conciliatory, even as he quizzed her about what Roy had told her when he left for England with his military unit. He'd made her find Roy's papers, letters, and photographs—searching for some clue he'd kept to himself. It wasn't until she was knee-deep in mud with the French Resistance that the fog of those days cleared and she finally remembered her husband's parting words at the tarmac. Roy Mercer, dashing young Army captain and aide to a highly placed general, had announced he was going out to change the world, one general at a time.

Pausing at Young Street, Lane watched the cars pass by and gave Roy's ghost a salute. He'd been cut down too young. At least that's what the Army personnel told her at the funeral. But then, so had thousands of other young men who'd volunteered to serve Uncle Sam.

Now another man was offering to share the journey with her.

Lane wasn't entirely sure she could trust the opportunity. The life Theo gave her in the OSS was one of hazards, but it also revealed skills and abilities she'd never dreamed she owned. Things that didn't fit the profile of a shopkeeper.

Pushing the pedals, Lane hopped on the bike to hurry across the street. She hoped that she knew what she was doing.

Chapter Fourteen

April 22, 1943 7:12 p.m.

"You have company," Zeke announced as he dropped a bag of trash into the alley's container.

Lane's gaze whipped from the box of barbecued brisket on her lap to the tall black man hurrying past the bank's back entrance.

"What's he doing here?"

"I couldn't say." Lane wiped her fingers of the tangy sauce. She folded the napkin into her lap and ignored the tension that turned her stomach into a hive of bumblebees. Her mind spun though a series of possible disasters.

"Can't?" Zeke set his Pearl beer bottle on the concrete step of the shop's back stoop. "Or won't?"

Lane steadied her breath. She glanced from Zeke's expression to Patrick's as he walked with his hat clutched between his fists—like he wasn't sure if she was his executioner or liberator. She wasn't sure either.

Sitting on the step, with sweat dripping down her ribcage, she was sure of two things. She was tired from installing the carpenter's new shelving and the work hadn't generated any answers for the questions that seemed to rob her of peace.

"There are things I need to tell you, Zeke," she murmured. "But please don't ask anything right now. Okay?"

"You know I can't make that promise."

She noticed the sunburn across the bridge of his nose and the perspiration that creased his golf hat and left a halo on his hair. He'd not been happy to find her still working when he walked in the door with the barbecued brisket—although he'd teased that he'd likely be thinking about her mopping the floor on her hands and knees during his lonely nights in New Jersey.

She'd been grateful he was too excited about his hole-in-one to ask too many questions about why she was behind on her chores list.

The box of BBQ seemed to override much conversation anyway.

"Would you rather wait for me inside?" She crossed her fingers, hoping Zeke would say yes. Keeping him away from her negotiations with Patrick would avoid an unnecessary confrontation.

One of Zeke's eyebrows rose slightly, much like it would if he'd cross examined an imbecile. "I saw that man hold a sword over a senile gentleman in a lobby not three months ago. I'm not letting you out of my sight."

Patrick stopped short of the bookshop's stoop. He shifted from foot to foot, seemingly unsure of what to say. "Judge Wyatt told me to come see you tonight."

Lane stood, brushing biscuit crumbs from her skirt, knowing she had seconds to figure a plausible strategy. "I thought he might."

"He said you'd know something about a job for me."

Lane propped one hand on her hip and shaded her eyes from the sun with her other. Taking a good read of Patrick's posture, the curiosity in his expression, the mayhem alluded to by the patch over his missing left eye, and the sweat stains around his collar, she was sure he was ready for a change from his current circumstances. Whether or not he was ready to put his life on the line for the United States of America was something altogether different.

"I have an awkward situation. . ." Lane tried to imbue the scenario with enough danger for him to take it seriously, but not so much it scared him off. "And I think you're just the man who can handle it."

Patrick's lone eye focused on Zeke, like an eight ball looking for a pocket.

"I have no idea what she's talking about." Zeke stood and reached down for his beer. "But knowing Lane, she's not going to want to have this conversation in the alley either. Y'all better turn inside."

Lane reached for the knob, but Zeke caught the door as it opened and held it while three people, absorbed in their own thoughts, walked into the relative coolness of a dark office. Lane fished around for the overhead light switch, and the bulb burned a yellow haze into the room. She noticed the quality of Patrick's suit. Most men had one suit they wore to weddings and funerals. She supposed this was his.

This interview wasn't worthy of such a wardrobe change, but she could guess there might be another woman he'd planned to impress before dark. Inspiration smiled on Lane, and without much provocation, Jewel Carter became a player in a skit that no one would ever ask to be repeated.

Zeke approached her desk and pushed aside a stack of catalogs to sit on the corner, swinging his leg like a metronome. He set his beer on top of the ledger and crossed his arms across his chest. She could almost hear the flutter of index cards as his thoughts arranged for a closing argument.

Patrick stood stock still, glaring at the newspaper cartoons stapled to the wall above Zeke's head.

Lane reached toward the desk, picking up one of Edith's hand-me-down handkerchiefs stacked in a basket, and wiped the fine linen across the back of her neck, buying a minute to gather her wits. Much like her spontaneous actions with the underground efforts in France, there often wasn't enough time to troubleshoot the ramifications. Faith, she'd learned, was hoping she didn't ruin something bigger than what she could see.

"Patrick, we all know you have a particular keenness—let's call it a skill set—that has been useful to Judge Wyatt," Lane said, keeping her back to the wall so she could watch the reactions of both men. "And to be clear, I'm referring to your people-management abilities, not anything involving illegal acquisitions or disbursements."

That lone eye roved between Zeke and Lane like it was watching a tennis match. "You two up to something secret? They selling moonshine at those golf courses now?"

Zeke barked a laugh.

"Mr. Hayes is not involved," Lane clarified. "Not at all. He's returning to Washington, D.C. this weekend. But I have something that's come up that's just giving me fits and I'm not sure what to do about it."

She didn't know how disconcerting it could be when a man with one eye narrowed his lids and aimed his razor gaze on her. He could be as frightening as a Gestapo agent.

"You see. . ." she paused, twisting the handkerchief between her fingers. "There's a censor, someone who's in authority about sorting out propaganda spreading in the States. He's coming to Longview. Soon. And he's going to try to shut me down."

Zeke turned on his hip to focus better on her, one hand cupping his chin, like he was fascinated by her acting chops.

"Well, to be frank—" She stood a little taller in her sandals so she'd look commanding. "My bookshop is small potatoes on this censor's radar of all things sinful and corrupting, but the thing is, he's aiming to shut down shops that sell perceived smut."

She hoped this assignment was over before the novelist, Roberta Harwood, ever heard of the scheme. If wind of this scheme leaked, it might lead to an actual reprimand by publishers, not to mention the congressional committee on un-American activities. There were a few senators talking about how they were going to stop Communism from corrupting the public through the entertainment industry, and she was going to play off those headlines.

"And clubs," she continued. "Speakeasies and nightclubs that offer jazz music are right up there with bookshops and newsstands."

Patrick didn't budge. Whether or not he understood the tale she was spinning was anyone's guess, but he hadn't turned around and left the office, either.

Lane slipped her ace from her sleeve. Every OSS agent learned how to leverage information, and nothing was more valuable than a perceived threat against a loved one. She hadn't known this was a tactic when she'd been recruited, or she might have resisted Theo's ways. But once she'd learned the maneuver, she'd used the ploy more times than she was proud to admit.

Patrick's Achilles heel was Jewel Carter, she was sure of it. Lane laid her only card on the table and hoped she was right. "For whatever reason, this man, this censor, is after the singers. Particularly lady jazz singers. He sees black women as sowing sedition and sensuality. I've read a report about him that implies he thinks clubs represent the downfall of civilization, and well, though I'm no expert on speakeasies, I don't want this guy to get a toehold in Longview, if you understand my meaning."

"He can be removed." Patrick set his hat on his head and prepared to turn around.

"No!" Lane grabbed his sleeve. "If this censor goes missing, the Senate agency will bring in the hounds." She bit her bottom lip, squinted with pain, and was reminded about the last time she'd let her emotions get away. "I've volunteered to let this man take lodging here at my bookshop. The old 'kill 'em with kindness' routine, as opposed to putting him up at a hotel, where he might talk to people. Where I could really use your help, Patrick, is keeping an eye on him throughout his three days here, just to make sure he doesn't get too familiar with the city. Certainly, we need him to stay away from all the clubs in Gregg County. Well, he'd ruin everybody's business."

That scary eye had glazed over, and she knew she'd gone too far.

She smoothed the bunched wool under her fingers and stepped back, feeling for the ledge of the chair. "Can I talk to you later about providing some basic bodyguard activity? Nothing obvious. Just sort of a quiet shadow, just you hanging out here at the bookshop, and then if things get out of hand, I would need you to intercede, but that's about it."

Patrick stared at her, like he was trying to solve a puzzle.

"Think on it." She pushed a stray lock of hair behind her ear. "I'd hate to lose the bookshop, my livelihood, so soon after getting it set up but eventually, I could reopen somewhere else. But jazz music. . .it's a creative expression that is just beginning to catch on. We need to protect and promote that sort of talent. Don't you think?"

The air in the office had thickened with lies like roux that had lumps of flour—the gumbo would taste awful.

"That's the job you have for me?" Patrick asked, propping one hand at his waist and exposing his sidearm. "Body-guarding someone from cutting off the lady singers?"

Lane fanned her face. "I knew it was a long shot. You're just so busy doing other things. I knew this would be too boring for you."

Patrick turned to leave, then stopped. "How many days do I got 'fore I have to tell you?"

"By tomorrow would be helpful."

Zeke stood, moving closer to her shoulder and whispering, "Lane, what are you up to?"

Patrick walked to the door, his hand resting on the knob. "So you don't want me to do nothin' about that man that's been asking about you down at the Cotton Club? Telling us all you're a spy?"

Lane's lips froze in a giant O.

This news wouldn't have been such a shock in France or Belgium, where everyone was wary but in the middle of America, the land of the free and the home of the brave, few questioned one's patriotism or looked beyond the surface of the image presented.

She'd have to tell Theo she'd been compromised. How, or why, was a mystery she couldn't solve in the moment.

Zeke's breathing made the hairs on her ear feel warm—enough of a contrast to the fear that zapped her momentarily speechless—and she remembered that Patrick was waiting for a response.

"Why, that's just utter nonsense," she said, dismissively. "It's probably just more name-calling put out by this censor I was telling you about."

Patrick opened the door, letting rays of sunset streak over the boxes and floor. "Okay, but if I was you, I'd want that man taken down."

She glanced toward the orangey colors, ignoring the panic that was curling around her heart. "Let's not kill anybody this week, okay?"

The door thudded closed, taking the sunshine with it.

Zeke stepped away and took a long drag from his beer, then turned eyes toward her that had seen known criminals deny theft. "When were you going to tell me?"

Lane swallowed, both her hope that he'd understand and the image of their future happiness. "I was hoping you would leave before this nonsense started, maybe even that the censor wouldn't even show up, but I've heard, from a reliable source, that he might be here in the next day or so."

Zeke's gaze hardened. "The censor, seriously?"

She glanced again to the door, begging Patrick to return with a quick yes. "The government is on a tear these days, rounding up those whom they perceive to be anti-American."

There was an odd beat, and the room fairly sizzled with the wheels turning in both their minds.

"And bookstores and jazz singers are on the list?"

The pressure of avoiding Zeke's eyes was almost more than she could take. It was one thing to zip in and out of churches and barns in France, passing information, tracking agents, sending Morse code messages, and reporting on German maneuvers. Now it was personal. And even more dangerous because it included the man she loved.

She dropped her chin and covered her eyes with her handkerchief. "I wish I'd never invited Mrs. Harwood to the shop."

Zeke wrapped her in his arms and pulled her against his shirt. "I wish I knew what I was supposed to believe, but for now—today—I'll go along with you. But if Theo Marks is behind this hullabaloo, we're going to have words."

It stole something from her to remain silent. She doubted she'd ever get the integrity back either. She wrapped her arms around his waist and buried her nose against his collar, breathing in his sweat stains like the odor was the only thing that made sense. "You're the best."

He kissed the top of her head. "As long as we're being honest, I'd like to revisit that moment when I walked in this afternoon and saw you scrubbing the floor."

Lane's breath whooshed through her lungs. That was it? That was the extent of her chastisement? She wondered if Zeke was playing a ruse or if he was really going to believe her. "Since when did maid work become memorable?"

"Since it was you, a bucket of soapy water, and a door with a lock."

A bubble of laughter pushed through the air still tight within her lungs. Zeke never failed to surprise her. His humor and his devil-may-care optimism were the antidote to her twisted, over-thinking tendencies. She needed him like she needed oxygen.

And tomorrow, she'd figure out how to shed this second life that was going to choke her happiness.

Leaning on her toes, she brushed his chin with her lips. "The crew has knocked off for the day."

He grinned. "Best news I've heard since I left the golf course."

As their kiss turned heated, the phone rang. She was close enough to the desk to pick up the receiver and leave it off the hook for the next hour or so, but those three short rings followed by a pause and three more short rings followed by a pause, could only mean that Theo was calling. She couldn't ignore the OSS if she wanted to keep the shop open. Pitiful cash reports and a renovation that had exceeded budget were reason enough to accept the government's interference.

Stepping away from Zeke's embrace, Lane breathed in a fortifying gasp of air. She held a finger up and said, "Just one quick second. I have to get this call."

"Are you kidding? Let it ring."

"I can't." She reached for the phone, knowing Theo would wait through four cycles. He'd programmed the operator to keep for the pattern, anticipating that Lane might be in a sales situation. "Between the Lines bookshop, on Fredonia in Longview."

"I'm looking for a copy of Mrs. Washington's cookbook. Do you carry it?"

She squeezed her eyes shut so she couldn't see the disbelief on Zeke's face. "Yes, I have one copy of Mrs. Washington's cookbook."

The operator paused. "Please hold."

A perilously long fifteen seconds endured.

"Lane?" The Bostonian accent was clipped like he was calling from a public location.

She watched Zeke swig the last of his beer, toss the bottle into the trash, and march into the storefront. The clatter of a box as it toppled to the floor followed. She was sure he'd find something else to kick before her conversation ended. Squeezing her eyes shut, she fought through the conflicting feelings that battered her brain.

Reality reminded her she owed a debt to Theo that was bigger than any joy Zeke promised.

Defeated, she turned her back, tucking the phone close to her chin, and answered Theo. "You have the worst timing."

"Like I have the luxury of a good script." His chuckle was as dry as toast. "That does seem to be the same complaint from our commander too. He's not too happy with our pass/fail ratio these days."

Lane held back the sigh. There just was no good news in the world.

Theo continued. "You can lash out at me about lousy timing all you want tomorrow night. I'm bringing Boris to meet you. Sorry we're coming in earlier than anticipated but that's the way it goes in this business, and we should be in Longview after supper. Make sure the accommodations are ready."

"By accommodations do you mean—"

"You know what I mean, Lane. We're in a dangerous situation, and we'll need all reinforcements in place. Don't disappoint me."

Lane set the receiver onto the cradle and lingered for a moment. Of course, Theo would appeal to her compulsion to help. The agency psychiatrist, Dr. Brown, had told her last year that her need to nurture was at the root of why she threw herself in harm's way without a thought for her own safety. She'd been protecting others since she could toddle, and it was not a faucet she knew how to turn off.

Theo was using her profile against her, but then that was what they did in agency work. It was what she'd done with Patrick not ten minutes ago.

Maybe this was why the only way she knew how to save herself was always to run. She'd never been able to stand up to those who took advantage of her nature, and her semi-retirement hadn't shown any improvement. She was a patsy.

Words weighed heavy on her tongue with excuses that she might make to Zeke, who wouldn't want to hear that their Friday night plans for dinner at Romeo's and dancing at the Reo were going to be usurped by a Russian's moving in. Maybe it was because she'd been thinking of her mother so much lately, but it was almost as if her conscience assumed that familiar South Georgia tone—Baby, just tell him. You can't start life together with a lie.

A winter snow wouldn't have shocked her more.

Those paper cartoons tacked to the wall melded into a teary mess as she stared ahead, wishing she had someone she could talk to about this struggle—a mother, an aunt, a friend who would offer empathy instead of judgement. But there was no one who'd understand the place she'd come to after all the years of wandering.

She heard what might pass for a cough and glanced toward the rounded archway dividing her office from the shop. Her mouth fell open.

Zeke leaned against the polished wood, his shirt unbuttoned farther down his chest, and a paperback novel in his hands. Reading glasses perched on his nose only added to the odd mix of signals he gave off.

"That's a Roberta Harwood novel," she said, for lack of anything else.

"Um-hum," he murmured, *speed reading through the pages of The Man from Positano.*

"It's one of her most scandalous yet a definite bestseller." Lane had sold more copies of the book than almost any other. "I wouldn't have thought that was your type of reading material."

"Well, when a censor is threating to bring down the woman I love, I'm going to find out what all the hubbub is about." He glanced up from the middle of the page. "I can see why Congress is afraid. This author can paint a vivid picture. I got all hot and bothered just reading about the artist so intent on finding a model to be his Madonna. His dedication to the arts knows no bounds and by going village to village, personally interviewing all those young maidens, why it's positively indecent how he conducts his research."

She swiped the book from him. "You're mocking a beloved author."

"Beloved?" His eyes rounded in disbelief. "My brain is so awash in adverbs and descriptions of sunrises that I can barely process how he got any girl to follow him to his studio."

Lane chuckled. "It is a little over the top."

"A little?" Zeke grabbed the book again, and turned the page. Assuming an actor's pose, he read, "Margarita's pulsing bosom swelled with love for the heartbreakingly beautiful species of manhood who bent down on his masculine knee to breathtakingly propose that she abandon her poor, pitiful family and follow him to his broodingly dark and weather-whipped castle on the hillside, barely and most decrepitly hanging to the rocks before crashing into the sea."

She covered her lips with her hand. The sentence sounded even more horrendous for Zeke's twang obliterating the vowels.

"I don't know if I'm more afraid of Margarita's bosom or the castle that is one swift breeze away from becoming a coffin in the sea, but either way, I hardly find this sort of fiction the thing that a censor is going to want to waste his time stopping." Zeke closed the book with a thud and removed the glasses.

She took the book and added it to the stack of paperbacks waiting to be displayed on the new pine shelves. "Remind me to not allow you anywhere near my ordering catalogs. You'd be bad for business."

"Come on, Lane. Level with me. What's up with this nonsense about offering Patrick a job."

Panic battled with truth.

Tell him, Louisa Jane.

The rate her mind was firing warnings, she had no idea what words might fall off her tongue. She reached forward and put her hand on Zeke's shoulder, smiling in a way that suggested she wasn't at all bothered by the nightmare of the recent phone call.

"Why would you want to talk about that when we have a whole evening to ourselves and a closed sign on the door?"

His eyes darkened. "Not that I don't love your distraction techniques, sweetheart, but you haven't answered my question."

There were downsides to falling for an intelligent man. Particularly when the hands he wrapped around her waist made her want to escape from responsibilities—even ones with national implications.

She pulled back. "I can't think when you do that."

"Oh, so two can't play this game?"

Lane whacked his arm. "We're not supposed to play games. We're going to be married."

"Exactly." His face grew serious. "So, tell me the truth."

Air seeped from her lungs like a balloon with a pinhole. Lane took several steps away from him, nearly knocking over a stack of books.

"I see your lips moving," he said, following. "I know you're trying out different methods to tell me something you don't want to actually explain."

She stared at him, regretting that she'd underplayed his experience with liars.

"I'm a master of this trick, Lane. You can't fool me," he said as he lowered his voice. "Just be genuine, for once."

As a widow with no obligation to another man, she wasn't supposed to clarify her plans, her movements. Sharing confidences was what got agents arrested or killed. The training had been too good for her to let it go now that she was not active duty anymore. But this man was her only hope. After she married him, theoretically, her lifelong friend. Couldn't she trust him with her story?

Her gaze swept the mess of books, rolled-up rugs, and knick-knacks left behind by the previous owner. After Zeke returned to Longview full time, the odds were pretty strong he'd discover what she was really doing with the apartment upstairs.

"You're not going to be happy with me," she said, turning toward the closet and double-checking the box with the vodka supply.

"Whether or not I'm happy with a circumstance will not change the way I feel about you." He reached to grab her waist, pulled her back, and kissed her hair. "Nothing you can do will change the way I love you."

Oh, to believe that was true.

Her childhood was a series of lessons on behavior guaranteeing affection or abuse. Everyone in her life had used her to further some agenda, and she couldn't yet believe that Zeke would be different. Even Delia, for all her faults, had never lied about the life she'd led. She owned her disaster.

"Did you bring any more of the Pearl?" she asked, making sure the back door was locked.

"You're stalling."

"No, seeking courage in a bottle."

Zeke sighed. "I've got more in this bag of ice." He stepped around her to pull open the sack and wrapped his fingers around two brown bottles, offering her one.

She shook her head. "I don't need it, but you're going to want both after you hear my story."

He propped the bottle on the sharp ledge of the desk and slammed his fist against the bottle neck, the leverage causing the metal top to pop off. He tossed the cap into the sack and hurriedly sipped the foam before it fizzed over her paperwork.

"Come with me upstairs," she said, walking toward the steps that were narrow and would twist on two more angles before they got to the top.

"I do appreciate the privacy, Lane, but we're going to need to have a talk before we get up to that kind of trouble."

She paused, her hand on the rail. "This is no decrepit castle by the sea, but I think I could explain myself better if you see what the carpenters have been doing here the last few weeks."

He followed her climb. "I thought they were building our love nest?"

"I told you from the beginning we're not living here," Lane said, flipping the new light switch at the top of the stairs. "I'm going to need a little more space away from my customers, if you don't mind."

Zeke stood next to her on the landing, surveying the large closet, the door to the bathroom, and the wall mounted kitchen. "It's like a magazine spread for Good Housekeeping," he said. "How to turn a shoe box into a home."

"Thanks, but it's not my home. And it won't be yours either."

He glanced at her as he pulled another draw from the bottle.

Her vocal cords were taut, and she wasn't sure they'd hold if she went through with a full confession. She was just going to have to spit it out.

"Theo Marks is paying for this remodel, not me." She folded her arms across her waist and walked through what would be the living room space to the bedroom underneath the half-moon window peeking out on Fredonia Street.

"Marks is moving here?"

Lane swallowed down the urge to lie. If she was going to be truthful, it was as much an all or nothing as the sunset glow coming through the window. "No," she said, tremulously. "Theo is using this space as a temporary accommodation for government agents he needs to move quietly across the country."

Zeke's bottle thudded against the kitchen countertop, and the echo was a clink she heard in a repeat between her ears.

"You retired from working for that man." His voice was quieter than she'd have expected. "I was there when you told him you quit."

She closed her eyes. "I did quit. From active duty, but when he proposed this simple option, I agreed. It's my way of staying involved but without getting in the line of fire anymore."

There was a lapse of long, sunbaked moments.

"And when were you going to tell me that you were still a government spy?" Zeke's breathing intensified. "Before or after you said, 'I do?'"

The sunset radiated through her eyelids. "I don't know," she said, being as vulnerable as she'd ever been since agreeing to Theo's request. "I've acted on my own for a while now. I don't know how to share any of this with another person."

"So, Mr. Mercer wasn't any more clued in than I was?"

Roy was as much a reason for her going into the agency as it was her own need to lose herself in a cause bigger than her pain. "He never knew. Roy died before I signed on with Theo."

Lane opened her eyes, blinking against the kaleidoscope of colors assaulting her retinas. She almost turned around to see what horrible expression must be on Zeke's face when she heard his footsteps cross the floor. He stopped behind her, his hands gripping her shoulders.

"Well, all's not lost, is it?" He tugged her back until she rested against his chest. "I think I can understand where you've been used to making decisions for yourself and might have overlooked the importance of including me in your process, but we can move past that."

He was going to allow her to carry on with this work?

Zeke kissed the top of her head. "I don't know how much all this cost, but we can repay Colonel Marks and get you out of this contract with no muss or fuss. It's not like you've started running the little hotel. He'll understand that it is too much risk to ask a young woman to keep track of those details, and he'll let us return to the business of starting our family." He paused and then added, "I'll just set you up on a golf course and you can probably swing enough long shots to not only repay this debt but buy us a little house down on Green Street too."

Lane bolted to the other side of the room. "I'm not giving this away."

His eyes blew up like a thundercloud. "Oh, yes you are. It's dangerous work. Too dangerous for any wife of mine."

Nervousness was replaced by fear of imminent loss for all that had held her up these past years. She was a trained and experienced agent—highly valuable in these dangerous days. She was not going back to being a nobody who hid in the caverns of the Library of Congress. She couldn't. "I've been living a hazardous life since I was an infant. I'm not scared of agents coming through town and needing a private place to spend a few nights. That's a piece of cake compared to what I used to do."

A muscle throbbed over Zeke's jaw. "See, you've never been real forthcoming on what it was exactly you did for Colonel Marks. I don't even know the name of the agency. Was it the FBI?"

Lane squeezed her fingers into her fist. "It wasn't the FBI. They don't allow women to work for them outside of being secretaries."

"Isn't that what you were?" His hands splayed out. "You were a secretary for Major Parson."

"I'm not at liberty to talk about my work. It's classified."

A strange tint colored Zeke's cheeks. She'd label it hurricane gray. "Classified?"

"Are you going to repeat everything I say?" She opened and closed the drawers on the kitchen cabinet for something to do with her hands. "I have to admit, I thought you were okay with all this. You seemed to be in February."

"In February, I thought you worked for someone in the Department of the Interior who wanted an inside man, or woman as the case may be, to make sure Parson built that pipeline to the government's code and didn't get mouthy about the president. You and I both know oilmen don't usually cooperate with the Feds." He followed her as she walked toward the bathroom. "Then I meet Theo Marks, Mr. Suave and Debonair, and I

*wondered if maybe Washington had a little more at stake than I'd previously thought.
But no, never did I think your work was classified."*

Shrinking into her shell, she murmured, "Prior to coming to Longview,
I had been in Europe for two years."

Silence wrapped itself around the exposed beams and teased out a few
tense moments.

"You were a part of the war?"

"On the frontlines." Her memory flashed a thousand photographs of
British, Dutch, and American soldiers slinking through villages with guns
up trying to outsmart the Germans. Blood and mud marked those photos,
as did tearstains, but also a spirit of humanity she'd never seen
demonstrated anywhere else. Strangers would hide and feed each other,
even if they were Jewish—a mystery she was forever grateful to have
witnessed. "Most of my work was with the French Resistance. I spoke
passable French."

Zeke looked gut punched.

"I was happy doing my part," she said with an earnestness she didn't
often get to reveal. "No one forced me to participate. It was my free
choice."

"So, what am I to believe? Are you going to get called up to go to Japan
next? And what was all that crap yesterday with Emmie Tesco's innuendos
about some old boyfriend of yours in town? And my God, how does all this
business with the Wyatts and their guard dog, Patrick, factor in? It's safe to
say there's a whole lot I don't know, Lane. And quite frankly, I'm not sure
you were ever going to tell me."

She reached for his beer and gulped a large draw of yeasty liquid. "I
wasn't going to tell you."

Zeke stopped midstride, his shoe finally finding a resting spot as he
blinked rapidly. "You can't be serious."

Lane better understood firing squads now. "In some weird way, much
like how I'd worked in France, I've juggled so many secrets that I thought I
could carry these too. I'd been pretty good at it, over there. Until some
rogue agent named 'the Grasshopper' went on a killing spree and, for
reasons that I may never understand, stole the lives of four men I was
working alongside."

Zeke stared at her like she was some zoo exhibit. "You worked with the
French Resistance?"

"I believe I already mentioned that."

"And you got to Longview. . ." He ran his hands through his hair,
forcing the sweat-stained strands into a salute. "How?"

"It was Theo's attempt at giving me time to recover from watching the
murder of my friends." She felt oddly calm now that the words were freed.
"I was working on an OSS assignment here, protecting Major Parson from

the Nazis who would have liked to dismantle the pipeline project—or just him personally—but either way, I was undercover on the job as his personal secretary. Or was, until I quit after the fiasco with Velma Weeds."

Zeke's hand clamped his jaw as if holding it from coming unhinged.

"I never wanted to tell you because I thought you would be so repulsed by the things I've done, the places I've been, the . . .experiences I can't unlive." She offered a frail smile of conciliation. "This little apartment is my way of still giving to the cause without going back into the field. Without being too close to the front. This seems so much safer."

He stared, dumbstruck.

She latched on to a previous conversation they'd had, hoping that would help him understand.

"It's like how you felt when you got that F4 medical exam that said you couldn't go into the military, but you wanted a way to help the troops, so you went to work for Major Parson and the Petroleum Administration Service." Her tongue grew thicker like maybe she was talking too fast and her brain would spin out from the energy. "I'm not really ready to say good bye to the agency that was so vital to me after my husband's death. I have to stay involved. It's what keeps me sane."

Zeke walked over to where she stood, reached for the beer, and gulped the last of the drink in one swallow. He slammed the bottle against the counter. "No."

She'd watched his movements, better understanding how, as an attorney, he could process gross information with little time to digest. But she wasn't sure she'd heard him correctly. Had he demanded her to stop?

"You are ridiculous to feel any obligation at all to this organization." He tossed the empty bottle between his hands like a first baseman with a ball and a runner on third. "You will have to tell Theo Marks that you quit again. And this time for good."

Chapter Fifteen

Edith snapped her pocketbook closed and wiped away the sample lipstick she'd applied. "You do pick the oddest times to want to go shopping, I'll say that for you." She folded her handkerchief into her palm.

Lane had risen with the hens and made multiple lists of things that needed to be done before Theo and the double agent arrived tonight. Tucked into her purse were three separate pages: one for the apartment elements still to be acquired, one for the construction workers so they could work while she was out gathering supplies, and third—what she was going to do for security if Patrick bailed.

"The manager wants a VIP meeting with Mrs. Harwood, the novelist, so they're letting me be the first customer of the day." Lane led her aunt through the J.C. Penney aisles, looking at more products than she could ever imagine having space to store. She'd once made snap decisions about weapons, so she wasn't sure why flatware was giving her fits, but she knew it was really the lingering pain from her conversation with Zeke that had clouded her judgment this morning. That and the rebellion she couldn't resist. "Besides, crowds give me the heebie-jeebies."

"That's why I've given up on us going to Dallas to shop for a wedding outfit. I think we can find something local, if you'll just set aside some time to try on clothes."

They'd argued this over coffee and toast at breakfast. Lane didn't have the heart to go through it again. "Maybe next week."

Edith stopped next to a display of hand appliances. "Now, that's a good idea. Next week, your fiancé will be back in Washington, and there won't be any of the distractions that have kept you away from wedding planning. And we can take advantage of the after-Easter sales."

Lane turned toward a mixer so she could roll her eyes without her aunt seeing her frustration. "Surely there's something besides my ceremony that you can get involved with, Aunt Edith—the Gray Ladies for instance?"

"Don't be silly. Why, my friends are already talking about booking showers for you."

Making arrangements with the sales clerk to have the bedlinens, towels, and kitchenware delivered to the shop, Lane turned toward her aunt, and decided it was time to stop dancing around the issue. She'd been liberated confessing to Zeke last night, and it was time to really go up against the bear.

"Edith, I'm not having my wedding at Trinity Episcopal on June twelfth."

The gong in the store's giant clock chimed nine bells.

Edith tucked her handkerchief back into the pocketbook. "You make me laugh with your stabs at independence. We both know that Mr. Hayes said last night that you and he were going to get this matter settled sooner rather than later, and I heard him say, right there on my front door step, that he'd rather get married at Trinity than in some pasture with Slim Elliott making up the vows as he went along."

Sadly, Zeke had said all that and more, and as he kissed her goodbye, told her he was playing golf again in the morning and that he would make reservations for their last dinner together before he left town. And then he'd warned her to put away all those foolish thoughts about hiring Patrick and courting Theo's wild ideas.

Later, Lane had taken a hot bath and tried to forget how much it hurt to live two lives. Theo's worldview was that she was to do as he had said without making up any of her own plans—a mandate of which she was clearly thwarting by luring Patrick into the agency's web and continuing with the bookshop remodel. Then there was Zeke's ultimatum to quit as hostess for the agency's bed and breakfast—of which she was planning to obstruct as well. What kind of person was she that she would floutt their instructions? It wasn't that she thought she was smarter than they were, it was just—it was just that they didn't live in her skin and know what she knew about the community.

Neither of them trusted her to know what was right, and maybe that was what hurt the most.

Edith would have no sympathy for this conundrum, so she wouldn't even try to explain it. She'd hope that Edith felt included enough in this moment that it would distract her from pushing wedding details for a few more days.

"Zeke has to go back to Washington this weekend, and we don't want to use our last hours together looking at bouquet samples. Please, let's put all the wedding ideas on hold for now."

Edith pursed her lips, as she propped a hand on her hip. "No."

"No?"

"Louisa Jane, I've watched you acclimate to Longview these past few months, and if I've learned anything, it's that you can't make up your mind. One minute you're working for Major Parson in that swanky office and then—poof—" She snapped her finger. "You're announcing that you're buying a bookshop." Edith glared at Lane, driving her words home much like Little Momma used to do. "You need someone who can organize you and set you on the right path. No more of this dilly-dallying around with finding yourself. I'm going to help you do the right thing and not make a mistake you'd live to regret."

Lane didn't realize she appeared so wishy-washy.

"You'll thank me for it too. One day," Edith continued, as she turned away from a toaster oven. "You can name a child after me. I think that would be appropriate."

The tittering laugh of the sales associate reminded Lane that they were not alone. She hurried to fall into step with Edith and whispered, "I've not been finding myself."

Edith sniffed a tapered candle. "What else do you call this roller coaster you've been on? You show up here without a single word to me that you're moving into my city. Then you get yourself kicked out of the most respectable boarding house in all of Gregg County, you move in with us, and proceed to fill Victor's head with all that newfangled conversation about a bigger world and whatnot, but you're never happy. You always look like you've lost your best friend, despite the fact that I've introduced you to respectable people in Longview."

Lane whipped her gaze into a mirrored column, trying to see what Edith saw.

"I swear," Edith went on as she inspected a matching set of casserole dishes. "I thought you were sick for the first six weeks you lived with us. But Victor kept telling me to give you some room, not make a big deal out of anything, that anyone who'd lived in Paris, France, would come back with their innards all crooked."

Edith had concocted her own version of Lane's events overseas for her friends, and somehow along the way, living in Paris had become part of the narrative. It was Lane's own fault. She should never have thought she could hide from such a relative, much less feed her snippets of details and think she'd be satisfied. There was an art to blending in with a community and she must have slept through that day in OSS training.

Her aunt moved on to table linens with an appraising eye to the stitching. "I knew the mess Delia led you through as a child, and the fact that you even have a head on your shoulders at all is probably due to the fact that you landed in with Little Momma and Big Daddy before permanent damage had been done. God rest their souls."

Edith set down the napkins, and as if unimpressed with the offerings, turned and walked toward the stairs leading down to the first floor. "But, enough is enough. When that Mr. Hayes proposed to you, against all odds that you'd ever find a man again after losing your first husband, well, I wasn't going to let that gift horse get away even if you didn't seem to appreciate how significant it was. Do you know how many widows in this town would give their eyeteeth to have a man take all their responsibilities on? No, of course you don't. You're too independent for all that."

Lane followed her down the stairs, wondering if every clerk in J.C. Penney could hear her aunt's voice.

"So, all that balderdash is behind us. You're going to own that little bookshop, and I guess, make it a going concern. Somehow, Mr. Hayes is going to indulge you in this and forgo ever having a home-cooked meal again. But as God is my witness, I will not let you drag out a wedding and tease us all that you're finally settling down. You're going to get married, and that's the end of that."

Lane stood on the threshold of the department store oddly entertained by her aunt's sermon. "Just so you know, I guess I did find myself when I came to Longview."

Her aunt pulled her fingers as she pulled gloves onto her hand.

"Living with you and Uncle Victor was a big part of feeling like I had a family again after all the years of wandering around after Roy's death."

Edith pulled the sleeves of her dress to cover her wrist.

"And. . ." Lane grabbed another breath. "I'm eternally grateful Zeke saw something in me he was willing to take on as a husband. This war has pulled the rug out from under all of us, and life is going to go on differently than it has ever been."

"Do you think I don't see that?" Edith signaled the doorman that she was ready to step outside. "I'm not so Victorian that I don't see the winds of change coming, but that doesn't mean a girl shouldn't be married. Besides, June twelfth is the perfect date."

Lane trailed her aunt onto the sidewalk, blending in with the morning customers scurrying to the bakery, market and banks before offices opened. A crew of soldiers approached, their uniforms starched, their shoes shined to a reflection.

Edith shaded her eyes against the morning sun, and said, "But don't you go getting involved anymore with that doctor out at Harmon. Victor said it's no big deal, but I have a feeling that Stuart Lemming is nothing but trouble, and you need to avoid him like the plague."

Stuart. Somewhere in one of her skirt pockets was a matchbook with his personal telephone number. He'd begged her to call him. Said it was something important. She'd have to add that to one of her lists.

At the corner of Green Street, Lane patted Edith's shoulder, and said, "They're so busy treating the crazy influx of soldiers at Harmon that I'm quite sure I won't cross paths with Stuart anytime soon. But I thank you for the warning and the help getting the kitchen things selected this morning."

Edith dodged a man pushing a cart loaded with mailbags.

"Does buying these home goods mean you're moving out of the house?" she asked. "Because it might be easier if you stayed with us until after the wedding. I'm not saying that people will gossip, but now that you're engaged, you can't be too careless with your reputation."

"I'm, uh, going to loan the apartment out for a few weeks until Zeke and I decide where we want to live." She glanced north along Green Street, remembering this route she'd walk when she worked at the Bramford Building. The woman selling pastries was still walking the sidewalk, hawking two croissants for a dime. "These were just the essentials to get things started."

Edith nodded. "I know Victor and I weren't Mr. Hayes's biggest fans at the start, but that young man has a good head on him. He'll make life better for you, I'm sure of it."

After their argument last night, she wasn't sure Zeke was thinking about long term anymore, but she wasn't going to borrow trouble. If she could keep him away from the shop today, she could honor her commitment to Theo without stirring up the wrath of Zeke Hayes again.

"Did you ever want to go out on your own?" Lane watched Edith fidget with her purse handle. "Do something other than laundry and garden parties?"

"Don't be ridiculous." Edith glanced at the faces of those who were passing by. "I live a perfect life."

"Uncle Victor is the one out doing whatever he wants to do, and you're reorganizing closets."

Edith's eyes snapped with an alligator's chomp. "I'll have you know that I'm perfectly content with my lot. I trust Victor—even after that strange phone call from a lady in Macon, and I'm quite happy to do his laundry, as you say, and not complain one whit."

Lane held her hands up in surrender. "Sorry, I guess I read more into your sadness than I ought."

"I'm not sad!"

"There's a permanent furrow between your eyebrows."

"That's called middle age, Louisa Jane, and I earned each one of the rows. Besides, we all know the Lord wouldn't give us more than we could bear. He never gives us anything too heavy that it would cause us to cave, or as in this case, develop wrinkles."

Lane gave up. "Fine. Just so you know, I won't be home for dinner tonight. Zeke said he'd make dinner reservations at Romeo's for our last night before he leaves."

"What? I bargained with the butcher for pork chops. I had to trade in three ration cards just to get something without too much gristle." Edith glanced toward the crowd filing off the city bus. "Now what am I supposed to do for dinner?"

"Will it keep for Saturday? I'll be at loose ends once Zeke goes back to Washington."

Edith turned around again and faced Lane. "I guess. I was hoping Victor would be home and we could have a nice meal."

"He's coming home." Lane reached forward to comfort her aunt. "One day."

Edith's lips quivered before her posture returned to stone. "Of course, he's coming home. Why ever would he not?"

Lane had seen similar expressions of resistance on the faces of mothers who'd just learned their sons and daughters were working for the underground in France.

"There's a USO dance tonight at the Community Center, and nobody loves to dance quite like Victor Thomas." Edith nodded like she knew a secret. "He'll be here."

Lane hoped Victor was keeping up with the Longview news from wherever he was and that he'd hurry back to Oakdale Avenue. He'd been gone longer than any business meeting dictated, and the tension at the house was thicker than the hallway rug Edith just purchased.

Edith stopped at the curb and looked back to Lane. "He's not like those other men, Louisa Jane. I won't let him stray."

Lane wasn't sure which other men her aunt was referring to—the ones who kept women like Delia strung along or the ones who just walked away from their responsibilities. With a war raging, it was getting easier to move around the country without too many questions about obligations. While working on the pipeline project, she'd met a few husbands who delighted in their "business trips," if for no other reason than it bought them some breathing room.

Victor's habits were getting complicated, but they were none of her concern—not beyond what level of stress it brought into the house. Edith seemed a little more aware that he might have fled for reasons that had nothing to do with Coca-Cola. Lane sighed, hoping the signs weren't pointing to another woman in Victor's life. She had enough worries of her own without adding the words of a private letter to her plate.

Blending into the traffic of Green Street, she walked toward the next intersection, dodging men carrying briefcases. Sparing a glance for the Gregg Hotel, she passed the shops that were opening for the day and was glad her aunt hadn't insisted on going to Riff's this morning. It would have been hard to leave the high-end department store without something appropriate for June twelfth. Turning left at Fredonia Street, she saw customers entering Perkins Dry Goods and J on the sidewalk of his haberdashery, watering the window box crowded with begonias. Scooting between cars backed-up at the intersection, she crossed the road to catch him before he took the can inside.

"Mr. Lassiter," she called out with a wave. "How's my favorite suit man?"

He turned and pushed his thick, black-framed glasses higher on his nose as he watched her approach. "Better be careful. There are several tailors in this town who'd like your trade."

She skipped up the curb. "I would only ever order a suit from you."

"Well, you're in a cheerful mood this morning." He set his watering can on the stoop. "I know it's not due to a big sales week because those carpenters create so much racket that most customers don't want to even peek in your window anymore."

That was why her savings drained faster than a bathtub—and why she needed Theo's financial help to cover expenses until East Texas readers returned to the sliver of a shop.

"I do see the end in sight. Mr. Crocker swears today he'll get the plates installed over the outlets, and then he's done." She glanced across the street to view her periwinkle door, sparkling bay window, and the wheelbarrow almost emptied of warped books. The pot of red geraniums looked quite fetching next to the tire. "The painter is finishing touch up work in the apartment, and I'm moving in furniture and linens this afternoon."

"Good for you," he said, with a nod. "Then it's all guns loaded for the grand opening, right?"

"I've mailed letters to the radio stations and newspapers asking them for coverage like you suggested."

"Your spruced-up shop will be just the thing to lure in the last of tourists lingering after the Friendly Trek." He pinched a withered leaf from his flowers. "A book is a lot easier to purchase than a custom-tailored suit."

"I heard Zeke say he's hoping to buy a suit from you when he comes home next." She'd remember him adding the codicil of after he got his bonus check from Parson's, too. Lassiter's haberdashery was a luxury. "So maybe I can drum up business for you."

"And what about the handsome man in the fedora? The one who stops by at odd hours."

He'd seen Theo? "I can't imagine who you're talking about."

"Can't you?" He turned to accept his newspaper subscriptions from the delivery boy. "I've seen you talking to Judge Wyatt too, and I'd never have imagined you knew him."

"My goodness, J, anyone would think you're spying from your storefront."

"I believe I mentioned that business has been slow."

Lane watched him scan the headlines. It was going to be hard to conduct agency business from the second floor of the bookshop if someone as attentive as J was across the street. She'd have to do a better job of making the alley entrance her primary door.

"I hate to run, but I've got three lists of chores to do today," she said, glancing up to the second-story half-moon window above her shop, wondering if the reflective film they'd installed would be enough to disguise the people staying in the apartment. She then glanced to the apartment above J's menswear establishment and guessed that anyone in his apartment could see the lights go and off in hers. That was unfortunate but outside of her level of control.

"By all means," he said, shooing her to the curb. "If you need any help, any at all, please know my staff and I are happy to oblige."

Discovering that her aunt, and now J Lassiter, thought she was incompetent was a tough wake-up call. She was left with no doubts that Zeke thought she was a notch away from a complete idiot, but this impetuousness masked a fierce determination to carve her own way. It was too precious to set aside because those closest to her thought she was fickle.

She just hoped she could hang on to it in all the chaos she set in motion by defying Theo and Zeke. Crossing her fingers, she really hoped Patrick would come through for her, too. If he didn't, well—

No, she wouldn't let her thoughts go there.

Squeezing the handles of her purse, she brought her attention back to Fredonia Street. "Thanks, J. You've been so helpful teaching me business ropes that I'm embarrassed to ask for anything more."

"I've done so little." His brow rose a fraction. "But you're a sponge, and it's been a pleasure to watch you invest in your business."

It was hers, wasn't it? At the end of the day, she paid the light bill. She paid the water bill. She owned a shop. For reasons that had nothing to do with the crisis that kept waking her up during the night, she looked again at the tall man scanning the headlines and tapped his arm.

"Can I ask you something? Something random." It was like a vice tightened on a worry she'd had for days. His answer could affect her future. "Do you think a woman can own a shop?"

His gaze cut to her from the bold newsprint, but he didn't say a word.

140

Lane swallowed the pill labeled with just how important this was to her. "I mean, I have no training and no real plan. So, I guess I've answered my own question."

J removed his glasses. "You didn't grow up with a burning desire to be in retail?"

She wasn't sure if he was joking, but it was frightening to realize just how poorly prepared she was to manage a store. Her childhood retail experience involved more stealing than it did cash transactions. "I made a snap decision in February, and I think I might have gotten in over my head."

"Are you speaking as a woman or as an investor who is looking at the income and expenses of the bottom line?"

Lane scratched at a mosquito bite and tried to ignore the feeling that she'd opened a line of conversation she didn't want to explore. The potential answers terrified her. Maybe she could run to Mexico before either Theo or Zeke discovered she'd left them hanging. "Both?"

"No," he said as he folded his papers and tucked them under his arm. "You are a business owner first. Your gender is immaterial for whether or not you can do this job. Always remember that. You either have the spirit to persevere, or you don't. Do not believe it has anything to do with the fact that you wear a skirt."

A rush of relief unlike any she'd known flooded her mind. This man, this new friend, had more faith in her than she had in herself. "But people expect me to stay home and take care of my husband. I won't be able to join the Junior League if I keep the shop."

J returned his glasses to the bridge of his nose. "Is this something you want to do? Go to teas and do good deeds?"

Lane shrugged. "I'd rather pull my hair out."

"I thought as much." J turned for his door. "Let me know when you're ready for your next lesson in inventory management."

She watched him enter the confines of his men's shop and envied him in his ease. She'd never begrudge another of his lessons. The man may have his own secrets and ghosts, but he'd become her champion.

Three cups of coffee put a buzz in her shoes, and she hurried across the street, dodging a delivery truck, and reached for the lock on the periwinkle door.

Slipping inside and hearing the rattle of the venetian blinds as she closed it, Lane surveyed her dark shop and knew she wasn't giving any of this up. After this fiasco with Boris, if Theo wanted to fire her, then she'd accept gracefully. By then, she'd have the grand opening behind her and could figure a way forward with customers. Maybe she'd rent the upstairs apartment for additional income.

And Zeke, if he wanted to stick with her after this fiasco with Boris, well, she'd walk the aisle. She loved him, and she was willing to do the hard work of finding a way to make all of their dreams come true. Even the ones about children, although that might be pushing it.

But for any of this to happen, she'd need Patrick to come through for her. She walked forward and set her purse on the counter, turning on the light in the green globe lamp. Patrick. Betting on him was like gambling the house with a hand full of small cards. Lucky for her, Big Daddy taught her how to play poker like he taught her how to play golf.

She just hoped she could bluff her way through the next few days.

Chapter Sixteen

April 23, 1943 6:39 p.m.

Lane shook out the new sheets, hoping the sweat pouring from her brow didn't drip onto the linens delivered from JC Penney. She'd followed behind the painter, putting supplies in the kitchenette, and when the McWilliams crew delivered the bed and living room pieces, she'd had to skip lunch to play with the positioning to take best advantage of the space.

She wiped her wrist across her forehead, wishing she'd bought more than two fans to stir the heat around. Maybe the Russian would think this was an acclimation process for the Nevada desert.

Knock, knock.

Lane whipped toward the echo of two knocks radiating off the wall downstairs. She checked the ticking hands on her watch and cursed.

"Lane?" There was a pause from the office below. "Honey, are you upstairs?"

She glanced at the apron she'd put on after the painter warned her that it would take a while for the baseboards to dry. She sniffed the skin of her wrist and grimaced.

Footsteps trod heavily on the stairs leading up to the apartment.

Zeke stopped at the top, his hand bracing on the jamb. His gaze tallied every dirt smear, paint stain, and trail of perspiration. There were enough for two columns.

Lane touched the bandana holding her hair off her face and shrugged, feeling like a child caught playing in the dirt before church. "I guess time got away from me."

His eyes had the flint that she was sure he gave when a guilty man tried to plead innocence. Zeke shook his head and glanced at his polished, wingtip shoes like he was trying to think of a reply worthy of this moment.

There wasn't one. She'd never heard from Patrick, and she was sure that Theo and Boris would see the small apartment with the minimal security and burst into a laugh. The best she could do was to honor her commitment to provide accommodations and hope that was good enough. Unfortunately, Zeke was expecting a dinner-dance for his last night in Longview. She was to have put on her prettiest dress and be ready by six.

"I can explain." She hurried toward him and accidentally kicked the Penney's bag, and a patchwork quilt spilled onto the hardwood floor.

His gaze latched on to that like it was stolen property.

"Don't bother." Zeke dropped his hand from the door and stepped back. "I've been willfully blind, but I won't be anymore."

She stopped short of reaching for him. His glare was enough to let her know a touch would not be welcomed. His eyes, which almost always radiated sunshine, stormed like a Texas thunderclap.

"I don't know what it takes to become a priority with you, Lane, but I'm far off the mark."

"Zeke, don't—"

He held his hand up, stopping her words. "During the last few days together, you've spent more time on this shop and this apartment than you have with me. And I now have empirical evidence that Theo Marks means more to you than I do."

"It's not what you—"

"Don't bother trying to justify." He threw his right hand, the one bearing a University of Texas class ring, toward the new sofa and chair. "This scene tells me everything I need to know about the choices you've made."

A voice, one that seemed to scream from the bottom rung of her conscience, urged her to beg for his patience. To remind him that she couldn't walk away from her obligations any more than he could. Her tongue couldn't do it. Despite the high she'd felt at J's encouragement this morning, her lists and the sick need to check everything off, had consumed every minute and she'd forgotten the one person who meant the most to her.

"The fact that you have no word, speaks volumes." Zeke shook his head, his eyes full of disgust. "I don't know how to reach you anymore. I'm not sure I ever did."

He turned, his heel clipping each stair like his wingtips were a battering ram.

A wave of regret flooded over Lane's heart. She hugged her stomach, and her chin dropped to her chest. Zeke was leaving her. With the surprise of a snap of thunder, her future crashed and shattered. A million broken pieces.

"Gawd Almighty!" Zeke's shout came from his gut and echoed up the stairwell. "Make some noise or something next time."

Her head snapped. She flew to the top of the stairs and peered down. Had Theo just walked in with the Russian agent? Were the spy world and her love life crashing in a head-on collision? Was Zeke going to punch Theo for ruining their life?

When her toe landed on the floor of her office, she grabbed the knobby handrail to stop before crashing into Zeke's back. The need to answer all those questions washed away from her mind.

Patrick stood next to her desk, clutching his hat between his hands.

Her eyes glanced to the locks on the service entrance, sure that she'd set the deadbolt after the painter left an hour ago. Maybe it was time to agree with J Lassiter about installing a bell over both doors to announce customers in the front and deliveries in the back.

"Patrick?" Lane's voice quivered, but she was going to hope that the reason he'd walked into her shop tonight was to tell her yes. There wasn't time to deal with a protracted lecture courtesy of Judge Wyatt's minion. "Have you reached a decision about working here?"

Zeke turned and stared at her. "A man just appears in your shop and you overlook all the necessary pleasantries like how did you get in here and shouldn't you have knocked?"

She blinked. "I didn't ask you those things."

"But we had a date." Zeke tapped the crystal on his watch. "And I was running late."

Chagrin flushed over her skin. There were too many complications in a week that was never supposed to have been this crazy. "You were here when I talked to Patrick about being a shadow for the man, the censor, sneaking in to Longview to stop jazz singers from, well, singing."

Zeke's eyes rounded. "I thought that conversation was all some sort of invention because you needed a bodyguard since those mafia goons working for Marco Abastini had slithered back into town."

Lane hadn't heard any gossip about the mafia returning to Gregg County—if they'd ever really left. They'd been run out of Longview last winter with the debacle over the assassination attempt on the Duffy newlyweds at the Gregg Hotel. She'd not even thought of them at all until Judge Wyatt brought up the men asking about her in the clubs.

"Remember," Zeke prodded. "Sherlock here implied that some creeps were hanging around the Cotton Club, suggesting you were, of all things, a spy?"

"You don't have to make it sound like a melodrama." Lane wouldn't look at Patrick while having this argument. It felt dangerously close to him witnessing the breakup of her heart. Zeke's color was high, and he had the tense movements of a man shaking a cage.

"It is a melodrama." Zeke insisted. *"No one would believe a spy is needed in Longview. Certainly, not a lady spy."*

She recoiled from his insult, silently pleading for him to keep his counsel. Lane wanted to cite client confidentiality, but she wasn't his client, and she had no way of knowing how far he'd go to hurt her if he was planning on calling off their engagement. The only way to stop him from confessing how badly she had betrayed her fiancé was to redirect the witness.

Lane wiped her sweaty hands on her apron. "Patrick, the man coming to this apartment is pretending to be Russian because he doesn't want people to know what he's really up to. I've heard he's very secretive about his maneuvers. So a vow of loyalty is the first step tonight. Silence about this effort, even to Judge Wyatt, is the second. If you agree, tomorrow, I'll show you the target—I mean, the man."

Patrick nodded, but his eye was moving between their two faces like the words and the facial expressions didn't match.

Zeke huffed. "You sound like you've torn a page from the Theo Marks's book of tricks."

Lane was going to need space to think fast, and she couldn't do that if she could smell Zeke's cologne. "I'm not very good at cloak and dagger," she said, as she scanned the front of the shop looking for any others who might have entered while she was upstairs. "Which is why Patrick could be so handy."

"Don't do it, Lane." Zeke folded his arms over his chest, his eyes narrowing like he was jury and judge. "This thing stinks like a bad deal, and getting involved with Patrick and Wyatt is about the last thing a girl like you needs to be doing. They run on both sides of the law."

She watched Patrick's one eye narrow on Zeke's profile. They weren't friends. Never would be.

Lane walked under the arched entrance leading into the main room and was glad to see the blinds still drawn over the door. At least no one would gossip that she was alone with two men. One of whom wasn't encouraged through the front door of many of the shops along Fredonia.

She stepped toward the sales desk and found a notepad under the stack of books. She scribbled a pledge that included phrases about blood oaths and a first-born male child being exchanged for breaking the contract. She pushed it across the desk.

"Okay, Patrick—" She glanced behind and saw him approaching the desk. "If you're willing to take your orders from me, sign here."

"I don't take no orders from no woman."

Lane pursed her lips, tasting salt. "I'm the only one who knows who this man is and what he's capable of doing to jazz singers."

She glanced at both men and knew that the only way she could pull off the mission for Theo was to hire Patrick—now, this minute. A Russian double-agent with information about possible German invasions was a higher priority than her immediate crisis with Zeke. And that was what she had to keep telling herself. Priorities. It was the backbone of any espionage mission.

"Zeke, did you know that the famous singer, Jewel Carter was performing in Longview this week? I can't imagine how a jazz singer of her renown was booked here, but I'd like to go hear her sing. Before she gets barred from performing here and maybe everywhere."

Zeke's gaze implied he wasn't sure who Jewel Carter was and why he should care to hear her sing. "Lane, stop this madness now."

"You know Jewel?" Patrick's marble eye narrowed on her.

It was disconcerting to be eyed by that black ball. "I read about her in the newspaper. She's very popular. And beautiful. The kind of jazz singer a censor would like to shut down, so that she didn't lure good, conservative folks into a wayward path."

Lane waited, and in the duration, her body odor circled around her like a wisp of moth-eaten silk. The closed confines of the shop were not kind to those in need of a bath. She inched the paper closer to the edge.

Patrick's glare took in the notepad and the pen. He didn't move.

"Oh, for Pete's sake, Patrick. Just do what Lane wants and end this charade. I can't believe the two of you even want to speak to each other after old Grady nearly died of fright in the Bramford Building, but at the very least, just sign and move on." Zeke pinched the skin between his eyebrows. "At least I'll know she's got someone in her corner when the bottom drops out of this thing."

Patrick stepped forward, and without bothering to read the contract, picked up the pen and wrote his name in large, circular letters.

A swallow of guilt clogged her throat. She was taking advantage of a man who'd learn to live by street smarts and was putting his life in her hands with his signature. She hated Theo for forcing this bind. Zeke was about to explode, and she wasn't sure if she'd have a fiancé in the aftermath.

As she so clearly remembered, she'd had a worse situation happen in Beaune. She squeezed her eyes to block the ghosts of the four men who'd trusted her to sneak them away from Beaune in the middle of the night. Their deaths had been because she'd not double-checked her details; she'd assumed she'd been given good information. A load of dynamite confirmed she'd been wrong.

Their blood was on her hands, and she'd never forgive herself the stain. That was why she wouldn't leave Theo helpless with a double-agent who may, or may not, cooperate with the U.S. government.

"I can't believe what I'm seeing," Zeke said, rolling his shoulders back and collecting his hat from the chair in Lane's office. "It's insane. You're all crazy."

He set his hat at a tilt over his hair and moved close enough to Lane that he could kiss her cheek, should he wish. Stevenson curled around her leg and meowed a complaint. Zeke's gaze shifted to the cat and his lip curled.

"Tell me I'm dreaming," he said. "Tell me that I'm going to wake up and you'll be standing next to me in a fancy dress with your hair pinned back, and we'll walk to my Jeep, drive to Kilgore for dinner." He waved his hand between her cat and Patrick "And this will all be forgotten."

She bit the inside of her cheek, wishing she could make that true for him.

"You can't do it, can you?" Zeke took three steps toward the front door. "I'm the fool. An idiot for thinking I can mean as much to you as you do to me."

"Please don't make this a test of my feelings." She swallowed salty gasps of air. "It's far more complex."

"Is it?" Zeke shot Patrick a gaze before his focus landed on Lane again. "Or are you hooked on some adrenaline rush from pushing every known boundary?"

Patrick held his hands in surrender. "Hey, man, don't throw me in with the break-up of your romance."

"This isn't the end!" Lane needed cool air, a bath, and a bracing tonic to free her mind of all the tangles Zeke knotted. "He's just angry that he's not included."

As soon as the words left her mouth, she knew they were wrong. Painfully wrong. Zeke had given her generous help at the shop this week, alternating between woodworking to sand the old stain off shelves and moving boxes of inventory around in between golf games to fill the hours of his brief vacation.

Zeke blew air from his lips, but it wasn't a whistle or even a plume from his favorite brand of smokes. It was defeat. He turned on his heel and jerked the knob, making the blinds shudder in response.

"Zeke, wait!" she called, as she followed him across the threshold. "I didn't mean it." She followed him, furious that she'd set something in motion that she couldn't dial back. "Zeke, don't leave like this—"

"Like what, Lane?" He turned at the spot where the bank's yellowed limestone edge came out to greet the sidewalk, nearly the identical footprint for where he'd leaned over the railings and called out her name all those months ago. Instead of hurrying down the steps with a twinkle in his eye and a con up his sleeve, he glared at her from a crack in the concrete. "Like a man who loves a woman and just discovers she doesn't love him the same? Like that?"

She covered her mouth with her hands and shook her head. "No, I do love you. It's just—it's complicated."

From her peripheral vision, she saw J Lassiter exit his shop, his hand shading his thick glasses from the glare caused by the late afternoon sun.

"Can't do it, Lane?" Zeke turned, took two steps, and then turned back, his hand reaching for support from a lamp post. "Can't be honest with me? Can't tell me, the man you promised to share life with, that you have some sick attachment to danger?"

"You don't understand," she said, trying to find a rationale that would justify defying his wishes for her to walk away from Theo and the apartment meant for missions far outside the realm of Longview. No words fit together. Her tongue felt twisted from the effort to marry her need to stay in the game with her desire to step away from the front lines.

"You're right. I don't." Zeke dusted his hands together. "I guess I never will."

He turned away again, marching along Fredonia Street until he stepped off the curb, dodged the cars passing through the intersection, and hopped up to the sidewalk beside shops that were jangled together along Fredonia like cards in a deck. He was disguised by a throng of people, but she'd pick him out in a multitude. His hair was a crown of sunlight, and his walk spoke of miles spent crossing hilly golf courses. His bearing set him apart from every other man she'd known.

And she'd just lost him.

Lane covered her eyes with her hands, buying a moment to think how she was going to step back into the shop and not lose her composure in front of Patrick. She blinked away the tears, stepped backward toward the door that was propped open, and saw J Lassiter beginning to cross the street. She waved him back indoors, begging him to give her a few minutes to process what had just happened.

With her left hand, she felt behind her for the knob at the same moment she noticed a sedan ease against the curb, the window rolled down to reveal the driver.

Theo.

"Hello, darling, was that young Hayes fleeing from here like his pants were on fire?"

Grit and an unshed well of tears glued her teeth together. She stared hard at Theo and said, "I refuse to acknowledge what you already know to be true."

"Perhaps—" Theo lifted his hand off the steering wheel to point out her obvious work attire. "It was the unpretty welcome?"

"You know full well what's at the cause of this, and you're not making anything easier by mocking me for it."

Theo dipped his head. "Sorry, but I have a special delivery for you, and I'd just as soon finish this business and move on. I'll drive around to the service entrance."

The rear window released on a slow crank.

A large, block-faced man stuck his crooked nose through the opening, his wide eyes and corrugated brow aimed toward the storefront.

"This is the place, Marks?" His accent strung Theo's last name into two syllables with a marshmallow in between. "It is too small."

"Beggars can't be choosers, Boris."

Lane shuddered to think what J would think of this unconventional conversation.

"At least she has a manservant." The Russian leaned back into the car, his arm with a cigarette dangling from two fingers, propped on the window's ledge. "I can be comfortable knowing I have an attendant to wait on me."

Lane whirled around to see Patrick standing in the doorway, tall and proud as any warrior, his one eye glowing with indignation.

"Patrick?" She wasn't even sure how to begin to explain what was transpiring. "The censor seems to think, mistakenly of course, that you are—"

Patrick had turned into the shop, his shoes treading silently on the wood floor. "We haven't yet discussed my pay for your project."

She followed him, pulling the door shut behind her.

"And if that is the man you want me to follow, my fee just tripled."

Chapter Seventeen

April 23, 1943 7:12 p.m.

Lane leaned against the bookshop door and put a knuckle against her lips, an attempt at keeping her feelings from erupting. Despite the hurricane that blew in on Theo's tailpipe, she first had to deal with the shock that Zeke had walked out. Possibly, forever.

Patrick stood at the sales desk, holding the piece of paper he'd signed, as if he was wanting to renegotiate.

A series of knocks rapped against the back door, and she flew across the shop to reach it before she had to explain anything more to her new employee. Twisting the keys into the locks, she opened the door.

"Emmie?" Lane nearly hiccupped in shock. "What are you doing here?"

The nurse was dressed in snug, black suit, black hosiery, and serviceable shoes. Rhinestones were clipped to her ears, and her hair had been curled and brushed into flowing waves.

"I tried to make it before Theo, but I can see he's trying to wedge into an open spot in the alley." Emmie entered the stockroom and looked around, seeming to notice the organized boxes of new inventory and polished floor. "Thankfully, I was just in the nick of time. He doesn't have to know that you couldn't secure a bodyguard."

Lane squeezed her eyes shut, guessing that Patrick had followed her to investigate. He might remember Emmie from the outcomes of that incident with Velma Weeds in the Bramford Building, but she wasn't going to assume anything anymore.

"Emmie Tesco, you may remember meeting Patrick LeBleu last year," Lane sighed, feeling a hundred years old. "He's my newly hired bodyguard. Unfortunately, the censor, seems to think Patrick is a servant."

Patrick made a very unservant-like noise of protest.

151

"I do hope," Lane continued. "That you will correct the censor of his false impression."

"How am to influence a censor? It's not like I can even imagine why there is one even here in this one-horse town in the first place." Emmie reached into her purse and pulled out a slim cigarette case. "Do you suggest I don a maid's costume?"

Emmie was like a hurricane following the heels of a tornado.

Lane could barely breathe for trying to keep up with the nurse. "No one needs to put on a costume," she spat. "I just want to make sure we're all on the same script for the evening."

Emmie flicked a lighter open, held a cigarette between her lips, lit the end, and flicked the lid closed. Blowing a puff of smoke into the room, her eyes narrowed and she spared a glance for Patrick before landing on Lane.

"You are under the mistaken impression that you're the author of the script," Emmie said.

Patrick folded his arms across his chest. "I don't know what's going on here, but I don't like it. Mrs. Mercer hired me to stay here and keep an eye on a man, and I don't know nothing about costumes."

Lane rubbed at the headache growing teeth behind her forehead. "There are no costumes," she said sharply. "I had a plan with Patrick, and you, Emmie, have upended it."

"Aw, that's too bad." Emmie blew another stream of smoke into the room.

Lane swished away the smoke that had drifted toward her face. "Just leave. You're not needed."

Emmie sat on the corner of her desk, much like Zeke liked to do when he was holding court. "You look horrid. What happened? Did Dr. Lemming ditch your Friday night dinner plans?"

Lane cut her gaze to Patrick, begging him not to interfere. "I haven't spoken to Dr. Lemming since that day you and I saw him." She should have called Stuart, but honestly, she'd not written the task on her lists. "And my dinner date for the evening has postponed. He's momentarily somewhere else."

Emmie shrugged like she really didn't care one way or the other. "Well, it's not like you were going to have a lot of free time anyway. It will be all-hands-on-deck to keep Boris from escaping."

"Boris?" Patrick turned his body so he could see Lane with his good eye. "That doesn't sound like someone from the government."

"Not our government, dear," Emmie cooed with saccharine. *"The other side. The bad guys. The ones everyone is having a hard time trusting."*

Lane ran her hands into her hair. "Patrick was told that the guest for the next three days is a censor shutting down corruption."

Emmie pursed her lips around the cigarette and then smiled. "I like that one. It's a good ruse."

Patrick scratched his scalp. "So, Jewel isn't in danger of being shut down? She's going to be mighty upset to not star in a drama. She once kept singing during a raid on a speakeasy."

Lane sat on the bottom stair, and dropped her head between her knees. "I think I'm going to be sick." She glanced up at Emmie. "Can stress kill a person?"

Emmie reached down to pet Stevenson. "Not tonight, it can't."

Lane hated that her cat was now curled around the other agent's leg. "Just go, Emmie. You're not needed here. Patrick and I have this under control."

Emmie's gaze took stock of Patrick's appearance. "Until Theo tells me otherwise, I'll stay for the show."

Patrick stepped into the bulb's light, a clear call that he was bored with the shadows already. "Do you need me to go?"

Lane pressed her forefingers against the pounding hammer behind her forehead. "You're about to meet the censor, so I'll need you to stay put."

"Censor?" Emmie repeated with disdain. "Seriously, you're going to stick with that?"

"I didn't believe it either," Patrick said to Emmie. "But it was what Mrs. Mercer is going with, so I'll play along. Judge Wyatt told me to keep my eye on her, what with the guy poking around the speakeasies calling her out as a spy and all. If doing that involves babysitting a Russian, then so be it. It's gotta be better than working as a bouncer at the club tonight."

Emmie pulled out the desk chair, rolling it backwards for better viewing of the door, and sat. "It's better than going back to the hospital for me. There's some country musician singing for the soldiers tonight, and it's a madhouse of people thinking they can edge in on a free concert."

Lane glanced between the two of them, wondering what she'd done to deserve such chaos. "This isn't going to work."

"Of course it will work," Emmie said, tapping cigarette ash into the trash can. "If Patrick is as much like the man I remember from that little episode last winter, he's not going to be too fond of Boris, and we can't afford for Boris to walk off into the sunset just because of a misunderstanding. I'm here to pick up the pieces."

"I don't need no woman picking up my pieces." Patrick folded his arms across his chest. "She's paying me, so I can put up with anything for a few days."

The weight of the past week pushed Lane to the breaking point. There was a cold perspiration dripping into her ear.

"So, this censor business?" Emmie asked. "What exactly do you have Patrick committed to do?"

Patrick turned on his heel so he could see Lane's reaction. "Yeah, what am I supposed to do?"

The series of raps, signaling that an agency representative was at the door, broke Lane's thoughts. She held her hand in the air, "Please," she pleaded as she stood. "Just don't make a scene, and we'll figure this out as we go."

"I make no such promises," Emmie replied. "I grew up knowing no other way to live than by scenes."

Lane clicked the locks to open and pulled the door to allow the last vestiges of light, and two tall men, into the room.

A brutish man was shoved inside, followed by Theo holding a revolver pointed at the Russian's back. "Don't let this one out of your sight," Theo grunted as he reached back to close the door with his other hand.

Patrick assumed a fighter's pose as Emmie sat upright in the chair.

"You amuse me, Marks," Boris said in heavily accented English. "But as you kept me blindfolded until twenty minutes ago, it's not likely I would know where to run." His gaze swept over Emmie with a wolf's intensity. "If I were still inclined."

Emmie stood from the chair, vamping a pose worthy of a pinup model. "Well, let us correct that unfriendly welcome."

Theo folded his gun into the holster under his arm. "We'll perform introductions later, but let's not waste a moment getting Boris up to his new abode. He's been yammering for the last three hours about his impenetrable levels of exhaustion and the uncivilized standards of American transportation."

Boris held his hand up as if he wanted to stop traffic. "I must eat."

Theo shoved his charge toward the stairs. "You'll eat when we provide it and not a moment sooner."

Their footsteps sounded like a death march on the stairs.

"My, how things have gotten more interesting." Emmie smiled as she looked at her nails. "I'm so glad I gave up the Singing Cowboy for this."

"That's the man you want me to follow?" Patrick asked, bending around the stairwell and seemingly following Theo with his good eye. "'Cause I'm thinking he's not going to take kindly to my directions. But I could probably get him liquored up enough so that maybe he won't notice much."

Lane pinched the bridge of her nose, trying to stop the flow of unproductive thoughts flooding from her mind to her tongue.

"Theo mentioned that he was going to send some special provisions for the guest." Emmie glanced around the boxes marked from various publishing houses. "If they arrived, it might be useful as some sort of bribery."

Lane regretted that she had been a little too industrious this afternoon. "I wish I'd thought of that. As it is, the vodka is already upstairs."

Patrick whistled. "Real stuff?"

Lane nodded. "Boris has discriminating tastes."

"Is he really expecting me to be his servant?"

Lane regretted ever waking up this morning.

She untied her apron and answered Patrick, "I'm sure he'd love that, but we don't offer those sorts of amenities at Between the Lines Bookshop. I will need you to cover the night shift and the hours I'm not here at work. I think our objective is to keep him from leaving the premises, and if he tries, then we're to forcefully remind him of his duties to stay."

"Jewel don't have nothing to worry about?" Patrick asked as he looked into the water closet and coat closet on the perimeter of the office.

"She's quite safe from Boris." Lane hated surrendering her leverage, but Emmie and Theo upended her plans, flimsy though they were. "But I can't speak for the rest of Longview."

"She's not going far," Patrick said, studying the locks added to the back door. "Judge Wyatt says she's going to pack the Cotton Club at night and work the bakery during the day, learning a real skill in case the music business ain't kind to her."

There was a wistfulness to his tone that she'd never have suspected. Unfortunately, Jewel Carter was no longer on her radar of people she needed to follow. Patrick had given her a much more compelling reason for his loyalty to her mission.

Wyatt was worried.

Patrick was at her place not because he really needed a job to get out of Longview but because the Judge was not happy about this mysterious person slinking around the speakeasies suggesting that Lane Mercer was a spy. Patrick could most likely add to the rumors now that he'd had such an informative chat with Emmie, but she felt a slight reprieve knowing that the Judge decided she was worthy of protecting.

"Maybe your lady singer can come perform for the men on the Negro ward at Harmon," Emmie said, as she wandered from the stockroom into the shop. "Lord knows they could use some special attention."

"Jewel doesn't give out favors," Patrick insisted, his voice rising. "And if she did, I'd be top of her list."

Emmie held her hands in surrender as she wandered into the bookshop. "Sorry to poke the bear."

Lane collapsed into the desk chair and propped her elbows on her knees, resting her chin in her hands again. "What am I going to do?"

"You gonna do what you always do." Patrick leaned against the back door like he was waiting for orders. "You're going to figure out some trick to get that man to do exactly what you want him to do."

Lane wasn't sure what Patrick remembered from that incident with Velma and the elevator, but there was not enough rope to salvage this mess. "I'm all out of tricks."

Patrick tilted his head to the side like he was getting a new perspective on the situation. "Now, as I see it, you got me, the judge, and that fancy man with the slick hat, and that's a whole lot of fire power. What else you need?"

A way to bring Zeke back? "Well," Lane offered a weak smile. "When you put it like that, I don't think I need anything else, at the moment."

"I have no idea what you really want with that Russian, but I'm pretty sure if you keep the other lady around, she'll be a lot more persuasive than those bottles of vodka."

"I heard that," Emmie shouted from the sales desk. "I'm flattered."

Lane had known she'd have to be crafty to keep Patrick interested in the job. Now she'd learned that honesty was a much more powerful punch. If only that had worked out as well for her with Zeke.

Theo came down the stairs, his tie loosened, shirt sleeves rolled, and his suit coat in his hands.

Lane stood, stunned that Theo seemed so cavalier about the lion upstairs. "That was quick," she said.

"Magic tea. The perfect end to a hard day of travel." Theo set his coat and his hat on top of a stack of book boxes. "Boris is out for the night, but we need to have a strategy for tomorrow and maybe the day after. His driver for the second leg of this trek has been delayed getting to Longview."

Lane glanced at Patrick, hoping he wasn't inclined to ask too many questions.

Theo spared Patrick a momentary gaze and then returned to business. "I'm going to need to move on to a higher priority issue than our Russian friend. Lane, we need to chat. I'm under the impression that your old friend, Dr. Lemming, is stationed at Harmon General."

She wasn't sure why that was a concern, but she wished Theo would use more discretion with Patrick around. "Let's take a walk outside," she said hurriedly. "There are details I need to tell you too. And to be honest, Dr. Lemming asked me to call him today and I totally forgot to do that."

Theo cocked his chin toward Patrick. "We met last winter in that debacle at the Bramford Building, but I'm guessing Lane has recruited you to babysit our friend upstairs."

"Something like that." Patrick pushed aside his suit coat, showing the pistol strapped against his ribs. "All I need to know is if it's ever okay for me to shoot him."

"As long as you aim for extremities, I can't say no. Boris is a handful, and I've already resorted to firearms myself."

156

"Um, Theo." Lane hesitated too long. "Patrick was just hired this afternoon. He's really not up to speed on, well, anything."

"I see." Theo took a hard, long look at the man with one eye. "Well, maybe I need to take a walk with him, instead. There's a lot he needs to know so we can protect the delicacy of your cover."

Lane closed her eyes, saying farewell to any last thoughts that she had control over this episode—if she ever did.

"There's no time to gloss over terminology, Lane." Theo reached into his suit pocket and pulled out a silver flask. "If you thought this man has something to offer us, I'm going to have to work with that, and make sure he's prepared to give us his loyalty, though this hire is not protocol. And you know that."

Patrick's one eye followed Theo's movements taking a long sip from his flask.

"I don't trade in loyalty," Patrick said, when he had Theo's attention. "I work for Judge Wyatt, and if you know anything at all about what's it like to be a black man in the South, then you'd know that we know how to walk and talk real careful. If you got something secret going on that involves moving people around undetected, then I think I can help you. If you're doing something else, then I can pretend like we never had this conversation and go home."

Theo considered Patrick's words.

"But if I was you," Patrick continued. "And you cared about Mrs. Mercer like I think you do, then you're going to want to talk to Judge Wyatt and bring him into your plans. There's some whitey asking questions and planting seeds that she's a sort of spy. We both know that's about the dumbest thing in the world, but you got to know, folks around here are inclined to believe some mighty far-fetched things. How else you think we ended up with an oil boom?"

Chapter Eighteen

April 23, 1943 8:45 p.m.

Lane turned the heavy knob on the Thomases front door and pushed into the foyer. She signaled to the cab driver she was in the house. Edith's conversation carried from the kitchen, and she wished she had the confidence to think she could escape detection and make a run for the solace of her bedroom.

"Louisa Jane, is that you?" Edith walked into the foyer, her arm entwined around her husband's waist.

Victor looked flushed. Like he'd moved too fast or was surprised to be caught being attentive to his wife—either of which were noteworthy variances from the way things had been a week ago.

"Look what the cat dragged in," Edith announced jubilantly.

Victor's flush deepened to beets. "You make it sound like you weren't expecting me to return alive."

"I told Louisa Jane it would be today. And here you are." Edith stood to her toes to kiss his cheek, an obvious disguise to any meddling she might have initiated to get the outcome she wanted. "And after we have a long talk about this mysterious cousin you were meeting in Georgia, I bet you'll never stray again."

Lane slumped against the back of a high-back chair, unable to understand Edith's strange confidence. Had she found letters too?

"Welcome home, Uncle." She met Victor's gaze, but his eyes darted to the floor. "There was a hole in this little house without you in it."

"Pshaw—" Victor stepped out of Edith's cloying hug. "A business trip, pure and simple. And I met lots of people. Including a cousin I hadn't heard from since childhood."

"Whatever you say. But I do have questions about relatives coming out of the woodwork. And you'll provide the answers." Edith clapped her

158

hands no longer looking like the woman who'd darned every sock inside the bungalow. "After that, we're going out to the USO dance tonight, to celebrate."

Victor's eye darted around as if that was the first he'd heard of her plans for a tell all.

Lane had no idea how Edith could look so calm, but that must be the mystique of old marriages. Maybe trust allowed room for forgiveness, too. Or, Edith had tapped into the Parrish women's book of slow revenge, but either way, she was too exhausted to work up much fascination.

She needed to soak in a tub and ponder—for twenty minutes—how she was going to process the reality that her fiancé walked out on her tonight.

"Edith, can we just stay in and have a sandwich?" Victor reached for the ledge of the phone niche, as if holding on for home base. "I've been on trains all day, and I just want to sit in my chair and listen to the radio."

"Nonsense." Edith patted her tightly curled hair. "I've poured a little bourbon into your coke, and you're going to sit down and tell me every detail, and I do mean every, of this business trip. And then we're going to put it behind us, and go dancing."

"Dancing?" Victor's sigh was one of resignation.

Lane pulled the soiled bandanna from her pocket, a reminder, if she needed one, that she was not fit company for socializing. "Y'all ignore me. I've got to get cleaned up."

"That's right," Edith said, with a generous smile. "You and Zeke have a dinner date, too. Romeo's, isn't it?" The evening shadows that settled over the foyer were alleviated when her aunt turned on the table lamp. "Shouldn't you have left about an hour ago?"

Lane had no strength to begin this conversation. "It's been postponed."

"What?" Edith spun around and stared at Lane. "Did you say something to scare him off? Did you bring up all the hullabaloo about the wedding date?"

She was tempted to invent a reason, but she was too exhausted to lie, or too burned by the mysteries of intrigue, so she went with the truth. "We argued about my intentions to keep working after the wedding, and then he needed to walk off his steam."

Edith's eyes rounded.

Victor put a warning hand on her arm. "Let them work it out. Don't go sticking your nose in other people's problems."

"Maybe you're right," Edith sputtered. "We've got enough to sort out on our own."

"Now, Edith. You're making things up. We've got no problems. Not anything a good night's sleep won't fix."

Edith's gaze narrowed. "You'll be sleeping on the couch, if you don't level with me, Victor Thomas."

Victor reached for the newspaper, ignoring the threat. "I'll be in my chair if anyone comes looking for me."

Lane took this as the best time to exit and headed to the hallway.

"Louisa Jane," her aunt called. "You can fix this. Tell Zeke you'll quit."

Lane stepped carefully over Edith's expensive new rug. She wasn't going to quit the bookshop business. And she wasn't going to apologize. She didn't know what she was going to do, because at this very moment, nothing made sense. Not Theo taking Patrick under his wing, not Emmie volunteering to keep the shop lights on until the men returned, not Zeke's bolt into the evening, and certainly not her mixed-up feelings about the future. All she knew was that she no longer wanted to think.

Slipping out of her shoes the same moment she hit the light switch in the pink-tiled bathroom, Lane felt weights hang on her ankles. Her feet hurt from the day's activities, her knees hurt from carrying heavy supplies up the stairs, and her neck was stiff from holding back the emotions forced to the surface by people who didn't understand that she was an operative working a plan.

Lane undid the buttons on her blouse and turned the taps over the deep tub. Opening the medicine cabinet, she found bath salts that might eat away the grime and soften the muscles that were already in knots. The eucalyptus fragrance bouncing off the hot water opened her mind to the possibility that there might actually be a future without Russians and the collateral damage they brought with them.

Boris wasn't really the root of her troubled mind, but he was an easier target than the man who was.

Sliding into the steam, Lane sank down until her chin splashed with scented water. Tenser than she could ever remember, she wondered how she was going to find the strength to shake this off. Water might buy her a few minutes of escape, but it was no solution for her real problems.

As her skin tingled, she forced her brain to turn off the slew of words that would define those problems and, no doubt, categorize them into levels of intensity.

She sank deeper, submerging her head until her scalp felt fully saturated. She held her breath, waiting until her eyelids relaxed, then slid back to the surface, reaching for a towel she'd piled on the floor, wiping her lashes dry.

Maybe the bathtub therapy was going to take more than thirty minutes.

"Knock, knock," her aunt called as she opened the bathroom door. "Phone call. It's that Sergeant Tesco, the one you brought to the Christmas party."

"I know who she is." Lane started to sink below the surface again.

"Lawdy, but it's steamy in here. You're going to prune."

Lane sat up until her shoulders were hovering at the water level. "Tell her I'm busy."

"She says it's important. Something about your friend, Dr. Lemming."

Lane did sink below the surface this time, grabbing a long moment to forget that she'd ever tangled with Emmie. With her eyes squeezed shut, she put aside every inclination to respond to a lure. Most likely Stuart was nowhere near Emmie's reach. After all, Emmie was supposed to still be at the bookshop, but maybe she was bored and knew she could pull that string to get a reaction.

"Please tell Tesco I'm not available," Lane said, spitting water from her lips.

"But I already told her you were soaking in the tub."

"Just tell Emmie that I can't come to the phone," she said, keeping frustration in check. "And don't imply that I'll be available in a while, either. She'll never give up if she thinks she can call back."

"Honestly, Louisa Jane. What's the matter with you?"

Lane ran her hands over her wet hair, adding warm water to the ache throbbing under her skull. She'd never have thought she'd miss the isolation of being an agent in France, but at least there she didn't have to dodge the well-meant intrusions of relatives.

Finally, Edith sighed, saying, "My word, it's just like Little Momma used to say."

Lane cut her gaze to her aunt, wishing she'd close the door to keep the warm air in the bathroom. "Little Momma?"

"She used to shake her head after having a conversation with you, not at all sure how you got to be such an old soul, even as a thirteen-year-old. It was like you didn't want the complications of getting involved in anyone's life, but your own."

Lane thought she had become more cordial by thirteen. She'd recovered from the jumpiness of always thinking she had to do something to protect her mother, and by then she'd been fattened up on the pies and biscuits always baking in the Parrish kitchen.

Edith stared hard at the ceiling like she was remembering a scene from the past. "Little Momma used to say you were an odd bird. Terribly polite but never really in the same room with a person."

"That was just because I was quiet compared to my cousins."

"No, I think she saw something in you that was cut from a different cloth. We suspected that you were just a strange seed from your daddy's side because Delia never had a lick of interest in reading." Edith reached back for the door handle. "Now all that bad blood is coming home to roost. You're never going to know love, unless you let it in. And I think love is the only thing that's going to save you—outside of the Lord. Although I guess the Lord is love, so it's all the same."

The door thudded behind her aunt, but it didn't shut out the memories that were free-falling in Lane's mind.

She knew who her daddy was, or at least who Delia told her was her biological father, and he wasn't someone known around Georgia as strange. As a matter of fact, his family's mill empire was respected across the state. Though he'd never made any claim to act as if he even knew that he'd created a baby girl bearing his coloring and propensity for seriousness.

Lane had loved deeply in her short life. Every single time, she'd been kicked in the heart for her efforts too. Delia, never fit to be a mother, kept a starving child's heart beyond arms reach. Unless she was sick and needy, she'd treated her daughter like a nursemaid—depending on the child for confession and care. Lane still couldn't look at castor oil without thinking of her mother.

Years later, and a few thousand miles from the memory of Delia, she'd given her stitched heart to Roy Mercer. He'd stomped all over the seams, never knowing that her generosity and trust were terribly fragile and sewn with bravery she'd learned in her grandparents' house.

Now, several seasons later, there was another man standing at the door of her heart and wanting to come inside. A good man with dents and scars of his own. Zeke knew she was odd, and he still liked her, loved her even. That was the difference.

To make matters worse, he actually expected her to give him something in return, and there was the rub—she was terrified that her heart had gone hollow.

Lane covered her eyes with wet hands, pressing her lids to stop the tears that would serve no purpose. Leaning forward, she wrapped her arms around her knees, drawing in close. Two long years, she'd been running from the specter of Roy Mercer, never wanting to have to admit that she'd had some role to play in his death. That her wash-out as a bride had turned him away before she'd found a place to stash the wedding china.

Splashing water onto her face, she told herself to stop this maddening circle of defeat. There was no good that could come from comparing Zeke and Roy. They were worlds apart. The only thing they had in common was. . .well, her.

Resting her forehead on her kneecaps, she did wonder what Zeke would get for his efforts at this romance. Would that small offering be enough to hold him to vows? She drew a circle in the water, knowing it wouldn't. He'd want children, three if his comments to Edith last night were worth much, and a wife who'd stay home to raise them.

Children.

Delia was no role model for motherhood, but even with that gap, she most feared bringing children into this world, knowing what they might inherit.

Lane stirred the water some more, seeing faint white whips across kneecaps from the switch her step-father had lashed on her when she irritated him. She glanced at her left hand, and couldn't remember where she'd left her engagement ring. Had she worn it to J.C. Penney this morning?

Zeke was better off without her. She wiped her lashes with her fingertips, wishing she could stop the flow of all that she'd lose when she set him free.

The weeping felt good, cleansing, and as she sank so low the tears flowed right into the bathwater, she hoped that breaking what remained of her heart and giving up the best man in the world would be the last of her atonement. That maybe, with this final sacrifice, she'd be free of the shame and guilt she'd carried for the sins of France.

Chapter Nineteen

April 23, 1943 9:12 p.m.

Emmie Tesco set the phone into the cradle of the nurse's desk outside the surgery ward. This time of night, the hall was nearly emptied of staff, as most patients at Harmon General were operated on under non-emergent scenarios. The silence made a perfect backdrop for clandestine meetings. Stepping over the threshold for the prep room for the surgery theatre, she ran her forefinger against her brow to smooth the fabric of a frown.

"She's not coming," Emmie said with the same dread she might have used to announce that Harmon General was under enemy attack.

"What do you mean, 'not coming'?" Theo turned quickly, his gin and tonic splashing over the edge of the beaker. He raised his thumb and sucked the precious liquid off his skin. "We need her tonight."

"According to her aunt, she's bathing. Something about a dinner being postponed and copious amounts of tears. I stopped listening when she told me that Lane was sobbing into bath water." Emmie tossed Theo one of the surgical towels. "We can presume this has something to do with that dust-up with lover boy."

Theo wiped his wrist, but as he glanced up, his eyes revealed just how irritated he felt to have to guess. "Just to be clear: that would be Lane's fiancé, not the pathologist who keeps tabs on her, right?"

Emmie shrugged, beyond caring about Lane's love life.

Theo had never denied that his feelings for Lane were more complicated than those he had for other agents. It still rankled her that after all their years of working together, and even their own misguided affair at the beginning of this mess, he still wore his feelings for the young widow much the same as he did for his long-lost fiancée—precious and spotless. Emmie had seethed with a twisted heart when she saw him fawn over Lane last autumn in the hullabaloo with the mafia gunmen, but watching his eyes round to saucers now because he was losing her to two men was a little much. Theo had killed spies in the line of duty. He was made of tougher stuff.

Emmie had been the one cleaning wounds and tending to soldiers all in the name of espionage. Didn't that warrant sympathy? But no, she'd get put on the shelf and, if lucky, a pat on the head for doing her job. Seemed like the only way to get respect with the upper suite of this agency is to quit, leave them high and dry, and then run off with the first civilian to show an interest. Without warning, Slim Elliott's bushy eyebrows, leathery skin, and a smile that hinted at dark, churning waters burst through her pity. Just as fast, she shut that image down. Slim added no value and no information to the mission at Harmon, and she was too old to waste time chasing a man who was nothing more than a distraction.

And that's what Slim was—a nuisance that she couldn't quite shake.

"Let's go with the fiancé." Emmie grabbed a towel and started dusting the sink where surgeons washed up for procedures. "I saw Stuart Lemming coming out of the mess hall ten minutes ago. If he'd had a date with Mrs. Mercer, he'd not have gone in for dubious offerings from the cooks."

Theo leaned against the glass window dividing the prep area from the theatre and crossed his ankles. "I hate it when people work against my plans. Lane has flipped this operation on its head."

Emmie unpinned her hat and shook out her curls. "Always the man for understatement." Personally, she was relieved that Lane had hired Patrick, making one less responsibility she had to cover in her god-awful schedule. "And, it's only going to get worse. It would seem Hayes is more aware of the OSS claws holding his fiancée than before. You'd better have a scheme for dealing with him too."

Theo's right hand went to the knot of his tie, and he worked the silk from around his collar.

Emmie heard the mutters of his cursing as he held the beaker in his left hand but gave him his time to work through the wardrobe change and the complications of an agent who was not following his orders. Or former agent, as Lane liked to remind. Emmie didn't see how one wasn't drafted into the OSS for life—once you'd heard and seen the things they were exposed to, there was no going back.

"So, have you read my latest action reports?" Emmie took his tie and added it to the hanger with his suit coat they were storing in the surgeon's closet. She'd hidden a dark pullover and black sneakers in here for him earlier, and now, set the shoes on the floor. "Though I had to condense the details, I've covered a lot of territory since this assignment began last June. You have to be proud of all I've accomplished, singlehandedly, no less."

"I hit the highlights." Theo dragged the last sip of imported gin from the glassware. Shaking off the burn in his throat, he said, "In the months you've been here, you were

right about a thief stealing penicillin. That soldier is now in custody. You were also right about someone altering the samples of penicillin mold being cultured in the laboratory, and the FBI is following that jerk because he fits the profile of someone with an ax to grind against the government." He unbuttoned his dress shirt. "That could be the same person altering reports on the Negro soldiers so that the malaria test results are skewed to show that the new treatments are failing, when we know they are not. But again, that conundrum is out of our jurisdiction."

Emmie took the shirt he handed her, but she had a bad feeling in her gut. Words like jurisdiction usually meant sharing the limelight. Not unlike the time she had to let some numbskull Italian police chief take credit for her recovery of stolen documents. "A by-product of our investigation into who might be working for the Nazis, right?"

The overhead light buzzed like the bulb was on its last burn. Theo glanced at it, and pulled the black knit shirt over his head, careful not to muss his hair.

"Right, Theo? I'm a crackerjack agent, and you're going to put my name in for a promotion." Emmie itched for a smoke, but if she lit up in here, the midnight janitor would smell the residue and investigate. "Just so you know, I'd like to get moved to agency headquarters in New York. I could adapt nicely to 5th Avenue."

"It's another excellent report." Theo tucked the shirt into his waistband but didn't look at her. "By the way, Boris says he heard the same rumors you have that the Grasshopper was heading west."

Boris. That lying, cheating son of a motherless dog. She'd crossed paths with him in Poland, and unreliable was the mildest thing she could say about him. When she had watched him walk into the bookshop this evening, she almost couldn't believe it was the same man she'd dealt with. She'd been sure some enemy spy would have annihilated him before now. That he was in Texas, under Theo's protection, and benefitting from Lane's naïve attempt at security was almost laughable, if it wasn't totally terrifying first.

Emmie ground her molars together.

And Boris had information Theo trusted. God, there was no justice in the world.

She was the one who gave Theo the tip. Her sources implied that the Grasshopper was alive and well and most likely, on their doorstep.

She hung Theo's shirt under the suit coat and draped his tie around the hanger. How insulting, she thought, that it took a man in handcuffs to confirm her intel about one of the most dangerous agents on the planet. Boris. What a stupid moniker for a man she'd like to see in a grave.

"Theo, not discounting that you haven't even read the finer points of my grade A report—" Emmie bit back the sarcasm she wanted to spill all over his bespoke suit. "I'm going to latch on to the better news, and that is my counter-intelligence experiment is working. My months at Harmon General haven't been wasted. My sources provided all the background for this new mission, and Boris showing up is just a hiccup in what could be a perfect net to catch the Grasshopper."

Theo looked around for a place to set the beaker. "Boris. The Grasshopper. Dr. Death, I can barely keep track of all the names we've been throwing around since beginning this mission at Harmon. But we're dealing with three different men, all extremely dangerous, and all with their own agendas they're working. Our job is to keep those three away from each other and somehow not set off another disaster in the process."

Emmie closed the closet with a sigh. "I know that. You know that. The agency chief knows that. But Lane Mercer has no idea what she's dealing with."

"And she's better off for that ignorance." Theo stepped closer to Emmie, and his breath washed over her ear. "I know you and Lane don't agree with how I've run this Longview operation, but I'm positioned at a higher elevation to see the whole picture. You two girls are on the ground floor. That distorts the view."

"I'm not a girl." Emmie whipped her face around and was nearly nose to nose with her former lover. "I'm very much an experienced agent and I don't appreciate being dismissed because Boris waltzes in with the same information I gave you three weeks ago."

Theo stared into her eyes, but stayed silent.

"So, that's it then." Emmie wanted to kick something, preferably a space between his legs, but she was too good at her job to give in to the madness of the moment. "You call the shots. I do your bidding. We're back to every mission played out in Europe. My months here were not about grooming me for a bigger role in the agency."

A color rose from Theo's jaw to stain his cheeks. "I may have been premature in suggesting that, Em. The agency isn't ready to see someone with bre—someone in a skirt—sitting behind the desk."

Her nightmare come true. "I could do the job better than the three men who are there now, and you know it."

"You could, I have no doubt. The president, though, does have doubts, and he authorizes our employment. The three in New York stay."

Emmie bit the skin on the inside of her mouth to keep her Irish anger in check. Lashing out at Theo would not help her cause, and with the time crunch they were dealing with, an argument would delay catching the criminal at Harmon. Catching Dr. Death, getting out of this hospital, and moving far, far away from Theo Marks were her new priorities.

"Lucky for you—" She winked with the hard flint of a diamond near a torch. "I have such a cooperative nature."

Theo rubbed her arm. "I know that this was not what you wanted to hear, but we're in deeper than you might have already guessed."

A wave of anger tasted bitter on her tongue, but this wasn't the time to give in to the long list of injustices she'd endured. There'd be time enough for that once they captured Dr. Death—which she hoped would be any day now.

"The FBI is here."

Emmie ignored the skip to her heartbeat and cut her gaze back to his face. "What?"

Theo blinked slowly, then took several steps away from her. "The President called them when he thought we—the OSS—had overstepped our bounds by investigating the possible theft of the malaria papers here at Harmon. He said the FBI are the ones with jurisdiction on American soil."

Emmie leaned against the closet door for support. "But this has international implications. The buyers are the Axis. We have a whole network of operatives positioned to intercept the papers when they're shipped overseas."

"Yes, but since you've been here, you've turned up petty thieves stealing from the pharmacy and a black-market channel for penicillin, all territory for the suits." Theo set his dress shoes on the floor and put on the sneakers. "On top of that, they're highly interested in the Grasshopper and Dr. Death too. Your report is now on the FBI director's desk, and when we walk out there tonight to stake out and wait for your suspect to come along, the FBI will be there too."

Emmie covered her lips with her hand. She'd been on missions before where they had to share intel and operatives among agencies, and sometimes other countries, but this was too personal. This was eight months of her life stolen right out of her grip.

"So, if you want to keep your spy tiara, you need to play nice with the Boys, and give them what they want." Theo held his hand out to her. "Your earrings please. Can't take a risk on those glistening in the shadows."

Emmie unclipped the rhinestones and dropped them into Theo's palm. "But we still get to go after our target, right? And the Grasshopper, he's ours too? I mean, he's a rogue OSS agent. Surely they'll let us take him down."

"If we catch him first, of course."

She had no idea how Theo could look so calm when all the plans he'd set in motion had the propensity to be commandeered by an agency that had despised the very notion of the OSS. He must walk a tightrope of political maneuvering that was more dangerous than any rooftop she'd skittered across in Italy.

Maybe she didn't burn with as much self-righteous anger as she had a minute ago, Theo's burdens might be heavier, but that didn't mean she was happy. No, she was even angrier with the Grasshopper, now that he'd hopped onto US soil, than when she was following him around the scene in Europe.

"Come on," Theo said tucking her earrings into his pocket. "Let's go see what's going on in the Harmon yard tonight, and then we'll move on to something far more to our liking than a midnight stakeout."

With trepidation, Emmie reached for the light switch. If Theo was running another operation under this one, she wondered why he'd worried about bringing Lane to Harmon General tonight. He'd not want her in the spotlight if the Grasshopper was anywhere near Longview.

Something wasn't quite right with Theo, but she was too pressed for time to figure out the odd pattern.

The room washed away in darkness, and she pulled closed the door handle. Blinking against the garish lights in the hallway, Emmie thought through the plan she'd envisioned this afternoon while taking the bus downtown. Motioning for Theo to stay closer to the shadowy lobby, she scanned the hall for any witnesses, then they hurried toward the staff entrance.

Though Theo would call her out as a dried-up, jealous shrew, Emmie knew there was one sure way to bring the Grasshopper out into the open and end the standoff before it ever started.

All they needed was assistance from the former OSS operative living down the street in a bungalow on Oakdale Avenue.

She stilled, thinking through the implications.

"Emmie," Theo growled as he urged her through the door. "I hear the clatter of the wheels turning beneath your gorgeous hair. Stop thinking and start moving."

"Yes, sir." She led the way past the windows where surgical patients were sleeping off their morphine. Every step confirmed that her instincts were spot on. Mercer was the right bait. The Grasshopper had tried to kill Lane in Beaune, France when he blew up the truck that would have moved her associates to an underground tunnel. Everyone who knew his legend, knew he was not a man inclined to leave witnesses.

Emmie paused at the corner of the barracks, her voice lowered to the level of whisper taught at the training academy. "We're going to crouch, hurry to the dumpsters on the left, at two o'clock. We can watch the penicillin lab from there."

Theo tapped her shoulder in signal that he understood the directions.

Dropping low, she hurried across the tar-topped surface, aware that the cooler temperatures were a credit to the cloud cover, and that was a benefit for hiding in the shadows. Theo crowded her as she settled on a rock outcropping that functioned as a stop for the dumpsters shared between the surgery and dental barracks.

The stench of disposed biological trash was enough to make her want to gag, but experience kept her stomach leveled.

Theo pulled a pair of specially lensed binoculars from his hip and searched the grounds.

"Theo, there's something I haven't told you," Emmie whispered. "It's not in the reports, either."

He grunted.

Emmie hoped he wasn't so intrigued by the night's movements on the military hospital site that he wouldn't understand what she was communicating. "Molly Kennedy, the owner of the boarding house where I rent a room, has a maid. Her name is Lola. She told me that a man came to the back door, offering to sharpen knives, and asked about an auburn-haired nurse named Tesco."

"That's pretty specific."

"Particularly since I only became a redhead again once I landed stateside."

Theo dropped his binoculars. "Anything else?"

"Lemming has received four long-distance calls from Birmingham in the last two weeks. He's been as agitated as a hound dog with ticks."

"So?"

"Lemming has no relatives in Birmingham."

"Old girlfriends?"

"None that I've discovered."

Theo sighed. "What are you suggesting?"

Emmie timed her words. "The Grasshopper has something on the good doctor, and he's using it to . . . get into the lab files about the malaria tests."

"You think the Grasshopper is the one the Nazis hired to steal the documents? Couldn't they have recruited someone stateside cheaper rather than bringing over a double agent from Europe?"

Emmie heard the strain in Theo's voice. Too many years of high stakes plots had left him ragged. Longview wasn't going to be easier. "You brought over a double agent from Europe, and he's sleeping above Lane's bookshop."

"Good point." Theo started flexing his knees. "I've been cooped up with Boris for twenty-four hours and I need to walk."

She checked her watch. "In ten minutes, the MPs will finish their patrol of this area. Then we can move. "

Theo crouched quietly as he watched the MPs through binoculars.

Emmie twisted her wrists to relieve the tension that she couldn't ignore. "Theo?"

"Um-hmm."

"Is it possible the Grasshopper is here for a reason other than selling the stolen malaria treatments?"

Theo lowered the binoculars and turned to study her face. "Do not say what I think you're going to say."

She was comforted by the knowledge that she wasn't the only one to think through the ramifications of Lane Mercer being in the same town in the middle of America as a notorious double-agent with an ax to grind.

"You're way too smart for your own good," she whispered, wondering if he'd see the wisdom of her scheme.

His face became a silhouette of anguish. "She's too fragile, Em. And if he knew she were still alive, much less here in Texas, he'd forget all about his pledge to sell the papers for Dr. Death and go after her with guns blazing."

Emmie wiped her forehead and touched pearls of perspiration at her hairline. "All the more reason to offer her as bait," she said, returning to focus on the crisis at hand, and not the bitterness that taunted from the vault. It wasn't like she despised Lane: she didn't. Not like she despised malaria. It just annoyed Emmie that the petite agent's perky self-reliance was catnip—from Slim Elliott to Theo Marks and everyone in between. That's what Emmie hated. The bravery of her spirit. It was stuff that couldn't be taught but was hewn from the bones of tragedy.

"The Grasshopper is irrational, and I think experts would say, criminally insane." Emmie spoke so quietly even the breeze wouldn't carry her words. "So, we should play to our strengths. After Lane somehow escaped his assassination attempt in Beaune, he'd be obsessed about taking her down. When he goes after her, we stop him in his tracks."

The pause of silence was so long that chain gangs could trip on it.

"Like he'd miss on his second attempt?" Theo's eyes squeezed shut as he shook his head. "There is no way that I'm authorizing Lane to walk onto that target. She'd never understand how I'd let her be exposed to that level of personal danger, and quite frankly, I don't think I could live with myself if he got to her before we did."

Emmie suspected that Lane didn't know the real reason she'd been recruited to the OSS all those years ago in the first place—and she'd most likely never know—but her personal danger had been a foregone conclusion from day one. Theo was searching for a loophole for his guilt.

"He's going to come after her regardless. How much better if we orchestrate it so that she's surrounded by all our firepower and less likely to be caught unawares?"

Theo grunted. "Our firepower being a one-eyed black man, you, and me?"

"And Boris. Don't forget your new best friend. He likes gun play too."

Theo cursed and then cursed again. He inched away from behind the dumpsters. "I'm taking you off this assignment. You've lost your perspective."

Gut punched, she choked. "You can't do that, I'm in too deep. My cover is rock-solid and we're inches away from saving Harmon General from becoming a footnote on the evening news."

"Then bring in your mark and do it this week. My advice is to bring in the pathologist on charges of colluding with the enemy, and we sort out the details after he's off the grid."

"That's messy." And a potential lawsuit, she added to herself.

"And what you're suggesting isn't?"

Emmie stepped up to Theo's shoulder and hissed, "Lemming is not our mark."

"All the evidence points to the pathologist. His signature is on the reports and test results. He travels to the conferences that would put him next to potential buyers of his information. He's had a questionable character report from his last duty assignment at Walter Reed Army Hospital. The same unit that turned in the reports for our Dr. Death in the first place." Theo's voice dropped to a frosty level. "Your own words condemn him. You told me he's had calls from Birmingham, and that's our last known sighting of the Grasshopper."

She wanted to throw up her hands and stomp off, the fulfillment of a return to her rebellious childhood, but this was not the tenth grade, and Theo was not going to ground her for backtalk. He'd terminate her contract and freeze her pension. Then hide her body.

"It's not Lemming." She ground her teeth.

"So, who is the man you've been following these past several months?" Theo checked his watch. "If it's not the pathologist?"

"One of the supply clerks in acquisitions with an addiction to gambling, prostitutes, and opium." Emmie had a long list of the soldier's faults, but none of them matched the profile of the one selling secrets to the enemy about treatment methods, drug protocols, and the military's strategy for combating malaria in the Pacific.

"And why have you ruled him out?"

"He died in a knife fight two weeks ago. Since then, we've had two more episodes of tainted penicillin administered in the wards."

"Why aren't you looking at the nurses or those orderlies? Some of them are German POWs, for God's sake." Theo glanced to the clouds moving fast and about to expose moonlight. "I can't believe someone in Washington thought shipping trustees from Smith County's POW camp was a good idea for bed pan patrol. Kegs of dynamite have less explosives."

"The patients don't like the orderlies either. But the orderlies don't want to do anything that might get them shipped to confinement or hard labor. They're happy enough here. A lot happier than our soldiers are over there in German POW camps." She rolled her neck, loosening muscles tighter than two-by-fours. "It's not the pool of nurses here, either. Most are Red

Cross volunteers. Some have actual medical experience, and most are half in love with every man who gets dropped off by bus or train."

"So," he mused, checking the face of his glow-in-the dark watch again. "It's not a nurse or an orderly."

"There are too many oversights for them."

Theo moved toward the line of trees. "Makes Lemming all the more likely."

Emmie didn't know how to prove it, but her gut told her Lemming had too much starch to fall for an enemy sales pitch. He didn't need the money—his family was loaded. He didn't need the fame either—he was shakes away from becoming internationally famous for the papers he was publishing in medical journals. The doctor had no discernable motive.

"Give me two more weeks. If I don't have my mark in custody," she hated to offer this prize, "then I'll frame Lemming."

"Two weeks is too long. I can't move Lane out of town because Boris is unreliable, and his driver for the next stretch isn't going to be here for at least thirty-six hours. After that, I can move her to a safe house, but that opens up a can of worms because of the people she's brought in close. They know too much, and if they don't know, they'll most likely guess."

"Zeke Hayes?"

"Patrick LeBleu too," Theo huffed. "The only upside to that is Judge Wyatt and company know just about everything going on in this town and they like her. They'll cover her back."

Emmie had no such fan club. She'd ticked off more people than she could count since coming to Longview, and the only one who sought her out was the human stovepipe named Slim. She wasn't sure if it was because she looked like a hard luck case or if he just had a thing for women with hearts of steel, but either way, he was the only man to show her interest in a way that wasn't demeaning or demoralizing. She'd bet he was gunning for another star in his crown.

Emmie started walking across the lawn. Not only would movement help her think through her strategy, but she needed space to let go of the dream that she'd had any real influence over Theo. He was incapable of separating his work from his heart, and there was no woman alive who could compete with Lady Liberty.

Except maybe Lane Mercer.

Hayes had put a ring on her finger and that seemed to subdue Theo's irrational protective streak for the widow. Or it would if they'd actually get married and Hayes moved her off the agency's radar. Until then, Theo would play the knight for Lane, and Emmie would always be the scullery maid—picking up the pieces of plans that hadn't gone the OSS's way.

The saving grace, for Emmie anyway, was that she knew a secret about them both. His was rather harmless in the grand scheme of things. Lane's was not. Though no one was going to believe pure motives were at work, Emmie was going to involve Lane in this situation at Harmon General one way or another. From one angle, it was almost a perfect opportunity to protect the widow from discovering a devastating truth and, at the same time, potentially save the known world from a homicidal maniac.

On the other. . .well, the other angle was a total disaster.

God, she hated this place. Texas was pinching her last nerve.

Chapter Twenty

April 23, 1943 9:50 p.m.

Emmie climbed the porch circling Molly Kennedy's house. April humidity made her skin clammy, her shoes pinched, and her garter belt had long since given up its ties. Did she smell creamed spinach? She sniffed again. Great. Another night of overcooked vegetables. Her kingdom for a potato that wasn't a yam and a green vegetable that didn't have to be saturated in fat in order to be edible.

She should have moved out of this place when she had the chance. Those weeks chasing the supply clerk, who later turned out to be a flake, was the one golden chance she'd had to have moved to a place not filled with snoring women. A new complex had opened on Birdsong Street, and she could have snatched one of the furnished apartments, if it hadn't been for the distraction of chasing that idiot all through the pawnshops and bars of Gladewater. Before she'd had time to file an after-action report, a sign had filled the manager's window bragging that all the apartments had leased in the first four days.

Now she was stranded in the house of misfits.

The women boarding at the house on College Street were reaching a stage of boredom that would soon set to stone if they didn't shake off some of their ideas about decorum. Sipping their lemon water, the lady boarders might complain about the sad state of men's behavior in the 1940s, but if the truth were told, she'd just bet they'd give their eyeteeth to have Slim Elliott turn one of his been-there-done-that gazes on them. And if there wasn't enough of Slim to go around, well, any specimen of manhood who wore a double-breasted suit and carried a hat would do.

Emmie almost smiled, imagining the cackling if one of the ladies actually gave herself over to a red-blooded male. It might bring life back to the sanatorium. Although, she'd gone so long without a man that she was inches away from turning to stone herself, so maybe she shouldn't be too quick to judge.

The ringmaster for Victorian standards wasn't quite up to her usual brand of righteousness due to a condition that only those used to indelicate discussions could abide. The ladies of College Street would never say "bowel obstruction" out loud, much less diarrhea.

Since Lola managed Molly's laundry, she was the one who knew the full extent of the damage, and the way she subsequently carried on about changed diets and special preparations, anyone might think a plague had descended on the house. Emmie tried to explain that colitis wasn't contagious, but like everything, she was dismissed for her Yankee notions.

"You're late."

She opened the screen door. Beyond the mesh, she could make out the frail form of the woman who stayed far enough away from the lamplight so the whole town wouldn't find out she was decaying.

"I'm always late on Friday." Emmie stepped out of her shoes and carried them across the cool cedar planks. "I'm the one who takes the dinner shift at Harmon because I couldn't care less about rushing off to Curly's with the latest officer assigned to Longview."

That wasn't entirely true. She'd gone on a lot of dinner dates to find out who was most likely to harm the penicillin supplies at Harmon. If she never ate another chicken fried steak, it would be too soon.

Bracing the wood frame from slamming, she saw another layer of illness grooved into Molly's lean face. She had her guesses about the pathology of this disease, but so far, the Kennedy wagons had been circled, and no one was talking about the illness that had twisted the starch right out of the house mother.

"You're not wearing your nurses' uniform." Molly glanced at Emmie's stockinged feet and black suit. "So, I'm going to guess you did, in fact, meet a man."

Nothing wrong with her eyesight, that was for sure.

"I just said I wasn't chasing an officer. I never said I wasn't entertaining otherwise," Emmie replied carelessly. "And before you harangue me about him again, no, I wasn't out with Mr. Elliott."

Molly folded her robe to cover her ankles. "I could probably overlook his pushy ways, but I have never met a person so consumed with making sure everyone he meets knows the way to heaven. Like we weren't all raised in Sunday School already."

Emmie didn't have the heart to tell her that Sunday School was something different in other parts of the world. Her brothers had all gone through confirmation, just like she had, from one of the most popular Catholic churches in the Hudson River Valley. But you'd never have known it from the way their lives had turned out. "You'd be cooler if you took off that robe and walked around in your housedress, like Lola."

"A woman of dignity can endure a little heat."

Emmie made a point to sniff the air. Lola left yesterday to travel to some Cajun voodoo shop in deep Louisiana and bring back the spices she needed for her roux and gumbo. The offerings in the duration were pitifully slim. "It smells like you asked Miss Florey to cook supper tonight."

"We cooked vegetables." Molly struggled to stand from her chair. "I could have used your help in the garden."

"Where were the other ladies?"

"The spinster sisters are taking the train to Chicago this evening, visiting family or some such, and the others are at the show, and someone said they were going to a prayer meeting."

She refused the bait of the spinster calling the spinsters out. "There's a prayer meeting on a Friday night?"

Molly waved her hand through the air like it was only a simpleton who wouldn't know. "You can find a prayer meeting on any given night in this town. Good Christian folks know how to bend the knee."

Emmie's knees had developed calluses from all the years she was forced to attend Mass. After her stint at the Catholic home for unwed mothers, her knees didn't bend anymore.

"I'm going through to make a sandwich." She'd long since stopped asking for permission. "Is there bread?"

Molly trailed behind, her heels scuffing the floor as she shuffled along. "I don't know why you persist in acting like we're beggars in this house."

"Because our ration cards aren't going as far as they used to." Emmie saw that whoever had cleared the table of dishes had forgotten to come back and sweep the surface for crumbs. Lola would have complained about that kind of carelessness. "The government is under the mistaken impression that females don't eat as much as men."

When she didn't get a reply, she held the swinging door between the butler's pantry and the dining room and turned back. Molly was crouched over the back of a dining chair as if it were the only thing holding her upright.

"Molly?"

Molly's head shook like she didn't want to be noticed in this condition.

"You need to get to the bathroom?" Emmie wouldn't wait for an answer. She walked back and wrapped her arm around the woman's waist, feeling more rib than sinew. "Come on. If we hurry we can just about make it."

Molly's lips were pursed so tight a squeak couldn't escape.

More dragging than walking, she hurried Molly through the parlor to the hallway and back to the rear of the house where the suite she occupied took up what had once been a library, study, and back bedroom. Emmie had scoped all the rooms her first week as a tenant and knew there was a secret panel in the library that led to a small basement where one could ride out a tornado or stash illegal products. The extent of Miss Kennedy's private holdings were cherry cordials, but at one time, someone had shelving made for a large inventory of wine.

She navigated the four-poster bed and got her charge into the small en-suite bathroom before Molly vomited. Emmie held Molly's long string of pearls away from the projectile bile and reached for a cloth that she could run under cold water.

When the wave passed, she helped wipe Molly's face and flushed the toilet before anyone could comment about the blood.

Ringing out the cloth, Emmie thought back to the last time she'd seen Molly full of spit and vinegar. Well, discounting her normal demeanor for treating everyone with disdain, it had been weeks.

"Let's get you to bed." Emmie curled her arm around the older woman and nearly lifted her off the floor to move her toward the bed. "I'll see if I can't find Lola's stash of gingersnaps."

Molly's lips looked dry as week old newsprint. "You're not supposed to know about those."

"Obviously, with the way they're hoarded. But my nose can find cookies hidden in a jar made of steel."

As they lumbered toward the bed, Emmie saw a footstool that had been moved closer to the mattress, an aide in getting in and out of bed when knees had grown stiff.

She'd missed too many of the family-style suppers that were served at six on the dot every evening to know if Molly was eating for nutrition or appetite, but she'd guess that it was a little of neither.

"Here you go, Molly. Let's get up on the bed, and I'll help you with your shoes."

"You used to call me Miss Molly."

Emmie analyzed the brittleness in the jaundiced eyes. "After you told your friends last fall about the pantyhose, I wasn't sure what we were. But Lane tells me we're all friends, and that friends take care of each other."

"Friends." Molly chewed the word like it was sawdust. She fell against the pillows. "I don't have many of those."

Emmie lifted bird-like legs to leverage her into a more comfortable position. She pulled the quilt from the foot of the bed. "You're the socialite of Longview. You have tons of friends."

"Do I?"

Emmie peeked to make sure this wasn't senility speaking. "Yes. I could read you the Women's Federation telephone register if you need a reminder."

"Then where are they when I need them?"

She glanced at the woman whose closed lids were a fragile tissue over a silhouette of alabaster. "You've run them off by waving with your frilly handkerchief, telling them there's nothing for them to see over here on College Street."

"I have not."

Emmie reached to remove the strand of pearls so that they'd not choke Molly during sleep. Lifting her shoulders, she smelled a fragrance not borne of any perfume bottle. Molly was rotting from the inside out.

Setting the strand on top of the Kennedy family Bible, a leathery book so broad it seemed to hold down the nightstand, she pulled the quilt to Molly's chin and stepped away from the bed.

"Emmie."

The word was too weak to be qualified a whisper. It was more of a sigh with consonants.

"Don't." There was a long pause. "Tell."

Emmie couldn't make that promise. Not as a nurse and not as a friend. But since she cared, she said, "For tonight."

And she did care. She saw a lot of her mother in Molly Kennedy. For that reason alone, she should have run instead of renting a room on the second floor of this big house, but there was something about the unbending backbone that felt comforting. Like she didn't have to save the world all by herself.

Her mother wasn't nearly as traditional as Molly, though she'd argue that point to a fault. No, Emmie had grown up challenged by a woman who struggled against the ropes of conformity and took out her frustrations on a daughter who was more like the Irish relatives than her upstate New Yorker father.

Her mother had eventually snapped, leaving for sojourns in the Adirondacks and forgetting her family for months at a time. By then, though, the pattern of pushing against authority was firmly set in the youngest child, and only daughter, and much to her father's dismay, Emmie wasn't at all interested in keeping up appearances.

Emmie had vowed never to be caught in a gilded-cage like her mother, but here she was, forty-three years old, living as an actor with a script written by Churchill and Roosevelt. Nowhere near the dutiful nun she'd promised God she'd be if he'd just make her heart stop bleeding from the pain of making bad choices.

She pulled Molly's door closed and walked silently to the dining room, hoping that there was still a bottle of bourbon hidden behind the soup tureen in the breakfront. It would take alcohol to dull the memories of a teenaged girl being driven away from house and family because she'd flirted with a college boy at a debutante ball and her party favor from the night had been a seven-pound baby with cherry-brown hair.

She opened the glass door, happy to find the small bottle Lane had discovered all those months back. Watching Lane take the brunt of Molly's outrage that long-ago night had signaled a change in her opinion of the younger agent. It was a short-lived admiration deep-sixed when she discovered Theo's fascination with the famed Mrs. Mercer. The intuitive female spy, who somehow managed to escape a bomb assassination, had become a beacon for men drawn to warrior types. Emmie's style was more Cleopatra with a little Mary Queen of Scots thrown in to keep it original.

She unscrewed the bourbon cap, smelling the seal to determine if the contents had been replaced with water. Thankfully, it wasn't too watered down. Taking a long swig from the bottle, she thought about how Molly was in for a rough end if she didn't get in to see a doctor who was an expert with intestinal issues, sooner rather than later. Particularly since all the good medicines were going to war-wounded.

Like a stray thunderclap, she wondered if her parents were healthy.

There'd been limited communication over the last four years, and she'd enjoyed the break from reading about the gossip of her sisters-in-law and how her brothers were managing houses full of overachieving teenagers.

Her letters home had always been brief. So brief, her mother had accused her of sabotaging what was left of their tenuous family relationship. That wasn't entirely fair, but with the OSS, one didn't get to brag about one's latest exploits or share the tidbits of a society with which it was criminal to associate. The brevity was meant to discourage letters from New York, but it had the opposite effect. Her mother had a gift for writing that was lost on a reader who just wanted to know the basics, not the temperature of Sunday's roast or the color of a granddaughter's hair ribbon.

She took another pull from the bottle to soften out the faces of those who'd sit around that Hudson River table eating that perfectly cooked roast.

Her hand started to shake, a quiver really.

It always did when she thought too much about regrets. She knew she'd have to go back, one day, if only to prove to her parents she wasn't still the girl they'd been ashamed to claim. At the ripe old age of forty-three, they'd have to see that she'd finally outgrown her hotheadedness and impulsive streak.

Or had she?

Based on Theo's icy good bye, it was likely she'd only perfected her techniques, not overcome the root problems.

Maybe, once this assignment was over, it would be time to return to the Hudson River Valley and find her way home. If for no other reason than to see if her parents were still alive.

Emmie glanced at the bottle, wondering how much more she could drink without having to refill it from a new bottle of bourbon. A sound from the front of the house made her think one of the spinsters had returned from church. Leaning into the corner, away from the reflection of the hall light, she listened for the telltale signs of heels clattering up the staircase. Putting the bottle back into the breakfront, she gingerly closed the glass and tiptoed into the kitchen.

As she reached for the light switch, a voice surprised her.

"Close the blackout curtains; do you want us to get reported?"

Emmie turned back, seeing one of the ladies who was sharing a room with her twin sister—she just couldn't remember which sister this one was. They were both school teachers, both had a propensity for wearing beige, and as best as she could remember, both had names that were spelled too similarly for any distinction. Since she couldn't remember which one was which, she fell back on her tried and true catchall. "Thanks, girl. I almost forgot."

"I'm not a girl, and neither are you."

Prune, that's what Emmie should have called her. Since her hand was still on the light switch, she flipped it off. She could make a sandwich in the dark if she had to.

"Just because you didn't pull the blinds the way we're supposed to doesn't mean you have to smart off." The woman stepped over to the sink and pulled the vinyl shade down and then walked back to turn the light on. "It's just curfew."

"God save me from the police." Emmie reached into the breadbox and found the heels of yesterday's loaf, wondering if there was anything more than bologna in the refrigerator.

"Stop taking the Lord's name in vain." The woman folded her arms across her chest. "You are too flippant, and He can hear you."

Emmie opened the refrigerator and rummaged around for the jar of mustard and pulled out a package of what looked like some butcher's idea of pressed ham. She flipped it over, wishing there was some sort of label so she could curse this, too.

The eyes of the other woman bored into her back, but she could endure. Ticking off roommates was not a federal offense, at least not yet. But the war was encouraging tattletales to rat out neighbors regarding ration cards, curfews, and recycling. Pretty soon there'd be citizen police.

"I actually want to ask you a question."

Emmie smeared mustard on both sides of the dry bread and slapped a few pieces of the ham product onto the yellow paste, hoping it would drown out the salt.

"Nurse Tesco, I don't think you're listening to me."

The grandfather clock in the foyer chimed ten o'clock. The echo of those pings bounced off the walls of the downstairs rooms, and even in the kitchen she could hear its Westminster chimes. It would have been rude not to wait off the last bell.

"I'm listening. It's not as if I have a choice, is it?"

When she didn't get a lecture for her bad attitude, she glanced over her shoulder and saw an expression that was both hostile and righteous. Emmie wouldn't put it past this woman to sell her out if Dr. Death rang the doorbell.

"I'd like you to give me Mr. Elliott's address. I know of a ministry he could get involved with, one that would benefit from a having a man of his experience to mentor the young men who are at risk."

Ah, so Slim's appeal was a commodity in this house of women. He'd be speechless. He had such a low opinion of his value, outside being a welding wizard, that he'd be surprised to find out he'd been discussed behind closed doors.

Emmie closed the sandwich and pressed it down to smash all the flavors together. "Let me get this right, Adelaide, you want—"

"It's Idaline."

Emmie glanced up. "What?"

"My name is Idaline."

Her mother must have not liked little girls to give the sisters rhyming names. "Ida, then. You want Mr. Elliott to come speak to some juvenile offenders because he's come out of a life of hard knocks and he's still upright?"

She rolled her shoulders back. "I have no idea what his life is like. I just know he can work his way around Scripture and he has a deep voice. People like to listen to men with strong voices. It implies an authority figure."

Hmm, maybe old Ida was right. "Are you sure there isn't something more to this request? Like maybe you want to spend time with Slim? He is handsome, in a crusty sort of sunbaked way."

A flush of red shot up from Idaline's throat to flood her cheeks. "Oh, my, no. Why, that's the farthest thing from my mind. We're just short of men who are willing to be role models, and he seems like someone who might be inclined to do that sort of thing."

Emmie picked up the sandwich. It hovered near her lips. "And you're not the least bit interested in Slim, as a man?"

"Of course not. I can't believe you'd even think such a thing."

Emmie chewed a bite. She was tired of this conversation, and after the turn her thoughts had taken a few minutes ago, she'd lost the will to argue. There were other men in this town, or soon coming, who would eat little ladies like Ida and her sister for breakfast. Emmie needed to save her strength for her final duel with the Grasshopper and whatever other agencies descended on Longview after Theo called in the sharks.

"I'll write down his address for you, but I make no promises that he's willing to be your guinea pig. He's got a way of doing things that doesn't follow anyone's ideas of orderly." Emmie pictured Slim's earnest face over the dinner candles at the Gregg Hotel. "He's got sort of a free spirit that has found his own way of going through life, and I'm not sure he'd be much good trying to teach others to follow his way. It's a 'latch on for the ride,' or fall away approach to friendship."

Idaline sighed. "I gathered as much, since the two of you were so close. You're both so. . .let's call it unconventional. . .that I can see why you're attracted to him."

If Emmie hadn't been in the process of swallowing the vile sandwich, she'd have debated her level of interest in the welder. But with a moment to remember how much he made her laugh, she thought maybe she liked him more than she realized. He was probably the only man who'd treated her with respect when he didn't have to—or wasn't afraid of what she'd do to him with a weapon.

Using one of Lola's dishtowels, she wiped her lips. "I'll leave a note for you at the phone. He's staying at the Gregg Hotel this week and will be on the road recruiting pipefitters next week, so good luck reaching him."

Ida turned on her heels and left the room as quietly as she'd arrived. Emmie leaned into the counter, looking at the lipstick stain on the towel. She ran the cloth under some cold water and tried to remove the red blot before it set. Slim Elliott. Her mind spun circles around his name, trying to determine if she was going to run from him or if she'd give him one more chance to convince her that there was a reason they should continue to see each other. He was the opposite of every man she'd dated, but when was the last time she went out with someone because she genuinely was interested and not because it was useful to the mission? That didn't deserve an answer. It was too embarrassing to admit.

She turned off the tap, and used the cold towel to blot her forehead. There were so many other pressing concerns she needed to think through that she felt foolish anticipating a long walk with a man who had a voice like liquid steel.

Chapter Twenty One

"You look awful," Theo growled as Emmie crawled into the car, scooting over the cracked seat.

"And I love you too," she said with bite as she encountered a spring that had poked through the leather.

Theo's fingers were wrapped around the steering wheel. "Have you been drinking, darling?"

She'd brushed her teeth before she left the house at College Street, but Theo's taunt proved that people who knew you too well were best kept at a distance. "A little sip for courage."

His brow cocked over his eye. "You've never needed a sip before."

She glanced at him, surprised he was wearing a different suit and that his hair was freshly combed. "Well, I do now."

"You're losing your nerve." He put the car in gear and coasted away from the Kennedy curb. "I should have replaced you with a twenty-year-old ages ago."

That one stung. "Is that what you say to all your agents, or just the women who've lost interest in being the kitten at your pajama parties?"

"Grouchy. I'll have to remember that the next time I defend hiring women to do field work." Theo shot his gaze toward her. "Maybe Hoover and the others are right. Women don't have a place doing the dangerous work at the frontlines."

She'd ignore his digs—he turned snippy when he was tense. "Sounds like you're getting grief for your budget overrides, and you're going to take it out on the only agents who actually follow orders, show up on time, and don't get into a pissing match about moving up the chain of command."

"Cranky too," he said with a sideways glance.

"Grouchy and cranky are the same thing." Emmie tugged the waistband of her slim-cut black pants, relieving some of the pressure where the elastic pinched. She'd have to lay off Lola's home-baked bread for the foreseeable future. "You're getting lazy reading the thesaurus."

She glanced through the window, seeing the lights of downtown Longview glowing bright. "I thought we were going to follow Colonel Lemming tonight," she said, looking twice at his wardrobe. "But you've changed clothes and I've never known you to conduct a stake out in dinner wear."

"There's nothing wrong with your eyesight, Sergeant." Theo pulled the car aside as a fire engine screamed up behind them, passing them with a crew of men hanging off the side. "It's been confirmed," he said as the sirens blazed ahead. "We have a grasshopper infestation in Longview."

That sandwich twisted in her gut. Maybe Molly's condition was contagious after all. "What is your plan, Colonel?"

He stared through the windshield, and Emmie wondered if he heard the question.

Finally, he pulled the car back into High Street's traffic and fiddled with the knob on the radio. "The FBI team is in place at Harmon General. They have your reports to know the campus protocols and usual list of after-hour vendors."

Emmie watched him drive the car around a stalled taxi cab then turned east on Methvin Street. They kept driving farther away from the Army hospital, so whatever he had in mind, they'd not be tracking the suits as they set a sting operation in motion. She was going to regret not being there when they brought in the soldier messing with the malaria test results. But she doubted that the man would be the infamous Dr. Death. That villain had avoided detection for eight months; he wasn't going to walk into their trap.

"How do you feel about a night on the town?" Theo glanced at her, the streetlight reflecting his fetching grin. "Just like the old days?"

Anyone else might think that meant an evening of cocktails and dancing. Emmie knew the code meant that though they'd be in a public place, they'd be working a mission of highest priority. And here she was, wearing her ugly stakeout attire.

She turned away from him to stare out the window and gather her thoughts.

Emmie had been intimate with Theo back in the days when the OSS's rogue agent made his presence known. She'd never seen Theo so distraught over his mistake in hiring judgment and the implied loss to the agency credibility. She could make the case that the Grasshopper ruined what was left of their flashfire relationship. Since then, Theo had been consumed with finding any clue as to the man's movements and, by association, taking him down before he could do more damage to the Allies. That it had been a two-year chase was grounds enough for Theo's ulcer, but that it had been a chess match played out over an international game board had also run up a tab that the U.S. government wasn't keen to pay.

Since the Beaune, France, incident, the orders were to destroy anyone working with the Grasshopper and minimize collateral damage.

Theo's bright idea had been to move the OSS agent in charge of the Beaune operation to Longview in order to recuperate and to disguise that she'd survived the explosion. The Grasshopper wouldn't have wanted any witness left to identify him. When the local papers started covering the Velma Weeds story and pending trial, Lane Mercer was exposed to the press. Theo could whitewash it all if he wanted to, but that had been a red flag to a bull that was ready to charge U.S. soil.

Turned out, Roosevelt's cabinet members weren't too fond of the espionage network, which meant if the secret department were to survive, Theo had to bring in the rogue agent. Preferably alive so he'd confess of his contacts in Europe and what information he'd passed to enemy hands.

Emmie didn't feel so inclined to restraint. That man had thwarted several missions and was responsible for the deaths of too many of her associates. If she could get her hands on him, he'd not survive.

"Are we going to snatch Lane from her slumber?" Emmie crossed her fingers. She turned her head and stared at his profile.

"We leave her out of this." Theo pulled the car into a darkened gas station. "You and I have handled this sort of thing before and we'll do it tonight."

At the height of their romance, they were super spies, slipping onto trains and planes like jetsetters. Their success record was the reason they were both lured back to Washington to set up a training regime for new recruits. Unlike Theo, she wasn't as well suited to chalkboards and roundtable discussions. She'd reapplied and was granted another stab at fieldwork. Until the fiasco with her girls and the Gestapo.

"But you're a desk man now," she said, forming a pout. "Have you even been to a gun range to practice this whole spring?"

"Testy." He checked his watch. "Never your best quality."

"Just finding out if I'm going to have to cover your rear end, should we get stuck."

"We're not going to get stuck," Theo snarled.

"Says the man who somehow let the Grasshopper escape France."

His jaw turned to brick. "Intel said he was as good as dead. Tortured by the Germans after the fireworks in Beaune exposed their local military unit to a fatal retaliation by the underground."

"And Birmingham?" Her fingers twitched, so she wove them together and planted them in her lap. "You let him live in Alabama for what, months on end?"

"Unsubstantiated rumor. The young physicist would have believed any name given to him, and we know plenty of copycats who'd love to have the reputation this one has garnered."

Emmie blew out a puff of barely restrained anger. She'd been with this agency since its infancy. She knew the OSS higher-ups were battling limited funds, red-tape, and a performance record that wasn't a brilliant endorsement of ingenuity—there'd been almost as many disasters overseas as there had been success stories. Its chief architect sat next to her and seemed blind to the notion that Longview was poised to be the end of that era.

Theo cut the engine. "You've got something you want to say?"

Startled she turned her gaze back to the window. "Not particularly."

"It seems like you're itching for a fight, and as one who knows the pattern well, I'd like to dispense with all the drama that precedes it and get right down to the issue. Why are you mad at me?"

For about a thousand reasons. Starting with the way he dumped her when he found a younger and prettier sidekick and all the way up to his assigning her to Harmon General, a thousand miles away from action. But really, it was because he was in so deep he'd lost all his objectivity to their risks, and the premise that short term losses sometimes meant big payouts.

"I'm not mad," she lied.

"You're the most defensive person I know. I've just told you I'm giving your stakeout of the penicillin lab to suits you've never met, and you're not angry?"

"I'm a little peeved, but I'm not livid." She channeled some of the disdain she used to see her mother posture when her father would complain about those 'little writing projects.' "Mad is reserved for you suggesting that I've lost my instincts about Stuart Lemming."

He blew out his breath. "Lemming is in the thick of this, you mark my words."

"Based on what, Theo? You've been so busy chasing Boris, and who knows what else while grounded stateside, that I'm not at all sure you've read any of the intelligence I've reported to you about Harmon."

Theo stared at her, processing her words without changing his expression. "Based on Lemming's background check. Doesn't it strike you as odd that he was such a good friend to the Mercers back in Washington, and then he gets reassigned here, following on Lane's heels?"

Emmie was feeling claustrophobic in the car's interior. "He's here because he's an Army doctor and this is an Army hospital. The surgeons call him the doctor's doctor because they can't make a diagnosis without his input. There aren't many here who are so universally liked."

"A perfect cover."

"A real cover. And since when did you lose your objectivity about Lane? She's what the Grasshopper is after, not Lemming."

Theo tapped the steering wheel.

"How did you get confirmation that the Grasshopper had landed here?" she asked, letting her gaze hone in on his profile. "My information was a bit of conjecture."

"I went to the source," he said glancing back to the windshield. "I tracked the lead on your maid, Lola, but she's out of town. So I called on Judge Wyatt."

Emmie blew air between her lips, hungry for a cigarette to calm the tension sizzling in her bloodstream. "Wyatt does have the largest network in the area," she said. "He's got ladies who will come visit the Negro ward, and from them, I've learned volumes about the way colored people survive in this neck of the woods."

"Part Robin Hood, part crazy King George, right?"

She'd never met Wyatt but based on what she knew of Patrick and what she heard from the ladies who brought in pies for the soldiers, she could see the parallels. "Mix in a little John the Baptist, and that's the leader that every colored person goes to in this town to get matters resolved."

"Well, Wyatt says he's met the man who's been stalking the speakeasies on both sides of the railroad tracks, gambling like an oilman, and asking around about you and Lane."

Emmie looked at the knot of her fingers and released the pressure by flexing her hands. Maybe she'd underestimated Theo. "And?"

"It's him." Theo sighed. "I showed Wyatt a photo. He confirmed everything."

"I would have thought he'd have changed his appearance by now. I know I would, if I'd have done what he's done."

Theo reached over the back of the bench seat searching for something on the floorboard. "Apparently, he's vainer than you realized."

Oh, she knew him, vanities and all. He'd been recruited to the agency back when she was teaching classes on basic medicine and wound care at the training academy. He'd fancied himself a lady's man and delighted to schmooze the faculty and staff in order to get a leg up on an early graduation.

As one who enjoyed men, Emmie had been more than willing to play along, until he'd gone too far and demanded a better grade on his tests. He'd turned ugly fast, and she'd told Theo to keep an eye on that one when handing out assignments.

Theo tossed a paper sack into her lap. "Here you go, love. Don't say I never gave you anything."

Unfolding the crinkled paper, a whiff of stale body odor tickled her nose. "Sequins and tulle." Pulling out a scooped-neck cocktail dress in canary yellow she grimaced. "You don't like me anymore, do you?"

"I adore you."

She held the yellow against her throat. "I will look like a flu victim wearing this color."

"Sorry, the girls at the workshop send what they can, but it's never runway worthy."

"You bought this at a second-hand store off Tenth Street, admit it."

"I will not, and you'll look great. There should be a barrette of some sort in there too. You'll want to do something fancy with your hair."

Emmie felt her hair that had started to curl with the damp evening air. "It's the humidity in this blasted state. I don't know how the locals ever tame their frizz."

"Where we're going," he said, reaching over her and pushing open her door. "I rather think you'll be a stand out."

She stilled, getting the awful premonition that grasshopper bait wore yellow tulle. "Theo, where are we going?"

His lips lifted in a half smile, but his heart wasn't in his eyes. "The Cotton Club. I hear they have a lady jazz singer who can really bring in the crowds."

The conversation between Lane and Patrick in the back end of her bookshop returned, and she could hear all that ridiculous business about a censor and someone named Jewel. Theo, mastermind that he was, had set his own operation in motion while she was grabbing a sandwich.

"I hate you." Emmie set her feet on the concrete and looked at the shady side of the station where he expected her to change into the getup. "I really, really hate you."

"You hate this world we work in." He winked. "But you love me."

Emmie wanted a cigarette and a bourbon more than she wanted to plant her face in front of an icebox, but she stepped out of the car clutching the awful yellow dress. "You used me."

The twinkle in his eye hardened. "We both use people. That's what we're good at."

Marching across an oil-stained drive, she hid behind the building and started to peel off the clothes she'd put on when she thought her evening was a stakeout and an arrest. A train gathered speed on the track behind the gas station, and a plume of steam rose from the engine as it barreled past for some far-off destination. A mutt peeked out from behind a trash can, as if wondering if she was much of a threat.

How long had she been changing outfits—and identities—behind nameless buildings? Too long, she answered as she unfastened the black blouse. And this might be the last time.

Before she shook out her auburn curls, she glanced at the ring that always had a place on her right hand. Borgia's needle was always ready to do its deadly work, even in a speakeasy.

Eyeing the dog to make sure he wouldn't decide she was dinner material, Emmie searched the bottom of the sack for bobby pins. Without a mirror, she couldn't vouch her hairstyle would be worthy of a nightclub, but she'd bet wooly sheep had more style than one she created with a fake rose glued to a barrette. She dragged in a scent of putrid air and wished herself luck.

She was going to need it.

Climbing into the car seat, she tossed the sack holding her clothes and shoes at him. "You've taken this outcome for granted, and I, for one, don't understand why someone hasn't shot you for it."

"Offering your services, Tesco?"

She brought her bare legs, outfitted with too-small shoes into the car. "I'd prefer something slower and more painful. Poison might be a fitting end."

Theo tossed the sack over the seat onto the floorboard. "As a personal favor, I'd ask that if you choose poison, please disguise it in a fine Scotch. I'd at least like to die with a smile on my face."

"The beauty of that request is that you'll never know if I honored it or not."

He leaned across the space and kissed her so fast it startled her. "I'd expect nothing less than torture from you."

She found a tube of lipstick in her purse and applied three coats of Riviera Rouge. The memory of how much she liked his kiss was fully covered.

"You'll regret those words, Marks. I promise you that."

Chapter Twenty Two

April 24, 1943 12:04 a.m.

Theo pumped the brakes with his foot and turned the car off Cotton Street onto a dirt packed road lined with scrappy pines and clapboard houses. The shrill hum of pump jacks provided a backdrop offset by the distant horn of an approaching train.

"If Lemming is still here, then his friend will be, too."

"What makes you so sure they'd come to a club like this one?" Picturing the pathologist in a place that must be regularly busted by the cops was a stretch. Emmie leaned her arm out the window, cooling the blood pressure that had spiked.

Theo pulled against a curb, put the car in neutral, pulled a note from his pocket, and scanned the paper for the address. "My sources called and told me the good doctor had arrived and was joined by a man in a white dinner jacket."

Her gut clenched. "That was a bold fashion move."

"I think the Grasshopper wants to be discovered."

Emmie glanced through the window to the row of houses that were alternately cared for or abandoned and wondered how often the residents' complaints regarding noise and traffic were respected by the business owner. A pack of dogs walked into the light of the car's headlamps.

"Why, after all he's done, would he walk into a very public trap?"

Theo folded the paper and tore it into bits, set it in the ashtray of the car, and lit the edges with his cigarette lighter. "We'll just have to ask him, won't we?"

She brought her elbow in from window then returned her gaze to Theo and noticed his lips planted like two-by-fours. "You're as terrified as I am."

"I am not."

"Of course, you are," she said, feeling itchy in the car's cab. Now that she knew she was going to get a starring role, she was ready to get to work. "He's always been more interested in one-upping you than in seeing Hitler win. He's followed you across Europe, and now, come right to your doorstep. You're as consumed with this twist in the game as I am."

Theo dropped the gearshift on the steering column from neutral into first and eased the car forward. "Imagine my promotion when I tell the chief that not only did we stop the sale of top secret information to the enemy, but we also nabbed a rogue agent who'd been double-crossing us for years."

A breeze stirred the air in the automobile as Theo drove slowly, looking for the turnoff among the houses.

"Thanks for letting me be part of this mission," Emmie said feeling an odd vulnerability at being the one Theo counted on, in the end.

He turned to her, his gaze communicating a legacy too heavy for words. "I can't imagine anyone I'd rather ride shotgun beside. You're one of the best, Em."

Embarrassed by the emotion, she felt her cheeks burn. "I'm sorry for thinking you sold me out to the FBI."

In a moment of candor she'd never have seen coming, he said, "I did sell you out. It was the only way the OSS could afford backup for Harmon. What started as a simple, one-step assignment had spiraled into a whirlwind with all those soldiers."

Soldiers of all stripes had called Harmon home, and not all were noble. "So, giving my work to the suits—"

"Merely a budgetary savings, not a pronouncement on the quality of your work."

A pop followed by a hissing noise surprised Theo, and the sudden deflation of a tire left him struggling to control the steering wheel.

"What did you run over?" Emmie stuck her head through the open window, checking the dirt road.

"If I knew, I would have avoided it."

Emmie sat forward, searching the street to see if they were close to a glow of lights and the thrum of music that would indicate she could walk to the club for help. "I hope you weren't planning on this being our getaway vehicle."

He cursed, steering the car to the side of the road.

She pushed against the door and set her feet on the grass. Though it was dark, the sight of the damaged tire glowed like a beacon. "It's flat."

Theo walked around the front end, crouched down to feel the rubber, and then glanced back toward the darkness, gauging the distance to the club. "If I drive another block, I may get a rock in the wheel, causing permanent damage to the rim."

She swiped at a bug flying close to her ear. "Do you want to walk to the club?"

"We have to change the tire."

She made a point of looking at her watch so he'd appreciate their predicament. "Lemming could take off any minute. What would they say seeing us here on the side of the road? Do you think they'd offer to help?"

"This isn't my car. I can't return it in this condition, much less take a chance on ruining the guy's wheel."

"Theo, there's not time and we're not dressed to change a flat."

"Pop the trunk and see if there's a spare."

Emmie's gaze darted between the pine trees and dark houses. "Are you kidding?"

"Do it."

She walked around the back end, fitted her fingers under the trunk's lip, and felt around for a latch, all the while muttering curses in a language Theo probably recognized. Once the latch was released, a giant metal sheet popped from the springs, and she shoved the trunk the rest of the way into the air.

"This is ridiculous. What are you going to tell Roosevelt?" Imitating Theo's voice she mocked, "You see old chap, as Boy Scouts, it was more important to do a good deed than ditch the thing for expedience."

Theo walked to stand at the edge of the trunk and patted around the interior. "I'd remind him that he doesn't like getting his tools returned in damaged condition either."

She watched Theo flip back the carpet that disguised the spare and the tire jack. "I meant about the mission."

Theo cut his gaze toward hers as he hefted the spare from its cavity. "Get the jack, will you?"

There was no arguing with Theo when he'd already made up his mind.

"Can we at least move the car to someplace level?" She went to the driver's door and sat in the seat, her hand on the gearshift. "I'll pull up three feet toward that driveway."

Theo motioned her forward and she kept her eye on his directions as she shifted into park and pulled out the grip for the brake. Walking back around the car's bumper she watched Theo roll the spare under the car—she'd guess in case the jack broke—and then helped him out of his jacket and tie.

"Do not write this in the after-action report," Emmie muttered. "I don't want the higher-ups to know we lost the Grasshopper because you have an overdeveloped sense of automobile maintenance."

"We couldn't chase a convertible on foot, could we?" Theo bent down and propped the jack under the car's frame.

"Lemming has a convertible? Nice. Must be that cushy doctor's salary." She walked into someone's yard and brought back a brick, propping it behind the rear wheel in case the car started to roll. "I wonder if someone that smart could change a tire?"

"I know what I'm doing," he said, loosening the bolts on the hubcap. "I worked in a garage as a kid and have changed plenty of tires in my Army days."

She held her palm to him to receive the lug nuts. "I'll save my breath. There's no point arguing with you when you turn surly."

"Pot. Black." He worked quickly, and within a few moments was trading the old tire for the spare.

"You want me to put that in the trunk," she asked, wondering if she could even lift the heavy tire. "Or kick it into the ditch."

"It's evidence. Better put it in the trunk."

Emmie grumbled but leaned down to set the tire on its side and roll it toward the back end of the car. As she reached her arms around the rubber some of the stitching at the side of her dress split apart. Mumbling more curses, she heaved the thing into the trunk and looked at the grease and dirt smeared into her palms. With nothing to wipe her hands on, she was tempted to use Theo's expensive suit.

Honk. Honk. Honk.

"Hey, Baby! You available?"

Emmie jerked to watch a pickup truck filled with teenaged boys cruise the street waving at her like she was one of the freakish things they'd hope to see on this end of town.

"Animals." She pushed down the lid of the trunk and felt along her hip for the seam that had split, finding a hole big enough to put her fingers through. Good thing the OSS budget wouldn't break because of this rag.

As the truck bounced along ruts in the road, turned around in a driveway, and its headlights indicated a return route, Emmie turned the ring on her right hand to its release position in case she'd have to defend herself from boys who thought she was for sale.

"You almost done there, Marks?"

Theo twisted the last of the lug nuts. "Five minutes, tops."

She watched the truck approach from the other end of the street. "We might have company. Are you prepared to deal with teenagers?"

Theo leaned back to see the road and the traffic thickening at one particular driveway. "Get in the car. We're almost to the club." He lowered the jack. "We'll have to improvise."

She hurried toward the passenger door. "You sure do know how to show a girl a good time."

He worked the tire jack off the rim of the car and tossed it toward the floorboard, near her feet.

Emmie closed the door, wanting to wipe her hands along the tulle of the skirt, but knowing that wouldn't help her cause. She'd have to wait for a bathroom and hoped there'd be soap and towels.

Theo jumped in the driver's seat and turned the key, firing the ignition. "Here's hoping that tire stays on."

"Yeah, 'cause that's the least of our problems tonight." Emmie couldn't believe he sat there staring down a truck that seemed to weave between both shoulders of the street.

The headlights of the truck aimed for their car.

"Theo?"

"I see them." He had his hand on the gearshift, but the car idled like it was waiting for flight instructions. "These boys need to learn it never pays to go looking for trouble."

Emmie closed her eyes, not wanting to see what he had in mind as a teaching tool. Holding on to the armrest, she could feel the engine throbbing and rocking as gasoline goosed the pistons.

Peeking through one eyelid, she saw the truck stop a few feet from their front bumper. Just as the passenger's side door of the truck opened and a pair of boots hit the pavement, Theo pulled the switch for the headlights, dropped the gearshift, and floored the gas.

The car leapt forward, barely missing taking the door off at its hinges.

Shouts of surprise was the only epitaph for a deed that could have gone so wrong.

"You could have hit that kid."

Theo tapped the brakes, slowing for the turn toward the speakeasy. "I didn't."

"But you could have." Emmie released a breath tinged with resentment, anxiety, and pressure. "That would have been another obstacle to getting to the Grasshopper. Police reports."

A pothole ruined the wheel's alignment, and Theo fought the steering wheel for control. "Sometimes you have to roll with the circumstances and hope you're smarter than fate," he said, aiming the car for the valet parking area.

Emmie let him have the last word. It might be his only bright spot, once they set foot inside a club that promised seedy adventures. The elected officials in Washington who wanted his head served to them for casualties, incidents, and crises that they thought could have been avoided had the OSS never been created had spies scrutinizing one of their own to prove their conclusions. Theo wouldn't get promoted for catching a rogue agent tonight, but he'd be reprieved from sitting before a congressional hearing.

As the car cruised to a stop near the entrance to the club, and the people at the door turned their way, her nerves ratcheted up. "Are we announcing ourselves?"

Theo's expression was grim as he reached over the seat for his suit coat and tie. "I'm not sure what we're doing, but we'll play it by ear. Kind of like that situation in Bratislava."

Emmie opened the glove box, searched around and pulled out a bandana, and wiped her sweaty hands. "You want to do that here?"

"It's noisy enough, and the crowds will be crushing. I'd prefer not to involve innocent people."

"What about Lemming?"

Theo reached into his pocket for cash. "He's hardly innocent, is he?"

"I still think he is, though the evidence is mounting."

"You're the one who's turned soft. I believe that Mr. Elliott has been a good influence on you."

Emmie put her purse over her wrist and reached for the door. "I'll remind you of that if we get out of here with all our limbs."

Theo stopped her. "I'm sure tonight is some sort of teaser. If—and it's a big if—he's trying to show himself, it means he wants to bargain. Let's not scare him off. Instead, we'll bring him to the table and interrogate him."

"He's too smart to fall for that." From her periphery, she saw two black men approach the automobile. "Besides, you hold the best bargaining chip of all."

Theo's brow rose over his eye.

"Lane Mercer," she whispered.

Wearing a god-awful dress gaping at her hip, Emmie leaned out into the midnight air and took in her first glance of the club that had been changing people's luck since it opened. As a beefy hand extended to help her stand, she smiled with all the sultriness of a movie siren and crooned, "Good evening, gentlemen. I've come to be entertained."

Chapter Twenty Three

April 24, 1943 12:23 a.m.

A line of men and women were stalled at the password-only entrance, and she wasn't going to win any popularity contest by being ushered ahead of them. They'd no doubt cite white privilege as a means for the woman in the canary dress gaining access, but she knew that what would go down in this club was not something they needed to witness, anyway.

Mere moments later, she'd been deposited inside a whisky barrel crammed with humanity. Theo had snaked behind the line of dancers ready to go on stage. She assumed they really were going to try the same complicated dance maneuver they'd perfected in a castle overlooking Bratislava. This was no ballroom, and that band wasn't playing a waltz, so she wasn't sure how a covert mission was going to work. But for now, she'd be still and get the lay of the club. Whether or not they were able to capture their prey was a matter for the fates.

Through a haze of smoke, a trio of women jiggling in skimpy outfits was singing the new song, Rum and Coca-Cola. Guests were standing, jiving to the rattle of a maraca. The noise level was so dense she could hear her heart beating in her throat. She surveyed the faces, polka-dotted by an occasional white person sitting at a table. The bodies crammed together left little room for fast exits. All the more reason to chuck Theo's idea to the trash bin.

He must have lost a screw somewhere on his way to Longview this trip. He'd been acting strange for months, no doubt pushed over the edge by the Roosevelt's cabinet members and the FBI breathing down his neck. Regardless, she had her doubts that the Grasshopper's Waterloo was going to be at the feet of a sweaty jazz band.

It had been drummed into her not to question her leaders, so despite tension turning her blood vessels into a harp waiting to be plucked, she

197

quieted her brain, observing more than facial types and overheated skin—looking instead for behaviors that would tell what words could never speak.

Waitresses hunched with the weight of carrying over-burdened trays around the tables crowded into the main room. The small semi-circle stage bounced with the pounding heels of the singers, and all the while, the band provided a nearly unrecognizable rendition of a popular tune. Based on the downbeat, the drummer must have missed rehearsal. She'd guess there were at least two hundred people crammed into a room a fire marshal would say had been designed for half that many. Along the perimeter were curtained alcoves fitted with tables, candles stuck into wine bottles, and velvet appointments. The men and women jammed into those spaces weren't interested in the music.

Backed against a wall too tacky to touch, she searched for her mark. Stuart Lemming had short brown hair and the kind of hazel eyes that could see beyond the surface, but the only reason he'd be memorable in a place like this was the color of his skin. He'd also wear that pained expression that screamed for an opened door. In the months she'd spent examining his patterns, he was the least likely military officer to attend a speakeasy. A library opening, a duck hunt, or a chess match, yes, but not a place with a stench that would lead a scientific mind to ponder bacteria-laced outbreaks.

Emmie would bet ten bucks that if the man was led here, he'd have found a way out through the backdoor and was most likely already behind the concertina wire at Harmon General. Theo should never have stopped to change that stupid tire.

She watched this crowd, remembering another jammed venue where she was sure she'd recognized the Grasshopper. The German troops rode into a French village and had forced most citizens out of the bars and restaurants, staring in defeat as Nazi tanks mowed over the cobblestones. There'd been one man, dressed as a farmer, who'd leaned against a bakery wall, totally unfazed by the horror around him, and that man had blanched when he made eye contact with her.

Had there not been schoolchildren packed like sardines between them, she would have killed him on the spot.

Behind her skirt, her thumb traced the top of the ring, feeling the ridges of the fake ruby, turning it so she could unlatch the hidden pin with a moment's notice. If opportunity presented itself, she might take things into her own hands and solve a potential international crisis while the FBI suits tracked mud into the penicillin lab.

"Beer?"

Emmie glanced at the waitress, whose eyes seemed fifty years older than her body. "Two, please."

The girl looked to Emmie's right, like she was wondering who'd drink the second beer.

"My date will be right back," Emmie said, with a world-weary sigh. "You know men. . .weak bladders."

Based on her expression, this girl knew plenty about middle-aged men. Emmie went back to surveying the club patrons, looking for curtained exits and partitions that led to back rooms.

A tingle crawled over her spine, and she glanced around to see who'd study her. No one seemed too impressed by her dress, and despite her track record in clubs across Italy and France, no one seemed to be drawn to her swagger either. She must look a wreck. That accounted for the awareness she'd discerned. Figured. Theo threw her into a mission with no time to prepare, and he expected miracles.

A static buzz invaded her eardrum—or maybe that was the pianist pounding down the keys in chaos—but she knew if she was going to be in position for "the maneuver" she needed to be near the dance floor. Moving away from the wall, she wove between couples clustered so tightly their bodies put off a heat no air conditioning could cool.

Emmie tried not to breath too deeply. The air recycling in this tight space was layered with cigarettes, body odor, beer, and something her momma told her never to smoke.

A door to her right was closed against the crowd but when a waitress knocked and entered with a beverage tray, Emmie could see men seated around a gaming table, poker chips stacked in teetering rows.

Her gaze surveyed the corners of the room, not seeing Theo tucked into a shadow. There weren't many places he could have escaped—a spot where he could sweep in and pull her into some sort of distraction-inducing dance, guaranteed to put all eyes on them and away from the smoke bomb he'd planted at the exits.

Her throat grew parched.

It had been hours since she had a drink, save that bourbon at Molly's. Now, she'd trade her kingdom for an iced water.

The energy in the room changed when a zoot-suited man came to the microphone to introduce Miss Jewel Carter. Emmie's antennae rose as the crowds shifted and attention was centered on the stage.

Raucous shouting and clapping welcomed a tall, well-endowed woman wearing a dress designed to show off her assets. Her wig and jewelry gave her the credibility of someone who'd performed for a far grander audience, and Emmie wondered if the costume was cheaper than it appeared from so far away.

Who was she to judge? She was wearing a secondhand dress that had a tear along the hip and satin strapped heels that cut into her bunions.

A throaty voice, like a human clarinet, cut through the smoke and the audience stilled, transfixed by a woman beginning a sultry rendition of How High the Moon. It was going to be hard to stage a dance exhibition if the soloist made up scat on the fly.

199

A finger tapped into her shoulder. Alarmed that she missed the cue, Emmie turned, seeing the waitress balancing two mugs of warm beer and a basket of popcorn.

"Your man ever come back?" the girl asked, handing off the glassware.

"He would argue he's not missing, but I'll take the mugs. You can keep the basket."

The girl seemed unimpressed that the popcorn wasn't a hit. What Emmie wouldn't give to have her bring back an aspirin.

Emmie surveyed the room as she maneuvered around, holding two heavy, sticky glasses of beer that smelled weak on hops. Elbows and knees made it hard to stay upright, but Theo needed her near the stage, and she'd go through with this farce because she was having a hard time imagining a better idea.

As if a radar pinged in her mind, she sensed footsteps that weren't in keeping with the top-tapping going on around her. Her posture straightened, and she narrowed her gaze, looking for a break in the pattern of her expectations.

"Nurse Tesco?"

Two little words spoken behind her shoulder proved she'd miscalculated her opponent. If she'd missed this clue, what else had she left to chance?

Turning on an unstable heel, she saw the hazel eyes that were famous for reading slides. "Dr. Lemming, what a surprise."

Color flooded his cheeks. "The surprise is all mine, I assure you."

She held the mugs a few inches closer to her breast, like armor, should she need the defense. "What can I say? I'm a huge fan of jazz music."

His gaze swept her outfit. "I can see that."

Sticky foam sank into her cleavage as she looked for his accomplice. "And you? I'd have thought these were late hours for a man who has to manage the blood bank this weekend."

"A friend drove in from out of town and insisted we come to this club." Stuart's gaze shot to the pulsating throng of people singing along with the chorus. "It's not my scene."

"Mine either, as it turns out. I've developed the rottenest headache. Any chance I could get you to drive me home? My date—" She raised the glasses for evidence— "has disappeared, and I don't want to have to hang around waiting for him."

Perspiration seemed to have marked Stuart's forehead like a Parcheesi board. "I'm obligated to stay. My friend, doesn't have a ride, and I can't leave him. . .unattended."

"I see." She let her shoulders droop as if this was the worst news. "Can you escort me outside for a minute, so I can breathe some fresh air?"

"Sure, that should be all right." Stuart smiled, like he wasn't sure of anything. "Have you seen Lane? She hasn't called like I'd asked her."

"She and I don't visit as often as you might think."

"But she's been with you every time I've run into you off base."

Emmie bit her lip. "That was a fluke. She travels a lot. I think she might be in Dallas this weekend."

"Dallas?"

"Yes. She's a big fan of the symphony." Emmie knew she was rambling, but it was her small effort at protecting the woman who didn't know she had a stalker. "Goes there a lot."

Stuart squinted with a blast of cigarette smoke blown near him. "Maybe that's why she hasn't called me. She's been out of town."

Emmie nodded. "Outside?"

He agreed. "Okay."

Emmie carried the beer like it was her weapon of choice. Stuart's breathing blew across the back of her neck and she guessed that if they attracted any attention at all, most would assume they were leaving for reasons other than a possible heatstroke.

Jewel started a song made popular in the Pinocchio animated movie and the crowd clapped along. Under different circumstances, Emmie could appreciate the woman's talent but right now her ears were filtering all sounds through a tin can, her blood racing with unforeseen complications and her mind was spinning with ways to outwit the pathologist.

Though she'd feel better outdoors, getting Lemming out of the building would create bigger problems, as Theo was unaware of these developments. She'd have to set up a stall.

Those thoughts hit the wall as Emmie's internal radar detected a missile tracking her through the crowd.

"Stuart, wait up"

Hair on the back of Emmie's neck rose in horror. She squeezed her eyes shut, for the briefest second, trying to prepare her facial expression to fit into a mask of indifference.

Stuart grabbed her elbow, and her feet skidded against the sticky floorboards.

"Introduce me to your friend."

Though that voice was eminently familiar she begged; Say no, Stuart. Say no.

"Nurse Tesco, I'd like you to meet one of my oldest buddies."

Stuart had failed her.

Rolling her shoulders back Emmie steeled her nerves. Turning and focusing her gaze through a haze of smoke, she saw the chiseled cheekbones of a man she'd thought—no, hoped—she'd never see again, outside of a firing squad.

His height and the elegant white dinner jacket gave him distinction compared to the sweaty locals, but it was his jawline, cleft in his chin, and cold eyes that marked him handsome as sin. An injustice against nature. But then he'd become the lead criminal in a caper that had such deadly consequences.

"Mary Magdalene Tesco." His cultured voice swooshed with an air that could have been disbelief, but more likely, a well-rehearsed line. "As I live and breathe."

"Roy Mercer," Emmie echoed, in frigid response. "Risen from the grave."

Chapter Twenty Four

April 23, 1943 12:41 a.m.

The piano, the metallic clang of snare drum, and a woman wailing about wishing on a star became the soundtrack for a moment Emmie thought she'd never experience. Prayed she'd never have to face. Even worse, she couldn't access her poisoned-tip weapon for the weight of glasses bearing a beverage she never intended to drink.

"You know each other?" Stuart's face swung right then left. "How is that possible?"

Roy's grin spread across his face like butter melting on toast. "It's a small world."

"Getting smaller with each second," Emmie said, even though her stomach was tighter than a sailor's knot. "That ghosts don formalwear."

Men hustling a girl to the front of the dance floor pushed into their shoulders and caused beer to slosh Emmie's wrists. She recoiled as if she'd been electrocuted.

"Let's take this conversation outside," Roy said, glancing at the bulky men crowding them against the wall. "I can barely hear myself think."

Stuart nodded, but his face bore the strains of having thought too much.

"No." Emmie knew Theo was here, somewhere, and she wanted him to know that the Grasshopper had landed on her shoulder. "We'll stay. Say what you want, Mercer, and then get out of here."

"Not so fast, nurse." Roy tried to move around Stuart's body, but the men surrounding them seemed to have formed a fence of spines. "I'm here to make peace. Find healing. I'm not asking for trouble."

Stuart nodded, his chin slack. "That's what he told me when he called last week. Couldn't have shocked me more. Imagine my surprise. I was at his funeral."

"I'm trying." Emmie hoped the doctor had as much integrity as she'd advertised; otherwise he'd be convicted of collusion with a traitor. In light of the other felonies going on at Harmon General, he'd be the scapegoat. The FBI liked prosecutions tidied up in a box. "I know we'd all want healing from the wounds we inflicted on each other in the name of war."

The floorboards bounced with the downbeats of the drums and radiated energy from the stage.

Stuart flattened his hand on the wall for stability. "That's why he's here." He looked back at Roy, as if confirming the statement. "To ask forgiveness."

"I've hurt so many people," Roy said, mimicking a choirboy caught filching from the offering.

Emmie didn't want to look Roy in the eye. It might be too mesmerizing, like when cobras strike. "Not to mention the people who are still alive."

She glanced to the place where a black handkerchief peeked from his lapel pocket, and searched for the bulge of a handgun strapped under his arm. If she'd learned anything from Slim's sermonettes, it was that people who'd repented of their old lives rarely returned to the locations that fostered their temptations. Roy's dinner jacket and black bowtie advertised a man empowered—not humbled—by his choices.

"I'm a new man." Roy held his hands out like he was presenting a clean slate. "You'll have to spend time with me to find out that I've turned over a new leaf. I'm no longer holding you and my dear wife responsible for selling me out to the authorities."

"You sold yourself, Mercer." She'd walk into solitary confinement before she volunteered to sit down for tea and conversation with this man. "No matter how many times a snake sheds his skin, he's still a snake."

Stuart latched onto Emmie's wrist with a grip that felt too strong for a man who handled glass slides of tissue and fragile microscopes. "Come with us."

Roy's eyes glowed with a light that didn't look quite sane. She knew most of the reports laid at his feet and suspected it was only a fraction of the misdeeds he'd claim, should he be interrogated. The psychiatrists at Harmon had a name for men with this condition, but she couldn't think what it was at the moment because Stuart's grip started pulling her tighter into its confines.

She wasn't going to be their shield in getting out of this club.

When she went down for the United States of America, it was going to be in a situation that would finally impress her parents.

Tightening her fingers around the grip of the glasses, she threw her elbows out and hands up, chucking Stuart under the chin with a splintering hit of glass against bone, and, thanks to the thrust of gravity, sent beer splashing in Roy's eyes.

Dropping what remained of the glasses to the floor, she shoved her back into the bodies of the men who'd crowded into the club and forced them to fall forward to their knees. Curses and a cacophony from a bleating trumpet rained down on her ears as she shoved more people out of the way, gaining scant inches before a hand clamped on her shoulder and jerked her backward.

She slipped on the floor, and her legs buckled.

As her arms windmilled, she hit Stuart Lemming's stomach and felt sticky blood on his evening shirt.

Before she landed on her bottom, Roy snatched her up by yellow satin and hissed, "You bitch!"

She'd either die with a knife in her back or be stampeded by the people closing in on the commotion. There had been worse brawls in Venice, so she wasn't going to let a two-bit speakeasy in Longview, Texas, be the end of her run.

Kicking off the useless shoes, her toes gripped the floor, and she used the leverage to push herself up and at the same time tossed her head back, snapping Roy's chin with a direct hit of tough, Irish skull. Her pain was a small consequence for being freed of his grip, and she spun around sinking her fist into the soft belly above his belt line.

Roy fell forward, and she dodged him, elbowing an unfortunate bystander in his private parts.

As the bodies started falling, she crouched down and barreled through an open space. Gasping for air, she pushed against the backs of people who had no idea that a skinny white woman was responsible for multiple men groaning in misery.

Her toes took piercing hits from boot heels, and she was sure she stepped on a nail head, but as she ran for the door guarded by bouncers, her only thought was escape. If Theo were still in there, he could finish off Mercer, but she was going to vomit and then she was going to call Lane and warn her to flee without a second's thought for Boris and the bookshop.

Roy was out for blood, and his wife's name would be at the top of his kill list.

Emmie barreled through the door and past the people lined up to enter the club, falling over herself as she hurried through the final door, a barrier guarded by the goons who'd been there fifteen minutes ago.

Stepping over grass tufts and stones, she made it to a lamppost and held on, heaving dry air and some spit.

Roy Mercer. When she'd heard the rumors that he, if it was really him, was on the move from Alabama, she'd harbored a fantasy of how she'd like to be the one to take the man to the grave for good this time. After his despicable behavior while in the OSS and the murder of one of his own fellow officers who'd threatened to expose his side dealings, she'd told Theo to send him back to the States because he was a court martial waiting to happen. But Theo had begged for patience two and a half years ago, as Captain Mercer was on the cusp of a great coup in exposing a mole inside the American Embassy in London.

Oh, Captain Mercer had exposed a lot of things in London. Countless barmaids, a few daughters of diplomats, and an undercover police officer posing as a prostitute, but he'd never delivered on the embassy employee because he'd decided at that point to get in on the lucrative game of selling secrets.

Faking his death during a bombing was a stroke of brilliant timing, but Theo couldn't risk revealing the truth of Mercer's demise for fear of ruining British and American diplomacy. Even more, the still-fragile shared resources of the OSS and the British equivalent of a spy agency, the SOE.

Instead, he'd recruited Mercer's widow for insurance.

"Ma'am?"

She saw the tips of shiny shoes in her line of vision. Turning slightly, she let her gaze climb the dark slacks, a three-buttoned jacket like the orderlies at Harmon General might wear, and a sincere expression on a young, black man's face.

"Can I help you?" he asked.

Great, a guy from Wyatt's Ambulance Services was seeing a potential fare.

"I'm fine, a little winded," she said, hoping he'd ignore the beer stains and blood on her dress and the unfortunate matter of lost shoes. The noise of a bar fight from the club didn't seem to register to him as anything noteworthy.

"No, I mean, I'm supposed to help you," he said, offering his hand to help her stand. "Judge Wyatt sent me out here to take you to Mrs. Mercer's house. It seems like he wants her moved to a private location."

Emmie stood, bracing her sore back with her hands. "The Judge has just decided this?"

"He and the Colonel made this plan a few hours ago. I was told to wait until a woman in a yellow dress came out of the club tonight, and I was to drive her to the next location." He couldn't hide his skepticism of her appearance. "I would guess that speed is of the essence."

"And your name is?" Emmie gulped fresh air.

"You can call me Arnold," he said. "Let's move this way."

Emmie walked beside him, itching to look back to the club and see what chaos was falling through the front door. "Is that what your mother named you?"

"No, ma'am." He smiled, showing straight teeth. "But that's the name I was told to use because sometimes things don't go well for colored men found in the company of a white woman."

She'd like to believe that it was Theo who had worked out the arrangements with Wyatt for this escort, but she couldn't rule out that

Lemming and Mercer were in cahoots with the Judge. "What code did the Colonel give you to use, Arnold?"

"He said to tell you that Boris sends his love."

That was not a known code, but it did the trick. "Which car are we using tonight?"

He pointed to a long, well-waxed hearse refurbished as a transport vehicle in the Wyatt's Ambulance Service company. "The ambulance."

"Of course." She deadpanned, as he opened the passenger's side door. "I guess I can be thankful you didn't suggest the back."

"That's where Mrs. Mercer rode the night we met her."

Emmie slid onto the leather seat and tucked her beer-soaked skirt around her legs. So, Lane Mercer had come into the Wyatt sphere of influence via an ambulance ride? She'd have to ask later what the circumstance was, but if she had to guess, it dated back to the night she and Theo rescued Lane after her meltdown in the lobby of the Gregg Hotel.

"And you know where Mrs. Mercer lives now?" She watched her driver pump the gas several times before he was successful at starting the vehicle.

"Yes, ma'am. Patrick and I have ridden by the house several times, making sure she got home safe, since she has a history of coming up on the crooked sides of folk."

"She does have that knack," Emmie said disagreeably, as she glanced back to the club's driveway and watched a few bodies be hurled toward the parking lot. Girls ran screaming from the club.

"We don't want no harm coming to her on account of how she's helped a few cousins find work as welders on that pipeline project."

Emmie stared at the Bible wedged between the dashboard and the windshield. "She's just a queen of do-goodness, isn't she?"

Arnold stole a quick glance at Emmie, and she regretted her sarcasm. Lane did have a penchant for helping others to the point it was sickening, but as Slim told her, everyone desires absolution for sins, so maybe job placement was Lane's. If anyone would ever acknowledge that Lane Mercer had sins.

Slim had called her on the jealousy, but Emmie wasn't sure it was as simple as that. Lane had something deep inside her, a keenness for survival, that was so much more elegant than anything Emmie had acquired in her years of foreign service, and that intangible instinct was the thing she could never replicate.

Emmie shook her head and tried to right the marbles running loose in her mind. She had too much to worry about tonight to start analyzing why she always delighted in thwarting Lane. It wasn't something she was proud of. She'd taught her agent trainees that they had to be able to trust each other no matter what, and that truism was something she needed to ink onto her own forehead.

Arnold pulled the ambulance against a tree-shaded portion of the curb along Hutchings Avenue, shifted into park, and let the engine idle.

Emmie thought through what she might say to Lane. Considering that she looked like a boozy prostitute, Lane might be resistant to believe anything. But, Emmie had a story to tell that wasn't going to go down easily, and it couldn't be told at an address surrounded by potential victims.

She needed to shake off her tendencies to go in guns blazing and instead use a little finesse in this situation. Theo had sworn that there was no way Lane knew that her husband had faked his death. He'd gone to incredible lengths to make the government's response as genuine as possible, even supplying death benefits. But after he'd recruited Lane to the agency, trained her in Morse code messaging, and assigned her to Europe, it became a concern that one of the other agents might mention a spotting of Roy to Lane and then the gig to use her to lure Roy out of hiding would be exposed.

Code-naming Mercer as "The Grasshopper" was both efficient and oddly accurate.

With a sliver of compassion, Emmie wondered, if the roles were reversed, would she want to be told that a man she'd been married to, and believed dead, had become one of the most despised double agents on the OSS's record books? Most likely, not.

Emmie ran a hand into her hair and found the barrette that was supposed to hold her hair off her neck.

"Ma'am? Colonel Marks said that if you weren't willing to go into the house and get Mrs. Mercer, that I was to remind you that you were made of better stuff than this and that you should think of one of your girls and pretend that Mrs. Mercer was one of the ones in France."

She turned on the seat and looked at Arnold like he was a rat fink. "That is awful. I was sitting here figuring out how I was going to break the news to her and you lay guilt on my head."

Arnold shrugged. "I'm sorry, but I'm just saying what I was told to say."

"Here I'd been thinking that you had such beautiful manners."

"My mother would thank you for noticing."

"And that you seemed so much nicer than Patrick, too."

Arnold's chin dipped closer to his uniform. "That's kind of you to say, I'm always aiming to be nice to everyone."

Setting her bruised feet against the curb, she climbed out of the seat and then leaned inside one last moment. "Don't judge me then. I'm going to handle this in the best way I know how."

He held his hands in surrender. "Judging is the Lord's business, not mine."

She could just imagine Arnold and Slim having a big old time talking about Jesus and the Apostles, but none of them had a place in her head tonight. Slim had sent her three letters and a Western Union telegram before he'd ever asked her on a date. It was time to tell him to stop wasting his stamps. Stubbing her toe on a brick in the grass brought less godly words to mind.

Focus, she chided herself.

Remembering a long-ago conversation about the smell of rose bushes and midnight sleeplessness, Emmie walked around the back of the Thomas household and looked for a window above a rose bush. It'd better be Lane's, because if she got called into a police station for being a Peeping Tom, she was going to have a lot of explaining to do, and she was too exhausted to think of convincing lies at this hour.

Standing in the moonlit back yard, she saw the chicken coop and, beyond the screened porch, what looked to be two medium-sized windows and a small window that must be the bathroom. Since all the windows had the requisite black-out curtains, a nod to national security, she'd have to guess that the window that was open to the breeze was the one she needed.

Leaning over a thorny branch, she rapped two quick knocks against the frame, careful to not wake anyone except the one who'd been trained to recognize patterns.

When there was no response, she repeated the sequence.

Lane's face appeared on the other side of a screen. Her hair stood on ends and her eyelashes were matted. "It's too late for a social call."

"Pack some things fast. We have to get you out of town."

Lane's eyes flashed wider as she focused on Emmie's face. "What's happened?"

"I can't tell you at the moment, but bring enough clothes for a few days."

Emmie worked on removing the screen while Lane stuffed things into a leather satchel. In mere seconds it seemed, Lane was wearing a skirt and blouse over her striped pajamas and handing her bag through the window. The ready-to-flee training, at all hours, was one of the first lessons learned in the agency.

"Papers?"

Lane nodded as she climbed over the sill. "Of course."

"Good." Emmie held back stems and saucer-sized blooms. "I have no idea where Theo will send you, but you may never come back to Longview."

Lane froze for a second, her eyes rounded to saucers. "What about—Zeke, and my relatives," she stuttered. "And Boris?"

"The only one of that menagerie that I know about is out cold at the moment, and we can keep Boris drugged if need be. But getting you into hiding is the priority."

Lane jumped to the dirt. "Does this have anything to do with someone outing me as a spy? Patrick said there's someone suggesting that down in poker rooms."

Emmie cast her gaze to the shorter woman, wondering if Lane knew more than Theo realized. "Yes," she replied cautiously. "This does have to do with that."

"Drat." Lane hugged her satchel close to her chest. "I thought that was all some sort of fishing expedition by those Mafia goons. If you're moving me out of here, then they must have put a price on my head after all."

Emmie made sure Lane had cleared the window with her belongings and then replaced the screen. "Do you have anything left in the room that might be an identifying lead on you, your work, or where you might have disappeared to?"

Lane pursed her lips. "Nothing significant."

"Not even a photo of lover boy?"

She patted her bag. "Grabbed it."

"Good girl." Emmie nodded to the street. "Follow me and stay low. There's a full moon."

They hurried, a little hunched and keeping close to the house just in case they had to drop to the ground if a dog barked or a woman screamed. At the curb, the ambulance engine hummed, but the headlights were off.

Lane looked at the vehicle. "Wyatt's man?" Then she glanced at Emmie's bruised feet. "And your outfit?"

"Oh, you know, just your friendly, neighborhood ambulance driver out giving us party girls a lift."

"I was sleeping."

Emmie wished she could sleep for a week, but these nights her mind spun so fast she could hardly shut the thoughts down for more than a few hours. "Well, lucky you. Some of us were working."

Lane opened the passenger door and slid across the seat, not stopping until she was sitting next to the driver. Emmie followed and closed their door.

"Good evening. Arnold, isn't it?" Lane set her satchel on her skirt, the pajamas underneath bunching around her hem.

"Mrs. Mercer." He nodded, as he shifted the gear on the steering column. "Nice night?"

"Not my best evening," she yawned. "And it seems things just got worse."

"Infinitely so," Emmie growled, as she rolled the window down to let in fresh air. "We've had a grasshopper infestation, and the darn thing is hungry for you."

Lane's jaw unhinged. "Me?"

"Deranged people rarely think straight, and this one is convinced you sold him out for crimes against society. Or something like that. I really couldn't say. He thinks I turned him in for murdering a general in his unit—which I did. So, who knows, maybe he's brilliant in his madness."

"But I've never sold anyone out." Lane seemed to have forgotten the warning about little pitchers having big ears, because she didn't tone down her voice for Arnold. "I only knew what I was told by my commanding officers."

"Yeah—" Emmie pictured Theo and his British counterparts in the espionage networks, rifling through their tidbits of clues as to what Roy Mercer might do, and where he might go with the secrets he collected in London. "The bust is we women are assumed to have skills in pillow talk that puts us at risk of everyone thinking we know tons, when in fact, we're sometimes the last to know anything."

Lane stared at her.

Emmie grumbled. "Don't worry. All will be revealed. Eventually."

Chapter Twenty Five

April 24, 1943 2:53 a.m.

Emmie picked up the fancy clock and squinted through eyelids coated with grit and flecks of mascara. Yes, those little hands were nearing three in the morning. She set it back on the shelf with more pressure than the porcelain shepherdess deserved.

"Hot milk?"

Emmie sighed, guessing her preference for bourbon would not be honored, and glanced over at the tall woman bundled to her neck in a housecoat, with a hair net over her curlers. "No, thank you. I'm waiting my turn for the bathroom, and, dare I hope, a shower. Milk would put me to sleep and make me miss that joy."

"My husband warned you might be surly." Mrs. Wyatt poured milk into a mug anyway. "Said I was to treat you how my momma raised me and not give in to the temptation to make you wait on the front porch."

Emmie wanted to collapse onto the sofa, but the white doilies would be stained by whatever gunk had taken root in this awful yellow dress. "How long has Colonel Marks been talking to Mrs. Mercer?"

The older woman's hands shook as she set the kettle onto the tray. "Half hour at least." She glanced at Emmie then to the bedroom door where little more than hushed conversation was heard. "I don't usually receive company at this time of the morning, so I'm not sure what's what."

A grandfather clock chimed three gongs.

"You've been gracious to let us barge in." Emmie had questioned Arnold when he'd pulled up to a house just three blocks away from the speakeasy where worlds had collided. "I can't imagine that Judge Wyatt had time to give you much warning."

"After thirty-two years, I've learned to adapt." Mrs. Wyatt's tired eyes surveyed Emmie's torn, beer-soaked dress, dirty feet, and hair that stood on end. "But you three were the surprise to top all surprises."

Maybe it was a stroke of genius to hide three white people in the den of the most powerful Negro family in Longview. Proof would show in the morning. Or whenever Stuart and Roy were stitched up and in the fighting mood again.

The mud stains on her legs and feet contrasted with the pristine condition of Mrs. Wyatt's floor, and it was all she could do not to ask for a towel to stand on. She'd be willing to wear a hand-me-down robe if she could just burn this dress, but no one had made any offers, save the suggestion of the bathing facilities once Theo finished his de-briefing of Lane Mercer—the woman no longer a widow.

The Wyatts' home was not spacious by Hudson River standards, but considering this was the first time she'd been inside a house owned by a man with whom she couldn't openly sit in a restaurant, it was noteworthy. Sparse but comfortable. From the entrance, she'd detected a few front rooms, one of which was most likely the Judge's office, based on the bookcases, note papers, and stacks of files. The kitchen was in the middle of the structure, and then there was a shotgun add-on that had this guest area and a bedroom that hosted Mrs. Wyatt's elderly mother—a fact she knew only because they were warned to keep the volume down. The irony for Emmie was that if she hadn't known of the Judge's complicated business endeavors, she'd have thought his home reflected the simplicity of an academic.

The door of the back bedroom squealed on it's hinges, a shell-shocked Lane emerged, and the temperature of the den dropped a few degrees. Her eyes were black orbs in a face of paste. She wavered in her serviceable shoes, as one pajama leg dropped to her ankle.

Theo walked behind her, wrapping his arm around her frame and moving her closer to the sofa.

She shook off his arm. "I'll stand, thank you."

Ah, so this was how it was going to go, Emmie thought. Stepping around the coffee table, she approached the former agent much like she would a wounded dog.

"Lane," she lowered her voice to the level she reserved for coded messages.

"Did you know, too?" Lane accused. "Were you part of the farce that circled around me like some sort of play where the actors were all given their lines—well, everyone except me."

"Now, that's not how it—"

"Was I just too stupid to be trusted with the truth?" Lane's body started to shake. "Or did you think that if I couldn't see through Roy's lies there was no way I would question you either?"

Theo wiped his hands across his jaw. "That's not what I said."

Lane held a hand in the air to stop any other words from Theo. "Emmie, tell me." She turned her back to him. "Which was it? Stupid or gullible?"

Emmie better understood firing squads now. She didn't dare break eye contact with Lane, or the game would be up for good. "Gullible. You're one of the smartest cookies around, but your default is that you always think there's some redeeming good in everyone."

Lane stared through Emmie.

"Take me, for instance," Emmie said, feeling Theo breathing down her neck, even though he was on the other side of the room. "I'm nothing but a secondhand rose, and you continue to think that I'm going to do right, regardless of my own self-interests. That I'm going to hold to a higher cause. Well, I hope you're cured of that foolishness, now that Theo has laid all his cards on the table."

Lane's knees buckled, and she caved to the floor.

Emmie knew what it was to have the wind knocked from your soul, and she also knew that mollycoddling was not the way to find it again. She glanced at Theo's face, drained of life. "So, you told her everything?"

He nodded. "The whole business."

Lane fell forward over her knees, mewing a slew of tears.

"And she figured out she's been the bait since day one?"

Theo stared at Lane's spine. "That sounds crass. Lane has many wonderful qualities that have been a gift to the United States, but she was useful regardless of her husband's penchant for not liking loose ends."

Mrs. Wyatt marched over to the sad tableau and threw her hands in the air. "You people are the coldest human beings I ever did see." She scalded both Emmie and Theo with her gaze. "Give this girl some privacy to weep."

Mrs. Wyatt wrapped herself over Lane's back, and within moments she'd pulled the young woman into her chest and held on to Lane like she might sink if someone didn't hold her against the tide.

Within Emmie, a sour jealousy rose up from a box sealed shut twenty-four years ago. She'd not gotten any support when the nuns yanked her baby from her arms, and no one had offered to ride the wave of tears that seemed to have no end. No, she'd been told it was for the best, and that if she had any common sense, she'd say a prayer of thanks that a good family wanted her baby. They could offer him what she'd never be able to create: family, stability, and a future away from the stain of his conception.

And they'd been right.

Emmie shook off that particular shade of blue and walked toward the bedroom. "I'm going to shower and try to put this nightmare behind me. I'd like to remind everyone that I'm the one who had to face down Roy Mercer tonight, and no one has even thanked me for leaving him with a concussion."

"Emmie, please," Theo hissed. "Compassion."

She stood in the doorway and looked back. Theo's despair was as tangible as Lane's grief. They were a pair. He might never be able to reach the agent again, and she was the only thing holding him true to his principles.

Judge Wyatt walked into the room, wiping his hands on a dishtowel. "Everyone ready to settle down for the night?"

Theo rubbed his eyes. "If you'll have your man drive me over to College Street, I'm going to camp outside the Kennedy house to make sure that Mercer doesn't show up to wreak havoc on Emmie's room or any of the other women sleeping on the second floor."

Wyatt cast his gaze to his wife, as she and Lane crumpled on the floor like a pair of repentant sinners at a revival meeting.

"I can see here that we got ourselves a crowd." Wyatt directed his attention to Theo. "Arnold will be around in five minutes."

Emmie shook her head, hearing marbles roll. "Do you people never sleep?"

"Us people," Wyatt repeated, "are saving your skins so you might be a little grateful that we don't sleep."

Theo interrupted, rumpled and weary as if he'd fought a battle of his own. "We're grateful, Judge. This is a delicate matter of national security, and we'd be dead if it weren't for you and your men at the Cotton Club."

"Feel free to include us in the report." Judge Wyatt turned around and headed back to the kitchen. "Don't keep Arnold out too long. He's got to work in the morning."

"Emmie." Theo looked at her like he wished she'd crawl under a rock. "Don't let Lane out of your sight. She's vulnerable."

"You don't say." Emmie yawned. "I'd never have guessed."

Theo closed his eyes with a slowness that belied the speed of his thoughts. "Be nice."

Of course, he'd want everyone to bend over backwards for the precious Lane Mercer, newly discovered to be not-so-widowed after all. That was Theo's way, despite his role with an espionage unit. He was a softie when it came to those who he thought had been dealt a rough hand, and since he was the one dealing the cards, it was mighty generous of him to want to baby her now. Not like she was going to thank him for it, either. Emmie had seen Lane's eyes. That girl knew she'd been used. The question no one was asking was whether or not that was enough to make Lane run for the border or want to get revenge on a husband who suspected she'd sold all his dirty laundry to the OSS.

Tomorrow would be soon enough to find out.

"She's going to be crying for hours, but I'll do my duty to make sure she's chained to the sofa. Don't you worry your sweet brown eyes over this one. No, sirree, Bob. Mrs. W. and I will pick up all the pieces and put Humpty back together again."

Theo shook his head in disgust.

"We have to," Emmie said as she reached behind her neck to unzip the dress. "Mercer is going to be coming for us with more than a chip on his shoulder. She'll need to be shipshape in the morning. Either that or she dies. It's that simple."

Chapter Twenty Six

April 24, 1943 7:22 a.m.

Emmie glared at the sign above the alley entrance and wondered if the so esteemed J Lassiter was really Texas's Finest Haberdasher. That seemed like a Texas-sized boast if there was one. Dawn's light was breaking on the horizon, and the hour gave her yet another reason, on an ever-growing list, to think Theo was running on wits—not any sort of actual plan.

"Miss Tesco," asked a dark-skinned Argentinean standing at the doorway, his accent giving the T a soft th sound. *"Won't you come this way?"*

Theo pulled another suitcase from the trunk of the cab. "Did you pack stones instead of shoes?"

"Of course I did." She carried three hat boxes over the threshold. "There's a trunk full of lead to follow."

He shouldn't poke her this morning. He, of all people, would know she was barely human without a cup of coffee or a good night's sleep, neither of which she could claim after her four hours as a guest of the Wyatts.

The cooler air of the boutique's stockroom welcomed her with the scent of money and sandalwood. Her shoulders relaxed a notch.

Theo stepped in behind her. "Go upstairs, Tesco. We've got less than an hour to get you set up, and then I'm moving Lane into the guest apartment with you once you have this place secured."

"What makes you think Wyatt is going to let her out of his sight? The wiry grandma came out of her bedroom with all the ruckus, and then there was some sort of church service going on over Lane. I walked out of the shower and swear I saw the grandma with her hand raised in the air, calling out every imagined demon that might be trailing in Lane's wake."

"That seems a bit odd in light of the Judge's line of work."

"Well, I'm here to tell you, the ladies in the Wyatt household don't cotton to the same philosophy as the Judge. Mrs. Wyatt runs the straight

217

and narrow, and she collects hitchhikers. Lane might have been baptized while she was passed out cold on the floor."

"You're sure she wasn't faking being asleep?"

Emmie shook her head. "As one who would trade a kidney for a good night's sleep, I can recognize the signs of those who've fallen hard. She's not waking up for hours."

They passed a clothing rack hung with chalk-lined, tailored suits, and she couldn't resist reaching to feel the superfine wool. "This reminds me of those suits you like to buy in London."

He dropped the luggage and felt the sleeve of a customer's suit. "You're right," he said, turning the fabric over and admiring the stitching. "The work of a master."

She glanced at the Oriental rug under their shoes and thought maybe J Lassiter wasn't over-bragging about his prospects. Was that ticket pinned to the corkboard an order from the governor's office?

The Argentinean held the oak-paneled divider open, and the clubby interior of the boutique welcomed her with leather chairs, dark paneling, and the unmistakable aroma of Cuban cigars. The mannequins modeling suits and the racks of expensive ties seemed secondary to the air of exclusivity in this oasis halfway down Fredonia Street. If they'd serve lunch, his customers might ditch the Brass Rail entirely.

"Don't tell Boris about this place," Theo said, cataloging the refinements. "He's hooked on bespoke attire."

"That man has turned into an expensive commodity for the government. I sure hope he lives up to his bill of sale."

Theo tilted his head to the side, getting a better look at the leather suspenders. "If I can get Washington to believe his intel, maybe he will."

"Do you believe his intel?"

He rubbed the whiskers over his jaw. "He told me Mercer snuck into the U.S. after being picked up by a lobster fisherman, who thought he was a downed airman."

"That's specific."

"Maine Coast Guard confirmed the story. I think it's solid."

She draped her hand along the back of a chair, relishing the expensive upholstery. "I hope the information I spread around Harmon General this morning doesn't get investigated."

Theo turned to get the rest of the belongings he'd hauled out of Emmie's room at the Kennedy household. "You made the phone calls from the Wyatts'?"

"No, there was a booth on the street corner. I called from there."

He accepted the trunk from the cab driver and tipped him extra for the weight.

"People need to wonder where Lemming is," he said struggling with the suitcase. "I want the MPs to get an all-points bulletin going."

She supposed she should help him with the luggage, but then she remembered how cruelly he'd treated her reports. Dismissive, and then handing over her eight months of labor to the FBI. She'd let him sweat. "He was supposed to be working the blood bank this weekend."

"What did you tell them about his broken nose?"

Emmie glanced to see where the Argentinean had disappeared to and then lowered her voice, saying, "He's got this med tech assistant, and I told him that the doctor was caught in a bar brawl and was last seen in a car heading for Gregg Memorial for treatment, although it was a known Mafia man's car, so anything was possible."

"Did the tech believe you?"

She remembered Peale's dead-eyed stare from the last time she'd talked to the man and wasn't sure if he was relieved to have the day off or worried about the incongruity of an Army doctor being treated in a civilian hospital. "Who can say? My hope is that Peale turned around and notified an MP."

Theo sighed and dusted his hands. "I'll place a tip with the Longview PD, and maybe that will net us two birds with one stone."

"You think the FBI will appreciate you bringing in the cops?"

Theo glanced around for obvious ears. "When I tell them that Mercer might be inclined to blow up their oil refineries or that federal pipeline project heading east, they'll be glad for all the help they can get."

Emmie set her hatboxes on a desk. "What makes you think they'll believe you?"

"If the Nazis were sinking oil tankers that cruised out of the Houston shipping channel last year, don't you think the Germans would have an interest in dismantling a 1,400-mile pipeline built above ground and straddling the middle of America?"

She hated when he pointed out what should be so obvious. "Go get 'em, Tiger."

He bristled at her sarcasm. "Em, about last night—"

She hated apologies. Especially when they came wrapped in a bow of failure. "We did the best we could, shooting from the hip."

Theo's brow rose over his eye. "I was going to say how impressed I was that you took down both men with nothing more than beer mugs."

Her breath caught in her throat.

"That's one for the record books," he said.

Emmie let air circulate over old scars. "Thanks."

"And I hope you still have some of those reserves left today, because we're going to need every ounce of creativity to stop this mess from imploding."

Her smile came a little easier than it should, considering her sleep deprivation. "Is that a confession that you have no real plan? That we're making this up as we go?"

Theo ran a hand through his hair. "Giving you a visual on the bookshop is smart. I'll visit the police chief on my way to the Wyatt's, and we'll tie up loose ends after that. Okay?"

She heard footsteps above and guessed that the famous Mr. Lassiter was finishing touchups to host his surprise guests. "You sure have gotten chummy with an unlikely cast of characters since coming to Longview."

His eyes were bleary, his hair mussed, and the circles under his eyes had circles. But one side of his lips raised as if the indomitable Theo Marks wasn't bested by the machinations of an enemy. "What can I say? I like this place. It has interesting people, and they can keep secrets. All the better."

Putting her hand on the banister, she looked up the stairwell. J Lassiter waited at the top. An already tall man made more distinctive for the angle and his charcoal suit, crisp white shirt, and royal blue tie. Even his wingtip shoes gleamed in the alcove. Maybe it was his hair oil or the aura of an expensive cologne, but the narrow space offered the airiest fragrance of almond oil and lemons. Like a plate of Mediterranean goodness had just passed under a window.

She grinned because she couldn't help herself. "Mr. Lassiter, what a welcome."

He smiled like someone who enjoyed solving people's problems. "Anything for a friend of Lane Mercer."

"She's a doll, isn't she?" Holding her head high, Emmie climbed the stairs and took the key J Lassiter offered, stuffing down another layer of resentment that Lane had won the affections of the haberdasher. "You're the gem for helping us out with this little situation."

"I hope you'll find everything to your liking," he said, as if the door he opened wasn't already twenty times better than her Victorian accommodations at Molly's boarding house. "I lived here until I built a little place over on Turner Drive. Now I keep this nook available for out-of-town guests."

Unlike Lane's shoebox, this was a plush apartment, boasting wall-to-wall carpet, expensive sofas, case goods, and a galley kitchen she could have all to herself.

"The bedroom is through that door, and there's a full bath, of course," he said, as if everyone's apartment was so generously furnished.

The luxurious curtains made the room feel like an extension of the club environment downstairs. Even the sweeping river scene painting poised over a sofa looked more old world collection than new money purchase.

Finally, something had gone right for Mary Magdalene Tesco.

"How will I ever be able to thank you?" she cooed, wondering if Mr. Lassiter was single.

Theo huffed as he dropped her luggage. "Mr. Lassiter understands that cooperation with the United States government is its own reward."

Lassiter stepped aside as Theo hoisted luggage onto the carpeting. "Perhaps dinner tonight will be opportunity for you to try, Miss Tesco. I'd like you to join me at the Gregg Hotel, about eight, if you're available. I hear the chef has found a supply of oysters and will grill them upon request."

Emmie would have thrown herself into his arms if Theo wouldn't mock her for it. "Yes, that sounds perfect."

"No, you can't." Theo corrected. "You have work to do this evening. Remember?"

She disguised the hit of his dart. "I'm not likely to forget, darling."

Theo reached to straighten a tie that he wasn't wearing.

They'd lost Mercer and Lemming, and the only thing the Colonel could do was move two of his agents into not-so-covert arrangements in the middle of a civilian community. It was a wonder he hadn't broken out in hives or developed an eye tick for the security risks he was heaping on Longview.

Lassiter bowed graciously. "My offer stands should your situation improve. It will be a pleasure to have you and Lane living above the store for the foreseeable future."

She winked, though with her dry eyes it might have looked more like a twitch. "We'll try to keep the racket down. You know how it is with the girls in this town—just a party waiting to happen."

Lassiter's expression remained flat. "I rather suspect the only noise you girls will make will be snoring. This war has about run everyone to the ground."

Not everyone, she thought. The real threat that Mercer might bring his firepower to downtown was a peril she couldn't ignore. She wasn't sure exactly of the story spun for Lassiter, so she'd play her usual role and hope Theo had laid enough groundwork.

"Having such a big, strong man around will give us all such peace of mind."

Lassiter's brow rose a notch. "I suspect you're quite capable of taking care of yourself."

Theo harrumphed. "You have no idea."

Emmie shot him a glance designed to scare him downstairs. "You have a cab waiting, right?"

Theo saluted, as he turned for the stairs. "She's a live wire, Lassiter. Don't let her shock you too much."

Kicking off her shoes, Emmie ran her toes over the rug. She'd only ever seen wall-to-wall carpet in an apartment in Rome, and there hadn't been a lot of time to admire the novelty when she was fending off the advances of an amorous politician.

"May I offer you some coffee?" J gestured to a silver tray set in the kitchen. "I had my man, Paulo, bring up some provisions. There's toast, jam and hardboiled eggs, if you're hungry."

She was starving—and thrown off her groove by a man showing kindness. "Thank you. I barely had time to brush my teeth this morning. If you'll give me a moment to freshen up, I'd love a cup of coffee."

After checking out the white-tiled bathroom, pale green bedroom with twin beds in matching matelassé covers, and a closet with plenty of room for luggage, she returned to the kitchen and found that he'd set a bistro table with china and silverware.

"You will spoil me, Mr. Lassiter." She sat in the chair he held for her, noting that his cologne was not too strong, a subtle hint of Capri on a summer's night. She liked a man who didn't need to announce his presence. And for reasons that surprised her, she was all the more intrigued by his reticence. Who was this Lassiter?

"It's probably long overdue that someone did," he said.

Staring at the rose print set offering toast and jam and a china holder boasting a boiled egg, she thought of the men who'd railroaded past her in the last five years, most using her to gain an advantage in some plot where she was treated as an accessory or someone who was an obstacle to be removed. But rarely was there one who stopped long enough to ask if she longed for anything. A coat for winter? More bullets for her revolver? A thirty-minute break to rest an old knee injury?

Scalding hot coffee and browned bread were her undoing.

Staring at the white egg shell, marginally cracked by the edge of a spoon, she almost teared up. "Maybe you're right," she mumbled.

"I think I am, Miss Tesco." He made a move like he wasn't going to join her.

"Please," she motioned to the other chair. "Won't you share this with me?"

"I have to get the shop ready for business," he demurred. "Saturdays are busy in my line of work."

"Five minutes?"

He acted as if he had to make a hard decision. Finally, he acquiesced and folded himself into the corresponding chair.

She piled jam on a slice of toast, and before she bit the corner, asked, "Why did you do it, Mr. Lassiter?"

"You must call me J."

Emmie winked. "As you wish."

Settling back in the chair, he wasn't exactly comfortable, but as his gaze drifted from the tabletop to the wallpaper, he softened. "I've watched Lane, and that store, for weeks now. It didn't take long for me to realize she was not the usual shopkeeper."

Lane, again.

"I meant—" Emmie held a triangle of browned bread close to her lips. "Why did you move to Longview when you could have taken your business to any major city and been a huge success?"

"Oh." Color tinted his cheeks. "You want to talk about me."

She chewed the toast and held back a groan of delight for the nutty flavor. Chased with the best coffee she'd tasted in months, she almost asked for his hand in marriage.

"I felt like I could make a comfortable life here." He watched her eat. "They had rich oilmen who'd have no idea how to dress for their sudden wealth. I think my gamble worked."

"You must be good at sizing people up then."

His head dipped a bit to the left. "Yes, I am."

She'd remember that he wasn't a braggart, just a forthright man who didn't feel the need to flatter. "Is that how you knew I'd been working so long as a nurse that I haven't taken a day for myself in a long time?"

"You are the epitome of a professional woman." His eyes were as calm as a morning lake. "Not even a hint of complaint."

The insight almost stunned her. She'd always heard that she was a whiner, with a penchant for creating a starring role in every drama. His serious demeanor engendered trust, and she realized she needed someone she could rely on more than she needed a man to fill her head with pretty compliments.

Maybe it was the toxic combination of sleep deprivation, adrenaline overload and exhaustion, but she liked that she could relax with this man.

"Then what made you say I need to be spoiled?"

Emmie watched his eyes and even the grim set to his lips, waiting for his pronouncement, as if it really mattered. Which, she supposed, it did. Short of Slim tallying her bad traits and short temper, there were few who even acknowledged that she had feelings, much less needs.

Crossing her knees brought her leg into conflict with the table, and the beautiful china rattled in protest. Embarrassed that she'd upset his effort, she reached for the egg and almost missed his silence.

He'd not moved a muscle to rescue his precious linens.

He was still thinking. Fascinating.

"I guess you could say, I noticed," J spoke as if porcelain was farthest from his mind, "that you looked small behind your eyes."

She stared back at him, trying to imagine what he'd seen when she walked into this apartment. "I don't understand," she murmured.

"The moment Lane Mercer's name was mentioned, I could see you shrink. As if for your whole life, you've been forced to share, wear secondhand clothes, and live a half-life, because someone else's needs were always greater than your own." He refilled her cup with steaming coffee. "I recognized that because I felt the same way before I moved to Longview."

"Tack on a heavy responsibility for others, and you would have nailed me to a T." Emmie was humbled by the observation. "The irony is my parents would have told you that I was too self-centered to have ever become a nurse. But it's my lifeline. I've been travelling with my instruments since I was twenty years old."

He set the percolator back on its stand. "This is why it's time someone spoiled you."

A stone dislodged from the groove that had been carved into her neck muscles. Had anyone ever suggested such a ludicrous thing? She was the brat—or so her brothers taunted. Even her parents had called her ungrateful and belligerent.

No one showed hospitality to a misfit. It just wasn't done.

Yet, this stranger did more for her in ten minutes than anyone had since her childhood. She was so chastened by the generosity that she almost wept. As it was, something bloomed in her heart that she'd long thought dead.

She stared at her fingers, wrinkled, scarred, and notched with stories from a life lived—maybe not running from something, like she'd always thought, but maybe she was running toward something better.

"Thank you, J." She almost hiccupped, like a suitor with too much emotion in the throat. "It was lovely of you to say that."

"You don't get a lot of lovely in your line of work, do you, Miss Tesco?"

A movie flickered, tracking frame by frame with shadowy rooms, blood stains, clothing that seemed to belong to an actress, expressions that never felt quite real, and fewer and fewer days of freedom. She used to laugh so easily, especially at herself. But now no one appreciated humor honed by hard luck.

"Call me, Emmie, please. It's a nickname for Mary Magdalene. And I almost never see the lovely in life."

He dusted his hands on the dishcloth from the sink. "Well, take this morning to indulge in a little rest and relaxation. Colonel Marks said that you and Lane were being stalked by a crazed man and that getting you out of your normal places would help keep you safe."

Stalking was as good a description as any, and it bathed the escapade in enough mystique to keep the questions limited. "Colonel Marks knows best."

"I would say so," J said, as he reached for the apartment's door. "The good news is that better days are coming."

224

Emmie turned in the chair to see her host standing on the threshold, both solid as a statue and yet a bit sad, like he needed some lovely too.

"How do you know that? We're in a bleak war that looks impossible to win."

He glanced at the window beyond her table, as if searching the panes for a message from the other side. "My nanny used to say, 'Everything will work out in the end. And if things haven't worked out, it's not the end.'"

With a tear hovering on her lashes, she hoped his nanny's words played out true. "Thank you, J."

He shrugged. "Think nothing of it. Small kindnesses are the least we can do for each other in these difficult days."

As he shut the door behind him, she pulled the pistol Theo assigned her from her brassiere and set it on the table, feeling a weight lifted literally and figuratively. This day was going to be one straight from Hades, but she was going to take ten minutes for her peace of mind and try to think like a woman who hadn't been scarred by loss, pain, and war.

Chapter Twenty Seven

April 24, 1943 7:53 a.m.

Emmie drew in a shaky breath and knocked the repeated pattern on the back door of Between The Lines bookshop. Her hands were icy, even though the temperature was nearing eighty.

Theo didn't know she'd sneaked out of J Lassiter's jewel box, and if she pulled this off he'd never have to find out. Lord knows how he was going to bellow if he found she'd upended his morning strategy. Lucky for her, Paulo—Lassiter's Argentinean butler—was susceptible to a wink. And in case that wore off too soon, a five-dollar bill reminded him to keep his mouth shut.

The door cracked open a fraction, a greasy bike chain kept it from opening farther.

"Who's there?" Patrick barked.

It wasn't code worthy, but at least she wasn't going to be solo with Boris. "It's me, Tesco. I'm alone."

The chain swept away, and the door opened for her to enter. She glanced at the door jamb. Patrick had modified his own version of additional security measures to the locks Lane had installed. Maybe she'd undervalued his role in this operation, after all.

"Mrs. Mercer coming soon?" Patrick closed the door behind her. "'Cause I'm not finding a lot of breakfast-making materials that will cover two grown men."

Emmie glanced at the pile of paint cans stacked like a pyramid on the stairs and then looked back at him, wondering how a man with one eye could get the balance so perfect.

He shrugged. "I sometimes fall into a fearsome, deep sleep, so in case that old Russian tried to sneak out, I figured he'd have to make some racket to do so."

"You show real promise, Mr. LeBleu." She turned around and saw the stockroom that was still much the way Lane had left it thirteen hours ago, short of some rolled floor rugs that had become a makeshift bed for first-floor security and an emptied can of saltine crackers.

"If my projections are correct," she said, without acknowledging his ingenuity. "Boris is going to wake from his magical sleep with the mother of all hangovers, at which point he will want to drown his sorrows in vodka, which, as we both know, will only increase his problems. But on the upside, it would keep him so sickened that he'd have no interest in food or wandering away."

Setting her purloined linen on the table, she added, "I brought you breakfast. It's just hard boiled eggs, toast and jam, and a thermos of coffee, but since Lane has been unavoidably detained, it was the best I could do."

Patrick unfolded the linen napkin and stared at the rose print china. "It won't scratch the surface, but I'll say thanks nonetheless."

"It's the small kindnesses, right?"

He looked at her like he didn't understand. And how could she expect him to appreciate the moment she'd had after J Lassiter left her to eat breakfast in privacy? Emmie barely understood how she processed the emotions herself. The hospitality a stranger gave to her had done more for her cold heart than any sermon ever could. The best amen she could offer was to repeat the kindness to another soul who seemed to have missed the boat on life's softer moments, too.

"Do you need to run out for a bit, maybe stretch your legs before Boris starts banging his metal cup?" She turned on the desk lamp, and set the saltines can in a box piled with Coke bottles and an empty potato chips can, waiting to be returned to the market. "I could tidy here, as long as you promise not to be gone too long."

He stared at her with that unnerving single eye.

"What you got up your sleeve, Miss Tesco?"

She regretted that her good deed didn't buy her a reprieve. It was wise to remember that the men of this town held her in a skeptical regard. "What a suspicious mind you have."

He didn't even flinch.

"You better eat while you can." Emmie waved toward the plate before she walked into the sales portion of the shop, wanting to give the man a second chance to accept the offering. "Then I have a story to tell you which is going to change the way we're doing business for the next few hours."

"The Russian is leaving early?"

"Oh, wouldn't that be bliss?" She flipped the switch to bathe the shop in warm light, seeing Lane's inventory still scattered in piles. "No," she said, deciding to weave Patrick into the net. "We've had another visitor who is going to be even more troublesome than old Boris. But eat first, and then we'll plot. I think someone with your skill set is going to come in handy, and lucky for you, I'm in the mood to share the fame."

While Patrick made short work of the contents on the plate, she turned her experience to organizing Lane's shelves. It wasn't going to be easy for the young woman to walk away from all this, considering the investment in the store. If the inventory had to be sold at auction, the least Emmie could do was make the process go smoother. As a pardon, it might keep Lane from feeling like she'd left something undone when Theo threw her on the first bus going to Wisconsin—or wherever he felt was far enough away to hide a target.

Pleased with her progress, she walked around the room looking to see if there was anything else she could do to work off her nervous tension. The floors had been polished, and she could unroll the rugs, but Patrick wouldn't thank her for removing his makeshift bed before anyone had announced whether he'd be spending another night on the floor.

She saw the promotional poster propped in the bay window and felt bad that Lane's celebrity author might get shipped on to Dallas instead of the much-anticipated layover in Longview. Propping her hands on her hips, Emmie sniffed, and didn't even sneeze from the dust in the air. Considering how appalling this place smelled the first time she entered, it was noteworthy that lemon oil now mingled with ink.

"Miss Tesco?"

Turning, she saw Patrick framed by the archway.

"I hear moaning from upstairs."

Theo wasn't going to be happy with her usurping his protocols, but it was the only way she could think to salvage international relations with the British, regain equal-footing with the FBI, and free their small OSS team of obstacles to take down Mercer. And Theo wanted a promotion? She was going to deliver the whole shooting match.

"Thanks, Patrick. Would you set some water to boil on the burner? Enough for a teapot."

He turned back without questioning, and she'd give him an A for obedience. That's more than some of the other recruits she'd had over the years. The one most difficult of them all was nursing his wounds somewhere in this town and no doubt plotting a most painful revenge.

Patrick unrolled the sleeves of his white shirt. "You want me to do anything else before we go up and see what's what?"

She hoped the "what's what" didn't involve bodily fluids. "Yes, but bring the teapot."

"Are you making more of that magic tea?"

"I am."

"You think that's a good idea? A body might die from so much sleep."

"He's Russian. Their whole winter strategy is hibernation." She walked into the stockroom, wondering if Theo left the tea upstairs or if she'd have to use one of the Mickeys she kept in a secret pocket within her purse. "He'll enjoy the sleep, and snoring will keep him out of our hair. I'm going to need you to be locked and loaded to protect this shop from someone who means to hurt Mrs. Mercer."

His eye narrowed. "Those mobsters have come back after her?"

Emmie hoped the FBI would round up the Mafia, but if not, well, she'd add them to the list of people she'd rather tangle with other than Mercer. "I don't have time to drag you through a history lesson, but suffice it to say, Mrs. Mercer's formerly dead husband isn't dead anymore—and he's out to kill her, me, and Colonel Marks before he engages whatever nasty plan he has for Harmon General. And who knows? With his flair for explosives, he might even want to dismantle the Big Inch Pipeline too. Wouldn't that be something, taking down the pipeline before it's getting Texas oil shipped to Europe?"

Patrick reached for the back of the desk chair to steady himself. "That's mighty bad."

"Yes, well, Captain Mercer is a mighty bad man. We're going to do all we know how to do in order to stop him before he gets around to stopping us."

"You need me to call Judge Wyatt?"

She wondered if the Longview Police Department appreciated the resources available through Wyatt and Company. Maybe the FBI needed to send a recruitment officer to the speakeasy.

"Wyatt knows," Emmie said, moving closer to the stairs. "He's got Mrs. Mercer safely tucked in with his wife and mother-in-law. We'll need to use you, Arnold, and any other men who are comfortable moving around town to help us track down this rat." She pictured the face of that sweet, teenaged girl who'd wanted to do her part to help the Resistance work in France. A girl who died in a public hanging because Mercer gave her name to the Gestapo. "Or as we liked to call him on the warfront, the Grasshopper."

Patrick reached behind his back and pulled a gun from his belt. "I've got a .38, but we're going to need bigger firepower. Can you shoot?"

Patting her bra for the pistol Theo assigned her, she smiled serenely. "I'm prepared to do whatever is necessary. This man has caused the deaths of people close to me and close to Mrs. Mercer too. We're going to take care of him as quietly as possible so that the good people of Longview never find out that a terrorist was on their doorstep. But first, let's go help Boris enjoy a sleep-in sort of Saturday."

Patrick grimaced.

"And one more thing," she said, holding the stair rail to cement her plans. "Whatever you do, don't call Colonel Marks. He doesn't believe that putting Mrs. Mercer in the target is the best idea, but it's the only way we'll get her husband to show his true colors."

"A skirt is thinking better than a man?"

Maybe she'd underestimated Patrick. "In this case, yes."

"Now, I don't know about that," he said, shaking his head. "I don't cotton to taking orders from a woman."

"You take orders from Mrs. Mercer."

"Not me."

"But I've seen you." She hated arguing with a subordinate. "Every single time, you do exactly what she asks you."

He turned the .38 to the side as if inspecting the safety latch. "You sayin' I don't know my own mind?"

"Good Lord," she hissed as she climbed the stairs. "All I'm asking is for a little consideration: an acknowledgement that maybe I know what I'm talking about."

"You want me to keep secrets from the man who's covering my pay."

"Lane Mercer is paying you."

"Marks told me to ignore whatever sum she promised and that he'd give me a big old wad of cash if I kept this here Russian from escaping the apartment." Patrick fitted the gun into his right hand. "He also told me to do exactly what he said and that I wasn't to take no lip off you or Mrs. Mercer if you came in here changing the instructions."

"He did not." Although, it would be just like Theo to undercut her before she even got her plan in motion. "What's the code word?"

"He didn't give me no word, 'cept he said if you showed up here without him, I was to hogtie you to the closet." He waved the gun toward her, motioning her back down the stairs. "He was real clear about the kind of knot I was supposed to use too."

The man was serious. "Patrick?"

He lifted the gun as if he was going to bring the butt down hard on her head. "I hate doing this, but it's the instructions."

The crack she heard reverberated through her own Irish skull.

Chapter Twenty Eight

April 24, 1943 7:55 a.m.

Lane packed her satchel with the few toiletries she'd brought. She hated to be such a cad regarding the Wyatts' hospitality, but she couldn't face them once they woke up. It was hard enough slipping past Mrs. Wyatt's mother thirty minutes ago while looking for coffee. Of which, there was none.

The Wyatts, she was told, didn't keep anything stronger than apple cider in their house, but the old woman with a bandana tied around her knobby head did want to pray over their Saturday efforts together, and for that moment of hand holding, she was thankful.

Scribbling a note on the pad next to the sewing machine, she tried to express her gratitude for the bed and an explanation that she couldn't forgive herself for bringing even more danger to their doorstep. Leaving without a word, though cowardly, was a self-preservation technique too. She didn't want to hear the Judge chastise "Red Bird" for thinking that they didn't know their way around a dangerous man. Since she had no idea what Roy was considering for her, or this town, she'd try to limit the damage.

Removing the black-out shade from the bedroom window, she checked the perimeter of the Wyatts' yard for anything suspicious and lifted the sill. At eight in the morning, there wasn't much moving, save the mist leaving dew on the yard. As far as Emmie and the rest of the house were concerned, Lane had gone to bed after Theo left with Arnold and was going to sleep off her troubles.

Like she'd ever been able to quiet her brain enough to rest. A person couldn't shut a broken faucet in their soul.

There was no precedence for what she'd been through in the last five hours, and she doubted there would ever be one, even if she survived to tell the story. There were too many twists for even her limited understanding, much more for someone like the OSS's psychiatrist who'd have a hard time choosing whether to conduct a case study on Roy Mercer or turn him over to an international tribunal.

Gently, she dropped her bag to the yard and eased her leg over the windowsill. Landing with a thud, she crouched against the beams holding the Wyatts' house firm, making sure a dog or a hen wasn't disturbed by her movements. As jittery as she was, even a sparrow might be alarmed by her actions, but if she could make it off the Wyatts' property without attracting the attention of their henchman, she'd consider it a success. What she was going to do with herself after that was more of a fly-by-the-seat-of-her-pants exercise. Right now, the only thing on her mind was getting Zeke, her aunt, and her uncle away from the line of fire.

Slinking past the automobiles haphazardly parked in the yard, she made it past the fence, covering her nose from the aroma of the chicken coop and a pile of food scraps that would get tilled into the garden. She couldn't afford to sneeze and wake someone. At the gutter, she chose to follow the graveled ledge along the road heading back to town, just in case she had to drop and roll into the culvert, should a vehicle return from some early morning run to the market.

Walking with her stomach crawling into her throat reminded her of some of the escapes she and Delia had improvised when the rent money ran out or the sugar daddy decided he'd grown bored. It wasn't something she'd deliberately recreated, but over the last few years, the feelings had returned more than once—today was the moment she'd never expected.

Glancing at her hands, she saw knuckles, blunt nails, and that scar along her thumb, not the raw tissue of someone so undone by a lie. How was it possible to feel so skinless and yet have the nervous energy to skip across grass like a steam engine fueled her feet?

Lane had no idea what propelled her forward—maybe the sheer terror that Roy Mercer not only lived, but he seemed impervious to the destruction he'd caused.

She'd given herself permission to not think through a lot of what Theo had told her during the night. It was just too much to comprehend. Locking in on Roy's betrayal of all things humane was enough for now. Anything more, and she might not be able to breathe.

Turning away from the dirt-packed road of Timpson Street, she forced her feet to move slower, more purposefully, as she clipped a yard at Clover Street. The paved road and tall trees made the journey simple enough, but she knew to avoid houses where the lights were switching on to greet the day. She hurried through the various blocks and potential shortcuts before she'd get to Melton Street. Zeke rented space from a family who had a sprawling home with a carriage house to spare, and she was going to catch him before he left for the Junction Depot.

They'd not spoken since their argument, and not only did she not want to leave things so undone between them, she also needed to warn him that he could be on Roy's radar.

Lane's gaze shifted to the pale orange streaks warming the morning clouds. Warnings sounded so inept, even as she tried a few in her mind. Zeke would snarl and think she was making it up to justify keeping the safe house. Lawyers were notoriously hard to convince without evidence.

All she had to offer were Theo's words. Secondhand accounts of a man who had, until a few hours ago, been conscripted to a grave. Maybe Zeke would hold her hands, kiss her forehead, and tell her that it wasn't as awful sounding as she'd made it. But that was a fantasy.

Her sapphire ring meant nothing if she was still married to another man.

An engine growled from the top of the hill. She jumped into a thicket of azaleas as a slow-moving car approached. Her heart pounded against her ribs.

The sound of air slicing in two, followed by a thump echoing off wet grass suggested a delivery man was tossing copies of the Longview Morning News. Giving his automobile time to inch along, and hopefully alert her to any stray dogs that might bark at intruders, she waited for him to pass by. Her shoes rubbed blisters against her heel, but she'd not grabbed stockings last night, and there'd not been opportunity to ask to borrow Emmie's this morning. Besides, the pain felt right. It meant she wasn't numb. If she could bleed, she was still alive and could take steps to solve her problems.

With all the conversations swirling in her head, a mistake would set a matchstick on fire, running flames through the relationships she'd cultivated with her aunt and uncle, Patrick LeBleu, and whatever J Lassiter had seen from his doorstop yesterday. She pushed hair off her forehead and tucked it behind her ears.

The better question was how many mistakes could she make and still control the situation? And control, she would. Theo had painted some picture about how he was going to round up the FBI and the local police to create a sting operation to catch Roy and Stuart, but that felt like a joke. How could men who wrote speeding tickets take down an international agent? Even with her experiences, she was stumped to imagine what sort of master plot it would take to catch someone as wily as that grasshopper.

If Roy were here to finish what he'd started by marrying her, then she'd find a way to lure him out and put him right in the line of fire. The thought made her stomach pinch, but she couldn't take the risk that Roy was also here to toy with Theo. Maybe even Emmie, too, since they seemed to have had some sort of history.

After Roy's funeral, Theo had asked if there had been mail her groom had sent—or souvenirs. Theo had said then that it was purely OSS policy to make sure that delicate information hadn't been included in a love letter or postcard—he wasn't being harsh. Lane had been chagrined to admit Roy had written only once, to say he'd landed safely in London.

Theo had still rummaged through their things, unsatisfied that Roy was so heartless toward his bride.

Looking back, she could see where Theo had his doubts about their lack of newlywed communication. That could explain why he asked if Roy had left uniforms behind—suits that might harbor movie stubs or even a favorite book he'd like to read. Lane had shrugged and glanced around their meager belongings, indicating there'd been no room for a library because they'd not had time to buy shelves.

The pieces of their life together had been so paltry. She'd cried about that void for weeks, until Theo returned to the tiny apartment with a proposal that would help channel her grief into something worthwhile.

With bills due and a bleak future, she'd accepted his offer to use her language skills for the OSS. After training at the academy, it was determined she had intuitive knowledge and an observation aptitude that shot her to the top of class rankings. These abilities also moved her into the pocket of Colonel Theo Marks, as together—with her unique skill set and his extensive experience—they could work quickly and successfully at intercepting intelligence communiques in Belgium and disabling information trains to the Germans. Their escapades had built a friendship and a trust that she'd have said was impenetrable.

Until, that is, at three o'clock this morning.

Now, she questioned everything.

Even Theo's intentions in befriending her.

He had known that Roy had faked his death but never divulged this news to her. Who could do that to a friend?

She scurried from the hiding place and tripped in a pothole, catching herself before falling to the road. Hurrying toward the stop sign for Melton Street, she grabbed for the pole, scanning east and south for witnesses. The sound of a car throttling caught her attention and she glanced toward the west end of Melton. There, five houses down at the Catons' address, was a man wearing a dark suit and fedora as he tossed his luggage into the trunk of a cab. She'd have recognized the shape of his body and the tilt of his head even if Zeke's walk didn't bear the marks of a man determined to escape. He slid into the passenger's seat, and the car door thudded against metal.

Breath lifted in her throat to call out to him but strangled in her vocal cords. As the taillights glowed like fiery eyes in the grey morning, she watched the cab pause at the intersection with Mobberly Avenue and then turned right, into the future.

She'd been five minutes too late.

Five minutes that would have been able to right the wrong of his impressions, and change the future of their relationship. She swiped at her eyes, feeling ten types of failure.

Lane squeezed her eyes shut to keep the hot tears from flowing. Once they were let loose, there'd be no seeing her way to Oakdale Avenue. She'd have to sit down on a curb and, like a school girl, bury her face in her knees and bawl. And there wasn't time for sorrow. Not today.

Lane decided right there, right then, she was going to change her fate. Zeke was safer on a train to Washington than if she'd found him in his apartment. Pained though she was by the memory of their last words, this situation was for the best.

A red fox skittered across the yard and seemed stunned to find her standing like an appendage to the sign. He didn't wink, just stared at her like he was debating if his curiosity about her was worth the effort.

"Shoo," she brushed him away.

She'd never set out to make Longview her home. That fateful day last July when she'd stepped off the Sunshine Special at the Junction, she was just as sure she'd get back on the train and keep going west to California. But some curative wind had blown through here, some elixir that was as much about finding a purpose as it was in finding people she wanted to live among, or, in the case of Zeke Hayes, with—forever and ever.

Her whole life she'd been looking for this sort of settling down place, a dream she'd barely been able to imagine when moving from town to village in tow behind her mother. Macon was all wrong. Valdosta wasn't right, and Washington certainly wasn't it either, but Longview. . .this town had grown familiar. And she'd not let Roy steal this from her, too.

Drained and exhausted beyond any level she could remember since France, Lane climbed the last incline and paused at the intersection with Young Street. A milk truck was gearing down for a turn, and she was careful to hug the garage of a house that had a deep overhang.

With an empty street both ways, she hurried across the road and into the yard of two sisters who tended the gravestones at Greenwood Cemetery. Scooting along Young, she turned south at Hutchings Avenue and, with a mountain of relief, eased into the backyard of her aunt's house.

Catching her breath at the stand-alone garage, she examined the street and didn't see a stray automobile staking out the corner. Looking around the Thomases' back yard, the black-out shades were still pulled low, as the chickens began their morning complaints.

Everything was as it should be.

In what seemed like the strangest farce of all, she climbed over the rosebushes and through the window of her bedroom, collapsing onto a narrow mattress that still smelled of damp bath salts. How had a few strange hours upended her world?

The toilet flushed in the bathroom, and she knew her uncle had started his morning rituals.

Changing out of the sweat-soaked clothes into denim pants that would give her more flexibility, she traded her leather shoes for socks and sneakers, stuffing cotton between her heel and the leather rim. She had to cram a few more clothes into her satchel and devise a plan to make her relatives leave town.

Her aunt's slippers made a shuffling noise against the heft of the new runner in the hallway, and Lane leaned out the bedroom door.

"Morning," she said, quietly, out of respect for her aunt's inability to be cheerful before coffee. There was a grunt in return.

She checked her watch. There wasn't time for formalities, so she stepped into hall to knock on the bathroom door.

"Uncle Victor?"

She heard the sound of his glasses crashing to the floor, like she'd startled him.

"Can't you give a man ten minutes of privacy?" he growled through the door. "Sheesh."

Lane knocked again. "I need to speak to you as soon as you're able. It's terribly important."

There was a snap of newsprint and she knew that she'd caught him before he settled in for a read of the headlines.

"Two minutes, Lane. And it better be good."

Hurrying back to her room, Lane scanned the space for anything that might give clues, should Roy sneak in after they were gone. She opened the top drawer, checking to see if she'd scooped Delia's cameo with her other OSS-issued belongings last night. The delicate, filigreed gold inset with an ivory etching of a Grecian maiden stared back from a cheap, pink scarf. Unpinning it, she folded the tiny hidden camera into her pocket.

Opening the closet, she checked the shelf over the hangers and behind the shoes where she sometimes hid cash in rolls of hosiery.

She ran her hand behind the mirror and under the dresser not taking a chance that a sales receipt or a list had somehow gotten away from her diary.

The bathroom door pushed open, and her uncle stormed the few steps, tying his robe around his waist.

"Yes, your highness?"

Lane motioned him into the room and was tempted to close the door for this conversation but it might go easier if Aunt Edith eavesdropped on the difficult things she had to say.

"Uncle, I'm going to try to breeze through an unbelievable story. At the end, I'm going to need you to accept that what I'm saying is true and then I'm going to need you and Aunt Edith to pack for an emergency stay somewhere far away." She grabbed a breath. "Maybe Dallas or Fort Worth."

He scratched his scalp, disturbing the stray hairs that were already standing from their usual comb-over on his balding head. "I don't understand."

"And you're not going to, most likely, but I'm going to tell you things that are confidential. Secretive. And for your safety and Aunt Edith's, I'm going to need to know that you trust that I have your best interests at heart."

He scanned her strange morning attire and narrowed his gaze. "Have you been drinking?"

She was terribly parched. "No."

"Did that Zeke Hayes take you to some hole-in-the-wall where people were smoking things that aren't legal?"

Lane didn't think her uncle knew of such places. "I haven't seen Zeke since five o'clock yesterday. He's in as much danger as you are just by knowing me but I have to trust that he's on a train heading to St. Louis and is for the moment out of danger."

"Danger?" Victor stood a little taller in his house shoes. "Does this have something to do with those soldiers out at Harmon? 'Cause I was one of the first to say at Rotary that those men coming into our town was going to stir up bad stuff for our womenfolk."

"Please, for Pete's sake." She held her hand like a stop sign. "Just let me get this out."

His mouth closed, but he was vibrating with insult.

"I've only just found out that my husband, Captain Roy Mercer, is not dead."

Victor's eyes widened. "Well, that doesn't sound so bad."

Oh, how little the innocent understood. "Roy is a trained assassin, and he's here to kill people. Me, friends of mine, and maybe you and Edith if you get in his way."

Victor collapsed on the edge of the mattress, his mouth gaping.

The hens clucking for attention created a beat in the air blowing through her window that her timing could not follow. She'd been transported to a place that hovered above the morning glories waking to the day and skated over the rose buds opening beneath her sill. Her mind wasn't even in this wall-papered room. Lane was a million thoughts ahead, running operations that would get Patrick and Boris away from the bookshop, and J Lassiter out of town too.

Victor put his clammy hand on her arm. "What do you think he'd do to me if he caught us?"

Lane took a step away from such a selfish thought. His robe barely covered his barrel chest and the pajamas that were faded from drying on the line. "Let's make sure that doesn't happen," she said, organizing a mental checklist of how she could double-check that her aunt would be protected. "Go pack for a week away, Edith too. And then call a few friends and tell them you've surprised your wife with a trip to make up for all the stress you've brought home with the war work."

Victor nodded. "I have been awful busy."

Edith stood in the doorway, her hand clasped over her mouth. "Do we really need to leave town? I have Shakespeare Club this week, a bridal tea, and I just signed up to be a Gray Lady out at the hospital."

Victor leapt from the bed. "Did you hear everything, you nosy-posie? A man is out to kill me, and you're worried about a tea party?"

Lane glanced at her watch. "Edith, if you'll pack some clothes for travel, I'll go rustle up some toast and boiled eggs for the road. You'll need to be out of here within an hour, at the latest."

Edith propped her hands on her hips, her big, pink curlers bouncing with momentum. "All I heard was that your husband had risen from the dead, but no one has said why we're in danger."

Lane wrestled with the truth. With Roy in Longview, her secrets trembled with exposure anyway. She'd have to hope that Edith was too scared to share her troubles with those who dealt in the hush-hush.

"Roy was a soldier, but he was also in an espionage network in Europe."

"A spy," Edith gasped, and the light that twinkled in her eyes gave the job description much more glamour than it deserved.

"He worked for our side until he didn't anymore." Lane didn't know enough of the details herself, and she was sure Theo had tempered the information last night so that she wouldn't implode on site. "He's sold out to the Nazis, the Japanese, the Italians, and I don't know who else. He's turned into a vile, wicked man, and for reasons that I don't fully understand, my husband thinks I know more about his dealings than I do." That was mostly true. "There's reasonable suspicion that he's here to. . . to silence me, should I want to testify at a court martial. And, one of the best ways to make me do his bidding is to hurt those I love."

The twinkle in Edith's eye tarnished.

Victor's chest puffed. "There's no way we're letting him in our front door, Edith Thomas, so you go throw what you need together and we'll go out to Chuck's cabin on Lake Devernia for the week. He owes me a few favors, and that will keep us close enough to pop in on work and stay out of the way of stray bullets."

Edith covered her lips and tears spilled from her lashes.

"Sheesh," Victor grumbled. "Did you hear the girl? Go. Get packing."

Edith opened her arms to Lane. "Come here, child."

Lane's gaze shot to her aunt.

Edith wiggled her fingers. "If anyone needs a hug it's you, Louisa Jane. I can't believe the Good Lord has let this happen to you, but baby, we're going to pray you through it."

Something cracked the hard shell of her childhood. It was as if Little Momma had been reincarnated to return the exact same words from that cold day when an orphaned child stepped off a Macon bus and into the arms of family she scarcely knew. Emotion gurgled in her throat and it took immense strength to hold those pieces together at their seams.

She walked toward her aunt and gave in to what, she hoped, was a quick hug of reassurance. Parrish aunts were masters at hugging. Like Little Momma, they had the touch that would hold a person still and let love cross cheek to cheek. It was Edith's most endearing quality.

"Thank you, Aunt Edith," Lane said, swallowing more memories from those days with her grandmother. There'd been no other person who'd communicated so much with a touch or a squeeze, and she dearly missed those nudges of confidence. "But I won't be able to think straight if I don't get the two of you away from this address. I have no idea what Roy knows about my life here, but it won't take him long to figure out that we three share this bungalow."

"Gawd-a-mighty," Victor shouted from his bedroom. "He'd better not mess with my rose bushes."

Edith started pulling curlers from her hair as she walked the hallway. "No one cares about your rose bushes, but you'd better pack your support hose. You know how your blood pressure goes up when you're worried."

Lane rested a hand against the doorjamb, relieved that the conversation went as smoothly as it had.

The phone rang its bleating cry, and she stopped thinking.

It was too early for anyone with a social purpose to call.

"I'll get it," she shouted and hurried to the telephone niche farther down the hallway. She put her hand on the receiver, feeling the cold handle.

It could be the Coca-Cola factory.

Or one of Edith's friends had been taken to the hospital during the night.

Or—

The ringing continued and seemed to echo off the walls as if they were living atop the Grand Canyon.

"For Gawd's sake, someone get that telephone!"

Victor's voice added to the chaos in her brain. Lane picked up the receiver and held it close to her ear, listening for some gasp or familiar voice. There was silence.

Well, not silence, exactly. Someone was breathing on the other end.

Edith leaned out from her bedroom door. "Was that him?"

Lane slammed the receiver against the base and squeezed her eyes shut. "I don't know, but y'all hurry up," she said, feeling her nerves shoot off sparks. "I'll need you to drop me off at the bookshop on your way out of town."

Edith stepped into the hall, her hair half undone and her robe gaping open at the snaps. "We can't throw a week's worth of clothes into a box and scoot out of here. There is the trash to put out, food to sort, and I've got to gather up the mending so I don't fall behind."

Lane ran her fingers against her scalp, all but hearing Big Ben tick off the seconds that were being wasted while she waited for people with no training, no warning, and no idea what they were up against.

"Besides," Edith said, unraveling two more curlers and stuffing the pink foam rollers into her pocket. "what are you going to do about Zeke? Does he know your husband has come back from the grave?"

That was a question with an easy answer but no simple solution.

"He doesn't know yet. But he's already left for the train station and will be on his way to St. Louis within the hour."

"Seems like telling him would be a priority." Edith turned, and talked on as if Lane followed behind her. "As much as I hate to admit it, looks like you're not going to be able to walk the aisle in June after all."

Chapter Twenty Nine

April 24, 1943 9:12 a.m.

Victor huffed and hit the steering wheel, complaining about being stalled at Cotton Street and Mobberly Avenue.

"It's a parade of German POWs," Lane said as she leaned forward to better see the details of the forced spectacle down Cotton Street. "I'm not sure if they've disembarked from the train station and are being marched to buses or if they're being publically shamed for their role in Hitler's army before they're incarcerated. I guess it could go either way."

"Folderol!" Victor banged his fist against the steering wheel again. "Just ship them off to their camp in Smith County and be done with it."

Edith nibbled her lip. "Take a side street instead."

"We're stuck. I can't move for those cars behind me." Victor leaned into his car horn.

"Look at those MPs on horseback." Edith pointed toward the militia supervising the march. "They're carrying some serious shotguns."

"It wouldn't break my heart if they started shooting a few, just to show 'em what we Texans are made of."

Lane changed the subject, not wanting her uncle's ire to circle back to her own paranoia of senseless killings. "I guess they'll move along in a few minutes, right?"

Victor pushed back the sleeve on his arm and tapped his watch. "It's been fifteen minutes of congestion already. I'm going to call the mayor about this, you mark my words."

The line of cars waiting for the POWs to pass was growing, and she suspected that the drivers felt much like Victor did, worried that a city that had already given up hundreds of millions of gallons of crude oil to the war effort was now going to be at even greater risk because the weather and remoteness of Texas was conducive to prisoner camps.

Glancing at her wristwatch, she could see it was forty-five minutes past the time she'd told Patrick she'd bring breakfast for him and Boris. At this point, she didn't know what she'd serve and hoped the Hollywood Café had their hash special on quick order.

"If you don't mind, I think I'll walk." Lane reached for the door handle. "I can manage my satchel."

Victor turned and looked over Edith's girth crammed into the middle of the seat, to nail Lane with his gaze. "Oh, no you don't, missy. We haven't gotten any more information out of you since this madness started, and if I'm holing up at a fishing cabin for a week, I'm going to need to know what I tell my staff."

An ache throbbed behind her eyes that had everything to do with diminished reserves of energy. She swallowed dryness in her throat and wished she could take the thermos of her aunt's coffee. "Tell people the least. Stick with the story that you wanted some alone time with Edith and that you had to make a snap decision to surprise her."

His eyes narrowed. "No one is going to believe that."

Edith slapped his arm. "They would if you were more affectionate or acted like were the least bit interested in me."

"I spend my every waking hour with you," he insisted.

"Wrong—" Edith corrected with a finger raised like she was going to rattle off a list. "You go to work and spend ten to twelve hours with your employees. Then there's the Rotary meetings and whatever other clubs you're in, and on the weekends, you go hang out at Pinecrest, even though you despise playing golf. But after Macon, we're going to change some of that."

Lane didn't want to air out their old wounds. She had too many of her own needing oxygen. "I'm going to skip out here," she said, glancing longingly to the Junction, wondering if Zeke's train had left on time. "Please call J Lassiter, at his shop, if you need to leave a message for me. I won't be at the bookshop unless absolutely necessary. And whatever you do, do not speak of Roy or how we're altering our lives to hide from him."

The Thomases' argument faded away as quickly as it rose, and all that was left was tension that seemed to make every breath flinch.

"He's not going to find you at the bookshop, is he?" Edith's mouth had brackets carved around her lips. "You've worked so hard to get that place spruced up. I'd hate for it to be marred. . .well, by a tragedy."

The thought of having to walk away from those shelves almost made her ill, but that was the codicil to her employment agreement: The government owned her steps. Lane would go wherever Theo told her, even if that meant never seeing her aunt and uncle again. But that obedience would be final.

Among the chaotic debris shattered in her mind was the truth that this day marked the end of her career with the OSS. The thrill of secrecy and patriotic duty had been hard to wean off of even with the slim connection to the safe house on her horizon. Theo's confession last night had released her fingers from that grip on a flagpole. She'd reached her tipping point, and if anonymity and obscurity were going to be her sentence for two years of service, then she'd take her lumps. No one had promised this business was fair. Most spies didn't survive Europe. She'd already outlived the odds—but that wasn't enough.

She wasn't turning in her badge before she had a chance to seek justice for those Resistance Fighters who died at Roy's hand. And, if in that act of revenge, she made him confess his betrayal to their vows, then those final seconds would be even sweeter.

Rearranging her expression so that her relatives had no idea of the monster beneath, Lane sighed.

"I have no idea what Roy will do," she said, regretting that all she had to offer was the truth. "I only found out hours ago that he was alive, and then to hear that he's in Longview, too, well, it was a little much to take in. He's extremely dangerous, and I care about you too much to let him try to manipulate you in order to get to me. If I have to leave Longview and the bookshop to protect you, then I will."

Victor's gaze shifted to the scene of POWs marching along Cotton Street but he didn't seem to see their uniforms and Army issued numbers. "I brought my hunting rifles with me, if you need me to go after him."

Lane swiped a tear from her lashes. "Thank you, Uncle. That means the world to me. You take care of Edith, and I'll do what I can to get away, too. If you don't hear from me for a while, don't worry. It's safer for you if you don't know where I am." She leaned back to kiss her aunt's cheek, "But I will get in touch when it's safe. Okay?"

Edith nodded with watery eyes. "We'll be praying for you, baby."

Lane heard an echo of her mother in her aunt's voice. "I don't want you to worry; I've survived worse things."

Stepping away from the Hudson, Lane checked the street and realized that being in the middle of America might be the most dangerous assignment she'd ever navigated. Despite flying bullets, landmines, tanks with automatic artillery, and grenades, no one had ever marked a target on her back before. She was being hunted on her home turf, and it was unnerving.

With dark sunglasses and a scarf tied over her hair, she hoped her attire and her satchel gave the appearance of someone on a Saturday jaunt to the train station, and not a reflection of someone running for her life.

Dodging the cars backed up by the jam caused by the POWs march, she knew it would be smart to stow her luggage at the depot, but for now, she'd catch a cab and rush to get Patrick and Boris out of the safe house and on to a place where they were less likely to meet Roy.

"Where to, miss?" a taxi driver asked, leaning from his window, his Economy Cab Company hat perched at a devilish angle.

Lane glanced around the cars idling in front of the depot. "Downtown, please." Climbing onto the back seat, she added, "If you'll drop me off at Hurwitz's, that'd be perfect."

"A mighty fine shop, that one is."

Lane nodded, like shopping was foremost on her mind. As it was, she could slip out of the cab and sneak down the alley, arriving at the back door of Between The Lines with few witnesses.

As they drove under the railroad bridge, she could almost hear Zeke shouting out his UT chant, and the echo of that memory made her wince. Three weeks ago, her biggest worry was how to tell him she wasn't ready to marry him in June.

She pushed her fingertips into the sides of her forehead, rubbing at the tight bands of worry.

Turning at Methvin, they passed beautiful homes and she saw a group of students wearing their Longview High School varsity sweaters, posing for a photographer. Further along, a man walked his dog, and a woman tended a flower bed that came right to the edge of the sidewalk.

"So, miss, what do you think of those POWs being ushered through our town?" He glanced at her over his seat. "Did you ever think you'd see such a sight here in Texas?"

"I never expected that."

"It's a sad day, for sure. This war has about flipped us on our heads." He put his arm out the window to signal he was slowing down for a stop sign. "Although I'm guessing adding some Nazis to the mix around here ain't going to shake up the millionaires too much."

"Maybe not."

"And I'm not so sure as we're ever gonna be right again. The average Joe is just tryin' to make a living, see, and as long as some Jap or German doesn't come in here and try to take our jobs, we'll just live and let live. You know what I mean?"

A black woman stepped off a city bus, her arms loaded with bags from the market. The woman limped along the sidewalk, engulfed by the exhaust of the bus as it pulled away from the curb.

The grocery bags had acted like a red flag.

"Stop, please." Lane leaned forward, double checking the intersection. She reached into her wallet and handed him the fare plus a tip. "I'm going to get out here because, until just now, I'd forgotten I was supposed to bring pastries to the staff."

He turned around again, watching her as she scooted toward the door.

244

"I'd be shot if I forgot to bring the girls some kolaches today."

He nodded like he understood.

Lane watched him pull back into traffic and then hurried into the corner bakery run by a Czechoslovakian couple. She knew their inventory well and ordered several each of the pastries offered. It wasn't the hot breakfast she'd hoped to provide Boris and Patrick, but the way things had unraveled, it was the best she could do under the circumstances.

Tense as she was, Lane could hardly make small talk with the baker, much less chew the sample cinnamon twist he was hawking. She paid for her purchases and then pushed open the door cluttered with concert posters advertising benefits for war bonds.

Theo mentioned that Stuart Lemming had been with Roy last night when Emmie clocked them at the Cotton Club. Stuart might have told Roy details about the bookshop and the hotel, but she doubted—as busy as he'd been at Harmon General—that he knew much about downtown Longview, and she'd use the alleys to her advantage.

Scooting across Green Street, she bypassed cars parked along the curb and made it to Bank Alley, unavoidably nodding to a janitor who whistled as he emptied trash cans gathered during the night.

"Mornin', Mrs. Mercer."

Lane did a double take, recognizing a man who'd worked janitorial at the Bramford Building. Someone she knew well from her days of working for the Petroleum Administration for War office. "Morning, Waldo."

The janitor propped the broomstick on his shoulder. "P-picking up extra night duty at the d-dry goods store here to help with D-dad's expenses."

"Grady's still at the Veterans' Home?" She pictured the old soldier, fallen to the floor of the Bramford Building that wintery night Velma decided she was out of patience. "And holding his own, I hope?"

"B-barely." Waldo nodded as he walked toward the door that was propped open from the dry goods store. "But that's more than some of us can s-say. Yes'm, that's so much more."

Thankfully, he didn't ask what Lane was doing slinking along the alley. She glanced again to Green Street, making sure she wasn't being followed, and dodged a delivery truck advertising fresh milk and eggs from Spring Hill.

Knocking in the pattern she'd taught Patrick, she waited breathlessly for him to open the back door of the shop. There wasn't a response, and she wondered if he'd actually stayed the night. Maybe Patrick had given up on her oddball request and decided he had better things to do than shackle himself to a Russian? Maybe he'd called Jewel Carter and skipped town with his ladylove? Maybe—oh any number of disasters could have happened, and she'd be unable to enact the frail details of a plan that was only just now forming in her mind.

Lane was going to kill Roy. She was going to do it today.

She knocked again. Sweat pooled around her fingers clutching the satchel and bags of pastries. Where was Patrick?

Lane knocked the pattern again.

A clatter of metal answered, and the door jerked open, caught short by what looked like a bike chain.

"Patrick—" she whispered with relief. "It's me. Lane Mercer."

"You women are going to be the death of me." The chain was unfastened. "I swear, you two are more trouble than wrangling frogs."

Women? Sucking in her breath, Lane slid through the opening before he'd fully opened the door. Paint cans were scattered on the stairs, rugs rolled in one corner to make a pallet, and Emmie Tesco was face down on the floor.

"What happened?" Lane fell beside the agent and lifted her wrist, feeling for a pulse. How had Emmie ended up on this floor, fully dressed in an agency-issued suit, when she was supposed to be sound asleep at the Wyatts' house?

"The Colonel told me to knock her out if the nurse returned and tried to mess with his arrangements." Patrick wiped the sweat pooled on his brow. "She returned."

Lane shot her gaze to Patrick. "So, you hit her with what?" She glanced around the room and didn't see anything that could double for a weapon, but sitting on her desk was a nice linen cloth and china she didn't own. "A tin of saltines?"

Patrick patted his belt. "My .38."

She set her satchel behind the tree stand. "Gawd Almighty," she hissed, knowing she sounded just like Uncle Victor. "Move Emmie someplace more comfortable. We've got a heap of problems, and having her out of commission isn't doing us any favors."

Lane glanced again at the china, thinking it looked like J Lassiter's pattern, and then down to the floor. How had Emmie gotten here so fast? When she looked back, expecting Patrick to do the heavy lifting, he stood stock still with his arms folded over his chest.

"Patrick?" Nodding to Emmie, she pointed to the floor. "Move her to a chair. She's not going to thank us for having paper clips pressed into her cheek."

"No, ma'am." Patrick's single-eyed gaze bounced around the room. "I can't do that. The Colonel said if you showed up, I was to hogtie you, too."

Lane untied the scarf from her hair and set her sunglasses on a stack of boxes, buying a few moments to think through what Theo would have told Patrick and how she could circumvent the instructions. She was clueless as to how Theo had communicated to Patrick so quickly, but if she underestimated his powers now, she'd be in serious trouble later.

Harkening back to the days when she ran operations with Theo in Belgium, she'd have to outsmart his chess moves. Remembering that he could set traps in the dark, while most people were sleeping, she'd need to play off her skills in building community support. Between Molly Kennedy and J Lassiter, Lane knew she'd be far more successful if she employed a human net. She glanced at the phone.

They'd both be awake by now.

Lane returned her thoughts to a man who'd proven he was far more loyal to men than to women. "Okay, Patrick, before you have to tie me up, just tell me—What is the status of Boris?"

It was hard to tell if Patrick blushed, but his mouth was slack when he said, "Oh, yeah."

"Did you forget about your primary assignment—not bashing women over their heads, but body guarding the man upstairs?"

His eye was jumpy, like there was too much going on and he was ready to bail. "We was heading up that way to put out some of that special tea, but it was too good a chance to knock out the nurse, so I kinda forgot about the Russian."

A thump on the stairs confirmed Lane's worst fears.

"Dobraye Ooto—good morning, Americans," announced a man with a Russian accent. "I'm so hungry I could eat a horse."

Lane and Patrick whipped around, both crouching in case Boris came down the stairs swinging.

Boris scratched the stubble on his jaw. "The U.S. government isn't going to get any favorable marks in my travelogue if they don't serve kidneys and eggs, but at least I found the vodka."

Patrick whipped his gun from his belt, aiming it at the man who appeared impervious to paint cans, the crowded office space, and the clear sign that there was no staff preparing breakfast.

"What happened to the beautiful redhead?" Boris asked leaning over to see Emmie's crumpled form. "Is she going to be out for long?"

A groan whimpered from the floor. Emmie rolled toward the desk, shielding her eyes from the glare of the overhead bulb. "Where am I?"

Patrick slashed his weapon through the air, as if he couldn't choose between the Russian and the nurse for his first bullet.

"Put the gun down, Patrick." Lane rubbed the throb at her temple. "No one is going to get shot on my watch, at least none of you." She gave her fickle assistant a moment to make a decision, and then added, "I brought pastries so maybe that can tide you men over while we assess the situation."

Boris walked past Patrick, seemingly un-intimidated by the firepower of a .38. "I prefer kidneys and eggs—kippers if you're feeling generous."

Patrick eased his locked arms, but didn't tuck away the gun.

"The offering today is kolaches, sausage rolls, and some sort of Danish that the baker threw in." Lane glanced again at the china. "But I see I'm not the first to bring breakfast."

The rumble of a morning train barreled through downtown, and its horn drowned out the complaints about pastries.

Emmie crawled to sit then folded herself into the chair, and laid her forehead against the desk's blotter. "No one expected you to be here, Lane."

Boris opened the bag and fingered all the baked goods, seemingly searching for something to appeal to his palate. Patrick returned his gun to his belt, and Lane walked over to the door to secure the deadbolts.

"Well, suffice it to say, I don't care a fig for what you and Theo might have planned." Lane grabbed a kolache and bit its end off. "But, if you're willing, I'd allow as how—now that you're all here—you might help me enact a little revenge."

Emmie moaned. "How naïve you are."

Boris had a sweet roll chomped between his teeth as he looked between the two women. "Prison hasn't been good for me, so I'm game to get involved, particularly if this has anything to do with Roy Mercer and his sneaky return to America."

Lane folded her arms across her chest to keep her heart from pounding through her ribs. "It would appear I'm the last to know about my husband's ill-fated resurrection."

"I just found out," Patrick offered. "So, you weren't the very last."

Lane finished the kolache without even tasting the sweet bread. "Patrick, are you sure the front door is secured?"

He nodded, leaned on his back heels to check the shop space. "There's still a chair propped under the knob and a bookcase jammed into the hinge."

Lane had controlled small operations in France, usually relegated to messages between the Resistance and troops on the ground—this one had even higher stakes and more moving parts. "Boris, sit down. I need to know your knowledge of this case. It can't be a coincidence that you're here the same time Roy decides to slink into town."

Boris inhaled the roll to the point he started choking. Emmie stood, slapped him hard between the shoulder blades and a chunk of bread flew across the room.

Emmie collapsed into the chair. "Way to go, Lane. Bring the bad guy into your scheme."

"Boris is a trained spy. He was going to know something was up when he was assigned a role to play." Lane rubbed her temple again. "Okay, here's what I know. You three fill in the blanks. Roy and Stuart Lemming

248

are in cahoots. Roy is in town to kill me. And there are FBI agents crawling all over Longview. Have I about got that right?"

Emmie's laugh sounded brittle. "Way to make it all about you. As it turns out, Captain Mercer is an international criminal with a list of kills that makes us all trigger-happy. He's responsible for the deaths of some of my girls, and if Boris were honest—and let's agree that would be a stretch—Mercer has probably double-crossed him, which is why he ended up in American custody in the first place."

Boris nodded. "Mercer is a soulless bastard."

Patrick swore. "I don't know this man, but if the FBI are in town, I need to let Judge Wyatt know."

"He knows," Emmie and Lane said in chorus.

Boris folded his girth onto the bottom stair and held his block-sized forehead between his hands. "Mercer is going to come after me, too. I may have traded his last known whereabouts for a free ride to Nevada."

Lane propped her hands on her hips. "Okay, so we all work together and lure Roy into a trap. I'm the most likely one to bring him in to the center of the light, because Stuart won't know that I know Roy is here. They'll think I'm. . .gullible."

"You are gullible," Emmie said, reaching for a kolache.

Lane wouldn't deny it. Her status reports with the OSS had never corrected a basic flaw in her makeup—apparently, once off the frontlines, she'd believe anything. Stuart had fooled her from that first moment on the steps of the Gregg Hotel.

"What we need to do is create a trap that has no escape clause," Lane said, thinking as she spoke. "Something where the two of them are caught, and the FBI can take the credit, thereby keeping the OSS out of the press."

"Loyal to the end." Emmie wiped her fingers on the linen. "You know, Theo has betrayed you too. You don't have to protect him."

"I'm not thinking of Theo," Lane barked. "Zeke is still working that pipeline project, and I don't want to alert the Nazis that our presence here means we're concerned about national security."

Emmie shrugged.

Boris lifted his head. "I don't have a weapon."

"We can get you firearms." Lane looked at Patrick as she said the words. "Right?"

Patrick nodded.

"And Boris—" Lane's eyes narrowed on the furrow between the Russian's nose. "If you flee this operation, you'll become a sitting duck. I'll take personal delight in telling Roy what you did to him, and then I'll notify every agency that a Russian has gotten loose in America. I hear they're looking for people to test nerve gas on—you'd be a perfect candidate."

His gaze turned cold. "You wouldn't."

"I would." Lane felt the old fire return to her bones. "And worse."

She'd protected foot soldiers with her maneuvers in Beaune. She knew how to play dirty. "So, Emmie, what do you know about the FBI positioning?"

The nurse laughed bitterly. "They're all over Harmon General, thanks to Theo turning my reports over to them."

"Good. We'll stage a reunion in their court," Lane said.

Emmie stood, but grabbed the desk for support. "This is way over your skill set. I don't like it."

"Is it, Emmie?" Lane's gaze narrowed on the woman who'd undercut her at every turn. "You didn't question my skills when you needed my help with Dr. Death, but now that I need yours, you pause?"

"Roy has no conscience; he doesn't think like you and I would think." Emmie looked away, as if not answering one question gave her a right to deflect attention to another topic. "Besides, Theo is working a plan."

Lane wouldn't think about the character of the man she'd married; it rocked too many worries regarding her cold feet with Zeke. "Theo might have a plan, but we don't know where he is, and he seriously underestimated us all to leave us unguarded in this most dangerous scenario."

Boris grunted. "Maybe Marks is trapping us all so he can erase our history from the war? Your government doesn't like messy foreign loopholes."

Patrick took a step forward. "I'll help you, however I can."

Lane released a breath. With the networks of Wyatt, Kennedy and Lassiter, she could rope in most scoundrels. "Thank you. As of right now, Judge Wyatt is going to blow his top when he realizes I snuck out of their house before breakfast. I'm going to need you to run interference with him and gather as many of his hired men as possible. You'll have the ability to get close to the Army hospital without raising Roy's suspicions. He's from North Carolina. He doesn't really see black people unless they're in his way."

"Wyatt's men are not going to get past the MPs," Emmie said with scorn. "They won't have appropriate ID."

"I doubt any of us are going to go into this with ID and permission." Lane defended. "Wyatt's men can drive in their ambulance, maybe say they're going to the Negro wards. I doubt the gate guards will give them a second thought."

Emmie leaned her hip against the desktop, crossing her arms over her chest. "And how are you going to lure Roy and Stuart into a meeting with you?"

Lane didn't have every step planned. Some things had to be left to spontaneity. "If I advertise that Boris is my escort, that might gather their interest."

"I can't do that," Boris said. "I have to keep my nose clean if I'm getting to Nevada. I've already promised evidence in exchange for forgiveness and a new identity."

Lane walked into the bathroom and filled a glass with tap water. Gulping it down, and refilling it twice, she finally returned to the crowded office space and said, "Saturdays are busy with visitors at Harmon. There'll be buses pulling in at all hours, and the cabs will be running Mobberly like it was a track. We'll be able to get you back here before Theo finds out you escaped."

Boris chose another pastry. "I'd prefer the magic tea."

Lane wandered into the bookshop thinking through the ramifications of trapping Roy at Harmon today. She didn't have the luxury of time. The longer they took to piece together a plan, the more likely that Roy and Stuart would have escaped their hiding space and enacted a plot of their own.

Stuart—how could she have misread his clues? They'd been friends for so many years. But with the proverbial slap to her forehead, Lane woke herself from that fantasy. She'd been wooed and married by one of the most dangerous men in the world—and she didn't know he even played tennis. There were volumes she didn't know about either man, and that vacancy was a liability at the moment.

Lane ran her fingers over the spines of books that were nicely shelved in an order that wasn't the system J Lassiter had suggested. Someone had helped with the inventory. And she was going to trust that phantom friend would help outwit the two Army officers with a bent toward international pandemonium.

Lane blew a tight breath between her lips.

As if he was close enough to blow in her ear, Lane remembered Zeke's voice chastising her for feeling she had any obligation to the agency. And she didn't. She knew that now.

Joining up all those years ago had felt right—like a secret gate had opened in a maze. Lane had walked through that gate, away from a tissue-thin life, and embraced what it meant to do something significant and brave.

The maze had since been crushed.

She'd never lose the confidence and intuition she'd gained in battle, but she no longer had to play by the rules, either. She was free. And as a civilian, she was able to do whatever she wanted without an explanation as to the secret operations that may—or may not—be going on around her.

Lane's stomach growled.

If she survived this afternoon, she'd find a way to explain her heart to Zeke. Depending on what happened, it may be months before she could reach out to him, but she wouldn't let him remember her as the waffling girl who couldn't choose between service to country and marriage. He'd know that this last burst of clandestine effort was about righting a wrong and cleaning the slate.

Maybe, if he ever spoke to her again, he'd forgive her for not explaining this passion when she had the opportunity? Or maybe not—but she was going to do it anyway.

Walking over to where the Roberta Harwood sign was propped in the window, Lane straightened the poster board but didn't take it down. Any change would alert J to something being off, and she didn't want him walking into a spray of gunfire because Roy brought his rage downtown. She shuddered.

Why was she Roy's target? There'd been nothing left in their apartment to incriminate him.

But Lane guessed, Roy didn't know that.

Standing behind the sales desk, Lane draped her fingers across the dates scrawled on the blotter and wondered if she had something tucked into one of these drawers; a post card or a book that might act as something that she could suggest to Stuart was a keepsake of Roy's. Something tempting that would lure them into the open.

Pulling open the cupboard and rifling through sales ledgers and letters from publishers, she looked for some of the travel postcards that the previous owner had kept nailed to the archway.

Boris yelled out, "Do you have more food? This paltry offering is gone."

Heavy knocking on the front door rattled the blinds.

Lane jumped, dropping the papers clutched in her hand.

Rap. Rap.

Had Roy found her already?

The repeating knocks grew more frantic, and a voice soaked in Texas sunsets and sausage gravy called between the door frame.

"Lane, answer this door. I know you're in there. I can see your shape through the window."

The scramble in her brain shot forward with adrenaline. She ran to the bay window and barely nudged the curtain, spying on the person at her door.

Rumpled, as if he'd slept in his suit, Zeke stood outside her shop with as much fire in his eyes as he did the last time she'd seen him.

"Damnation, Lane. Don't do this to me."

She closed her eyes for a brief second, trying to run through the consequences if she opened that door. When she heard footsteps from the office, she glanced over her shoulder.

Patrick entered the shop, staring at her. His brow cocked over his one good eye as if he was waiting to see if she'd answer the door.

Lane shoved the chair away from the knob, and pushed the bookcase away from the jamb.

Jerking open the door halfway, she reached her hand out and pulled his sleeve, making him trip over the threshold.

Zeke stumbled. "What the—"

"Get inside quick." Lane locked the door and stilled the bouncing blinds with her palms. "You were supposed to be on a train going east this morning."

Zeke shot his cuff back into shape. "I couldn't make myself get on that train, having left things the way they were between us." His gaze raked her T-shirt and jeans. "I'm sorry, honey. I lost my head last night. I don't know how to fix the problems we have, but I want to know that we can at least try."

Oh, to have had this conversation without an audience. Lane fidgeted with her belt loop before reaching out to pet his sleeve. "I do too, Zeke, but this is not going to be that moment. You need to get on the next train leaving Longview."

He reached for her, wrapping his arms around her waist and dragging her against his chest. "Baby, we're too smart to let something stupid derail what we have going."

Happy though she was to see him, his timing couldn't be worse. Speaking into his lapel, she said, "Zeke, this won't work. Something awful has happened." She pushed out of his embrace, clamped her hands around his jaw, and said with as much compassion as she could, "I love you, but you have to leave. Take a cab, jump a bus, I don't care. But you cannot stay in Longview for one more minute."

He kissed her fast as if her lips had scalded him. "I'm not leaving. I called Parson from the depot and told him I had to stay and make this right between us. I have until Monday before I have to meet up with the team in New Jersey."

Emmie walked in from the stockroom, clapping. "Goodie. The gang is all here."

Zeke's chin grazed Lane's hair as he looked up. "What's she doing here?"

Lane gulped air, hoping her brain cells would catch up with her racing heartbeats.

Boris joined the menagerie. "Hallo," he said sounding less Russian than usual.

Zeke removed his hat. "This isn't at all the reunion I was expecting."

Lane sighed. "Zeke, there's something I have to explain—"

"Her husband is alive, he's descended on Longview, and he's basically out to kill us all." Emmie grinned like a child caught peeking under the Christmas wrapping paper. "Oh, and welcome back. We can use your help."

Zeke's eyes were as wide as golf balls, when he dropped his voice and asked, "Honey, what's the crazy woman talking about?"

Lane rubbed at the furrow grooving between her eyebrows. "Emmie's not entirely crazy, and if you're going to stay, we will need your help."

Boris walked up to Zeke with his hand extended in greeting. "Welcome to the team, I hope you brought firearms."

Chapter Thirty

April 24, 1943 10:00 a.m.

Zeke collapsed into the desk chair, his cheeks chalky, his eyes glazed.

Boris handed him a shot of vodka. "I'm only sharing this because your lovesick news is more pitiful than mine. I deserve what I get. You're just a man who fell in love with a married woman."

Zeke downed the liquor and pinched his eyes shut. "This tastes terrible."

Boris looked dubiously at the glassware. "It isn't the best brand. But I guess it's all the FBI could get their hands on with short notice."

Lane paced the crowded floor. "No more alcohol. We need everyone in top form if we're going to pull this off."

Emmie interrupted. "I suggest we put lover boy on the bus going to Shreveport and get him out of here, pronto. Once Roy hears that you're engaged, he'd take sick delight in torturing a fiancé."

"I agree," Lane said, glancing back at the man she loved so much that she didn't want to see him die under Roy's hands. "Zeke, you're going to have to leave. This is bigger news than that I'm still married."

Zeke stood, but his legs wobbled. "No ex-husband is coming after you without going through me first. I don't support the stupid mix of danger Theo has created, but I'm sure not letting you go into it without backup."

"Charming," Emmie groaned, leaning her elbow on a stack of boxes. "But technically, Roy Mercer is not an ex. He's a spy who is working off a play-book that only makes sense in his twisted mind and the rest of us are going to have to guess at his movements."

Boris poured another finger of vodka. "I think you do not need to rush this moment. The man just found out his woman is married to her first husband. Give him time to recover from the sucker punch."

Emmie grumbled, "A romantic Russian."

Patrick stepped away from the shadows. "I think Hayes should stay. We'll need another set of eyes and someone who can talk the authorities into thinking we're not half crazy. No one has a more silvered tongue than this here lawyer."

Everyone turned their gaze toward Patrick. He'd not spoken during the discourse educating Zeke to the difficulties presented when Mercer faked his death, but now he looked around like he enjoyed the attention.

Patrick ran his hand over his close-cropped hair. "Since we don't know where Marks is hiding, Hayes can be the one to go to the FBI and inform them of our plan to catch Captain Mercer."

Lane wanted to crumble, but part of the OSS training was to not fold under pressure. "Nice to hear from you, Patrick. But Zeke isn't going to be part of this mission." She checked her watch. "It's safe to say Theo is working his own plan and he's decided we're not on the need-to-know list. So let's get Zeke on the road to Shreveport, or Tyler, and the rest of us can start acquiring our tools to do our own thing."

Boris shook his head. "I don't like the sound of that. Marks has run operations all over Europe."

"And I know Longview." Lane swallowed the bravado. "The only place I'm not familiar with is Harmon General, but Emmie can draw us a map of where we can best stage a meeting with Lemming, and hopefully draw out Roy as well."

Zeke's gaze swept Lane's commanding posture. "I know Longview too. And I'm staying. I have a short list of every mucky-muck in this town and I can call the police chief too."

Emmie yawned. "The police chief was playing poker with Roy, so don't waste your breath on that call."

Lane picked up a rag and ran it across the desk, scooping away the pastry crumbs. "Zeke, this isn't a game. Roy is demented, and Stuart Lemming is involved as well. Emmie encountered them last night and they're dangerous. We don't even have a concrete plan for how we're going to stage this, but I do know there's no time to train you in espionage."

Wounded, Zeke's face lost more of its color, but he threw his arm toward Patrick. "And he's one of your recruits?"

Lane weighed her options for dealing with untrained counterparts. "He is for now. But none of us has a guarantee of tomorrow."

The truth of her words circled the small room, reminding them all of the stakes. Three of the four of them had survived the odds for getting out of the war theatre, but their good luck streak could well end at Harmon.

"You have a death wish?" Zeke accused.

"No," Lane said, softening her tone, remembering those early days at the academy when they were trained for kill-or-be-killed maneuvers. "We have a calling. And when you're ready to put your life on the line for liberty and justice, you go in knowing that death demands a paycheck."

Patrick gasped. "It's funny business for me to hear womenfolk talking about stuff like that. You're not supposed to be toting a gun."

Emmie smiled, but her gaze was unbreakable. "I'll remind you of that as I'm saving your butt later."

Boris shushed everyone. "Mr. Hayes," he said, speaking slowly to keep his accent in check. "I know this is difficult for you to understand, but we have made our peace with this world. You, it would seem, have much to live for. If you could pretend you didn't know about this meeting, I would suggest you go someplace far away until. . ." —Boris glanced at Emmie— "how do they say it in the Westerns? Oh, yes, until the dust settles. That will be all so much better."

Zeke's gaze hardened. "I'm not leaving. So, either you give me a job to do, or I'll make up one as we go along."

Emmie was shaking her head like she wished this nightmare would end.

Boris swigged the vodka and panted to let the air cool his throat.

Lane knew that she was fast losing control. Resigning any worries she had for Zeke, she decided to assign him a task that would at least keep him away from the potential strike zone. Folding the emptied sack of pastries into a shape that would fit inside the trash can, she glanced again at the phone. Tempted to dial Theo's secure phone number, she bit back the impulse.

She'd call Molly instead. The Women's Federation could stake out the main city center and possibly the route to Harmon.

"All right," Lane said, sounding more confident than she felt. "Here's my plan."

They all moved in closer as she pulled out a sheet of paper and started sketching a map of the major thoroughfares around Longview. Fifteen minutes later, and not without some arguing, the group had agreed to her scheme.

Lane checked her watch. "Let's synchronize and make sure we don't make a mistake simply because we got the time wrong."

Patrick was the only one to not lift his wrist.

"Theo said he was going to network with Wyatt, the local police, and the FBI, so we can't be obvious, as we don't know exactly what he's set in motion." Emmie pushed a strand of hair behind her ear and winked. "But I bet I can find out."

Zeke put his hands in his pockets and rocked back on his heels. "I'll check into the Gregg Hotel and make that my base of operations."

Boris leaned his shoulder into the wall and folded his arms across his barrel chest. "I'm not staying in this rat trap, so give me a task."

"You're staying here for the immediate future, and you'll be on your best behavior," Emmie ordered. "And while you're at it, finish Lane's chores in the shop. Might as well be useful until you're needed."

Lane pinched the bridge of her nose and squeezed her eyelids shut. "I'd almost forgotten, I have my grand opening Tuesday night. There are still books to unpack for the event."

"If you're around to even host the event. If you're not, Theo will sell this shop to the highest bidder." Emmie didn't apologize for her frankness.

Boris's shoulders drooped. "I don't do housework."

Zeke wrapped his arm around Lane's shoulders. "You're shaking. Are you nervous?"

She glanced at him, still unnerved that he was here and willing to put aside his misgivings to help. "Terrified, but don't read anything into my tension. My mind is sharp."

Zeke squeezed her close to his side. "I'm not sure who you are right now, but I like this lady."

Lane grinned. "I'll remind you of that when I asl you to take out the trash and you backtalk me."

"Don't mind me folks." He shuddered like he'd been shocked. "I'm a little turned on right now."

"Optimistic to the end," Emmie droned. "Let's get this show on the road before one of us bails, or gets killed."

Zeke turned his gaze on Emmie. "I wish you'd quit implying that Lane is not going to make it."

Emmie set the pen down carefully, as if treating the instrument with caution was important to making her point. "I watched Roy Mercer learn the ropes of becoming a spy. I saw him at his best, and at his worst. And that was before he'd become a turncoat on his country. I know exactly what that man is capable of doing, and Lane is not even in the same league."

Lane hated that Emmie was right. She had no advantage over Roy in strength, experience, or deviousness, but she had one benefit that he couldn't possibly hope to gain. And she'd use it to the fullest extent.

"So we split up and meet at the Junction Depot at three?" Lane knew that wouldn't give her much time to recruit friends and neighbors to form a grid across Longview, but it would be a good start. Roy couldn't dodge the eagle eyes in this town. "I'll be in the Junction's café with a scarf and dark sunglasses for our check-in. If I don't see you there, you're on your own."

Zeke pursed his lips and shook his head. "I don't feel good about letting you out of my sight."

Patrick stepped forward. "I'll get over to the Wyatts' place and fill them in. The Judge will have his own ideas and he can probably tell me what Colonel Marks is planning, too."

Lane reached her hand to stop Patrick from leaving. "The Judge knows what Roy looks like. He warned me that he was scouring the poker games and gathering information. Give Wyatt full rein to tell anyone and everyone that the man with the cleft in his chin has a price on his head."

Boris stepped up onto the stairs but before climbing he reminded Patrick— "Bring me a gun. I don't trust these women to find me an appropriate weapon."

Patrick nodded, then unlocked the door, glanced both ways down the alley, and disappeared into the busyness.

Lane turned the locks behind him. She leaned against the wood and looked at Emmie. "What do we do about Theo?"

Emmie struck a match and lit the corner of the paper instructions, watching the inked plans turn to ash. "He'll track me down at Lassiter's in about an hour. I'll find out his intentions, and then I may, or may not, tell him ours."

"Why would you not?" Zeke asked with surprise. "It would be foolish to work against him."

Lane almost couldn't believe that Zeke was on Team Theo after the words they'd exchanged last night, but she'd chalk that discrepancy up to the idea that men who practice law were sticklers for authority figures.

Emmie stared at the crumbling paper and dropped the last of it into the trash bin. "He would never agree to putting Lane in the line of fire. Yet she and I both know that it's the only way we'll draw Roy out of hiding. He's selling some bologna about wanting to make things right, that he wants to heal from his mischief, but it's a ruse. And still, it's all we have to work with. If he wants to confess, we'll make it easy for him."

Lane glanced at Zeke. "These operations are more complicated on American soil because of federal laws and local enforcement. Theo is smarter to those policies than we are because we've spent most of our OSS life in Europe." She broke eye contact, feeling weird for clueing him in to the work that had been as intrinsic as breathing less than a year ago. "It might go easier on us all if we ask for forgiveness later, rather than permission."

"As an attorney, I'd advise against that."

Emmie picked up the china and wrapped the linen around the cup, sauce, cutlery, and plate. "And no one really expected you to be a part of this, did we? Since you volunteered, you play by our rules."

Zeke sighed. "It's going to kill me to walk out of this bookshop knowing that a maniac is running around this town and the love of my life is unchaperoned."

Lane leaned on her toes and kissed his cheek. "I know the nooks and crannies of Longview. Lots of places to hide. Lots of people who can be turned against an outsider."

Emmie rubbed the back of her scalp. "I hope Lassiter has a handful of aspirin in that medicine chest. Patrick is going to owe me for this goose egg."

Lane glanced at the collection in Emmie's hand. "You've been to J's house this morning?"

"His apartment over the shop. You probably already know the stairs are near the stockroom. Theo made arrangements for us to stay there and we can take shifts spying on the bookshop. Although I'm feeling so spoiled, I may not ever leave."

Lane clinched her fists, exhausted already from dueling with Emmie. "I'll come over as soon as Boris is secured and you can slip out to get to Harmon and set the stage pieces in order."

"Hang on—" Zeke put his hand on the banister and stared up the stairwell as if tracking Boris's shadow. "You don't trust him to stay put?"

"Not at all. No offense to Patrick, but Boris could have snuck out of here with our measly security measures." Emmie finger-combed her hair around the bump on her head. "But since he stayed, I also have to think he can't resist a chance to claim fame either. If he can get credit for bringing down Mercer, that will go a long way to redeeming his dicey record with the British."

Zeke reached for his fedora on the desk. "This business is bad, and I'm not ashamed to say I'm frightened it will blow up in our faces."

Lane sighed. "That's the same feeling I have on every assignment."

"But you're not supposed to be on assignment, are you?" He turned toward her and looked tortured by a truth. "You had quit. You'd told me you had."

Emmie unlocked the back door, holding the knob in her hand as she glanced over her shoulder. "No one anticipated Mercer coming to America, Hayes. Deal with it or go to Shreveport. It's your choice now."

Lane deserved every wound Zeke wanted to thrust, but she was powerless to stop the need to see justice done for those four French Resistance officers who died because Roy sold his soul to the devil. Principles didn't make a roomy platform, but they'd be strong enough to hold against the winds blowing their way.

Zeke kissed Lane quickly then stopped, as if stung by an electrical current. Hurrying to the door Emmie had opened, he said, "I'm leaving before good sense talks me out of collaborating. But you'd better have an ace up your sleeve like you did that day at the golf course. I want us to have a story to tell our grandchildren."

Chapter Thirty-One

April 24, 1943 11:06 a.m.

Lane hovered at the corner of Tyler and Fredonia Streets, leaning against the wall of the dry goods store as if it were a prop on a stage. Flies swarmed the baskets of flowers displayed by the door, and the fragrance of popcorn wafted from a street vendor's kiosk. The traffic cruising the Tyler Street was too crowded to see who was gathering as the downtown train depot across the park. Not that she expected Roy to hop onto one of the coaches lingering before its departure merely because Emmie attacked him at the Cotton Club last night. He wasn't the type to be intimidated by a bar fight. But employing reconnaissance techniques revved her engine. And she needed to have all her wits sharpened and her brain fully engaged in counter-espionage technique if she was to complete the steps needed to confront Roy and Stuart.

This wasn't the day to analyze how she'd been married to a sociopath, but one day, and it'd be soon, she'd get to the bottom of that mystery and maybe in the process find the peace she needed to move forward.

Lane checked the time on a downtown clock, glanced at the train as it coasted out of the depot, and looked across the street to the Palm Court Tea Room, seeing Molly positioned outside the door watching the shoppers, with Lola holding her elbow for support. Molly had said she'd wave a pink scarf if she saw someone matching Roy's description.

Even from this distance, Lane could tell that her mentor in all things Longview was too ill to be outdoors, but there'd been no talking Molly out of surveillance after the phone call that would set Women's Federation on high alert.

Waldo was positioned at Bank Alley, and he'd recruited other custodians to look out for either of the two men that Lane had identified as armed and dangerous.

Her heart kicked up as foot treads padded against the sidewalk behind her, slowing in approach to her position. She'd surmise that the sound came from thick Moroccan leather, as opposed to the crisper taps made by men wearing boots.

"Hello, J. Happy to see you rather than someone else," Lane said, spinning around to see a tall man wearing black-framed glasses and a finely pressed suit.

"You seemed a million miles away, I didn't want to sneak up on you."

"I have a lot on my mind, but you wouldn't have scared me." She loosened her fingers from the pinch they held on each other as she tried to appear calm. "Did Emmie bring my luggage to your place?"

"Miss Tesco arrived in the shop and said I was to expect you momentarily. Paulo let me know that you'd not arrived, so I came looking for you." He glanced along the busy street to the blue door beyond the bank. "Your shop is closed. Again."

Lane exhaled and tried not to begrudge the untimely dig about her business priorities. "I'm going to ruin my profit projections for this month, aren't I?"

"I think we both know sales are the least of your problems today."

She stole a second glance at J's expression. He was more intuitive than she'd expected. Someone had briefed him. "What did Miss Tesco tell you, exactly?"

He stepped aside as a man pushing a delivery cart crowded the sidewalk. "Colonel Marks mentioned you had personal problems and that you'd not be occupying the bookshop this weekend. Miss Tesco was staying with you to make sure a stalker didn't get close enough to harm you."

She wasn't sure when Theo had spun this tale for J, but he'd not given her the cheat sheet. What else had the spy set in motion, and not told her the details of? With more tourists downtown than she'd expected, the risks for collateral damage felt exponentially increased and Lane added a new worry to her burden for a place that had opened its front door to strangers, and had inadvertently issued an invitation for terrorism too.

"Which is why I find it odd," J gestured to the bus idling at one of the busiest intersections downtown. "That you're standing on the corner—at peak time, no less. Seems like you would have sought solace in the apartment, like Miss Tesco."

Her business professor was so good with reprimands, a ringmaster with a silk whip. But he didn't know she was coordinating a network of informants who all had easy access to the police department. "It's like I said, I have things I need to take care of."

"And taking care of yourself isn't the top priority?"

Lane scrutinized the people stepping off a city bus. There wasn't time to debate the pros and cons of bringing Lassiter into the center of her operation; too many innocent people were already in danger.

"This stalker," she said. "If I were to describe him to you, do you think you could help spread the word to the other shopkeepers, alert them to call the police and have him picked up? I don't know on what charge, but we'll think of something."

J patted her shoulder as if he could remove this burden. "Already done. Colonel Marks gave me a photo that I've passed around. Paulo took it to the alley doors making sure everyone is aware of the man who is causing problems for you. Small business owners take care of each other, and you're one of us now."

Stunned, Lane's voice dropped. "You're too kind."

He tilted his head deferentially. "It was nothing."

"Well, it means the world to me."

A photo. The last time she'd seen Roy was at the military airfield, a veritable walking recruiting poster in his starched Army uniform, million-watt confidence, and a duffel slung over his shoulder—smiling as if the world was his to conquer.

Drained of that similar moxie that she'd tried to copy and carry into every fearful mission, Lane asked, "Do you have that, um, photo? Can I see it?"

J's glasses couldn't shield his surprise. "You don't know what this man looks like?"

Lane swallowed of a rush of saliva that tasted of sorrows, anxiety, and dreams that had never come true. "It's been a while since I've seen him, and I guess I wondered if he'd altered his appearance."

Lane had thought nothing of the kind until this moment. She'd been in such shock when Theo held her hands last night and told her Roy was alive that she'd still pictured him as she'd last seen him—waving good bye from a tarmac.

As J reached into the inner pocket of his suit, Lane held her breath. Would Roy have lost weight from the strain of running traitorous operations? Would he have scars from the torture he'd supposedly endured at the hands of the Germans? Would he wear the mask of a turncoat? Or would he still have the look that beguiled women with no more effort than a twinkle in his eye.

J handed her a photograph, grainy as if taken from a distance and enhanced to focus on one man's face in a crowd. As she took the paper, she wondered if her fingers were shaking or if the photograph were teased by a breeze.

Looking at the shadowy image that had caused her heart to unmoor the first time'd met Roy, a coldness replaced any past notions that she'd thought he was dreamy. Something righteous flared in the remnants of her courage and brought all the pieces of brokenness and shame into a single focus of resolve. He was her enemy.

"Is that the man you were expecting?" J removed his glasses.

Disconcerted that she'd forgotten J was standing there, she rubbed her finger over Roy's face. "Yes, he looks exactly as I remembered."

"Handsome." J took the photo and returned it to his pocket. "That cleft in his chin in distinctive."

"Dangerous," she said, shoring herself to see his shiny blond hair and chiseled good looks in the flesh. "Please exercise as much caution as you can. Believe nothing he says and wear a handgun at all times."

A troop of Boy Scouts marching through the crowd caused Lassiter to step against the dry goods store and allow the line to pass. A shrill whistle resounded from the center of the street, and Lane noted the policeman at the intersection motioning for crowds to cross Tyler Street. She'd talk to him after his shift change.

"Why don't you come back to the store with me?" J glanced again to the intersection and then back to Lane. "You look like you could use a lie down."

There'd be time enough for naps once Roy was neutralized. In the meantime, she was sharpening every tool the OSS had ever taught her to handle—including observation skills.

"Thank you. I'll be there shortly." Lane smiled with a calmness she didn't own. "I have to notify a few more people to be on guard, and then I'll come through the alley to the back door. Tell Paulo to expect three solid knocks. That will be my signal."

J nodded. "If that's the way you want to proceed."

In a moment she'd probably regret later, she decided to be candid about the bookshop's revolving door. "You should know there's a man staying in the apartment over my shop. If you see a large, Russian-looking fellow slinking in and out, just know, he's supposed to be there. For a few days anyway."

"A friend or an enemy?"

Lane glanced to the blue door sharing space with the emptied wheelbarrow. The pot of geraniums had been stolen. "I wish I knew for sure, but I'm going to treat him as a team member for now."

J rubbed his hand along his cleanly shaved jaw. "Lane, what is going on?"

"I can't tell you everything, but I do hope you'll trust me when I say, it's for the best that you don't know the details." She pushed her twitchy fingers into her pockets. "You are protected, if you can honestly say that you don't know."

"I will help you in whichever ways I can."

She looked into the earnest expression, regretting that their friendship put J in peril. "I know you will, which is why I need you to be vigilant about watching for Roy to appear downtown and turn him over to the police the moment you see him. Lay the sandwich board face down on the sidewalk if you've seen Roy, and that will be my clue that he's nearby. Okay?"

J agreed.

Lane needed breathing room from the chaos she was setting in motion. While J was distracted by a former customer who'd stopped to chat with him, Lane tucked in behind a trio of women gossiping about a movie star who was scheduled to attend a film premiere at the Arlyne next week. All thoughts of the Friendly Trek were forgotten for the lure of a bit of Hollywood flash and glamour.

As Lane hurried along the sidewalk, knowing she needed a better observation deck—like maybe the top of the Bramford Building—she sensed someone aiming for her. Ducking into the doorway of the K. Wolen's store, she felt a hand clamp onto her upper arm, pulling her to stop.

"Slow down, lady," a woman squawked.

Lane spun quickly, jerking her elbow to give her freedom and momentum should she need to uppercut the attacker's chin. The face that stared back at her had dark, dewy skin, and wore red lipstick. Sweat rolled down from an oily curl pinned to her scalp.

Like film in a projector, various images flew through her memory, and once they landed on a remembrance of where she'd seen this woman, the breath trapped in her lungs released.

"Miss Carter, what are you doing here?" Lane swallowed the weirdest sense of wrongness. This jazz singer was not on her list of people she expected to encounter today.

Jewel Carter dusted her hands like there was something sticky on Lane's arm. "I can be downtown if I want."

She was too stressed to deal with a tourist. "I wasn't implying anything, just surprised to see you. Now, particularly."

Jewel used a finger to motion Lane closer. "As it turns out, this isn't quite the casual meeting you might suspect."

Lane's lungs closed in again. Hadn't Theo told her that Stuart and Roy had gone to the Cotton Club last night—where Jewel was singing? Like a flashbulb exploding, Lane put Roy's timing and Jewel's arrival together with painful clarity. He'd always needed a helper to accomplish even simple tasks, and women were his default. This singer could be his latest accomplice.

Lane wouldn't wait around to ask. She took off marching, practically skipping, she was moving so fast, and tried to remove herself from the center of town where too many innocents were enjoying a Saturday in the stores.

"Hey, wait up!"

Lane wouldn't linger. If Jewel was the lure to bring her to Roy then the singer would have to catch her first. Hurrying past J's shop, she dodged slower couples and children staring into the candy shop as she aimed for the sweeping lawn of the courthouse.

Jewel wore spiky heels, and Lane heard the tip-tapping clatter keeping up the pace. Glancing back, she saw Jewel hurrying—her purse clutched to her chest. Once they reached the lawn, the thick grass at the Courthouse might be the natural end for a chase begun in high heels.

Lane scanned the sidewalks and lawn, looking toward the giant square belfry at First Presbyterian for her next landmark. If she could dodge between the alleys of the church and businesses, she could better hide from Jewel and whatever plan she was hired to carry out.

A slow-moving bus stalled in front of the courthouse, and Lane had to stop fast to miss crashing into the people filing out to admire the statues and shrubbery in spring bloom.

That warm hand clasped her arm again.

"Wait, I can barely breathe," Jewel huffed as she sank her fingernails into Lane's skin.

With wild energy, Lane glanced at the red-tipped fingernails then up to the eyes that were blinking rapidly to keep perspiration out of her vision. Old men on walkers barricaded her between the bus and her escape from Jewel.

"Judge Wyatt sent me." Jewel wheezed. "And if you make me break my legs in chasing you, he's going to be furious. I've got back-to-back shows tonight."

Trapped, she had no choice but to cooperate for the moment, but that didn't mean she trusted a word the woman spoke.

Lane's gaze darted to the sidewalk in front of the bank, searching the faces for anyone that resembled Roy. "I don't believe you."

Jewel's breathing grew difficult and her other hand fanned her face. "I don't care. Mrs. Wyatt was furious you'd left without saying good bye, and her little peanut of a mother about hit me with a frying pan when I said I wouldn't come find out what had happened to you. So, you better give me a good excuse to take back to them 'cause I'm in the dog house with all three of them if you don't."

Lane processed those words twice before she realized that there wouldn't have been time for Roy to have determined her situation at the Wyatt home and then recruit Jewel to twist the facts. The woman must be genuine, though it went against Lane's instincts to admit that.

"Did they even give you time to drink a cup of coffee before they sent you off on this mission?" Lane pulled her arm free and studied the fine lines around Jewel's eyes, watching for muscle twitches.

"Fool that I am, I didn't think to check that they don't keep coffee in that house before I agreed to stay there. I have to pay good money to the baker every morning if I'm to be clearheaded. And just so you know, I'm up three hours before I like to rise after a late show. For you. So, don't make me run again."

"Thank you for the sacrifice." Lane's breath eased behind her ribs. Jewel was telling the truth. "Why did they send you?"

The bus coughed smog into the air as it pulled away from the curb in front of the courthouse, and Lane led Jewel onto the sidewalk. She still wanted to seek the sanctuary of the Presbyterian church. Those thick walls could keep firepower at bay.

Jewel opened her bag and pulled out a handkerchief. Wiping her brow, she looked down at Lane like she was getting angrier by the minute. "They were worried for your safety. Mrs. Wyatt was sure some man had snatched you from the bed, so imagine her surprise when I tell her that you were walking free-as-you-like around the downtown this morning. Grandma Wyatt was in tears—worried sick—just so you know."

Guilt tightened Lane's throat, but it didn't affect her focus. "I'm sorry. I did leave them a note."

"A note." Jewel's sarcasm was thicker than the humidity. "Well, they didn't find your note so they woke me from sleep and made me come down here to drag you back. They're going to hide you in their church basement."

Lane waited at the curb while automobiles drove through the intersection, searching each driver and desperate to know if Roy had stolen a vehicle and tracked her movements.

"I'm not going back with you."

Jewel followed Lane across the pavement and up the curb to the sidewalk. "Oh, yes you are," she said, huffing as she talked. "That frying pan will come after the both of us."

Lane knew the First Presbyterian side doors were always open, and she ducked behind the shrubbery guarding their sidewalk. Darting toward the entrance, she motioned for Jewel to follow. She wasn't sure if the chapel was going to be filled with worshippers or mothers timing wedding marches, but taking her chances with them was safer than standing on a public sidewalk making plans with a woman who was memorable for so many reasons.

Jewel stopped at the threshold, staring up at the First Presbyterian signage and establishment dates. "I don't know about this."

Lane pulled her into the narrow hall that would lead around to the sanctuary. "Don't go shy on me now."

Knowing that if there were people in the sanctuary, it might get a bit awkward for Jewel, Lane mentally walked through the map of the church in her mind, searching out a quiet corner.

Once they were in the hallway, Lane pulled two folding chairs out from a closet. She collapsed on one and watched Jewel tentatively sit on the edge of the other.

"Level with me," Lane said, wiping her sweaty palms against her pants. "Why would Mrs. Wyatt send you to track me down?"

Jewel's gaze darted around the dark ceiling, the thin lights tucked into wall sconces, and the shiny floor that would usher children going to Sunday school. "It's pretty here."

Lane hadn't spared the décor a second thought. The sanctuary's stained glass was memorable, but they weren't going to have this conversation on those wooden pews. "Not a church goer?"

"Not in a church like this."

Lane nodded, better understanding Jewel's awe. "Sorry, I can't give you a tour but you're in danger if you're seen talking to me, and I don't want to put you on a target."

"I know, it's not so bad in Philadelphia but folks here don't like blacks coming into their churches."

Lane closed her eyes, putting herself in Jewel's high heels for a moment. "That's not what I meant, but you're right. The quicker we get a solution in motion, the quicker we can both go on to do the things we'd rather be doing."

"I'll need a nap."

Lane's body had not more than three hours of sleep, yet she felt capable of scaling mountains. "In the meantime, I'm not going back with you. I don't know what you'll tell Mrs. Wyatt but she knows what sort of danger I'm in and I'm surprised she sent you into the middle of it."

Jewel's gaze dropped to the floorboards. "To be honest, it wasn't Mrs. Wyatt who sent me."

Fear froze her heartbeats. Lane listened to hear if her husband's foot tread was falling behind her. "Jewel?"

Clatter from glass shattering caused Lane and Jewel to both jump, and turn toward the hall. A florist shouted for help as shattered glass, water, and blooms spread across the floor, seeping to the carpet running from the chapel.

Lane gulped fresh air. "Come on. We'll have to get out of here."

Jewel stood, but she was shaky. "Mrs. Wyatt's mother sent me. Said she knew you'd probably snuck out and were off to go looking for the man who was after you." She reached into her purse and pulled out a pistol. "She wanted me to give you this, in case you didn't have a means to protect yourself."

268

Lane looked at the handgun, heard the commotion in the hallway, and knew there'd be a contingent of church wardens in seconds. "Put that back in your purse and we'll leave the same way we came in. Don't pull that out again."

Jewel nodded and followed.

As they hurried the corners and returned to the exit that would lead out to the side yard, Lane cracked the door open and stared out into sunshine, searching for anyone that might be waiting on them to exit.

A cold, metal nose poked into her ribs, and she stilled. Her breath stalled behind her teeth.

Finally, the truth would come out.

Lane didn't move. She wasn't sure if she'd have to bolt or whip Jewel's arm from her socket in the end, but for now she'd wait another second.

"Don't think about leaving." Jewel growled the words in a quiet rage.

Lane hoped this might be the singer's first attempt at shooting someone at close range. Most found the intimacy too daunting to carry out. "You have my full attention," she confessed, plotting how she could hurt the woman and steal the gun.

"We're not going back to the Wyatts'." Jewel shoved the gun deeper against Lane's kidney. "You're going to take me to Patrick, and I'm going to have my conversation with that man. Those Wyatt women can't keep him hidden from me any longer."

Lane's fingers released from the door's ledge, wondering why Mrs. Wyatt didn't foster a reunion between the old lovers. No doubt, she didn't want to be responsible for mixing together crazy and dangerous. "I don't know where he is at the moment."

"Bah," Jewel groaned. "I know he's working for you, so I know you can take me to him. This doesn't have to be complicated."

It was sad that her spontaneous lie invoking a censor to stop this jazz singer was so off base. She should have invented something far more nefarious, now that she realized how badly she'd misjudged the woman she'd met on the Wyatts' front porch. "Is that even Mrs. Wyatt's gun?"

If she kept Jewel talking, it might buy her a moment to figure out how serious that pistol could be in the bigger scheme of things.

"Her little prune of a momma dug it out of a tin of oatmeal this morning, said she was sure you weren't armed and wanted you to have it. But the gun is useful to me at the moment, so you'll do what I want instead. And I want Patrick. That man should never have left Philly without me. Don't know what he was thinking."

Jewel was man hungry.

Lane would hope she also didn't have an itchy finger. "You think I can take you to him? He's not known for predictability."

"I heard those old biddies talking, and they said you got Judge Wyatt wrapped around your finger."

That was a doubtful conversation for another day. At the moment, Lane needed to finish this madness and get back on her schedule for tracking Roy to the ground. "I don't know where Patrick is right now," Lane said with all the significance she could imply. "But I know where he's supposed to be in a few hours."

"All right then." The gun eased off her back. "You tell me where I can see him, and I'll let you go."

Lane would use Jewel's hesitation to her advantage. "Do I get to keep the gun, since the Wyatt women wanted me to have it?"

"No. It's an insurance policy." Jewel stepped back a few inches. "I know you're in trouble and I'll need something to protect myself if things go catawampus."

Since the knife she'd removed from its hiding place in the bookshop's office was limited to close proximity to its victim, Lane would need to acquire that gun. She hoped it was loaded.

She paced her breathing. There wasn't much room in the small hallway to gain speed, so she'd have to count on surprise working its magic. Closing the door against the sunlight, she shifted her weight foot to foot, finding a balance.

"You've been thinking too long. I can tell." Jewel insisted. "Just tell me where can I find my man."

Lane lifted her shoe off the ground, flexed her foot so her toes pointed to the door, and shot her heel into Jewel's kneecap.

The woman cried out in pain and collapsed to the floor. Lane bent down and removed the gun from her slack grip, tucking the pistol into the waistband of her pants.

"Sorry, dear." Lane said, without real sympathy. Friendships didn't grow between the cracks of petty theft and blackmail. "Patrick is going to be too busy this afternoon for a social call."

She opened the door again, sunlight washing over Jewel's pained expression. "I'll tell him we saw each other though, I'm sure he'll be astounded by the lengths you were willing to go to reconnect."

Jewel's hand reached for Lane's ankle.

Dodging the fingers that would have brought her down, Lane stepped over the threshold, smelling honeysuckle growing near the sidewalk.

"But I love Patrick," Jewel moaned.

Lane glanced back to the woman cradling her knee. "Nothing quite says devotion like harassment and abuse."

Jewel whimpered.

"You don't deserve Patrick." Lane stepped into the sunshine. "And friends take care of each other. Which is why I'll do everything in my power to stand between you ever getting close to him again."

Hoping the church wardens found Jewel, Lane hurried from the building and ran along the sidewalk, dodging shoppers until she stopped at the corner looking south on Fredonia. There, a few doors down, was a man wearing a khaki uniform who held his hands cupped around his eyes and leaned against the glass of the bay window, peering into her shop.

A new layer of anxiety bubbled through her bloodstream.

Lane wouldn't swear that soldier was Stuart, but she wouldn't take any chances either. Backing up, she eased into the shoppers and went the long way around toward Center Street, hurrying toward the alley that would lead her to the back entrance for J's shop.

It was time to find out what Emmie had learned from Theo, and if her strings to the OSS were well and fully cut.

Chapter Thirty-Two

April 24, 1943 1:45 p.m.

"Did you eat the sandwiches Paulo left on the table?" Emmie asked Lane as they finished dressing for their various destinations.

Lane nodded and watched the other agent fasten diamonds to her earlobes. "They were tasty and will keep me fueled for a while."

"You're going to need every ounce of energy." Emmie turned away from the mirror. "Are you sure about going through with all of this? It's not going to be pretty, no matter how it ends."

Lane finished packing one of Emmie's special OSS purses, borrowed for the occasion. It boasted a new tape recording device that she had no experience dealing with, but that Emmie thought would be beneficial if Stuart confessed to war crimes. Lane glanced at her black Mary Jane shoes, sure that she looked like a teenager compared to Mata Hari at the mirror.

"As sure as I can be," she said, feeling the full weight of the possibilities for failure. "As long as you promise to get Zeke out of danger, should he decide to follow us to Harmon."

"Hayes is the least of your problems. Theo is the one with his hair set on fire."

Lane sat down on the edge of the sofa, wearier than she'd ever imagined. "Zeke will be my number one priority until my last breath. I know that now."

Emmie smoothed a tissue over her lipstick. "And Theo?"

Lane glanced up, trying to convince the other agent that there was no going back. "I'm grateful you were able to have a heart to heart with him and swear him to our plan, but I'm not sure I can ever see him again. I'm still too hurt by how he dangled me before Roy over these past two years."

"It was a means to an end." Emmie handed Lane a small coil of rope to stuff into the purse. "You shouldn't take it personally."

272

"But Theo was my friend, or I thought he was. Now I know I was just latching on to him because he looked stable. I've been searching for a man I could trust since I learned to walk."

Emmie affixed a bracelet to her wrist that had a homing beacon built into the bauble. "Honey, haven't we all. But let me tell you that Theo meant well by you. I've known him a long time, and he made darn sure you were always kept far out of Roy's reach—until the Beaune incident. That's why he scooped you out at Marseilles and sent you to Texas."

Lane wanted to believe Emmie's endorsement, and maybe one day— with hindsight—she would. But not today. "And yet here is Roy again. In Texas. To finish off the job."

"Yeah, well, Roy was smart enough to knit two endgames into one. Getting his hands on those malaria papers to sell to his contacts, and taking you down once and for all." Emmie grinned. "I'm joking," she said, with lightness. "He's not going to get to you. We're all running interference."

Lane wouldn't laugh. "I've got so much I want to say to Roy, not the least of which is to ask him—why me?"

Emmie brushed her hand through the smoke drifting up from the cigarette balanced on the edge of an ashtray. "Don't waste your breath. He'd not be honest even if you could get him to talk."

Lane stood, and walked to the window overlooking Fredonia Street. She could easily see the front door of the bookshop and the lights of the apartment from one simple angle. So much for her covert safe house. It was as exposed as any other apartment on the street.

"In case I don't get a chance to say it later—" Lane drew in a ragged breath. "Thanks for running interference with Theo and making sure we had his assets trained on Harmon this afternoon."

Emmie walked over to stand next to Lane, her cigarette perched between two fingers. She put it to her lips, drew in a drag, and then released the tainted air, watching the smoke disguise a frame of glass. "I did it for me, as much as I did for you."

Lane didn't glance at Emmie, she'd at least learned that honesty came easier if they weren't looking each other in the eyes.

"I was mad at the way he'd called in the FBI to take over my work," Emmie said. "And I wanted him to know that his 'little women' would prove, once and for all, that we could be counted on when the chips fell."

Lane didn't know the backstory that led to that frustration, but whatever it was, it had worked in her favor. "Regardless, I'll say thanks."

"And regardless, I'll say you'd better not choke." Emmie turned, leaning her shoulder into the windowpane and stared at Lane. "You're going to be shocked when you see Roy. If he lets you see him. So don't let the surprise faze you. Pretend like he's some faceless stranger, otherwise you won't be able to goose him with your stiletto."

Lane nodded, reaching her fingers to graze her sleek knife tucked into the waistband of her OSS-issued pants and imagining how she'd react if Roy played along with this plot.

"I'll do what I can," she said, picturing the man she'd seen in that photograph. "But he holds no real power over me. Not anymore."

Emmie took another drag on her cigarette, blowing it away from Lane's face. "I hope to God you're right about that."

"You'll see my signal at Harmon this afternoon, and you'll know Stuart is booked for the meeting in the chapel. It will give me confidence to stay strong knowing you have my back."

Emmie chuckled. "You sure have shaken off the poor-little-miss routine from when you first came to this town."

Lane hardly recognized herself from the quaking mess of an agent she'd been when she stepped off the Sunshine Special last summer. It would be hard to define the pinches that cracked her, making her wake up from the stupor of grief, but somewhere along the line, she started to stand taller and overcome the bleak wave pummeling her back under the covers most mornings at Molly Kennedy's boarding house.

She drew in a breath, tasting the tobacco from Emmie's cigarette. "All the opposition to the pipeline project and now, Harmon General, has refined me. It's kicked me in the seat of the pants, to be sure."

"And if Theo sends you to Timbuktu after this episode, are you going to stick with the agency?" Emmie glanced at Lane's black top and black pants, as if she approved the trimmer approach to stakeout attire.

Lane ran her hand over her hair, smoothing the stray strands. "I wired Theo my official resignation an hour ago. Once the mess is cleared from Harmon, and depending on if I survive, I'm out. For good this time."

Emmie gasped. "And the safe house?"

Lane glanced toward the window that, beyond the curtains, would have a bird's-eye view on the comings and goings of the bookshop. "If the Longview operation isn't exposed in this process, then yes, I'd give up the bookshop to let someone else run the safe house."

"And Hayes? What are you going to do about the attorney?"

Lane sighed, wishing he'd never walked off that train this morning. She could have met him in Washington or New Jersey with a fake identity and new hair color, and they could have at least picked up a thread of life.

She patted her heart and felt the Wyatts' pistol in the cup of her bra. "When Zeke walked into the bookshop this morning, I felt a love that I didn't know I was capable of. But I'd not be able to live with myself if he took the brunt of Roy's anger and I somehow survived. I guess a part of me hopes he decides this was not the life he signed up for when he asked me to marry him—and locks himself into a hotel room."

"You're sickening, you know that?" Emmie moved over to the table and collected her purse, another OSS-created bag filled with as many tools as

Lane's. "I can't even seem to find one man to like me, and you've got people tripping over themselves to line up for your float parade. I hope you rot."

The chuckle that bubbled out of Lane's throat was as much tension relief as it was hysteria. "Ever the one for understatement."

"Do you not see it?" Emmie propped the purse on her arm like it was a high fashion accessory for a catwalk. "Patrick, and Boris, and, I'd throw J Lassiter into the mix too. They are bending over backwards to help you because somehow you've wheedled your way into the center of their worlds. You've built a network of support in this town, and that's not the way it's done in the O.S.S. We're lone operators."

Lane had to overcome huge misgivings to open herself to friendship. But that's the part of the civilian life that had become a beacon for her. And, if she had to be relocated to someplace new, it was the lesson of Longview she wanted to repeat.

Steeling her tongue so she didn't tease another battle with Emmie, she remembered that their stress levels were already at a maximum, and it was time to leave.

"This day is about Roy and his sickness with power. He's the central figure in this tragedy, not me." Lane's legs were jumpy, like she needed a track to run. She moved away from the window. "And if you're half the woman I know that you are, you'll forget you ever said that to me. This isn't a popularity contest. It's about right over wrong. That's why we're going to go out there and we will defy the odds. We—you and me—are going to outwit one of the best OSS agents on the planet."

Emmie's color had faded. "Roy isn't that smart."

"I was talking about Theo!"

Emmie backed up a bit, startled by Lane's ire. "Okay, him too."

Lane marched across the room, spritzed herself with some of Emmie's expensive perfume, and then turned toward the doorway. Before she put her hand on the doorknob, she whipped around and pointed her finger toward the agent. "You're in charge of Wyatt's men and Zeke, and if they don't show at the depot by three, you come to Harmon without them. Do you hear me? I'm trusting you, Mary Magdalene. Do not let me down."

Emmie saluted. "Yes, ma'am."

Lane stood at the door to J's apartment, wavering before she left to begin the assignment they'd decided was the only way to solve the problem of Roy Mercer.

"I'm afraid," she murmured into the wood panel.

In a voice as quiet as Lane's, Emmie replied, "I am too."

Lane turned slightly, the light from the lamps casting the room in a hazy yellow glow that made the elegant surroundings so comfortable and welcoming, like a tea party was planned for the afternoon, not a coup to overthrow an assassin.

"If we're not successful—"

Emmie interrupted. "Balderdash! You stop that foolish thinking this minute."

Lane blinked as Emmie marched across the remaining space, her black suit a fashion statement for female agents still hoping there was glamour in this business.

"You are going to follow through on these plans," Emmie announced. "I'm going to corral those Wyatt men, Zeke, and Boris, too if he'll let me, and this will work."

"They don't really know what they're dealing with in Roy, do they?"

Emmie swiped a strand of hair off her cheek. "None of us knows what we're dealing with. Roy is deranged. I saw that in his eyes last night."

Lane shuddered. "I guess we all are, to even think of going after him?"

"Bah!" Emmie turned around and searched under one of the chairs for her shoes. "That's the problem with you, Mercer. You're too sensitive. Stop overthinking things and do your job." Coming up with a black pump, Emmie shoved it over her heel. "If you want to have a moment around the campfire when this is all over, fine. Have a party. I will be long gone."

"You're leaving Longview?"

"It's my hope that this sweep that scoops up Roy will also implicate Dr. Death, and we can get a two-for-one discount with those senators that would criticize our methods."

"Is setting this scene at Harmon going to mess up your plans?" Lane asked, regretting she'd not thought through the implications earlier.

Emmie polished her ruby ring on her skirt. "I'm not going to worry about those details, or who gets the credit, right now. If we can get the job done and Roy's accomplice at Harmon is outed, that's enough for me."

That didn't sound genuine from the woman who'd wanted praise for buttering the bread when they'd shared kitchen chores at Molly's boarding house. "I'm sorry. For getting in your way and maybe derailing your plans to capture your target."

Emmie glanced up, her gaze free of the usual insincerity. "It will all work out."

"But—"

"I said, don't worry about it. You get Stuart and Roy in through the front door, I'll take care of them at the back door." Emmie walked around Lane. "So, get out of here and tell Molly Kennedy to go back home. She has no business being out on the streets."

"Emmie—"

"I swear, if you speak again, I'll have to hurt you."

Lane's lips lifted in what was some semblance of a smile. But she waved goodbye instead of speaking and moved over the threshold. Stepping on the treads of J's stairwell, she hoped she'd always remember that there had once been a moment when they weren't at each other's throats.

Standing in the haberdasher's stockroom, Lane glanced to her left and heard voices of customers debating suit details. She wished J a day of big sales and turned for the back door.

Paulo, J's butler, stood near the door, holding a silver tray bearing a snifter of brown liquid and an ash tray for a cigar. "Leaving for the afternoon?" he asked.

She might be leaving for life, she thought. "Off to the races, as they say."

And because she didn't know what was ahead, she propped the OSS's purse into the crook of her elbow, took the glass off Paulo's tray, and tossed the beverage down the back of her throat. The scald of smoky bourbon gave her a kick that was both medicinal and a benediction.

"Thank you," she said, replacing the glass as if he'd intended the drink for her all along.

"Godspeed, Mrs. Mercer." He nodded with a priest's certainty. "You're going to need it."

Chapter Thirty-Three

April 24, 1943 2:20 p.m.

The chugging sluggishness of the train leaving the station acted like a gong on Big Ben. Lane folded the newspaper closed, approached the phone booth near the depot platform, and closed the glass panel around her. The relative silence of the booth contrasted with the busyness of the travelers wandering away from the downtown train station.

She gave the platform one final sweep, and dropped coins into the meter, dialing the rotary for the number at the Campbell's boarding house. Her stomach clenched into a knitter's ball of yarn.

She hoped everyone was where they needed to be, and that her aunt and uncle had made it to the lake house safely.

Only a few stragglers remained as the 2:10 train had left the station. Still, she gripped the handset with a force, trying to control her breaths so she wouldn't sound unnatural when she spoke into the receiver.

After telling the housemother she was calling for Dr. Lemming, Lane waited, thinking through the last of her steps before she was due at Harmon. Her tension was doubly increased because Zeke had proven he wasn't the type of man to stay in a hotel room while his fiancé was gearing up for a face off with a spy. Molly had reported that Zeke had bought her a cold Coca-Cola and flirted with Lola. Lane would have to hope he was really on his way to the FBI's stronghold at Harmon, since he'd told Molly that he was heading to the hospital to look up one of his law school buddies. Something she knew he'd already done.

"Hello, Lane?"

Snapped back to the moment by Stuart's cultured voice, she swallowed and tried to sound like any friend dialing in on a Saturday. "Sorry it's taken me forever to get in touch with you, but I have been swamped at the shop. You wouldn't believe what I've been up to."

"Don't apologize. My world has flipped upside down too." His voice was nasally and muffled, like cotton was inserted in his nose. "But I've been desperate to talk to you. The most outrageous thing has happened, and I have to see you. Today, if we can. Really, it's shocking, and you're not going to believe me when I tell you the story."

Lane watched a woman, who looked very much like the Mrs. Robertson she'd met on Sunday, peruse the departure schedule for the next southbound train.

"You sound sick," Lane said, imagining his face with a broken nose. "Do you have a cold?"

Stuart's pause was a heartbeat too long. "I, uh, have a broken nose. An unfortunate accident from last night."

"We can try again another time, if you're unwell. . ."

"Timing is of the essence, Lane. I need to see you immediately."

She glanced at her watch, hoping he'd want to meet when she wanted to meet. "I'm terribly busy today."

"Lane, please. You don't understand. This is really a matter of urgency."

She wasn't going to have to lie about having an old photo after all. "Well, I guess I could meet you this afternoon. I'm dropping off books at Harmon about four. Can I catch you at the hospital? Maybe grab a cup of coffee at the cafeteria?"

"No, that won't work at all. I need to talk to you some place private."

She double-checked the hospital map Emmie had drawn for her. "Well, how about the chapel? I hear it's lovely, and I've never seen it."

"The chapel at Harmon?" Stuart paused and coughed, like blood and phlegm were clogging his throat. "Yes, that just might work."

"Perfect," she cooed. "Say about 3:45, if the buses run on time."

"I should be able to make that."

Her fingers were icy, but she gripped the handset as if she had the strength to break it in two. "We have so much to catch up on, and I'll look forward to your story, too."

Lane hung the receiver on the handle before he could say goodbye. There was a man waiting for the phone booth, and she side-stepped him as she left the partition opened behind her.

Would Stuart bring Roy to Harmon, or would they go somewhere clandestine to meet him after the good doctor confessed his role in the treachery? There were too many variables for her to plan every step, but she was going to hope that Emmie roped in her MP buddies and Wyatt's men to stand sentry around the chapel.

Upcoming train departures were announced and a man refilling the newspaper stand with afternoon editions called out headlines to her.

Stepping into the sunshine, she walked to the curb and raised her arm to flag a cab. Feeling a degree of anonymity in the crowds, she scanned the streets one last time to see if there was anyone watching her who would wreck her calm. Nothing seemed unusual save a skinny white woman and her black maid who were sitting under the shade of an oak tree sipping Coca-Colas. Lane waved at them. Molly winked in return.

She slid into the backseat of the taxi and gave the address for the Junction. As the driver pulled away, she stared out the window, watching the habits of those lingering along the south end of Fredonia Street. She worried for the innocent bystanders.

There were pits in her stomach, thinking about the danger Zeke and Patrick would walk into, and they had no prior training for dealing with the potential trauma. She squeezed her eyelids together hoping that they'd not have reason to be scarred by today.

"You're mighty quiet, miss."

Lane caught the cab driver's gaze in the rearview mirror. "Just thinking about a golfer I know, hoping he gets a good round in soon."

"Perfect day for playing," the driver said, replacing his attention back on the road. "Wish I didn't have to work."

So did she—she'd be willing to walk any back nine Zeke chose if it meant she didn't have to go through with this fishing expedition.

The shops and businesses along Cotton Street passed in a blur and she wondered where Roy was hiding. He wouldn't be at Stuart's boarding house—that would raise too many questions—but that didn't mean he wasn't close by. The homes south of Cotton Street were addresses of some of the deepest pockets in Longview and if his tastes were the same as she remembered, he'd be drawn to the bright lights of homes with amenities.

Roy had coveted the prestigious neighborhoods in Washington, D.C., and she'd bet he'd never lost the hunger to have one of those addresses for himself. She turned on the seat and looked down Green Street as they passed through the intersection. Poker games, Judge Wyatt had told her. Roy had been surfing the private games and speakeasies. How had he gotten through closed doors so fast?

The cover charge alone would have taken money, and lots of it.

The announcer on the cab's radio was a KFRO regular, and he was broadcasting baseball statistics from area colleges. She let her mind wander back to where Roy might hide, and how he'd defined himself. Had he played off Stuart's role as a physician? Was he wearing a uniform?

The driver turned left at the intersection with Mobberly and nearly cutoff a truck as he made the quick right for the Junction Depot. Not as many people filled the covered patio as on a weekday, but every bench was claimed by luggage, children, or in one case, a cage that seemed to be stuffed with squawking chickens.

Lane paid the fare, put aside her thoughts of Roy's disguise for the moment, and studied the prospects for meeting Patrick and Boris in the café. Her watch showed she was early, and she decided to take cover inside the Mobberly Hotel's entrance area. Glancing up to the striped awning, she wondered if Roy had checked in to the popular hotel under an assumed name—better able to watch the comings and goings of people and still have a short commute to Harmon General.

Removing her sunglasses, she reached into the purse and pulled out a scarf. Turning around to face the brick wall, she fitted the floral silk over her hair and tied it behind her neck, a nod to fashion, coolness, and secretiveness. Replacing the sunglasses, she hoped that if Roy were watching the depot, he'd not recognize her. She wasn't keyed up for a confrontation yet. She needed to know her team was in place first.

A cab idled near the depot, and she watched a large Russian emerge from the backseat. Here was the first test. Would Boris run? He clutched a satchel in one hand and his hat in the other. As the taxi pulled away, she saw him survey the drive before stepping up to the platform. He disappeared behind the rail station doors.

Lane rose from the bench.

As she crossed the street, she hurried ahead of an automobile and skipped up the steps to the station doors. Reaching for the handle, a hand wrapped around her wrist and stopped her from entering.

"What in God's name are you doing?" Theo hissed in her ear.

Lane gathered her wits, stunned that she'd not sensed his approach. "I'm shopping. For a new employer."

He tugged her arm again, forcing her to turn toward him. "You've just set free one of the most notorious double agents in this war."

"Have I?" She spun her gaze to his leaden face. "Then we have two of those types running around Longview. How did that happen, Colonel Marks?"

Stung, he let her arm go. "I can't believe you released Boris. That's treason."

Lane pulled the handle of the Junction's door, relieved to disappear among the crowds and clatter of travelers. To her left, the directional arrow blinked on and off, advertising the Western Union telegram office. The opposite direction was the café where she hoped to find Boris waiting at a table.

She ignored the man trailing her across the marbled floor.

Once inside the café, she pinpointed an open table near a window overlooking the train's departure platform, but there was no known Russian waiting in the room. She scanned the shoulders of those at the bar top—he wasn't there either.

A fissure broke through her calm and chunks of her master plan crumbled to the black and white floor. With an energy she didn't label, she moved toward the table near the window.

Theo pulled the other chair across from her and sat down too.

"If you're going to be a nuisance," Lane growled, "I'll take a cup of coffee, black, two sugars."

"You don't drink sugar in your coffee. Who is the cup for? Lemming?"

Lane set her purse in her lap and glanced through the window. "Lovely day, isn't it? The tourists got a perfect week of spring for their efforts."

Theo tapped his fingertips into the table top. "Don't do this, Lane."

She met his gaze across the menu propped into the napkin holder. "What would you have me do? Wait on you to save me? Sorry, Colonel. I'm saving myself."

He groaned. "Between Boris and Roy, you're a marked woman."

"I wonder if you aren't my worst danger. At least with them, I know who they are, what motivates them. You? I'm not so sure."

Theo stared as if he could communicate volumes of information without batting an eyelash.

"I'm immune to you, Colonel Marks." Lane meant it too. "You had your chance to tell me the truth too many times for me to swoon now because you're worried my husband has found me."

"You don't know what you're saying."

"Of course, I don't. I'm a trusting, naïve girl you wrapped around a patriotic flag pole." Two years of confidence and skill had been reduced to a post script on a much bigger plot. "I put myself in uncountable layers of danger because you directed my movements, and you couldn't tell me the truth about Roy?"

"A matter of national security."

Her lips stretched with cool indifference. "Well, let that be your comfort. You held company policy until the very end."

Theo pushed back in the chair. "I can't protect you if you go off half-cocked."

"How about cocked? I have a team."

"And they are—" Theo waved his arm toward the tables filled with tourists. "Where? You're sitting here like a candle burning in the dark."

"Please don't insult my intelligence." Lane knew that without Boris, her strategy at Harmon was compromised. She glanced at Theo's suit— crumpled during the last twenty-four hours of crisscrossing Longview. "You were really only ever after Roy. I'm just fulfilling the mission of my recruitment. Lead him to you, and you'll take care of the messy details, right?"

Theo glared. "Then I guess we've said all we need to say."

"I guess we have."

Lane watched him rise from the chair and disappear into a gaggle of teenagers considering the café's chalkboard specials.

She blew out a strangled breath.

A waiter delivered a cup of coffee to her table. "Coffee with cream and sugar?"

Lane felt a measure of relief that the server wore an eyepatch. She'd not been entirely abandoned.

"Wyatt said that he's not going to get involved in your domestic dispute." Patrick set the cup and saucer near her hand. "He has his limits."

Lane moved the cup nearer the napkin dispenser so it would be the signal she'd promised Boris. "But—"

Patrick grimaced. "Wish I had better news." He held the serving tray carefully as he set a sugar and creamer on the table too. "I'll be at Harmon by four and I think Arnold will go with me. He's already on the schedule for the ambulance this afternoon; that made it easier to rope him in."

Lane put a few coins on the tray and leaned back in the chair.

Patrick backed away from the table.

Checking the immediate vicinity to see if anyone was studying her, Lane flew through curses, chasing chinks her scheme was taking on. She played with the sugar dispenser as if she had full intentions to drink the coffee, but couldn't fixate on the task for the slew of new worries.

She didn't have Boris. She didn't have Wyatt's army. And she'd just insulted the man who—with one phone call—could have called in the Texas Rangers.

But as she'd learned in past missions, when a plan falls apart, you create a new plan. Her assets list included Emmie, Zeke, and Patrick. And she had no way to let them know that a significant portion of their firepower had vanished. She'd have to hope they were able to wing it.

Lane watched children squabbling over a biscuit; the mother resolved the dispute by tearing it in half and giving each child a portion. Maybe she was too close to the problem? She wasn't seeing the right solution, because she needed someone at a higher elevation to tell her what to do. That would have been Theo. But he was working his own plan.

She pushed back the chair and stood.

Glancing through the window, she saw where a ray of sunlight was illuminating dandelions growing in the cracks of the platform. Something so incredibly delicate enduring the shoes, wheels, and energy of traffic. She watched the weeds bend and blow, seemingly dodging the obstacles with ease.

There was a lesson in those dandelions, if only her mind could solve the riddle.

A train's whistle blew as the rumbling of the building heralded a new arrival. She watched the station master step onto the platform, his pocket watch held in his hand as the train cruised into the station.

That might be the train Boris planned to hop in his bid to disappear.

Tucking her purse close to her ribs, Lane walked out of the café, pulled the sunglasses over her eyes, and headed toward the patio on the other side of the ticketing area. She'd never intended to take a bus to Harmon, but she'd thrown that out to Stuart in case Roy was planning to follow.

Trailing the line of those waiting for a taxi, she raised her arm and signaled that she had one fare. A traffic director whistled at her, waving her toward a vehicle waiting on the far side of the drive.

Climbing into the cab's backseat, she announced the direction as Harmon General about the same time a man shoved her from behind and announced he'd share the fare. Lane righted herself on the bench, worried that she'd underestimated that someone was following her within the depot, and turned to see Boris's broad face sweating with a perspiration that bordered on clinical.

"I'm going that way to check on a friend of mine," he said with a flat American accent. "Drop me off at the PX, will 'ya, buddy?"

Lane stared a hole into his profile, willing him to communicate with her. He'd upended the agenda too.

Changed the plans to suit his purposes. And he was ignoring her.

"You can drop me at the PX, too, driver," she said through a clenched jaw.

With a nod, the driver took off and blended into the traffic going south on Mobberly Avenue.

Staring straight ahead, she was grateful that Boris hadn't slid out of town on the train, but she wasn't sure what had transpired to make him go off script—and clearly, she couldn't ask him, for the nosiness of the cab driver. As the business district faded into residential, Lane beat the last details of the scheme into her memory.

"Hey, mister," she asked Boris. "You got the time?"

He pushed back his sleeve and turned his wrist so she could see the watch. "You late for a meeting or something?" he asked, not looking her in the eye.

"Not yet, but I'm cutting it close."

Boris was supposed to be at the chapel ahead of her so that he was already in place when she arrived to meet Stuart. She hoped that sweat-soaked wad of paper in his hand was the map Emmie had provided him and that he planned on sprinting ahead to the chapel when the cab pulled to a stop.

As the cabbie showed his ID to the gate guard at the hospital's entrance, they pulled into a courtyard that fanned out to encircle the massive complex. Slowing to the posted speed, the driver stopped for nurses pushing soldiers in wheelchairs across the street, and later for a group of Gray Ladies carrying baskets laden with goodies.

Lane's nerves were squeezing her windpipe closed. She coughed to relieve the pressure.

Boris said, as if in reflex, "Gesundheit."

The cab jockeyed for a position in the drop-off area for the post exchange. Boris handed the driver coins, before he shoved his shoulder against the door. Lane checked her watch and knew she had ten minutes until she had to be at the chapel. Paying her fare, she stepped into the welcome breeze blowing over the base and said a prayer that the same Being that protected that dandelion at the Junction would protect her, too.

Boris had blended into a foursome of people moving toward the PX. With that, she had to assume, that sprinting to the chapel was not his first priority.

She pinched her fingers together to relieve the stress of imagining that maybe Boris was going after Roy himself—either to warn him of the trap or kill him before he caught up with Stuart Lemming.

Channeling anxiety into her footsteps, Lane tucked her purse close to her ribs and followed the memorized turns of Emmie's map. There was nothing she could do to rope Boris back in, not with a timeclock ticking.

Surveying the grounds, Lane nodded to a soldier with an eye patch, as she turned on the sidewalk following the marker for the chapel. Being on this campus brought back a flood of information Emmie had shared over the last few months. The barracks seemed like file folders crammed into a cabinet, all bursting with stories and developments infinitely important to the work of medicine and recovery, but none of the facts meshed with the arrival of Roy Mercer. Maybe her husband was in cahoots with the Dr. Death character. Was that why Emmie seemed like she'd been stung with a cattle prod?

Lane paused, adjusted her sunglasses, hoping that the villain wasn't Stuart. It couldn't be, could it?

It was bad enough that she'd misjudged the man she'd married; misjudging one of her best friends would kill what remained of her spirit. How could she be so gifted in her academy tests and miss identifying two men so incredibly close to her?

She swallowed the dryness in her throat, knowing that this was not her problem to solve. First, she had to convince Stuart that she was stunned by the news of Roy's return, and then, secondly, have him lead her to her husband—hopefully without leaving the Army base.

The need to hear Roy confess was stronger than almost any desire she'd ever felt. Churning her tension into energy, she controlled her steps and hoped that if anyone noticed her, they'd think she was a family member coming to visit a soldier.

The white clapboard siding and narrow steeple drew her eye like a magnet. Maybe she wouldn't be alone with Stuart. Boris was supposed to be praying like a penitent, and based on the bulletin board announcing the chapel schedule, there would be a musician who'd be giving a piano recital at five in the afternoon. Could she be lucky enough to have a large group of witnesses?

She hoped not.

If things turned desperate, she'd have a hard time distracting Stuart—or Roy, for that matter—away from the notion of taking hostages.

Lane's heart rate kicked into high gear and she glanced around the parking lot, looking for a Wyatt's Ambulance. There were a few vehicles and an Army bus.

Dread pooled in her stomach.

Arnold might have had a problem driving on post after all. Lane climbed the shallow steps, surveying the industrious post one last time, hoping that Boris had made it here. Seeing soldiers hobbling over the grounds and nurses pushing wheelchairs brought home the danger she'd set in motion with that phone call to Stuart.

None of the men in uniform looked like Theo's counterparts in the FBI either.

Standing on the stoop, she watched the last vestiges of her plan curl up in ash. Something, somewhere, had gone badly wrong. She couldn't put her finger on it, but sensing that her backup support was gone was the first clue that other elements had unraveled too.

The white and pink petunias in the urns beside the chapel doors seemed to wave and cheer her on. Her fingers grazed the petals as she dropped her scarf into the planter. If Emmie saw the wildly colored silk, she'd know Lane had walked inside.

Winding her fingers around the brass handle, Lane hoped there was borrowed strength in the iron, she'd need every ounce of it. Quaking a bit, she drew in a breath and let the oxygen move through her lungs unfettered by fear.

She was doing the right thing, for the right reasons, but she was just doing it alone.

Pulling the door open as quietly as if it had been laced with grenades, she adjusted to the calm offered by a chapel built to redirect soldiers from their pain to their higher calling.

A scent of beeswax polish rushed forward, as well as a cooler temperature, courtesy of the high ceilings and shadowed space.

Lane removed her sunglasses and stepped quietly onto the wood floor that echoed the pianist's rehearsal efforts. Fluffing her hair, she took a moment to study her surroundings as the door whispered shut. Seeing nothing amiss in the narthex, she eased toward the double doors propped open to reveal the sanctuary.

Hammering melodies that sounded a bit like a Bach concerto reverberated off the walls as a dark-headed man teased complex notes from the piano in the far-left corner of the chapel. Pews and iron chandeliers were the only adornments to a ceiling braced by roughhewn beams. A witness would keep things calmer, she thought. Stuart wouldn't manhandle her in a room if there was a musician who could identify him later.

Her gaze swept the altar area, but the Russian, who was to have been praying for forgiveness, was not on his knees. Or anywhere else that she could see. Lane ground her molars. It had been foolish to hope Boris would have slipped into the chapel from another entrance. When Stuart arrived, he'd not recognize the double-agent, should Boris walk in—most likely, the large man would be dismissed as another of the more than hundreds of guests allowed on post during the weekends.

The music soothed her and, like a kite caught in the wind, she let go of the anger for Boris and his unpredictable behavior. There was nothing she could do anyway.

Scooting toward a pew about halfway between the rear of the room and the pianist, she eased onto the cushion so as not to disturb the man concentrating on sheet music. Her fingers released the catch on the purse so she could reach inside and set the switch that operated the tape recorder built into the base of the purse. Placing the sunglasses on top of the handcuffs inside, she listened for the next bar of music.

Silence.

Glancing to the piano, Lane watched the man's hunched shoulders straighten, wondering if he would launch into another Bach piece or drill through practice measures for his recital. When he didn't do either, a strange echo, repeating of frenzied breathing and energy, circled around her in the stillness like an otherworldly net swirling in smaller and smaller measures until it had her in its grip.

Her fingers stilled over her purse.

A flash from her childhood—when her stepfather hunted for her with a whip in his hand and she'd hide from him under the sink cabinet—came back to shake her spirit. With no effort at all, she was thrust back to the cabin in Macon and the fear she'd never be allowed to leave there.

Evil had a scent that couldn't be disguised, and for her it would always reek of mildew. Even though muted sunshine glowed through the windows, a decay—something that resonated of bones and wet moss—floated on the dust motes. She could feel her throat close up, s it would when she was eleven and petrified that Delia's husband would whip more lashes into her thighs for making him hunt through the house looking for her.

She ran her tongue over her teeth, teasing her voice back from that grave. Delia and Darol were both long gone. They couldn't punish her for leaving the lights on, the jelly jar opened, or telling the mailman that Darol lost his job again.

The pianist jammed the keys of several chords in a chaotic ode to anger. His shoulders spiked and he repeated the frenzied punch of notes that made no sense. The reprise of madness, after his last display, seemed to make the walls blanch.

Before the musician turned on the bench, she knew that Roy Mercer had never told her he could play the piano. There was a growing list of things she didn't know about the man she'd married, but the dark hair dye and affinity for the ivories was the least important of them.

"Hello, my dear," Roy spoke as he spun his legs around the wooden bench. He wore a twisted grin that spoke of thoughts best left to the nether world—a place she would have sworn he knew well. Had he still been dead.

A million thoughts flew at her, but no words settled on her tongue. She couldn't even work a response to his outrageous greeting. What did one say to a man believed buried? Small talk felt so feeble when she wanted to unleash a torrent of emotion and a list of questions to justify every tear she'd wasted on him. Still, words lay fallow in her throat. As if that eleven-year-old had wrapped a hand over her lips reminding her not to taunt the monster.

Lane stared, astonished by the changes that wickedness had worked into Roy's face, his carriage, even his voice. He was a desiccated version of his former gorgeousness.

"Shocked speechless, are you?" Roy rose from the seat and made his way around the pews closest to the piano. Diffused window light gave him the advantage of a shadowy approach, a cloak for someone with no soul.

"Stuart swore you didn't know I was alive, and I guess your stunned expression proves he was telling the truth—at least about this."

Lane watched Roy's stealth with the same caution she'd use when a panther stalked its prey. Though her nerves bounced like kettle corn at a carnival, she was careful to keep her expression impassive. Her movements frozen. Her breath held captive in her windpipe.

If he knew she was wary, he'd pounce.

Stopping one row short of her perch, Roy slid onto the cushion and curved his posture so that his back was to the pulpit, his arm stretched along the pew, his gaze leveled to her eyes.

She cut her eyes to the piano as if this person could not be the man who'd played Bach. The Roy she knew had been too busy jockeying his way up the chain of command to ever slow down enough to learn complicated musical patterns by memory.

Fast, so she wouldn't be scalded, she glanced again at his face, surprised that he sat so still, but he was anything but silent. His gaze seemed to peel from her every layer of clothing she'd chosen for a mission. She was sure he licked his lips.

Though she wanted to rebuff him, deny his right to claim anything from her, arguments were lost in the folds of her soul. She'd been rendered mute.

Lane hurried through a survey of his body. Not searching his muscles with a lover's anticipation, but instead for the shape of a timed bomb or a bazooka hidden under his lapel—anything that might reveal his real intent. This prelude was only one of the many tortures he would have planned for her. God only knows what would have happened to Stuart.

Beside the gauntness of Roy's cheeks, there were a bracelet of scars wrapped around his wrists and the casing of his skeletal fingers bore the pallor of a man long denied nourishment. The photo J had showed her must have been during healthier days because his hair had thinned—and was dyed midnight for disguise—but his shoulders poked through his suitcoat as if he'd lost his appetite for food.

But then demons didn't really eat cake, did they?

"You look good—great actually." Roy's voice rattled, but the agedness didn't take away from his awe. "The years have treated you better than they've treated me. I like what you've done with your hair. I wonder if it's as soft as I remember?"

Lane flinched, as if afraid he'd try to touch her hair.

Calming her nerves, she would guess Roy knew exactly what those years entailed, since he'd have studied her whereabouts in order to sabotage the mission in Beaune. Shivering as if someone had left the door open in a snowstorm, she ignored the tremble in her bones to think through the schemes he would have planned for today. Clearly, Stuart and Roy had laid a trap for her and she was the foolish one to have walked right into the chapel thinking she was the one in control.

There wasn't time to nurse the irony. She needed to plot an escape.

"Oh, for God's sake, say something." Roy slammed his palm against the back of the pew. "I know it must be killing you to sit there and see me when you expected me to be decaying under a headstone."

She stared at his chin—the cleft appearing bottomless by a scarcity of tone not welcomed on a man who'd once bragged about his prowess as an athlete. Instead of pondering the incongruities of Roy's health, she'd honor the faces of the men in the French Resistance who'd trusted her to transport them to the new underground tunnel. They felt more real to her than the ghost of a man she'd once loved.

"You were always the worst conversationalist," Roy spat. "Young and dumb, you could do nothing more than gawk at all the socialites at the dinner parties—sitting around a table and being a little sponge. Stuart thought that meant you were a great listener. I thought it meant you had the intelligence of a grade school girl."

Lane hoped he still felt she was that naïve. It would make a coup so much more of a surprise.

Using her thigh, she pushed the end of the purse with the microphone closer to the edge of the cushion. Better for recording his low-pitched threats.

"Don't you want to know how I found you?" Roy looked at his fingernails like he had a script embedded on the bones. "I'm sure you're just dying to know how I tracked you all across France to end up here, in Nowheresville, U.S.A."

She watched a bead of sweat drip down the side of Roy's temple, landing in the inner circle of his ear.

He must be anxious.

Her mind leapt through hoops, anticipating how she could use this information.

"But no, if you're not going to play along, I won't indulge you." He sighed with a breath scented of whiskey and withdrew his arm from the pew. "I can see that despite you looking all grown up, you're still that pitiful girl wearing hand-me-down clothes. And the rude thing is, you haven't even asked me how I am. Not very Southern of you, Mrs. Mercer."

Lane resisted his baiting. If he was insulting her, he was playing a game for which he was the only one with the rulebook. She glanced along the perimeter of the altar area looking for Stuart, and dare she hope—Boris. Neither man had entered. She was as alone with Roy as she'd been on their wedding night.

Lane fingered her waist, finding the opening that would give access to the stiletto.

Roy whipped a pistol from inside his suit and aimed it at her forehead. "You're boring me, wife," he said, standing. "After all you've done to ruin my career, I should have shot you the moment you walked through that door. No one takes down a spy without paying a price for it."

Lane's mind whirled with the memory of Theo's confession last night. He'd said Roy was obsessed with her because he believed she'd sold him out to the agency in a fit of jealous pique. None of that was true, almost the opposite, but Roy believed it and no matter how much she protested, he wasn't going to change his mind. Theo had said that Roy blamed Lane, and Emmie for that matter. They were both his scapegoats for denying the truth that he'd compromised himself with botched operations.

The delusions had sounded so frail in the middle of the night, but looking into the gaze of a madman today, she found the story believable. One thing she had known about her husband—he never, ever accepted blame. Not for missing the train schedules, not for bringing too little money to pay for drinks, and certainly not for failing to communicate his plans to her. She'd learned fast that it was easier to accept the fault than fight for the truth.

But not anymore. She was done being Roy's victim. If he didn't pull that trigger first, she'd find a way to turn the gun on him.

His eyes, once so quick to charm, narrowed with censure. "You didn't even grieve me, did you, little wife. You just moved in with Theo and became his pet. Did you think I wouldn't see you with him while you paraded across Belgium, posing as his wife? What a phony ploy. As if Theo, with all the women he's had, would ever be interested in Delia's little bastard."

Stung by how casually he'd turn her intimate confidences into knifepoints, Lane focused instead on how he would have tracked her, and why he'd kept at it for two long years? Why not snatch her early in her career—why wait until Beaune?

Unless he was lying about that too.

Maybe Roy wasn't as good at tracking as he'd wanted her to believe. Maybe he'd lost her scent. She'd embedded herself with the French Resistance, and he'd lost her in the maze of families, secret passages, and private meeting places.

He cocked the gun. "You were compromised weeks before the truck bomb. Not by me, but by one of the girls the Germans picked up. She's the one that outed you. And then they hauled me out of my prison cell and set me up to kill you and destroy the underground network. Wasn't that mean of them? To taunt me that I couldn't even kill my own wife."

Roy Mercer was long past rational thinking. He was bent on revenge, and she was the center of the bullseye. It was a wonder he didn't shoot her now. But then, as she well knew, sociopaths enjoyed toying with their victims. Another lesson learned courtesy of Delia's rotten husband.

"You've got that blank expression, Louisa Jane. I bet that doe-eyed look has fooled a lot of men, but it doesn't work on me. I had no idea you'd survived that bomb explosion in Beaune. It was set to be so thorough. But when the Gestapo picked me up afterward, they said a woman had crawled out of the wreckage." Roy's façade cracked and he looked as miserable as any concrete gargoyle forever frozen in agony. "It could only have been you, right?"

Lane rolled her shoulders back, hoping she could access the pistol stuffed in her bra, or the knife at her waist, if she only had room to move without attracting his attention.

"What's the matter? Can't find the right words to justify why you've been such a bad, bad wife?" Roy's eyes narrowed to slits. "You were such a minx in Washington. Leading me on, all the while plotting to hand me over to the authorities. Tell me—had Theo recruited you to the agency while you worked in that rabbit's warren of books, or after our engagement—to test me regarding my loyalty?"

With a precision that would be the envy of a surgeon, he moved the barrel of the gun against her forehead. "Your skin is so beautiful. It's going to be awful to see it splattered all over this chapel."

Her hands were sweating like faucets, but she forced her gaze to the center of the bridge of his nose, not looking into his eyes, or giving him the satisfaction of staring at the gun. If he was going to murder her, it would be without any of the flailing that he clearly expected.

"Were you and Mary Magdalene working together in D.C. too? Had she poisoned you with her hatred for me, or was it just a twist in Theo's fertile imagination to bring the two women that I most detest to within a stone's throw away from each other in Texas?" The gun pushed into her skull.

"She's next, you know. I'm sure she's followed you here and will swing in on some contraption so she can burst through the windows and steal my show. But, you won't see any of that. You'll—" he laughed bitterly. "Be dead."

Roy whipped the gun from her forehead and slammed it against the side of her head. Lane's skull cracked with a blazing pain that ricocheted through her entire body. She fell forward, clutching the bones above her ears, eating every scream that wanted to rip through her body.

"That's for not answering me," he said coldly. "A woman is supposed to obey her husband, and you have forgotten your vows."

Her teeth chattered and her jaw felt splintered, but she could hear his breathing and knew he hunched over her. Despite blinding pain, she released one hand from clasping her skull and fingered her waistband for the knife she'd used so skillfully in backrooms and war zones, just never in a chapel.

His whistle cut across the sanctuary and caused a flutter of shuffling footsteps in the narthex. Though she shouldn't have, she rose from the pew, and curved toward the door, seeing Stuart thrust forward from a bathroom. His face bruised like a raccoon's mask, his nose swollen and tilted to an awkward positon, a gag over his mouth and torn sheets binding his arms against his side.

His lab tech, Peale, pushed him again, and Stuart stumbled into the sanctuary, falling across a table stacked with communion trays.

Gasping, Lane realized how wrong she'd been to think she'd had Roy Mercer figured out. She would no longer believe that Roy was even sane.

Stuart looked her way, flinching in agony, communicating a silent message of apology in his gaze. Peale stood straighter than he had before, a haughty demeanor exchanged for the one she'd witnessed days ago.

Roy jammed the gun's barrel between her shoulder blades. "Don't you want to go to your champion? Stuart cares more for you than he does for me. Me, his fraternity brother.

Say he has principles and that his principles wouldn't let him sell his research. Don't you know I'll be envying his principles when I'm sitting pretty in Brazil."

He nodded to Peale, who then took delight in kicking Stuart between the legs and watching him cave to his knees in anguish.

Roy sighed with practiced drama. "This is going to take too much time, so I'll just have to kill you both now. Peale has a vehicle waiting, and if we don't get out of here soon, Dear Old Colonel Marks will have this case cracked, and track us down."

With one hand, he held the gun against her spine, while the scent of his hair tonic filled her nose as he bent to tip her purse over and dump the contents onto the pew's cushion. She hoped he'd not paw through the contents. The tape recorder was too fragile to withstand much jostling.

"What a good little agent Lane has become," he mocked. "She's brought handcuffs." He lifted the metal clasps and showed them to Peale. He then leaned his lips against her ear. "Maybe I won't kill you just yet. These could be handy for later use."

Recoiling as his beard stubble rubbed against her ear, she rolled her shoulder backward hoping to distract him from the contents of the purse. He'd once been easily diverted by a bit of flesh—she'd bet everything that he still was.

"And what is this we have here?" he asked, dropping the rope and reaching around to stuff his fingers into her blouse, trailing his thumb along the lacy edge of her bra. She flinched but let him pull out the pistol.

His laugh rumbled like an avalanche. "Oh, this is not going to be helpful to anyone."

While he was turning over the gun to look at its marking, she repositioned her body so she could kick her heel between his legs, a move made fruitless as he jerked her and held her with a bear grip under her chin, his fingers tightening around her throat.

"Now, darling wife, we have what they like to call in the training classes, an 'impasse.'" He pushed her forward to where Stuart had crumpled against the table, Peale holding a .38 to his back.

Stuart fought against the bindings, but Peale punched him in the kidneys, causing him to cave again.

"How sweet, he's still trying to protect you from me even after all these years." Roy tsked like he delighted watching Stuart waste his energies. "Peale, go ahead and shoot him in the head. My wife needs to see the execution. Now that we have his papers, he's useless anyway."

Peale stepped back a bit so he could cock the gun, and as he did, Lane knew this would be the only moment she could change Stuart's destiny. She reached into the waistband of her trousers, slipped the stiletto from its hiding place, and thrust it across the room with a strength she'd not accessed since field training.

With a sucking thud, the knife pierced Peale's shirt and perforated his intestines. Peale threw his arms over his injury and must have pulled the trigger as the gun shot a bullet sideways where it hit a limestone wall and reverberated toward an iron light fixture.

Shards of glass rained down from the chandelier. Stuart rolled away as Peale fell forward onto the table, sending the knife even deeper into his body.

Roy jerked her chin higher, causing vertebrae to crack. She could only see the wood beams bracing the ceiling, but assumed Stuart was freed.

"Let her go, Roy." Stuart gasped. "It's over."

Lane frantically searched the perimeter of the ceiling from her position, hoping that the doors would burst open and armed MPs would storm the chapel. In what could have been seconds but felt like hours, Roy's grip on her throat cut off her oxygen. In a last-ditch effort, knowing his hands were otherwise preoccupied, she widened her palm into a baseball mitt, threw her fingers up and backward into where she thought his eyes would be, and felt the moisture of his soft orbs collapse under the fierceness of her defensive move.

He dropped his arms, yelling obscenities, as she leapt. Reaching down for the pistol he'd so carelessly dismissed, she refitted it into her palm and released the safety.

As he wrapped his hands over his eyes, she raised the small handgun and fired, aiming for his knee. Bone and tissue splintered into a million inoperable pieces. He screamed and fell, clutching his leg.

A righteous anger fueled by the faces of four men who died too soon empowered her steps. "That was for killing those men in Beaune." She raised the gun, and aimed for his other knee, and cocked the gun a second time. "And this is for all the self-doubt and grief you brought into my life."

She fired, but he rolled away from the trajectory of the bullet.

"Lane!" Stuart leapt on her, crushing her to the ground.

The doors of the chapel flew open, and men filled the narthex, shouting commands. Shoving Stuart off of her, she looked up as Emmie drew her gun, aiming it at Stuart's back.

"He's innocent!" She rolled away in case Emmie shot anyway.

Behind Emmie, Zeke stood in his creased blue suit, like any shell-shocked soldier, his face ghostly, his eyes wide and blank as he stared at her crouched in a self-defensive position, her gun aimed at Roy who cowered between the pew and the communion table. Before she could process what Zeke might think, Boris pushed through the crowd, marched over to Roy, lifted him off the ground by his collar, and punched his face with a powerful right hook. Snot and splintering bone shattered off the walls.

If Roy hadn't already been moaning, he'd caved into a wailing child. Emmie, seemingly emboldened by Boris, forgot Stuart, and walked over to where Roy lay crumpled on the floor. She lifted her right arm and swiped at his throat as if she were swishing away a bee. It was a silent maneuver, and Lane wasn't sure what the nurse had done, but Roy's eyes widened and he turned on the nurse with spite.

Emmie leaned close to Roy's quaking body and yelled, "That was for my girls."

"Not here." Theo broke through the crowd and jerked Emmie away, tossing her toward Boris. "Mercer doesn't die. We need the names of his contacts."

Lane watched Roy's blood seep into the wood floor as Theo jerked him up and tossed him like garbage to the MPs who stood close. "Take this man to the jail and deny him any medical treatments."

Theo fell to his knees in front of Lane, taking the pistol from her hands and setting it on the floor.

Commands about Peale's incarceration were shouted, and Stuart was hauled off, too. The cacophony was deafening, and Lane felt herself crumbling inside, as if she'd been the one shot and left to hemorrhage.

Theo wiped his hand along her forehead and stared into her eyes. "You're in shock," he yelled, but his voice sounded like it was coming from a room that drifted farther and farther away from her perspective. "Stay with me, Lane. It's over. He's not going to hurt you now."

She nodded, so that Theo would stop shouting, but her neck felt held together with gelatin. A commotion behind Theo caused her to glance beyond his face and watch as Roy reached into the MP's holster, drew out a weapon, and aimed it at her.

He was going to kill her once and for all.

A haze of blue clouded her vision as Zeke flew at Roy, knocking his arm backward and causing the gun to fall to the floor before it fired off a round of ammunition. Theo turned and leapt to stand, tossing himself over Zeke to protect him from retaliation.

Like flies on a honeypot, men hustled to contain the chaos in the chapel, but with a strength that defied understanding, Roy rolled to his good knee and limped for the doors.

With strength that didn't come from her own power, she pushed her hands into the wood planks for support, grabbed the back of the pew, and stood. Running for the door, her ears filled with the barks of soldiers and agents yelling for her to stop. Grabbing the jamb, she saw Patrick and Arnold running away from the parking lot.

Outlined blindingly by a ray of sunshine stood a Wyatt's Ambulance Service vehicle idling at the curb. Roy leapt into the opened passenger door.

Just as MPs rushed from the building, an explosion ripped the sky, and fire spewed from the belly of the ambulance. MPs crouched to the sidewalk, covering their heads as the crackle and pop of overheated gasoline against metal rang louder than church bells. The vehicle, and by association, Captain Roy Mercer, were lifted off the concrete, twisted into the metallic pyre, and shattered into a cauldron of flames.

Emmie caved around Lane's shoulders, yelling into her ear. "Did he make it into that car?"

Lane nodded, barely able to support their weight as the heat radiating off the scene scalded her vision and reminded her too eerily of what she'd seen in Beaune.

"Damn," Emmie sighed. "We're going to owe the Judge a new vehicle."

Chapter Thirty-Four

April 24, 1943 4:12 p.m.

Smoke spiraled into the sky, creating an arrow pointing Harmon General's attention to the east end of the campus, the train spur location for the troops. Throngs of people hurried from the barracks to watch the spectacle, and the onlookers grew from police officers to a whole band of medical personnel, patients, and civilians—some covered their noses from the smell of burning tires, and others just stood immobile, seemingly fascinated by the arc and colors of flames.

Lane turned her head to see Boris's wrists circled by handcuffs before he was stuffed into the back of an unmarked vehicle, bound for some location that she supposed would be far removed from the plains of Nevada.

She scanned the grounds, looking for Patrick and Arnold. No doubt, they were well away from the fireworks and hopefully finding a way to get off the campus, now that their vehicle was in shards. Theo and Emmie escorted Peale's gurney toward an undisclosed ward, Emmie snapping instructions to the FBI agents like she planned to take over the interrogation and dispense justice before the man was charged with a crime.

Lane closed her eyelids, exhausted beyond any level she'd thought she'd known. Zeke huddled her close, clasping his arm around her waist and holding her like he'd never let go. She rested her head on his shoulder as she wondered what would become of Stuart's career, now that he was being led away by the MPs and an emergency room doctor.

Hopefully, if the tape recorder built into the purse worked, it would exonerate him, but until an investigation was conducted, he'd be guilty until proven innocent.

"I have aged twenty years in the last hour," Zeke growled. "I never want to live through anything like that again."

She didn't either. And hopefully, she never would. With Roy's actual demise witnessed by troops, nurses, and even a grease-coated railroad engineer, she could bury the guilt and questions that had haunted her about what she could have done differently in Beaune. No one would suffer at his hands again.

Turning into Zeke's suit, she wrapped her arms around his waist, breathed the threads that bore a scent memory from the last twenty-four hours and said, "Thank you for saving me. If you hadn't jumped on him, he might have shot me in front of everyone."

A rumble that sounded like a cousin to a chuckle rose under Zeke's ribs. "I'm quite sure I did very little to 'save you.' You'd already disabled the guy and that he even had a brain cell working to reach for a gun was about the strangest thing I'd ever seen."

"Evil thinks itself invincible." She wished she'd aimed for Roy's heart instead of his knee. Roy's contacts, confessions, and gloating of past mission were forever lost, but maybe in the bigger picture, with Boris and Peale still alive, they could piece together enough to figure out what information Roy had already sold abroad. "I'd like to have seen him tortured," she said quietly. "Waterboarding would have been a good start."

A nurse approached the chapel steps and headed for Lane. "Ma'am, I'm from the emergency ward, and I need to take your vitals. Are you injured?"

Lane sighed. "I'm fine."

Zeke interrupted. "She'll need a full workup, but she's stubborn."

A headache pounded through Lane's skull, and she was sure a bruise had purpled her cheek from where Roy had hit her and maybe loosened some teeth. All she wanted to do was sit down somewhere cool and drink a gallon of Dr Pepper.

"Nurse Tesco warned me to anticipate a certain, shall we say, resistance," the nurse said. "That's why she had a room prepared in the ladies' ward. It's been ready for days now and is quite comfortable."

Tesco had expected this outcome? Had the woman planned every detail of this operation without letting in the others?

"Come on, Lane. Don't fight it." Zeke took her hand and led her away from the bulletin board stand. "Let's get your things and go see about this room. I hate to think what your aunt would say if you were to walk home looking like you'd been on the wrong end of a bar fight."

Lane stuck her fingers in her hair, mussed from the pandemonium, and then gingerly touched her ear where the pain had rocketed through to her face. No bones were sticking out, but she was sure she looked like someone who'd been eaten by a coyote and dumped over a cliff, as Slim would have said.

There was a lightness lifting the chains in her soul as she moved, and that dawning outweighed the pain. Delia's voice wasn't even taunting her for thinking a cruel childhood had been any to blame for this madness. Stepping back, she looked at Zeke's ashen face like he was part of her freedom.

"You look like you're seeing a ghost." He waved his hand in front of her face. "Could be a concussion."

"I'll do the evaluating, thank you very much," the nurse said, wrapping her hand around Lane's wrist and feeling for a pulse.

"Well, if you'd let her sit a spell," Zeke said with firmness. "I'm sure Lane would let you exam her."

"Sir." The nurse faced Zeke. "We'll treat her with kid gloves as soon as we can get her settled in the ward. I will not conduct an exam on the sidewalk."

"And to be clear, all this care is going to be free," Zeke insisted. "Lane Mercer just saved this post from World War III."

The truth shall set you free. Lane wondered why that phrase flitted through her mind now.

An echo, from a long-ago conversation in a pickup truck, and she could see Slim driving his beat-up truck, the wind stirring his hair, as he was telling her his secret for enduring the cycles of blame his wife had levelled against him before their divorce. It might be years before the layers of secrecy Roy had built allowed for truth to shine, but she didn't fear the facts anymore.

"Zeke, I'm going to marry you."

The nurse and Zeke stopped talking and both stared at Lane.

A giddiness that might be some sort of reaction to the firetrucks descending on the chapel parking lot caused her to shout. "I'm going to marry you! I can—now that he's dead!"

Zeke kissed her and lifted her off the ground, spinning her around.

"Sir, you have to put her down." The nurse tapped his arm. "I'm serious. You could be adding to her injuries."

"Do you mean it, sweetheart?" Zeke settled Lane's feet on the sidewalk. "That was what was standing between us?"

Lane's focus had a hard time narrowing in on his bright eyes, but her heart was full of emotion. "I didn't know Roy was alive, but I'm free of the worries that I'd been a bad wife."

Zeke bent to be at her eye level. "You were not responsible for that man becoming a monster. Promise me you know that."

Lane nodded, but letting go of Roy's influence was going to be as hard as letting go of Delia's. She'd cling to Slim's promise that the truth would set her free and start from there.

"Ma'am." The nurse stepped between Zeke and Lane. "I need to get you to the ladies' ward now."

Zeke stepped back. "Go with her, Lane. You need to be checked out. God knows what the last twenty-four hours has done to your blood pressure."

Tenderly patting her cheek, Lane wouldn't rule out that she'd need a dentist by the end of the exam. "I promise. I'll go with you," she told the nurse. "But first I need to get my things from the chapel."

Before either of them could protest, Lane aimed for the doors knocked off their hinges. Entering, a surreal feeling washed over her as if she could do over the last half hour of her life. Her shoe kicked a piece of ceiling tile across the floor, and two MPs turned to see who'd entered the secured space.

"Just coming to get my bag," she explained, as she walked to the left side of the chapel. Keeping her gaze away from the place were Peale had bled on the communion table, she weaved a bit and reached for the back of a pew to steady her balance. "It's just right up here."

"I'll escort you," one of the MPs said.

Lifting the OSS bag, she held the base of it to her ear listening for the soft whirring noise of the tape. Flipping open the false bottom, she saw the small reel-to-reel tape spinning loose and flapping against the zipper. She reached for the knob that was disguised as the purse clutch and turned the machine off. As the reels slowed, she wondered what, if anything, this contraption had captured. Closing the compartment, she hoped never to see another purse made for spies.

Emmie could keep all the toys.

Lane held the purse against her chest like it was a talisman of a life she'd once lived but was willing, once and forever, to give away. She blinked tears too dry to be from her soul. This was the normal letdown of a mission that proved more dangerous than anticipated.

The white light streaming through the window was pockmarked by the red spiraling lights of emergency vehicles, and Lane regretted that her plan had brought danger to the hospital.

She wiped another tear from her cheek, grimacing that her bones were too tender to touch.

Drawn by an elusive pull, she walked toward the front of the chapel, wanting to make amends to someone for the chaos she'd brought to a sacred place on Harmon General. She stopped at the altar, staring at the simple rustication of a chapel that was free of any denominational embellishments. No icons, just a wooden cross.

Her heart weighed tons, and she wasn't sure that kneeling here would be appropriate, but she was consumed by the need to confess that her desire for justice had put innocent people at risk.

Lane's legs ached as her knees bent into the unfamiliar position on the raised floorboard and chin dropped to her chest.

Kneeling, she stared at a thin red carpet, hoping forgiveness would reach out and wrap itself around her like a shawl.

She had so much she needed to clear with God, so many sorrows and sins, that she didn't know where to begin, but since He'd let her live through this afternoon, she'd guess that she wasn't at the end of her life. There'd be more to come, and in the more, that there'd be something deeper, something real that she could use to frame this journey.

"Ma'am?"

"Yes," she responded, looking up to the cross nailed to the wall.

"Colonel Marks sent me to collect you."

Lane knew it hadn't been God calling out to her, but for a moment, it brought a ripple of peace to imagine He knew where she was and was willing to lead her away.

"Did he?" She turned around, seeing a young man wearing heavy-duty military gear. The uniform swallowed his whiskerless chin.

The solider glanced around the chaos inside the chapel. "Said I was to haul you to the emergency ward and have the docs see to your injuries. I'm not to take no for an answer."

She rolled back onto her heels to find leverage to stand. "That sounds like something he would say."

"Do you have everything you need?" he asked with the earnestness that comes from someone frightened by the thought of dealing with a hysterical woman.

She glanced through the open church doors to see Zeke standing in the sunlight. His hair unglued from pomade, his jaw lined with more stress than he'd ever carried, and a suit that might have to be stitched after the activities it had endured. But he was smiling at her.

"Yes," she said, as she approached the soldier. "I have everything I need."

Chapter Thirty-Five

April 27, 1943 4:30 p.m.

Lane gripped the novels to shove one more copy of Ever My Beloved *onto the shelf. Ordering Roberta Harwood's runaway bestseller had put her in debt to the publisher, but she crossed her fingers that tonight's grand opening might help recoup the expenses.*

"Where do you want me to set up?"

She glanced at the man clutching a violin case with a music stand propped over his shoulder. This must be the musician her aunt had secured, suggesting a performer would be the perfect touch for a book party. He'd agreed at such short notice, on the condition he could have an autographed copy of a Harwood novel in addition to his fee.

Lane scanned the space already crammed with a buffet table and punch bowl and more folding chairs than she thought the fire marshal would approve. "I think the only option is for you to try to squeeze into that corner near the archway."

He followed her gaze and saw something that caused him to freeze. "There's a cat sitting on the buffet."

She was so used to Stevenson claiming some perch never intended for felines that she'd gone cat blind. "He's the guest of honor, didn't you know?"

Lane walked over to scoop Stevenson from the table.

Edith hurried in through the front door, burdened with baskets and a silver tray covered in cloth. "Lawd, I didn't think Victor would ever find a parking place. That silly Sherlock Holmes movie is debuting tonight at the Arlyne, and you'd think everybody and their brother had come to town to see that English movie star who's here for the premiere."

Lane set the cat on the floor, shooing him under the tablecloth. "I could have brought some of this food when I was at the house for lunch."

"Like you had room in that Jeep for lemon squares and cheese straws." Edith hurried toward the table centered with a vase of yellow roses. "You were a hillbilly with all that furniture tied down, and don't even get me started about how you just threw Little Momma's china into a hamper and thought that looked like smart packing."

Lane had moved some belongings upstairs to turn the safe house into her personal abode since the security status had been compromised with so many civilians aware of the apartment.

"Nothing broke in the move, and the old club chairs fit perfectly." She studied the way her aunt stacked the cheese straws like logs on a timber barge. "I'm rather pleased with the arrangements."

Edith harrumphed. "We'll finish decorating tomorrow, after this book party. There's a sale at Northcutt Furniture, and we'll get you set up right."

Lane knew there was no point arguing that she liked the apartment like it was.

Edith glanced around the bookshop. "Where is everyone? It's almost five."

Lane untied the knot of her apron. "Zeke walked over to collect Mrs. Harwood from the hotel. Emmie has gone to see if Miss Kennedy is well enough to attend. She's been seen by a specialist that Dr. Lemming recommended and we hope that a new treatment will put her back into spirits."

"It's the least he could do after all the pain he's caused you." Edith pursed her lips. "I knew that man was trouble the day he tried to weasel his way into our car."

"Stuart is not trouble." Lane wiped her fingers of the lemon curd clinging to the silver tray. "But it may be a while before his name is cleared. I hope they let him return to practice. He was discovering some good research, and I've heard talk they may create a specialty center at Harmon just to focus on malaria now."

"I dreaded seeing the Easter newspapers. It was bad enough that your name was listed as a witness, but now big city reporters are poking around town asking questions and I hear that some radio station out of Shreveport is going to start broadcasting a special program featuring the soldiers at Harmon and their stories after all this."

"Why does that bother you?"

Edith shot Lane a look of dismay. "We're just quiet people around here, who don't want a lot of attention, certainly not from those city slickers who have opinions about their country cousins. It was unfortunate that the ambulance blew up, but surely we don't have to keep reading about it in the headlines."

Lane straightened the stacks on the book table. Her mind needed busy work. Patrick and Arnold had set the dynamite in the ambulance and, thankfully, had gotten away scot-free without damage to them or any other bystanders. Theo had hauled Patrick and Judge Wyatt in for secret reprimands, but Lane rather thought that Patrick had sealed his long-term contract with the OSS in the process.

She'd been shuttled into a room at Harmon for the weekend and attended by the doctors and nurses who specialized in psychiatric disorders for those who'd been fighting on frontlines. They'd ruled her stable and released her Monday morning with a free pass to come see them anytime the memories were too strong.

She wasn't sure what defined "too strong," but she didn't feel as crippled as they'd all suggested she would.

"Ma'am?"

Lane glanced at the violinist.

"There's a reporter who's arrived and would like to ask you some questions." The man pointed to a young woman wearing a fancy hat, a chic pink suit, and high heels.

Lane glanced beyond the plaid skirt of her dress to the sensible shoes and, for the first time in a long time, regretted that she'd ignored the impulse to doll up a bit. She lifted the apron over her head and dropped it on the sales counter. "How may I help you?"

The lady offered a card embossed with the logo for Tyler Morning Telegraph. "I drove here a bit before your event so I could interview you and, later the famous Mrs. Harwood, is that all right? I'm going to catch Mr. Rathbone after the movie's premiere and really make my trip worthwhile."

Lane had not contacted this paper and wondered if Lassiter had made a few calls on her behalf. "Yes, of course. How about we go into my office?"

Lane pulled in a folding chair and made room beside her desk. Settling in her chair, folding her hands in her lap, she smiled at the earnest reporter uncapping a new fountain pen. Smoothing a pleat in her skirt, Lane looked at the quality pen and wondered if writing utensils and fine papers were something she could sell in the shop too.

"Can you tell me," the reporter asked as she opened a flip top notepad and poised the pen between her fingers, "how you felt being at the site of a major explosion at Harmon General Saturday afternoon?"

Strong feelings circled her mind. Not the kind that needed a medical evaluation—the kind that interrupted fanciful thoughts of ink pens. The commanders at Harmon were labeling Saturday's explosion an "internal military investigation." She'd been classified as a spectator, and that was the story she was sticking with.

"If you don't mind," Lane channeled a bit of Molly Kennedy. "I'd prefer to talk about the shop and my excitement about bringing a bestselling author to Longview. It's my hope that this is the beginning of a longstanding tradition."

"But my real interest in you is what it must have been like to be at the scene of a dramatic car explosion. Were you really just a bystander, or had you been there for an event?"

Training advice from her early days with the OSS returned to calm her tongue. They'd said to give short, mostly true answers if ever questioned by broadcasters and to not encourage more exchanges. Lane guessed this reporter was hungry to prove herself to the men at her newspaper and wouldn't let go until she either had a statement or something she could work into a testimony, be it true or not.

Lane glanced to the tin ceiling tiles for inspiration. "It was a total surprise. I'd been to the chapel to meet a friend, and when I walked out, it was just a matter of seconds before the vehicle exploded. Quite shocking."

"I'm sure it was." The woman nodded sympathetically. "There's some scuttlebutt that it was a Negro ambulance service that had been packed with dynamite, maybe in protest for the way the Negro soldiers have been treated at the hospital, and that the man caught in the explosion was just one of the protestors. What do you think?"

Lane covered her mouth with her hand, as if traumatized, but really to buy a moment of thought. "I really couldn't say anything about that. I'm not even sure I saw the particulars of the vehicle before it blew up."

The reporter bit the top of her pen's casing and studied Lane. "I can't seem to get anyone to confirm or deny that report, but sources are saying that it's a real possibility."

Lane would let Judge Wyatt know about the gossip. "I was under the impression it was a mechanical malfunction."

"I'll get to the bottom of this, one way or another." She glared at the notepad like she was hoping the scribbles would materialize into a new source. "In the meantime, can you comment on having seen a Russian double-agent in the crowd? My source said the FBI were there that day to trap a tall, thick-chested Russian wearing an eye-patch and that the blast was intended for him."

Widening her eyes, Lane tried to look astounded. "I've never heard such a thing. Short of the quick response from the MPs at the scene, I can't say I saw anyone unusual at all."

"Hmm. . ." The woman tapped her pen against the notepad. "That's a bust. I guess I can ask you a few questions about the book party." Her gaze scanned the room filled with opened boxes and the ingredients for Edith's famous punch. "Are you expecting a big turnout for Mrs. Harwood's talk?"

"Not at all." Lane had tried to dissuade Edith from borrowing chairs from First Methodist, but her aunt insisted more people would come as a result of Sunday's bold headlines—if for no other reason. "But it's my first grand opening, so I don't know what to assume."

The reporter rattled off a few questions that didn't take much thought to answer. Lane was grateful that Theo peeked his head around the back door and provided a distraction.

"Hello, darling," he said with a wink to Lane. "How's my favorite girl in the whole world doing today? Feeling chipper?"

It wasn't the first time she'd seen Theo since the explosion, but it was the first time she'd acted as if he hadn't set her world on a collision course. Part of that counseling at Harmon General this weekend was about not assigning blame and becoming bitter. She wasn't sure if the doctors knew quite how deep and tangled her anger for Theo could travel, but it was enough to know they were right. Part of healing from Roy and his second demise was in setting free the questions and hurts that could never be answered.

Theo would have to be a part of that resolve. And in time, she'd work through those feelings. Just not tonight.

As Theo removed his hat, placing it on the coat rack, the reporter forgot all about questions regarding the party while admiring his movements.

"Hello, there," the reporter cooed.

Theo looked and did a double take.

Lane rather thought he'd been struck speechless. She stood, seeing the inevitable return of Theo's charm and made introductions, carefully omitting his rank. "He's a former co-worker and here for moral support," she said, picking up the clipboard that had her list of last-minute tasks. "One of my oldest friends, a veritable geriatric."

A color, similar to freshly bloomed apples, tinted the reporter's cheeks. "Oh, certainly not old."

Theo stared, started to move, and then just sort of froze, the toe of his wingtip nearly nicking the damp mop propped against the wall.

What a surprise, Lane thought. She'd have enjoyed watching more of Cupid's antics, but she had heard guests arrive during the interview. Stepping toward the archway, she was stunned to see twenty or twenty-five people gathered in a space that could comfortably hold ten. Stevenson bolted between her legs. She couldn't even hear the violinist play his instrument for the chattering of female voices.

"Emmie and Miss Kennedy are on their way," Theo called out. "Patrick was going to chauffeur them and drop them at the alley entrance for Miss Kennedy's privacy."

Lane glanced at her watch. Zeke and Mrs. Harwood were due to arrive in minutes. "Then I'd better start selling books."

Theo's and the reporter's voices mingled, as Lane glanced toward the front door and saw J standing at the threshold, holding a bouquet of flowers. He raised them in salute to her.

Lane had not talked to him since Saturday and wasn't sure what he knew, or had guessed, about the newspaper story identifying the tragic mishap at Harmon General. Emmie had promised Lane that she'd take care of getting Lane's luggage moved to the bookshop apartment, but there'd been no more comments about leaving Longview. Even with Peale in custody and his confession as the mastermind behind the malaria papers going on the market and the failed test measures for the local administration an official part of the debriefing transcript, Emmie had lingered.

Lane wasn't sure why Emmie stayed the weekend, but since Molly was benefitting from the attentions of a private nurse, she wouldn't complain either. Instead, Lane pushed all those thoughts out of her head for the moment and concentrated on navigating a path to the sales counter.

Edith gestured around the room as she talked with three ladies gathered close. "I was telling my niece that bringing in a celebrity author was, in fact, the only way to get everyone's attention. I mean, with the way business is booming these days, you've got to make a big splash. Really, I don't know what she'd do without me, guiding her along the ropes of society."

Lane coughed loudly.

Edith turned, blushed a bit, and carried on. "Why, look. Here she is now, the brilliant young businesswoman." She leaned in close to the women who were keen with fasciation. "Louisa Jane is shrewd. She's giving a ten-percent discount on her sales tonight, so buy lots of books. You'll never get a better deal."

Lane hadn't planned on giving any discount. As it was, she hoped she'd gotten enough cash from the bank to make change. If sales produced what this crowd might generate, she'd be up all night balancing her ledgers.

There was a commotion at the door, as J stepped aside to let a woman enter. A stately lady with highly-styled, auburn hair wearing a green suit and a triple-strand of pearls, smiled with the grandness of a queen entering a ballroom. Voices hushed, as Roberta Harwood was welcomed into the crowd of adoring fans. Zeke followed, his sunny disposition clouded over by a set to his jaw she'd not seen since the MPs questioned him Saturday for being at Harmon General without a visitor's pass.

Zeke patted J on the back as he slipped around a book table to step behind the desk to squeeze Lane with a side hug. "Be warned, that woman is a handful," he whispered. "She had the concierge in tears with complaints about bath water temperature and the selections in the fruit basket left in her suite, but I can guarantee you'll have a memorable event. Half of the lobby at the Gregg Hotel will be trailing over here any minute to buy her books. I don't think any of them remembered there was a movie star in town."

Lane nodded, trying to get a second peek at the author.

Edith leaned into Lane's other shoulder and whispered, "Why, she doesn't look like a strumpet at all."

"That's what you were expecting?" Lane watched three unfamiliar people enter the shop behind the author. "Someone racy?"

Edith cupped her hand over her mouth so no one could read her lips. "I started one of her books last week. I nearly died of shock, but I couldn't put it down either." She fanned her face. "Victor is reading it in the car as we speak."

J wound his way around the sales counter. "Good job. This turnout is even better than I'd imagined."

She smelled cloves on his breath and glanced at his jaw, shaved of the usual five o'clock shadow. "I'm blown away. Will you help me turn these curiosity seekers into shoppers?"

"Of course," he said, seeming to take pride in his student's success. "All it takes is presenting them the opportunity."

She followed his gaze as it bounced around the room. Book shoppers were admiring titles on the shelves. The musician pushed the bow across his violin but Lane couldn't hear a tune for the volume of voices, and those inspecting the desserts had already nibbled away the cheese straws.

"Edith is helping with the register, and she's advertising a discount. I hope I don't lose money tonight." Lane brushed her hand on her skirt and rolled her shoulders back. "Cheer me on. I'm going to meet my special guest."

Zeke nudged J's elbow. "I brought something to spike the punch."

J's gaze landed on Zeke, patently ignoring the flask advertised inside his suit pocket. "That won't be necessary."

Zeke raised his brow but closed his jacket nonetheless.

Lane spoke with a few folks as she made her way behind the buffet and tried to come up on the quieter side of Mrs. Harwood. She managed to find a spot and waited while a fan asked questions. Theo and the reporter looked in on the scene from the archway, but they were sharing a conversation that Lane would suppose had nothing to do with books.

From the alley entrance, Patrick ushered Molly into the office and trailing behind, a subdued Emmie. Patrick pulled the desk chair over for Molly to settle on the cushion, but he didn't look inclined to stay long. Emmie looked doubtful, too.

Lane was sure the only reason Emmie came tonight was to say goodbye. Theo had whispered earlier that he was leaving on the morning train, and since Emmie was here too, it could only mean she was going to follow. Saying good bye was going to be much harder than she would have imagined a month ago.

Putting her hand on Mrs. Harwood's elbow, she steered her to the office area. "This way please," she said, speaking as she walked. "I'm the shop's owner and would like to have a word with you to discuss when you'd like to begin your remarks."

"Of course, dear," Roberta replied, with the tones of a well-educated New Englander. "I'm looking forward to chatting with everyone. I've never been to Texas before, and I find it enchanting. Why, that young man who you had escort me to the shop might be the candidate I've been searching for as the role model for the cowboy hero in my next book. I'll have to spend a little time with him later, to—" She smiled with delight. "Study his attributes."

Lane nearly choked and tried to disguise the surprise as a cough. Zeke would have a word or two to say about his attributes being studied. Just as she started to reply, she heard a gasp from Mrs. Harwood.

"Mary Magdalene?" Roberta's voice bore the stretch marks of heavy baggage.

"Mother?"

Chapter Thirty-Six

April 27, 1943 9:51 p.m.

Lane closed the door behind the last customer and turned the lock. Placing her hand on the blinds to silence their rattle, she glanced around the bookshop littered with crumbs, fallen receipts, and punch spills. Sagging into the jamb, the thrill of a big night carried the exhaustion of entertaining a crowd of shoppers who didn't quite get what they'd bargained for in the meet-and-greet with Roberta Harwood.

Edith pushed the sales drawer into the register and its thud caused Lane to momentarily forget the drama played out for guests and a reporter who'd been looking for a juicy exclusive.

"A fortune!" Edith pushed a pencil into her hair, tucking it behind her ear. "I wouldn't have believed the sales had I not counted them myself."

Lane picked up the receipts from the rug and stacked them on the desk. "Not bad, right?"

"Calling in the police was a stroke of brilliance. That brought some of those movie fans over from the Arlyne, and I didn't think you'd have a book left on the shelves after that."

Squeezing her eyes shut for a moment, Lane blocked out the memory of the chaos that erupted after shoppers, anticipating a domestic disturbance, ran for the officer directing traffic at the movie premier. It took negotiation skills she'd hadn't used in months to separate the policeman from the mother-daughter reunion that defied the common therapy that talking about the past was healthy.

Zeke ushered the two women to the apartment upstairs where they could at least have some privacy for their argument about whose responsibility it had been to stay in touch. Although when Lane took them two glasses of punch and some lemon squares later, the conflict seemed to have dissolved into tears. Roberta's face had crumbled, but Emmie's expression was belligerent.

"Someone must have thought there was going to be a catfight."

"You handled it beautifully," Edith said, as she signed her initials to the sales ledger. "Getting them upstairs to work out their differences, sending that gorgeous Colonel Marks and Zeke with them to mediate was good thinking, too. Women tend to control their anger better if they think men will judge them."

Lane was sure that Theo knew all of Emmie's secrets, but that hadn't stopped anyone from treating him kindly. During the five minutes she'd stepped upstairs to remind Mrs. Harwood of the fans waiting on a book talk, she'd seen him glower—as if the threat of a thrown pitcher was a real possibility.

Edith pulled small-framed glasses from the bridge of her nose. "So, what do you think will happen next?"

Lane collected the punch glasses that had been stacked behind the sales counter. "Molly Kennedy suggested that everyone take a break, and meet in the morning to see if cooler heads would allow for some sort of healing to the rift."

Edith nodded. "When Mrs. Harwood—or whatever her real name is— came downstairs and mingled with her fans and carried on as if nothing major had happened, well, I knew I'd be buying more of her stories. That's grace under pressure. I think the other ladies saw that too, and that was what was behind your sell-out tonight."

Lane glanced to her denuded shelves, still stunned by the strange turn of events. "All I know is that I need to get on the telephone in the morning and see if I can order more inventory."

Edith turned off the globe lamp and followed Lane to the office. "I'm going to head on home. Victor said he'd pick me up at 9:15, come hell or high water."

Lane grimaced, remembering those first few moments after Emmie and Roberta discovered that, despite years of avoiding each other, they'd collided, and there were witnesses. "I think you had a little of both tonight. But on the up side, the ladies did agree to see each other tomorrow. Molly was insistent that the rift be righted."

Edith reached for her hat, saying, "Molly Kennedy could negotiate warring tribes."

Lane was grateful Molly had color in her cheeks and vigor in her spirit again. Whatever treatment the doctor prescribed had helped Molly turn the corner. That meant better days ahead for the boarders on College Street, Lola, and the friends who relied on Molly for entertainment and direction.

Edith reached for the doorknob to the alley exit. "Are you going to be okay, staying here tonight?"

Lane nodded. "Zeke will be back any minute from walking Mrs. Harwood to the hotel. He'll help me clean up."

Edith's eyes narrowed. "Just don't let him linger too long. That Mr. Lassiter might gossip about the two of you still here when he leaves his shop later."

"We'll be good." Lane caught the door as it was opened and leaned out, seeing Victor's Hudson idling at Bank Alley. "Y'all don't get up to any trouble now that I'm not living at Oakdale."

"Pshaw." Edith stepped onto the stoop. "We're quiet as little lambs, no matter what Victor's friend said after the fishing boat capsized Saturday."

Lane waved to her uncle sitting in the driver's seat. "I guess that's a story I haven't heard."

"It's best left at the lake." Edith's heels clicked like typewriter keys as she hurried past the dumpsters. "I'll come back tomorrow to see if you need help at the shop."

Lane waved goodbye as her aunt settled into the passenger seat and Victor's slow drive away led them from the alley. Lane sagged. The apron string connecting her to the Thomases was made of leather.

"Hey, good lookin', what you got cookin'!"

Zeke, singing that ditty as he ducked around the corner of the alley where the Hudson left a contrail of exhaust, made her smile.

"Hey, yourself." She admired how fingers of moonlight stroked gold and silver into the waves of his hair. It wasn't a surprise to her that Roberta Harwood thought he was hero material. "You sneaking in the back way tonight?"

"Your front door was locked." Zeke reached for her waist, picked her up, and swung her around, kissing her as her heels settled on the stoop. "And I'm not one to give up easily."

She hugged his neck. "I'm so glad for that. I don't want to imagine what the last few days would have been like had you boarded that train Saturday."

His kissed her forehead, her cheek, and then nibbled at her lips.

"Let's take this inside," he said, reaching for the knob. "I left a bottle of bubbly chilling in the upstairs icebox, and I'm itching to see if it's any good. I bought it off a crook with a secret stash."

"Life with you will never be dull." Lane followed him into the stockroom. With all the horrific memories from the showdown with Roy, one of the best parts was the relief she felt when she stood in Zeke's embrace as flames closed the final chapter on Mr. and Mrs. Mercer. History had been corrected, and she was freed from vows that nearly strangled her. Trinity Episcopal wedding bells didn't make her shiver anymore.

"Lucky for you, I like Champagne."

Zeke's lips lifted on his smiling side. "See, that may not be a plus because I can't promise this wine is French. It might have been bottled in Louisiana."

Lane stepped over the papers and cans of emptied ginger ale as she wrapped her arms around his waist. "We have a lot to celebrate. Edith says I made a fortune tonight. And I'm sure I heard Mrs. Harwood promise you a starring role in her next book."

"That might not be the reward it seems. I'm kind of particular about how I want to be remembered for posterity." He kissed her quickly. "And more important, we need to have a long talk. I'm due on that train tomorrow. Parson isn't going to let me claim one more calamity for missing the last leg of the pipeline project. The ribbon cutting will be here before I can blink."

The glow of the evening dimmed as she imagined him leaving her for the next several weeks. "I know," she said, feeling a hollowness that only he could fill. "I will miss you. Terribly."

His eyes brightened and the smile that had beguiled people into putting large sums of money on his putts aimed its full wattage on her.

"To be clear, I am coming right back." His finger traced the greenish curve of the bruise on her cheek. "I've told the Major I'm not interested in continuing on with Washington work. Once we get the oil pumping in New Jersey, I'll be on the first train home."

He'd be giving up a goldmine in earnings, but she'd never heard anything that sounded so good. "You're ready to buy that farm and hang up the lawyer's shingle in Gladewater, so you can write wills and trusts?"

"I'm going to entertain an offer I was handed from the District Attorney's office first. Seems like they're hiring, and a courthouse job would keep me closer to you." He glanced around the messy stockroom. "If this is where you are, then it's where I want to be too."

Whether from surprise or a letdown from an unbelievable weekend, tears swarmed her eyes and she couldn't blink fast enough to keep them contained. Maybe the most stunning revelation was that, for the first time in her life, someone was putting her first. Zeke was rearranging his life for hers, and that opened a door for love that she'd not known she'd padlocked.

"And," he said with the gravity of a judge, "I'm going to give you the key to the pleasure mobile as a sign of my commitment."

She watched him pat his pockets, looking for the narrow bit of iron.

"This is serious." She laughed, swallowing tears that were running down her cheeks. "You didn't even let the Catons drive that Jeep."

"Well, that's because I had to start stashing my clubs under the backseat." He found the key and reached for her hand, turning the palm upward. Placing the iron on her lifeline, he folded her fingers over it. "I've never given my clubs to anyone before, so not to worry you or anything, but my entire career is now in your hand. If I can't hack it in the DA's office, I'm sure I could keep us off the streets with my golf winnings." He turned her hand over, running his finger over the scar near her thumb. "That is, if you don't lose my lucky clubs."

Lane wiped at her cheeks, and placed the key in the pocket of her skirt, sure that she'd lock the sticks in a closet here at the shop before she'd leave them in the back of a rusted-out Jeep. "I won't lose them, I promise."

He lifted her left hand, looked at the stones shining from her third finger, and sealed the symbol of his pledge to her with a kiss. "I take this as a good sign."

Her finger tingled from warmth he breathed onto the sapphire and diamond ring. "It feels right to wear something that shows the world how much I love you."

All Zeke's vivacity faded as his face fell into a childlike expression of someone who'd just been given his dream come true. "You mean those words, Louisa Jane? This isn't some sort of emotional crash from the last few days."

She blinked away the surprise that he didn't know the depth of her feelings. Perhaps she'd been so consumed with finding herself after France that she'd never really confessed what his faith in her had grown. That daffodils had sprung up from the grave of her past, that sweet fragrance had replaced the decay she'd known so long, and that the light that drew her forward—to that place where she saw a future—was as much the glow of his confidence in their relationship as it was the very real idea that she didn't have to live in fear anymore. When someone lets go of the darkness, it was easy for love to bloom.

"With my whole heart." She reached forward, cupped his cheeks with her hands, bringing his lips to hover near hers, and whispered, "I hear being a June bride is quite special. How does the twelfth, at Trinity Episcopal, sound to you? Aunt Edith already reserved the chapel."

His lips brushed hers. Then he froze. "We can't get married that weekend, I have a golf tournament in Carthage."

Oh, Edith would kill him.

"Are you sure about the date?" She pulled back to see his eyes. "Absolutely sure?"

He nodded. "I've already heard there's big money riding on me making the final cut."

Lane sighed, feeling better than she thought she should, considering that her fiancé just deep-sixed their wedding date. Breathing room expanded her lungs and she could enjoy the idea of setting their own plans in motion, on their own calendar. "Edith is going to be so mad at you."

"That's without even considering the fireworks I set off when I go ask your uncle for his blessing on our marriage. He hates me, so he won't make this little tradition go easy either."

"I hardly need his permission. I've been married before."

"Sometimes the blessing process is really the forgiving process, and that's too important to skip."

Lane knew she had a lot of forgiving she needed to ask for, and even more she needed to offer. That part of owning her truth was going to be painful, but it would be necessary if she was ever going to be free of the ghosts who spoke with the voices of Delia and Roy—and forever release their hold over her heart.

Zeke didn't seem to mind that she was a work in progress, so she'd pack his love, and her growing network of friends, along with the confidence she'd gained in navigating this life, and walk through the bower of wedding bells and white roses. Even if it meant honoring Victor and Edith as her closest relatives—and the ones who felt responsible for her protection. She'd do it, because family was important too.

Zeke grabbed her hand and tugged her toward the stairs. "But let's not think about your relatives right now. I've got a better idea for how we can celebrate."

Chapter Thirty-Seven

April 28, 1943 7:26 a.m.

Rain clouds were moving in. Barometric pressure kept the steam from the *St. Louis Sunshine* Special's churning at the rails. Lane pulled her jacket's collar up around her throat to keep the chill at bay. Maybe a hundred people were gathered around the Junction's portico and platform, waiting for the last possible moment before boarding the train. She'd be among those remaining, those who'd wave off the travelers and then return to the cabs and buses idling at the curb.

"I wasn't sure I'd see you this morning."

Lane turned at the sound of that familiar Bostonian accent and saw Theo adjusting his fedora. She wouldn't wonder how he'd walked so quietly that she never knew he'd approached her side until he was ready to announce himself. He'd been the one to invent that technique, and he was a master spy.

She saw the briefcase at his feet. "Zeke is in line to buy his ticket too. He's taking the train this morning. I would imagine you're both heading back to Washington?"

Theo nodded. "I'm sure we'll have much to commiserate. But at least he's coming back to see you. I'm not sure when our paths will ever cross again."

Lane wasn't going to fall for Theo's guilt anymore. He'd had two years of her life, and for that she'd savor the good memories, the high adventures, and the surprises of humanity—carefully editing out the danger, loss, and terror.

She looked around the faces gathered under the portico. "Is Emmie going with you?"

He shrugged. "If you see her get on the train, then the answer is yes. After last night, she's not inclined to speak to me."

316

"Holding you responsible for not telling her that her mother had become the infamous Roberta Harwood?"

"Among other things."

Lane's mind opened a memory from her earliest conversations with Theo about how the bookshop could serve as a cover operation for the agency's safe house. "You're the one who gave me the idea for inviting Roberta Harwood to my grand opening. You'd given me the article from the *Washington Post* detailing Harwood's southwest journey to meet a real cowboy for her next novel."

Theo shrugged, looking bored. "I have no recollection of that."

"Of course you don't." Lane shook her head, feeling all sorts of foolish. "And Roy—did you circle Longview on a map and mail it to him after you had the FBI and Boris in your playbook?"

"Now that—" Theo sighed with a release that showed his age. "That was the riskiest fire we've ever put out. Can you imagine what would have happened if he'd set bombs at the refineries?"

Lane had spent just enough time with her husband to know he'd not given two figs for the refineries, if he even knew what caused that distinctive odor in town. He'd had one mission, and that was to kill her for crimes only he had imagined. Peale was the mastermind behind selling the malaria papers and was just biding his time to raise the price point for his cooperation with Roy's contacts overseas. A washed-up middleman with a terminal disease, that's what Roy Mercer had become in the last year—a pale shadow of the man who'd flown away from D.C. thinking the world was his to capture.

And she was sure Theo had known every detail of that sad demise. No doubt using Roy's mental condition against him in a final trap so elegant that Roy didn't recognize the breadcrumbs.

Theo opened his suit jacket, reached for the inner pocket, and pulled out a narrow packet. "This is a thank you from your government, for putting yourself in danger to save Texas citizens from a terrorist. It's the deed to the bookshop property, including the apartment. A check will follow once I turn the paperwork into accounting. Consider it part of Captain Mercer's death benefits, if that makes the official separation easier to swallow."

She glanced at the envelope, knowing that when she accepted it, she'd be released from any official obligation to Theo or the OSS. "You've given me benefits once before."

"Call this a severance package then. I've decided I never want to put you in the center of a bullseye again."

She accepted the envelope, holding the heft of legal documents and wondering if she could go cold turkey from the pull of missions and covert operations. Time would tell, as her aunt liked to say. Time, and a separation from Emmie Tesco. Thankfully, without the OSS agents in town, she could better wean off the mysteries and settle into her life as a business woman.

Lane had made her choice, and she was glad of it. Her heart was at peace, and when she looked into Theo's face, she didn't feel any of the normal compulsion to know what was spinning behind his eyes. She could release him, just as easily as he was releasing her. "Thank you—for everything. Even the things I'm too angry to understand."

He winked, but the twinkle didn't sparkle. It was a farewell. "My pleasure."

Lane tucked the envelope into her purse. "You can always come back here. If things—your situation—changes."

Theo glanced at the thick clouds mixing with the engine's steam. "To Longview?"

Oh, how she'd hated the depot, and herself, that first day she'd arrived. "It's been good to me."

He returned his gaze to her for a long second and then backed away, as if it would take distance to make the emotions of this moment fit into an exit strategy. "I wouldn't make a good Texan. Wide open spaces frighten me." He lifted his hand in salute. "But I'm grateful it's been good for you. Ever grateful. Good bye, my friend."

Lane watched him back away and then dive into a sea of suits and fedoras. Her heart hiccupped for the severing of a tie that had kept her stable and connected to something vital. She might despise how Theo used her, but she couldn't entirely despise him. He'd been a rock, and she'd latched on to him like a barnacle. Tearing away now left wounds that touched deep emotions.

Staying behind would give her much-needed breathing room. And eventually she'd forget that she'd invested so much of herself into Theo's world.

An oily stench from the steam engine wafted in the rain-heavy air, a fitting epitaph for her thoughts. She snapped her purse closed, and rolled her shoulders back. Staring at a harmonica player hovering along the depot wall proved an effective distraction for the tears she felt she owed their friendship.

Forgiving Theo would be part of her healing process, but it wasn't fair to her fiancé to roll that puzzle out now.

Lane glanced around the crowd, looking for the face that had replaced all others in her memory.

With a jaunt that defied the early hour, Zeke walked through the throng, waving a ticket in the air. "I was able to get a sleeper car." He walked around a man balancing on a cane and stopped in front of Lane. "You have no idea how miserable this commute to Washington can be."

She'd ridden packed shoulder-to-hip in trains across France. Her brow rose, and she wondered how well Zeke would endure travel that didn't include a diner car, fresh sheets, and a private bathroom.

"Okay." He kissed the tip of her nose. "Maybe you would know."

She smiled, feeling so much lighter than she had when Theo disappeared. Zeke knew her so well he could read her expressions too.

"I'm glad you found good use for your golf rewards," she said, stepping closer to his side. "I'll feel better about the distance if I can picture you in the lap of luxury."

Zeke nudged her shoulder. "There's only one lap I'm interested in."

"Scamp," she scolded.

His gaze shifted to the engineers running the checks on the train prior to departure.

"I hope this is the last time we have to say good bye like this. When I come home after the pipeline's ribbon cutting, I just want to settle into the predictable boredom of a married man."

"I'm scratching predictable and boring from our vows."

He chuckled. "I expect to see Slim in New Jersey, so I'll get him a draft of the critical points before you see him next."

"You just need to know you're supposed to wait on me with a butler's devotion, and after that, we're set." She winked at him with the same disarming charm he'd perfected. "I'll keep my calendar open for the first weekend you're free of golf tournaments."

"Could be late fall. After we endure the Velma Weeds trial, I will still have to go through some sort of training period with the District Attorney's office." He squeezed her waist. "Can you wait that long?"

"For boring and predictable?" She kissed his cheek, remembering every remnant of goodness she'd enjoyed from this past year. "I could wait forever."

The engineer called out across the crowd, "All aboard."

Zeke glanced at the man, sighed, then turned back to Lane. "This is it, then."

Fat raindrops pinged off the porch's roof.

"I'm a big fan of ripping a bandage off," Lane said, enjoying this tradition of seeing a fiancé off on his travels. She wasn't sure what sort of travel an attorney in the DA's office might have, but the awareness that his schedule would be part of her ebb and flow was nice to consider. "The slow peel is gruesome."

His eyes widened, like he'd seen something gross. "So just like that, you're kicking me on to the train?"

"Onto first class, no less." Lane stood on her tiptoes and wrapped her arms around his neck. "I love you, and I'll be here when you return."

"I wish I could believe that you're not going to get swindled into some new OSS drama while I'm on the east coast." He kissed her. "Stay away from Theo Marks, you hear me?"

The settlement from their arrangement was tucked into her purse.

Lane didn't doubt that the secure line linking the OSS colonel's whereabouts to her bookshop desk had already been disconnected. With Emmie by his side, he'd have more than enough entertainment, and Lane rather enjoyed the notion that her name would fade away like a paper doll that had come too close to a fire.

She saluted Zeke. "Yes, sir."

"Harmon General, too." Zeke started to step away, but hesitated as if he wasn't sure he'd left enough ground rules after the latest episode in Lane's life. "They've got plenty of pretty nurses out there. You don't need to feel sorry for those soldiers. They don't need your books or your pies. They're well taken care of by the Gray Ladies."

She smiled, remembering the application Edith had brought by the shop, suggesting they both register to become Gray Ladies.

"I make a horrible pie, and my inventory has been plucked clean from the shelves."

"It's not your pie-baking skills that worry me." Zeke clutched his briefcase and glanced to the rain falling between the porch and the train's door. "Oh, I don't know why I even bother. You're going to do exactly what you want to do whether I'm here or not."

Despite the way events ended at Harmon, she did want to go back to the hospital and find a way to volunteer. She had too much of a soft spot for those willing to fight on foreign soil.

"Zeke?" she asked. "What is it you're afraid is going to happen? I'm not going to leave you."

He stood there, his face drained of demands, rain sheeting behind him, splattering his pant legs with splotches.

"I guess—" His gaze narrowed on her. "I can't believe I've ever done anything worthy of you, and if I'm not careful, you'll be gone as fast you arrived."

Lane had never heard those words, and her heart expanded with the confession. "You don't have to worry, Hayes. You're the only man for me."

"That doesn't mean you'll stay out of trouble." He glanced back to gauge the downpour between the porch and the door. "You could live without a man quite fine." He blew her a kiss. "It's me who would die without you."

She watched him run for the gaping door of the nearest train car, and returned his wave once he found her from a window's view. Even as she watched him disappear among the train's compartment, she couldn't let his words settle.

Quiet and self-reliance had become drugs Lane was addicted to, and the withdrawals would prick as she found a way to share her life with someone who trailed grass stains, golf balls, and other people's' legal briefs in his wake. Though she couldn't promise she'd stay out of trouble—she'd been born with one hand on the doorknob of misfortune —she didn't see how selling books would create much of a stage for drama.

Down the car, a window shade was lifted, and Zeke waved good bye to her.

"Final call," the engineer yelled down the platform.

Lane sighed, tightening the belt of her coat. Giving up some of her hard-won freedom might not be so difficult after all.

Depot officials came along the platform to check that doors were locked as the engines puffed clouds of steam into the already rain-drenched sky. A clap of thunder followed by the *pop-pop-pop* of a car backfiring caused her to flinch.

A year ago, she'd have broken out in hives at the horror such sounds caused. Today, she looked at her palms and saw no flop sweats. The past was going to stay buried.

Smiling for reasons she couldn't even label, Lane twisted to look for a city bus to transport her downtown.

"Gad, you make me sick. Staring off like a love-struck teenager."

Lane whipped around to see Emmie wearing a pale blue trench coat, a waterproof hat disguising the auburn curls, and holding a piece of luggage worthy of a long-distance trip.

"Aren't you supposed to be going to Washington?"

The chugging motions of the train wheels turning caused wet exhaust to fill the platform.

Emmie watched the engine pass, as if the industrial beast was the most fascinating invention on the planet. "I seem to have changed my mind."

Lane tried to read the other woman's expression, or at the very least, the darkness smothering the brown of her irises. "You couldn't wait to leave this town last night. I can't imagine anything that would make you stay."

"A big box of cash could do the trick."

Lane doubted Emmie was motivated by money. If what Roberta Harwood announced last night was true, there was a trust fund in New York beyond its tipping point.

"A man might," Lane corrected.

Emmie peered at her like a skunk had just skittered too close. "Not hardly."

"Not even one that you could see prosecuted? Are you waiting for Peale to get escorted to Fort Knox?"

Emmie blew air from her lips. "Quit with the questions. I'm starving." She checked her watch. "It's past my breakfast hour."

Lane created a short list for an interrogation, and after these months together, she was well aware of how to navigate the moody agent. "There's a café in the depot."

"Their coffee tastes like brown water."

Lane saw the caboose pass the platform and knew that Zeke and Theo were well on their way to St. Louis and then on to the intricacies of Washington. It would take weeks for them to find their way back to the piney woods, if Theo ever got off at this stop again.

"On the other hand, the Mobberly Café does a wonderful breakfast," Lane said, remembering a Sunday she'd splurged on a brunch menu. "I was going to pop in across the street and see if I could find Arnold's mother there. She's one of the cooks, and I need to get her approval to sign him up with a counselor at Harmon General. He's underage and what he did Saturday couldn't have been easy to witness."

"Arnold?"

"Don't act like you don't remember your chauffeur from the Cotton Club. You were practically demanding he go back and find you a pair of shoes."

Emmie pinched her forefinger and thumb together. "I recall the teeniest bit of that conversation, but just so you know, his given name is not Arnold."

Lane propped her purse in the bend of her elbow. "So, how about I buy you pancakes, and you can explain why you chose to stay here when you could have fled the opposite direction of your mother."

Emmie shuddered. "She, who shall not be named, is still here?"

"Mrs. Harwood says she has unfinished business in town and changed her booking for a train later in the week. I can only guess she's thinking of seeing you again."

"She can think all she wants—won't make it happen."

Lane sized up the tension woven between Emmie's brow. "Believe it or not, but I understand not wanting to spend time with your mother. If mine were living, well, let's just say I can't imagine we'd be friends."

Emmie sighed, her gaze flitting off the hats poorly shielding rain from those who dodged the cabs and buses. "Not that I don't appreciate the kindred spirits moment, but my feelings for Roberta are a little more complicated than anything you could imagine. I'm only just now coming to the point where I might be willing to accept part of the blame, and for a gal like me, that's saying something. But it doesn't mean I'm ready to endure one of my mother's talks."

The twists in Emmie Tesco's OSS assignment jumped to the forefront of Lane's mind. Despite the end to the mission, there had to be another reason for her to stay in Longview other than the ever-so-slim possibility of a reunion. Theo would know, but he was off limits to her now. She'd have

322

to hope that the glue of Harmon General was strong enough to bind her to Emmie, and that Emmie would be truthful should she ever feel inclined to confess her intentions.

"Breakfast then?" Lane glanced toward the other side of the Junction's drive and saw a line of people hurrying under the striped awning. "I did mention it was my treat."

Emmie turned away from the melee exiting the portico. Her scrutiny bounced over the vehicle tops to the Mobberly Hotel's neon sign blinking a yellow vacancy message through the mist. "I could eat a horse."

Lane felt the first strings of non-agency friendship. "Where there's hunger, there's life. And where there is life, there is hope."

Emmie's red lipstick distorted with a lemon's tartness. "That's the most awful drivel I've ever heard you spout. Don't keep reading those books in your shop or I'll set Slim on you."

"Maybe Slim said this to me months ago."

"Then he should be shot. That man thinks way too highly of his own opinions."

Lane bit back the smile that tugged her cheeks. She'd bet good money that Slim Elliott had a tighter hold on Emmie's affections than either of them suspected.

"So. . ." Lane nodded toward the hotel's entrance. "Breakfast?"

Emmie shifted her luggage to her other hand. "Pancakes, you say?"

"The best in town. My uncle swears they're made with cream."

Emmie seemed to weigh her options, and then straightened her posture. "Well then, let's not dawdle. Nurses aren't served pancakes in Harmon's mess hall."

As they walked toward the edge of the porch, waiting for a break in the traffic, someone tapped Lane on the arm.

"Ma'am? Are you Mrs. Mercer?"

Lane regarded the Red Cap worker who hauled a dolly filled with trunks and a duffel stamped with MAIL. He didn't look familiar, but she chided herself—she needed to stop thinking that every black man in Longview worked secretly for Judge Wyatt. "Yes."

He reached into his uniform's pocket and withdrew an envelope. "I was asked to give this to you."

She read her name scrawled in a bold script across airmail stationery. "Who gave this to you?"

The Red Cap's expression was blank. "I didn't ask his name, one of the passengers I guess."

The worker's hand was still out and Lane remembered that she should compensate for the delivery. After she dropped a nickel in his palm, she took the envelope and slipped it into her coat's pocket.

"Aw, love notes, and Hayes has barely left the station."

Lane shook her head, her mind spinning toward various possibilities. "That wasn't Zeke's handwriting."

"Theo then."

She cut her gaze to Emmie's. "It wasn't his either, and I won't know who sent it until I open it. Which I won't do at this platform because someone may be watching to see my reaction."

Emmie propped open her umbrella. "Ever the good agent, I can see."

"Former agent, thank you very much."

Lane followed Emmie across the drive, dodging the city bus that was slowly inching away from the curb, spewing oily film from its tires. Once they were inside the lobby, Lane hurried past the concierge desk and its radio, broadcasting Glenn Miller tunes, and pushed the door of the ladies' room. Sitting on a plush chair pulled beside the powder room counter, she wiped her damp hands on one of the monogrammed towels, and pulled the envelope from her pocket.

Sliding her fingernail under the seal, Lane opened the fold. She had a sense that she wasn't going to be happy with the letter.

The scrawl was not one she recognized, but the message was clear enough: *Don't testify at the V. Weeds trial, or it will go bad for you.*

Lane flipped the paper over, looking for any identifying marks.

Emmie pushed through the door, blinking against the lights circled around the mirror as if movie stars regularly powdered their noses in this room. "I knew your curiosity would get the better of you. What does it say?"

With a dread she'd not felt in days, Lane handed Emmie the note.

Emmie read the threat then folded it back into the envelope. "So, my little angel with scorched wings, you have another enemy."

Lane collapsed against the chair's back. "This is never going to end."

Emmie grinned. "And for girls like you and me, that's what we live for."

Epilogue

Emmie snapped her purse shut, taking the package of cigarettes she'd conned from the grocer in a concocted two-for-one deal, and tapped the menthols against the picnic table's ledge, letting the smooth tips slide to the front. Smiling with anticipation, she selected one and set its papery end against the lighter. Breathing tobacco into her mouth, she barely let the cigarette touch her lipstick—sure that the wrinkles she'd seen fanning from her lip line were payback for this habit.

"Those things will kill you. You mark my words."

She glanced to the sky, dotted with fat clouds and an occasional screeching bird, choosing to ignore Slim Elliott and his pithy predictions of doom.

He slid onto the bench next to her, bumping her hip with his.

Slim propped his elbows on the table, seemingly staring at the scene of summery bliss. Reaching across her and into the grocery sack, he stole a cherry tomato, popping the treasure in his mouth.

"Thief."

"A kinder person would have offered to share vine-ripe tomatoes."

Emmie would give him points for accuracy. Staring at the lawn that rolled in swells to the small lake where children were skimming rocks, she cocked her ears toward the car lot off of Marshall Avenue and the music blaring from someone's radio. Duke Ellington's trumpet offered a bouncy jazz to complement the moment. Blowing another puff of smoke, she realized that the afternoon had become an almost perfect example of the tranquility one could muster when one was in between assignments.

It wasn't entirely a lie. She'd just never had more than a long weekend off, and that was usually part of the transport from one country to another. This sojourn might be labeled a sabbatical if it lasted much longer.

Theo had called yesterday and told her the three-month suspension, brought on by territory infringement charges from the FBI, had been lifted and the OSS chief had appointed her to a mission working field hospitals in Guam—including looking for an agent who'd been shot down from a plane surveying the island—*if* she wanted to don her nurse uniform and take anti-malaria precautions. She'd chuckled at the irony but hadn't ruled out the Pacific. She had until midnight to make her decision. Theo already had fake identification papers ready to go, not wanting to take the chance that Roy Mercer had sold her name to sweeten some deal with the Germans.

Emmie watched a farm truck amble along Marshall Avenue and envied the driver. Without turning to Slim, she asked, "Why are you stalking me?"

Ellington's band kicked in and gave kick to the air sizzling around her.

"I'm hardly stalking. I just got to town, so I can't be held responsible for whatever terrors you invited these past few weeks," Slim said, reaching for another red prize from the vine. "But there's no denying—you're like a box of chocolates set on a high shelf, and I've always had an incurable sweet tooth. If I'm not careful, I'm going to tip off the ladder and split my head open for trying to reach."

"Charming," she deadpanned.

He shrugged, and the denim work shirt he wore bunched around his suspenders. "No one ever said the truth was pretty."

She folded the sack closed, not wanting Slim to discover the makings of her meager dinner. Living in J's apartment above the haberdashery was luxurious, but the flat didn't come equipped with a cook and Emmie's pay was too thin to afford dining out more than necessary to stay informed of the comings and goings in this town.

"So—" Emmie gave up thinking Slim would wander away like a stray dog that realized she didn't have any scraps. "Back from Washington or wherever your latest travels have taken you?"

"Went to the Big Inch's ribbon cutting in New Jersey then scooted over to Kansas and spent some time in Montana. I've got more pipeline projects than I can reasonably build." He gazed at her like he enjoyed soaking up the details of her face. "But nothing I saw in those places could hold a candle to what was right here in Longview all along."

She ignored the crackle in his gaze. "Spoken like a man who doesn't have a life outside of work."

"I think the bags under my eyes testify that I haven't always lived a life of virtue. But I can see well enough, and I like your sharp edges and broken bits, Em. They fascinate me." His gaze shifted to stare out over the lawn. "Although, I was surprised you hadn't left town after that hullabaloo at Harmon."

Emmie blew a shaky ring of smoke into the air. It was less potent to think about those days after she turned in her uniform than it was to remember the long walks she'd taken with Slim later—his attempt at comfort after her experience witnessing the ambulance's explosion.

She'd spun a tale on those strolls that included running away from her mother—again—and finding a way to help young women discover a path toward nursing school, and how much she'd come to care for Molly Kennedy. But none of those conversations touched on the truth at the center of her stall.

She was hiding from frailty.

If she didn't move too far or too fast, maybe her bones could reset and the things she remembered while in Longview would disappear like a slipper of childhood. Despite Slim's attempts otherwise, she'd battened down the errors of her youth and pinned closed the memories that were pushing against their shrouds. Facing the past was highly overrated.

Besides, though Emmie couldn't tell Slim, she'd lingered because the threat Lane had received was too real to ignore. The OSS didn't have authority to get involved in something more appropriate for the Texas Rangers, but Theo had suggested Emmie stay close to Wyatt's people, regardless. Keeping tabs on the underground, while the Weeds case geared up for a public trial, made Emmie's gather of gossip top priority communiques.

All of which, Lane was—hopefully—unaware of, thinking Emmie was caring for Molly's ongoing recovery and enjoying J's friendship.

The only catch would be if Arnold had squealed.

Patrick and Arnold had both been debriefed after the Harmon incident. Patrick had leveraged his experience into a position within the OSS. Arnold had chosen to stay in Longview, finish high school, and then he ridiculously volunteered for the Army.

She tapped the cigarette ash onto the grass, bringing her attention back to the man whose body heat seemed to make her skin melt. "I can't believe some woman hasn't snatched you up by now. Miss Kennedy assures me that men with all their limbs are a highly-prized commodity these days."

Slim chuckled, a sound that echoed like marbles in a well. "Well, at least I have that working for me. Although I am missing a fingertip." He flexed his left palm and showed her a stubby forefinger. "Welding accident, back in '36 I think it happened in El Dorado."

"That'll cost you points," Emmie said, admiring how his silvery hair glistened in the sunshine. "Best improve your dinner repartee to make up for the deficiency."

Emmie thought about the women Slim would have met in New Jersey. They'd be attracted to a rugged man without any of the refinements associated with pencil pushers and politicians. That mystique was part of the reason she'd entertained an apology from him after their disastrous encounter at the Chamber's award dinner for the pipeline project.

Men with character etched into their faces were hard to snub. Even harder to forget.

"You're going to go out to dinner with me tonight," Slim announced as he reached again for her grocery bag. "So, you don't have to be so greedy with those tomatoes."

She laughed before she could stop herself. "Conceited."

He stopped his reach and seared her gaze. "Hopeful."

"Hope," she said, breaking his eye contact by glancing to the mother rounding up her children from the lakeside. "The elixir of fools."

A stunned expression gave a catch to his breath. "How can you say that? You've treated people wounded in horrific conditions."

Emmie shrugged, but it wasn't with indifference. It was with the dense weight of guilt—and because she was so raw from listening to Molly and her cohorts rehash the names of Longview boys who'd died in battle, she remembered that baby she'd held a lifetime ago, not knowing how to care for him, other than to give him away. Yes, her life was proof that hope offered no guarantees.

"There's no magic in medicine," she said quietly, stuffing blue baby blankets into her mental vault. "Tools and techniques can only take a patient so far." Emmie faced him, letting him see the ravages she'd witnessed in field tents at war zones. "I've held so many dying men that I can't remember where having hope has made any difference at all."

He reached for her hand, swallowing her slender fingers inside his grip. "You were the hope, Emmie. You and that smile that can make a man forget his sorrows. You have so much energy that you make people believe that danger is just a passing ghost."

The memory of the whispered thanks from those soldiers who'd died in her arms nearly ripped her heart in two. Tears streaked her vision. "Bah."

Slim held on to her fingers even as she tugged them. "You and I both know it was never about medicine," he said. "And it was never about technique. What people want, at their end, is to believe there is something better in the beyond."

Emmie had to break his mesmerizing stare before she fell in love with him. "You think that is Heaven, don't you?"

"I'd rather believe that than argue that this life was just a vapor." Slim's eyes rounded with earnestness. "If I'm wrong about God, then I've just wasted my days meditating on a good book, but if all that I've told you is right. . .Wouldn't you want to know what I know?"

"I know plenty."

He kissed her knuckles. "Do you know that you're not alone?"

Emmie jerked her hand from his grip. "Quit trying to save me, Slim Elliott. I'm beyond help. The things I've done would scare you back to Montana for good."

Wiping her eyes, Emmie stubbed the cigarette on the picnic table, gathered her purse and grocery sack, and climbed over the bench, all while plotting an escape from this collision of summer sky and her own miserable saga. The car blaring big band tunes looked unoccupied, unless there was a couple in the backseat. She could steal it, as there was bound to be a key in the ignition since the radio was working. A fast getaway was what she needed. No use prolonging a line of thought that was bound to end in sorrow anyway. Slim was too good for her. He believed in things that she'd proven—time and again—that she was unworthy of.

Thunder clapped in the distance.

A shimmer skittered along her spine.

Maybe it was the stubborn Irish in her that made her glance back at Slim sitting at the picnic table. But with tears filming her gaze, she knew the constriction in her soul—this regret—was going to stay with her a long while. Longer than she deserved.

Emmie had abused a good man's heart.

Slim might appear as flinty as rock, but underneath that exterior was a man whose character had been mined from veins of pure gold. In her line of work, she'd known a lot of men who shimmered in the sunshine, but they were fool's gold. The man who'd found her in this park was the kind of man who'd stay true. He'd not toss her over when her hair turned grey or her skin pruned. He'd love her through the worst that this old world could offer. She knew that—because he already did.

Grateful that she could escape without him trying to whitewash her life, she took three giant steps toward the parking lot. As her watery gaze focused on that car, the heel of her shoe caught on a stem. Tripping, she fell across the arthritic roots of a magnolia tree's base, and her sack of tomatoes spilled across the maze of brown tangles.

Tears spurted from her eyes, not because of the scrape to her skin but from the leak in her soul that she'd patched with thread and glue, until the stitches finally ripped. She wiped her fingers across her lashes, stunned by the damp mascara smearing her skin.

Slim had loved her when there wasn't anything to gain by the commitment. Though he'd made no pronouncement of his feelings, she knew, and she'd rebuffed him every time he'd come close enough to kiss.

Those black slashes of makeup wavered in her vision until they resembled the dash she'd seen on so many headstones—that ever-so-small link between dates that was supposed to represent one's life on earth. More tears dripped from her cheek, taunting that *her* dash, and all the mayhem she'd crammed into it, was too heavy on misery and too lacking in happiness.

A life lived angrily spilled into the soil.

This town of misfits and millionaires had become her Alamo. She was surrendering to an army of memories that would not be denied any longer, and she had no resources to guard against them, save the love of a man who she'd rebuffed.

She covered her face because she didn't know how to contain the onslaught of tears, particularly when she was supposed to be so hard and stubborn. Slim would see her like this, weak, and a victim of emotions she could no longer control.

Emmie blinked hurriedly against the light, trying to gather all the pieces of her life and stuff them back in the box of her past. Cooling breezes seemed impervious to her plight, it was as if the universe was working with the tide of her waterworks—maybe using gravity to bring more salt-wrapped hurts to the surface. She crawled to her knees, aware that flight was her only salvation.

Twitching like she'd been stung, Emmie felt warm, big hands settle on her shoulders. "Leave me alone," she shouted. "I don't need you. I don't need this."

Slim knelt on the ground next to her and pulled her against his shirt front. "Let it go, Em." He crooned like a parent to a child. "Just let all the trash wash away. You can't heal until you recognize you can't handle it all on your own anymore."

Hiccupping, she tried to glare at him, but the fight wasn't there. "You don't know what I am. Forget you've ever met me."

He smoothed his palm over her hair. "You don't scare me, Mary Magdalene."

Ever since she'd met Slim, she'd been trying to shock him with her behavior, but he seemed impervious to her moves—even today. As faces from her past flitted through her memory, she was unable to resist crying for their loss any longer. Despite scars so deep they had their own connective tissue, Emmie caved into Slim's embrace and gave sorrow free course.

Slim leaned back against the magnolia's trunk, bringing Emmie with him, and for a time, they stayed together—her alternately weeping, and occasionally talking about names that had never been discussed outside the spy circle. He'd given her a bandana from his pocket, and she'd wiped her face free of makeup.

As various vehicles came and left the parking lot, taking their summer tunes and exhausts with them, Emmie learned the rhythm of Slim's heartbeats and fell into a dreamless slumber that was so deep she'd not felt any change in the weather.

Waking against the dripping tedium of rain that seemed to flick against her cheek, Emmie pushed off of Slim's chest and saw heavy clouds so low she could almost reach them. A summer shower bathed the park, as she wobbled to stand on knees stiff and bloodied.

Slim blinked like he was waking from a long nap too.

Emmie kicked off her shoes and found her footing, walking onto the lawn sloping toward the lake and inviting the rain to fall against her puffy and tear-stained face. Soon her hair was flattened of its curls, and her blouse was glued to her slip. Holding her palms out to puddle the water, she didn't see any of the nerve tremors so often felt quaking when stress stirred her blood pressure. Putting one hand against her heart, she felt a steady beat, and a calmness centered the fragments in her mind.

Sadness didn't echo in the repeat.

Staring at the lake, she watched small waves crash against the shoreline and a flock of geese huddle under the dock. Mentally running through a checklist of her body, she searched for signs that this feeling of tranquility masked some organ failure. But she was unusually fine.

An exhaustion that felt eerily like the aftermath of a battle grounded her, and she felt like—for the first time in her life—maybe she was strong enough to take a hard look at who she'd become and not shudder in disgust. There was work to do, but if Slim didn't tick her off too much with his religion, maybe she could ask him how he recovered from the hard knocks of his life. Emmie didn't want to reinvent herself, but she was willing to let go of some of the anger she'd churned and see if there was a better way to live going forward.

Slim walked to stand behind her, wrapping his arms around her waist and pulling her close to his body. Burying his nose against her collarbone, he kissed the hollow of her neck.

Emmie inhaled clean air into her lungs, accepting this grace she couldn't begin to understand.

Leaning back into his embrace, Emmie decided that maybe she'd been too hasty before. Her eyes batted away raindrops as her skin absorbed the warm bath brought on by silver linings.

She folded her palms over his hands knitted at her waist and acknowledged that women of a certain age were allowed to change their minds, and maybe their hearts too.

Emmie decided she didn't hate Texas after all.

A Final Note

When dealing with big history and a local story, there are so many places to go to mine the nuggets of truth—and though I found many, I'm sure there were places and people with anecdotes that I overlooked. That's the temptation of history—there's always some new source, an additional interview or an eye witness that someone refers me to, and the lure of these leads can take me into unchartered places. But in good faith, I do eventually have to sit down to write. It's with no small prayer that I finally begin, hoping I don't clutter actual history too much.

That was the way of it for the active military base that was known as Harmon General Hospital during the World War II years. When I had stretches of time, I'd lay out the old Longview photos, documents, archived interviews, and notes gathered from the Gregg County Historical Museum, *Longview News Journal* archives at the Longview Public Library, LeTourneau University Library, and files found at the Army Medical Museum located at Ft. Sam Houston, Texas, and try to fit it all together into a high-speed lane that meshed fiction and reality.

I attempted to give credible justice to the men and women who made military hospitals the state-of-the-art facilities they were in a time of national crisis. Those pre-fabricated barracks were far from perfect, but the very real Harmon General had such a high number of success stories and created so many modern medical methods that the accolades are long overdue. More than 25,000 soldiers were treated in the brief time Harmon General occupied those 156-acres in Gregg County, but the legacies tell quite a story. As a result, a diverse group of Americans chose Texas as their forever home after treatment at Harmon General, and the medical practices perfected there went on to become the leading edge in teaching hospitals for generations that followed.

The impact of Longview opening its arms to outsiders might be a little harder to document, but the people in Texas with stories from Harmon bear their own testimonies.

The beautiful second chapter for Harmon General Hospital is also a story worth telling. In a divine series of appointments, American entrepreneur and inventor, R.G. LeTourneau and his wife, Evelyn, were touring, by airplane, possible locations for their next manufacturing plant, when they saw the decommissioned Army hospital and decided in a spontaneous moment that the barracks and treatment rooms could be retrofitted into a technical institute training displaced WWII GIs in the new arts of large-scale mechanical equipment that LeTourneau Inc. would use to change the face of a dirt-moving industry. Buying the grounds and the building "as is" for one dollar, Mr. and Mrs. LeTourneau set a foundation for a Christian education that has blossomed into one of the nation's leading private universities, and the only one with a Christian Polytechnic distinction. All that remains on the beautiful campus still bracketing Mobberly Avenue in Longview, all 156 acres intact, is the echo of those vital military days, heard in the walls of the Speer Chapel. Lives are still being changed on that campus, long after the medical beds and ambulances rolled away, and I encourage you to take a good look at LeTourneau University and listen for the resonances of its former life. Longview, and LeTourneau University, would welcome you to follow the trails of the characters from these pages and see the gumption of how an East Texas town, with two big World War II efforts, went on to change the face of history.

Dear Readers,

Thank you for buying this book. If you finished it, I hope that means you enjoyed it as much as I did in writing it. If you did feel satisfied at the end, I'd be honored if you left a review on various social media sites where readers chat. Maybe, you want to know what happens next in Longview during the WWII years, or you want to register to receive email about this and other Fish Tales books? Please, visit my website, **www.kimberlyfish.com** to read about the backstory regarding this research and news related to the next novel in the Misfits and Millionaires series. And for those of you with friends who prefer audio books, *The Big Inch* is available on my website and read to you by a gifted narrator, Sydney Young. I so enjoy staying connected to readers, and hope you'll join me at the website to keep in touch about these novels and the contemporary ones that I write that are set in the Texas Hill Country.

Kimberly

About the Author

Kimberly Fish started writing professionally with the birth of her second child and the purchase of a home computer. Having found this dubious outlet, she then entered and won a Texas manuscript contest which fed her on-going fascination with story crafting. She has since published in magazines, newspapers, and online formats. She lives with her family in East Texas. Please visit her website **www.kimberlyfish.com** or follow her on Twitter, and Face Book @ Kimberly Fish or on Instagram @ fish_writer.

Made in the USA
Columbia, SC
22 January 2019